Lost Hollow

Shay Lawless

Lost Hollow—

ISBN-13: 978-1-940087-32-0
ISBN-10: 1-940087-32-5

21 Crows Dusk to Dawn Publishing, 21 Crows, LLC

Thanks, Sue, for the inspiration and giving me a treasure from West Virginia's past and the days of mine camp baseball so I can share it with others.

Chapter 1

It all started with six Ball Mason jars, an antique wooden trunk with a dead baby inside, and a guy named Trevor Woods. The story behind the Ball Mason jars and Trevor Woods would come long after the antique wooden trunk was found. It had originally shown up on the damp steps of the Grace Fellowship Church in Lost Hollow, a small mining community along the New River of West Virginia, on a rainy Easter Sunday morning in 1934. It was Annabelle Easton, the sixty-eight-year-old church organist, who stumbled upon it while she was banging her white umbrella with black polka dots against the wall to rid the canopy of any remaining rain droplets.

In the early 1930s, the steamer trunk would not quite be considered an antique. It just wasn't old enough yet. Instead, the chest would be regarded as an outdated suitcase, something passé. Possibly the only value would be that it was once treasured by a dead, beloved aunt, so it was shoved into the back of a shed or in an attic and filled with other items of like-character. It was made in the mid-1800s of oak and tooled metal. It had a domed lid with bent wood slats along the top. It must have seemed a peculiar item to be settled on the wet, bare porch. Perhaps, at first, Annabelle believed the trunk was a donation and was mentally trying to figure out how to dispose of it without hurting the feelings of someone in the community.

Annabelle dropped her head to the right and saw it plopped below a window. As she would later report to the local sheriff, she had been curious and taken two steps toward the chest before leaning over and flicking open two hasps on either side of the front with her fingers. Then she had turned the skeleton key settled into the lock in the center. She opened it wide. Much to her chagrin, a horrid smell enveloped her. Annabelle stumbled backward until she nearly fell off the top step. She quickly keeled forward and extended her right hand as close as she could get to the trunk. Then, Annabelle flicked the lid with her outstretched fingers, and she used the toe of her modest pumps to close the lid tightly.

It would be forty minutes later that the lid would be opened again when a chubby Reverend Andrew Mills worked his way in a lumbering step from the parsonage down the muddy street. Reverend Mills was an infantryman and had been shot in the right knee in the World War I Battle of Saint-Mihiel in France on September 12, 1918. He never quite recovered and was fondly dubbed Limping Andy when he returned home thirteen months later. Close behind was Clyde Hatfield, the local sheriff who had been helping his wife, Sharon, set out Easter eggs for their six young children when he got the urgent knock on his front door. These two would be standing overtop when the trunk was opened for the second time that day, exposing the dreadful contents within. While they stood overtop, their mouths would drop in utter horror—

"It was a newborn baby carefully swaddled in a homemade, pink quilt," I am telling Mister O'Sullivan's ninth-grade class softly while I sweep my hand downward and follow the same sequence of movements of Annabelle Easton. I unlock the hasps, turn the skeleton key, and then after a deliberate and painfully drawn out pause to prolong the anticipation, I open the trunk with two fingers.

I'm hardly much taller than the students with my teeny height of five feet and two inches, so they nearly knock me over moving forward to gaze into the trunk. I suppose they probably lack a bit of respect for me—I could be one of them passing as fourteen or fifteen, although I have a good thirteen years on most of them. I've got these too-big, buggy blue eyes that make me look like a cherub on steroids, a scrawny figure, and these pouty, puffy lips that should be sexy, but instead make me always look like I just got done with a big cry. I blend in so well with the students; two weeks ago, one of the fifth-grade teachers started herding me toward the school bus with her class.

We're in the Lost Hollow Historical Society Visitor Center. It's the last week of school. It is a tradition for the students in all grades to come here for a field trip. And yes, I did say Lost Hollow. It's where I was born and raised because my grandpa and my grandpa's grandpa were miners during the town's heyday when there were two bars, three groceries, a hardware store, and about fifty families living in the dusky, forested shadows at the bottom of Brandy Mountain and along Long Creek, a tributary of the New River Gorge. It's not so big anymore. It would give us the appearance of being a ghost town. Not so. There are forty-three rundown homes on a rutted, asphalt and gravel street and more than a handful of houses heading deeper into the overgrown forestland left over from the coal mining days that are too tumbledown to occupy. Oh, and there's our little schoolhouse that is now used as a church (New Grace Fellowship), and an old church that is now the local historical society for the three other nearby almost-ghost towns. The historical society is where I am working right this moment. I'm volunteering, teaching local history to kids from up at the Brandy Mountain School system on their end-of-year field trips so I can finish my college degree.

Twenty-five sets of eyes are wide with anticipation, and twenty-five bodies lean forward to peer into the contents of the trunk and what could easily pass as a brown, papier-mâché head. It isn't. There, swaddled in a pastel pink blanket are the petrified remains of a three-week-old baby complete with a thick wad of black hair still on the head.

"Okay, guys, move back a little. This isn't Spain. You don't have to be a herd of bulls running over Miss Davidson," Mister O'Sullivan instructs the students while they almost overcome me to get a closer glimpse inside. The softness in his tone contradicts the man's huge size. My Uncle Zach, who hangs around with him, told me once after his friend bounced his auburn-haired head off my grandpa's front door frame, he is six feet and four inches and something like two-hundred and eighty pounds. He's a gentle giant, built like a semi-truck carefully making his way down the right lane of the highway compared to all the other compact cars, tailgating and zooming rudely in and out of the lanes and through the traffic.

I know him like the back of my hand, although we ran in different circles. If he'd been in one of the old yearbooks that are stuffed into the back of the museum, his face would have been plastered on every page with a sport, the cool clubs like student council and theatre, and then on the now politically incorrect page of awards with a superlative: Most Likely to Succeed. And, not to mention: The Cutest Couple. He dated his high school sweetheart, a cheerleader and volleyball player, from ninth grade. He ended up marrying her. Me, on the other hand, didn't get picked for any team or was I chosen for any of the cast in the school plays. I was one of those somewhere-between kids, not considered athletic enough or from a powerful enough family to get recruited for a structured school sport. But I could ramp my skateboard or bike off most inclines with the prowess of a pro when I got home. I would have probably been deemed Most Likely to Win the Lottery and Lose the Ticket.

Beck (we used to call him Beast in high school because he even towered over the teachers) hasn't changed much except that his once curly brown-red head of hair is clean-shaven down to a ducktail haircut. He's got a scrubby, dark stubble-beard complete with stubble mustache that must take him hours to groom because it always looks perfect. He's still got the heart-shaped lips the girls used to die for and oddly green eyes. He wiggles his bear-paw hand between those nearest the trunk to gently goad them to take a step back. He looks up and smiles at me guiltily. He was just as eager as the kids, taking the deep lean forward, and he almost knocked two over. But I'm certainly not going to scold him. When he came into the historical society this morning, I called out a *Hey, Beast!* forgetting all unwritten proprieties about addressing teachers with their nicknames when students are around. Fortunately, he was easygoing about it even when the kids mimicked my call and giggled. For just a second, he traded in his high-school-teacher-poker-face for a lopsided grin and waved at me across the room. *Hey, Flea.*

Flea. Yes, that's my nickname. I earned it when I was four. I was a biter. I was too little to do much damage. At least that's what my grandpa, who raised me, told my preschool teacher when she brought it to his attention. When she held up her arm with fourteen, tiny tooth marks dotting her skin, my grandpa said: *You got to be kidding me.* He'd stared flabbergasted at Miss Thomas's thick glasses that made her look like a beetle. *You made me leave work for that? I seen her bring blood—*

The students don't bother to work eyes to mine when I continue. They are spellbound staring into the trunk. "Old Doc Bobby Brown was called in," I say softly to the backs of their heads. "But you know the story. I'm sure your mamas and daddies have told you. Doc Brown examined the baby. It had been dead nearly three months. He figured it was just one of the babies from the mining camp. Girls married young back then at fourteen or fifteen, just about the same age as some of you right now. If their babies got sick, some of them weren't so good at taking care of them. But Doc Brown, he placed the baby back into the blankets. Mimi Edwards was a rich lady who was married to one of the mining owners and lived up on top of Brandy Mountain above us. She came down and took the baby, said she would give it a decent burial and a sweet name—Margaret Josephine. She called her Little Margie for short. But the burial never happened."

I pause for impression, listen to the silence of enrapt students. "Two days later," I go on, my voice softening. "Reverend Mills died, and everybody up on the mountain got scared the baby was carrying smallpox, or tuberculosis, or whatever killed the preacher. Then, Annabelle Easton dropped dead on the back porch of her house putting seeds into the bird feeders she kept there. Just boom!" I slap my hands together, and two students gasp, turn and give me a glare for startling them. "She dropped dead. The sheriff, he just vanished a week later. Gone. He left a pretty wife and six little kids under twelve, and nobody saw him again. Some say he ran off with Mimi Edwards because she disappeared too. The people of the town said the baby was cursed. Cursed. For the next three weeks, every time someone made plans to bury Little Margie, someone in the mining community died— almost six people in all. They were afraid to bury her. So instead, someone bundled up the baby, stuck her back into the chest, and hid her in the rear of the church. That is until she was found again in 1974, while they were digging around the basement when they opened the historical society. And maybe it *was* just tuberculosis sweeping through the town that killed the rest. That's what old Doc Brown put on the death certificates of all those who died. But those who were around when they found Little Margie, well, they see things quite differently—your grandmas and your great-grandpas. They passed on the story and told the misfortune that fell upon those who disturbed her eternal sleep. They tell us it's the baby. She's cursed. Since that day she was found, those who touched her have—died."

It is completely silent for ten seconds. Then, one chubby girl in jeans and a short sleeve t-shirt with a pink turtle on the front takes in a deep gasp. I look up just in time to pass the teacher's face, and he is hiding a grin behind his hand. "It's not real, Bethany," chides another student who has moved up in front of me and two steps from the trunk. I look over the head of a boy to take in the tiny girl with elf-like facial features and self-dyed, too-black hair. Willy Dunn is her name. She is Lester Dunn's daughter, a local man who is best known for a record number of times he's listed in the local paper for drunken bar fights and other miscellaneous run-ins with the law that are just a fraction of an inch beneath the threshold limits of what the courts can legally consider felonies. She rolls the one eye that is not hiding beneath a well-worn blue hoodie, doesn't make eye contact with me. "God, you're so stupid," she says to the other girl. "It's one of those cheap dead-looking dolls you can buy at the

Halloween store." She switches her gaze back to me. "Why don't you tell us something we'd rather know, Miss Davidson. Like maybe you know where that old, crazy guy buried his money."

"That *old crazy guy* was Hans Branntwein, the man who started the coal mine here in 1866," I grunt impatiently. Everybody wants to know about the damn treasure. There's supposed to be a million dollars' worth of old coins buried in Ball Mason jars, up the mountain where the rich folks lived to get away from the noise of the coal works and the smell of burning coke ovens. Hans Branntwein disappeared four or five years after he opened the mining operation. Some say his partner murdered him in cold blood for the mining rights. But Hans knew it was coming, so he hid all his earnings in glass jars and buried them at his home for his family. That's why Grant Lebowski, the part-time museum curator/part-time Brandy Mountain accountant, gets to do the talk on it and not me, a meager volunteer college intern.

"You'll learn about our town founder in less than five minutes when you visit Mister Lebowski in the next room," I divulge to Willy. "And you know Hans Branntwein disappeared too, don't you? He just vanished into thin air a few years after he started the town. Poof!" I slap my hands together like a firework explosion and let my fingers wiggle toward the floor like the colored flames floating downward from the sky. "But it's real, Willy." I drop my voice to a whisper. "*She's* real." I push my way through the bodies who have worked their way around me to peek into the trunk, take in the scent of mothballs and the fetid odor of something old and dead. I nod toward the trunk. "You want to touch her and see?" I murmur to Willy, lean in, and nudge her elbow with a knuckle. "Go ahead." I make the sign of the cross, give her another nudge, and whisper huskily. "Do it."

"No way." She looks pale, shakes her head.

I take a step back and make a dramatic sweep of my arm toward the next display in the tiny visitor center. "Good answer," I make a deep sigh. "I was hoping you'd say that.

My ninety-five-year-old Nana Nisee used to tell me: *Let sleeping dogs lie. A sleeping dog don't bite.* I'm thinking it might be best to let Little Margie sleep. So, we should let the dead baby get her rest." I reach over and push my hand on the lid of the trunk and slowly close it. "If you kids will move on to the next room, Mister Lebowski will continue your tour." I watch them all lean in as if they believe the little mummy is going to clamber out of the dark confines and snatch one of them inside. It is nearly silent when I let the lid fall the last six inches, and it slams shut loudly. Everyone jumps in a startled reaction while I try to bite my lip to stop from laughing out loud. Willy rolls her unconcealed eye at me before she pulls her gaze to the rest of the class.

Old Grant Lebowski has a sour look on his face; his lips are pursed beneath his gray 1960s mustache. He doesn't approve of the heart-hooped earring I have in my right ear. I have to hide it behind my hair. He shuns my eyebrow ring and tells me I really need to take out my opal gold nose ring. He'd shit bricks if he knew I had six tiny baby blue butterflies running up my back and stopping on my shoulder. He criticizes the way I dole out my history spiel. And he chides me relentlessly while he dabs a moisturized facial tissue beneath his nose and sneezes six times. "You have to wash your hands before work, Harley. I am allergic to cats. You cannot pat your cat and then come into work. Or get rid of the thing since you are working here. It makes me miserable." But I don't have a cat. I've told him that a hundred times. He doesn't listen. He only sneezes another six times. I think he's allergic to me. I don't care. I'm mentally flipping him off in my head while I blink innocently at him in physical form.

"Everybody please give Miss Davidson a thank you before we move on to Mister Lebowski's talk," Mister O'Sullivan goads his class. He claps his hands together, and they follow a bit less enthusiastically. Then before he goes, he loses his fake, teacher smile and awards me a real grin. He lingers, watching his students file through the door while I carefully fasten the metal clamps on the trunk.

"You really make history come alive for them, thanks," he says in almost a whisper like if he talks in a loud voice, he will break me. "They aren't an easy crowd to please. Or keep awake."

"Dead babies help," I whisper back lightheartedly.

"You think you can come up with a little paper with more information on Hans Branntwein for me to use? Grant has asked me to help with presentations this summer to supplement my teaching income during the off-months. I'm supposed to come in for training this week."

I snap my gaze upward, surprised. "He's paying you to work here?" I must have shown my bewilderment-slash-disappointment because Beck returns with a slightly guilty dip of the chin, brow furrowed.

"Oh, you didn't know? He just said he needed me a few times a week. I don't think I'm replacing you."

"I don't get paid. It's volunteer work for a class I have to complete to graduate," I mumble. "I guess that's it, then."

"So you don't plan on sticking around anyway."

"I was told there wasn't money for a paid position." I feel sick, but don't want him to see my distress. "Listen, I need to close up shop. I've got to get to my paid job."

"I didn't mean to—"

"I know." Bullshit. Now, I'm mentally flipping off Mister O'Sullivan with my middle finger while he pivots on his feet slowly and follows his students into the next room.

Chapter 2

"God, you like that way too much."

I jump. I didn't hear anyone enter the room as I follow the last of the students stepping through the entrance of the doorway. Grant Lebowski is impatiently waving the kids around him with a crooked arm so he can begin his boring pitch to them. The voice from the shadows echoes in my ears like the scent of chocolate chip cookies fresh from the oven gives me a melancholy ache. My grandpa raised me since I was two years old. I call him Pop Pop. He used to make me chocolate chip cookies with sugar sprinkled on top every Monday when I'd come home from school because he knew I hated Mondays.

But it isn't my Pop Pop's voice. I turn, take in the man standing at the door with deep auburn hair and a distinctly expensive-looking designer haircut. He's the kind of pudgy that comes with late-twenty-somethings who have turned in their play shoes for work shoes. However, his suit coat and tie are certainly tailor-made and flatter his physique. Even if the voice had been recognizable, the man standing there is a stranger. Oh no, wait a minute, I can see the boy I remember beneath the man—his always-laughing, abnormally piercing, slate-gray eyes were almost hidden beneath his glasses. *Max.* In the five years that have passed since I saw him last, he's gone from a skateboarding boy in ripped blue-jeans to a conformed mainstream society adult.

I'm dumbstruck. It is my ex-boyfriend's best friend. His first and middle name is Maximus Alexander. If that isn't long enough, his last name is huge and hyphenated—Matthews-Branntwein and they've tagged on a suffix, III. His mother was a direct descendant of the Branntweins. She married John Matthews, our town mayor. It's always been rumored that the reason his family kept both names for the kids was that they were descendants of Hans Branntwein, a multimillionaire and town founder. They wanted everybody to know their hands were in the pot for his money. I'm sure that's what helped leverage his dad to the position of Brandy Mountain Mayor, not that the job position is such a big deal—he's only part-time and has his own construction business. Besides, Brandy Mountain, population 1172, and its tag-a-long little brother Lost Hollow, population 182, isn't that big. I didn't care so much for all that drama. Max was just kind of like the big St. Bernard, the family pet that padded along behind me and, when I started dating Trevor, him too.

I'd dangled the nickname of Mateo sometime in Junior High over his head, and he was more than happy to take it. He latched on to it like a teething puppy eager for a bone, and everybody just followed suit. Well, except his family. They prefer to call him Max and amplify the *Branntwein* whenever they are asked their last name.

"Max," I say this time, losing the slight smile I was carrying on my face. He's no longer *Mateo* to me. I fiddle around with the trunk and see him narrow his eyes to fine slits at me beneath his glasses.

"*Max*?" He chuckles beneath a hesitant smile and pushes his glasses along the bridge of his nose. "Is that who I am now? I'm not *Mat—teo* anymore?" He draws the last part out like I always used to do with a hard thrust to my lips and tongue. I shake my head slowly back and forth. He sniffs sarcastically. "You're not going to ask me if I'd rather say hello to you or go out with a hundred old fat ladies with warts on their butts?" It's an old game we play where I measure his friendship to me by tossing out a list of the last things he should choose over me—dead dogs, pieces of coal, ugly women. Max has always teased me by choosing anything but me.

"No. You chose your side," I tell him bluntly.

"Whoa, whoa—side?" He holds out his hands in front of him. "I didn't choose anything. It was chosen for me." He reaches out, wiggles his finger in front of my face. "Wow, what's all this?" I'm assuming he's pointing out the eyebrow ring like everybody else does like it's something new and way too radical for our little town. "Your Pop Pop know you've got all that—stuff?"

"It's an eyebrow ring, if that is what you are referring to, Max. Stop. Yes, he does."

Max sniffs a patronizing laugh like Pop Pop gave me when I was twelve, and I wanted to pierce my ears—a knowing *she'll-eventually-grow-out-of-it* kind of snicker. He nods toward the room next to us. I look up, and Beck must have been eyeing us because he quickly turns away. He never liked Trevor or Max. Trevor and Max are from up on top of the mountain where the big money is. They are like bad January sleet storms and were always quick to make subtle, under-their-breath jokes about him. Beck is from the same neighborhood as me in the bottomlands. He's just the opposite of my ex-boyfriend and his best friend and more like a mild day in June. He just let their remarks roll off him. "Can you believe that dumbass is a teacher?" Max leans in and asks me.

I ignore him. "I need to pack up. What do you need?"

"Trevor and I were driving past. I saw your car."

"Huh?" His words rip me away from my thoughts. "Trevor's here?" I feel the blood drain from my face. Five years. It has been an entire sixty months (give or take a month or two) and Trevor Woods, who I was two months away from marrying, snuck-sexed my best friend and I'm still hung up on him. I guess. Maybe? Why do I feel like I would rather run off the edge of a cliff than see Trevor now?

"Yeah, he's helping some old lady unload a bunch of stuff from her car," Max tells me nonchalantly, suddenly seems like he doesn't want to be here at all either because he's looking behind him as if he's panning out an escape route. I suppose it was Trevor who was the glue that held us three together. He's gone. Like a porcelain coffee mug shattered on the floor, we're just another broken friendship tossed out into the garbage. "So where did you disappear to?" Max asks.

"I went to school and got my degree." Now I'm looking

over his shoulder as if I'm searching for a way out. And yet, I still smell those chocolate chip cookies in his voice even if the air between us screams we are like two strangers riding an elevator down twenty floors together trying to decide if we should talk or just remain quiet in the stale, silent air between us.

"I had a couple internships," I babble on. "And this one. I've got to do this last one to graduate. Once Grant Lebowski signs off on my intern form, I'm free and clear."

"Things are going well for you, right?" Max looks behind him like he wants to run. "I mean, you're working here now, living the dream? That's what you wanted to do, history stuff."

"*History stuff,*" I repeat with a slightly cynical laugh. I suppose it is boring for him. But to me, it is the light at the end of my long, dark tunnel. I have been volunteering at the Lost Hollow Historical Society Visitor Center since tenth grade. Grant Lebowski, who is running it now, is sixty-two years old and swears at every quarterly meeting, he's going to retire. Let me explain it how my cousin, Randy, has summed it up: I'm trying to earn a living doing something I hate so I can volunteer for free doing what I love. It's a lose-lose situation. So that's why right now I'm looking over my shoulder at the clock, so I can slip out the front door and get to the Givens Hotel and Conference Center for a meeting for my real job which is being a Central Independent Realty sales agent.

"Listen, I'd love to stand here and chat with you, but actually, I have to go. I'm getting an award tonight at the conference center at my real job." Why did I say that and it sounded like *na-na, na-na, boo-boo* as if I'm six years old and we both reached for the same cookie, and I got it? I might as well be cleaning the portable toilets for as much money as I'm making. And it's an overstatement, really. My award is akin to a participation trophy; at the end of a ball season, each and every player gets, no matter if they hit the ball or not. I've *not* hit the ball—well, I've not sold a house yet. But I've completed the 90 hours of pre-licensing education required by the state. The company I am working for requires a year of training and working with their associates along with all the requirements the state demands of realtors. I'm one of the few that haven't dropped off like dead flies on a window since we started. That, alone, is enough to warrant an award in my backup field, I suppose. "What are you doing down here, slumming?" I ask a little caustically.

"We were down here looking at the old ballfield—"

"You're putting in apartments there too?" I cut him off. I wave a hand at him. I shouldn't be so mean, but my Pop Pop said Max's father has been buying up a bunch of properties and building big houses for rich people who want to raise their families far from the city. They move in and start complaining our houses are eyesores just because they might need a slap or two of paint on the exteriors. They call the police about the ATVs running up and down the roads.

"Listen, he's buying those homes for fair market value for redevelopment. It's called eminent domain." Max stiffens a little when he says those words. "We get the property in the name of public use and build expensive homes. Those homebuyers actually pay taxes. We need more money here, Harley, or the entire place will go to nothing but a ghost town. You live in a blighted area, and blighted areas are up for grabs. It's called an aging tax base. There just aren't enough tax-paying people living here anymore. They are old. With the view of the river, he can build a subdivision there and really help this town."

"*We* like the view too. Are you insinuating that poor people don't deserve beauty? What's wrong with that? Why should we let rich people take our homes just so they can have *our* view? You can't do that."

"Why sure we can. There isn't a house down here worth more than a couple thousand bucks. People don't want to look at it. We can make it prettier and make more money for the city. It happens all over the United States."

"Well, it's not going to happen here."

"It is already happening here, Harley. You can't stop it." I know he can see the anger in my eyes. His shoulders drop. "Listen, it's my dad and his committees that are working on it. It's mostly on paper. I'll tell him how you feel, alright? Maybe we can work something out." He nudges me with his knuckle. "I won't let anything happen down here." I don't meet his smile. "Regardless, we're actually trying to find someplace to practice for the ball tournament—the Brandy Mountain Classic Big Ball Tournament. My dad's dedicating a new ballfield in town for the little league and an adult league. While they build the ballfield, we need a practice field. Please don't be snarky."

"I'm being snarky to you because Trevor is a shit. And you are a shit through association." I stop, tap my chin and feign mulling that over in my head. Then I shake my head adamantly. "No, you're just a shit all by yourself. And don't come down the mountain and take what's ours. Go take your stupid-ass rich friends and—" It is suddenly silent. I realize that the kids have stopped their chatter so Grant Lebowski can start his talk. So *stupid-ass rich friends* echoes in the air while twenty-five sets of eyes, plus another set from Grant are settling hard upon me.

"What's *yours*?" Max snaps back. "None of it was ever yours or your family's. You all worked for all of us up on the mountain, you get that right? We owned the company and the houses your family lived in—"

I just put up my hand. "Whatever." I look at the clock and prepare my exit. "But you don't own us anymore. I don't have to pretend to be your friend through association. I don't have to stand here and listen to your bull crap." I hear footsteps coming. Fearing it is Trevor, I slip out behind Grant's group to escape. I come to a standstill long enough to turn slightly and tap my finger on the doorframe, crane my neck, so I'm looking up at Max. I give him a long gaze, hear the doorknob turning. I shrug and leave.

Chapter 3

Pop Pop tells me there's a meeting for anybody who wants to play in the Brandy Mountain Classic Big Ball Tournament. It is to raise funds for new baseball fields at the old mining communities. It's at the Brandy Mountain Baseball Complex. He hits me with that when I walk into the open garage behind his 1930-ish, 2-story white company-built coal camp house left over from the town's mining years. It's just like the forty-three others on the five blocks remaining in the town, Lost Hollow. Pop Pop's house, like the others, is tucked behind a rundown downtown that's a little white church, an old company store, a superintendent's house, and a few abandoned brick buildings.

I mutter an indifferent *uh huh, I heard*. It doesn't strike me odd that the motive for the tournament he has given me—to help the old mining community fields down in the bottomland does not match Max's, as a promotion for a local league on the mountain. I don't care. Women have never been a part of whatever secret baseball society exists in this part of my world. We are excluded. My eyes are set toward the rear of the garage to the warped cardboard boxes stored there on one rusted, blue metal shelf sandwiched between six more shelves of tools and toolbox roller cabinets.

"How the heck did you hear me coming in, Pop Pop, with that stupid drill running?" Sneaking in would be more like it. I had hoped to get in and out. I had not expected him to be lying beneath a truck with his splayed legs hanging out. He must have seen my shadow cross the floor. He slips out on the mechanic's creeper he was laying on and sits up.

"Zach told me you just pulled in." Oh. He waves a finger to the far side of the dark garage. I narrow my eyes. Sure enough, my Uncle Zach is settled into a green, woven lawn chair. Zach is a foot taller than me and two months younger than me. Like all my uncles and me, he's skinny and has blonde hair and big, blue eyes. Unlike me, he's tall. Zach has a buzz haircut, tattoos on his arms, and a grudge against me for always trying to be Pop Pop's favorite.

He's the surliest of Pop Pop's seven sons. We grew up side by side, such he treats me with the same kind of respect an ornery brother gives a bratty sister who isn't afraid of fighting back. None-the-less, as we've grown older, instead of punching and kicking, we've resorted to negotiating our way through almost every situation for which we come into contact.

"So, is it true what Max Matthews-Branntwein told me today when he stopped at the museum?" I ask him. "They are using eminent domain as an excuse to buy up houses here?" He doesn't answer. Suddenly my grandpa can't hear either. But I suppose he's stuck on the ball tournament. He gets like that the older he gets. Everything he wants to hear is funneled in. Everything he doesn't just lays in the air.

I'm assuming Pop Pop got the information about the tournament from Zach and two of his buddies sitting next to him almost hidden in the dark too—T.J. Atkinson and Beck O'Sullivan. They are all three couch potato sports watchers with Pop Pop during whatever ball season is in at the time. Both are divorced. I wouldn't give either of them a thumbs up on character and personality. I ask Zach all the time why he hangs out with them. T.J.'s just lazy and half the time, doesn't have a good job. Beck's a teacher, and he's got the personality of a cardboard box. No surprise. He was, perhaps, the most popular boy in high school regardless of his personality. Peel back the ability to play any sport without having to work at it, and he's just corrugated paper and an empty package beneath.

Beck hasn't liked me since third grade. Yep, we go back farther than that, but that's when I beat him up on the playground, then told Miss Feininger that he hit me. Of course, my own uncle, Zach, ratted me out and the two became best friends. I always remind him blood is thicker than water because of it and he's a traitor. He tells me to go to hell. People change. But I know better. Lots of times, the three of them hold secret, guy-talk meetings in here with a game on the old boombox in the corner while Pop Pop tinkers on cars or trucks or ATVs. Whenever I come in, the chatter stops, and they all stare at me with Martian ray gun eyes until I dissipate out the door again feeling left out. I mean, what could they possibly be talking about that I can't be included? Girl butts and tits? No, because my Pop Pop wouldn't allow it. Ew, maybe he does when I'm not around.

"You're not saying hi to any of us?" Zach mutters a bit sarcastically. "That's rude. Can you hand me my beer on the table over there?" No, rude is tossing my stuff into a box and shoving it into the garage. Rude is Beck taking my volunteer position and dream job and getting paid for it. Beck and Zach don't deserve a greeting. T.J.'s just left out because he's with them.

"Can you have a little respect for my stuff? No, you never do. So no, I will not get you your beer."

"Oh, come on. It's five steps away."

"No, you took my stuff out of the basement where it was safe and shoved it out here in the garage." I can see my box from my standpoint. I've got Pop Pop's good LED flashlight he uses when the electricity goes out. I had to dig it out from the kitchen drawer full of odds and ends and buried beneath a screwdriver and hammer. I flashed the light on two of the boxes that say: HARLEY'S JUNK on them in my Uncle Zach's hard-to-read, first-grade-looking scrawl. "And you called my treasures *junk*. It's a good thing I was looking for it before my stuff gets ruined out here because half the time, Pop Pop forgets to close the garage door, and somebody could steal it."

"The question is, *would* somebody steal it?" T.J. asks with a chuckle like my stuff wouldn't be worth anything. I glare at him.

"I got more stuff than you do, Atkinson." He's difficult to stay mad at long, even if he has always been on Zach's side just like Beck. He's got this big, white-toothed grin that is only more predominant because he's also the warmest shade of toffee brown with freckles dotting his face and skinny arms reminding me of the cinnamon Pop Pop used to sprinkle on my toast with a little sugar. Still, I hold my ground with those three. "I was looking for something from my room before I left for college." I don't tell them I'm looking for something of Max's, a box of his stuff I'd had laying around my jeep and my room. For some odd reason, it seemed important to find it, get it out from the darkness it had been hiding and poke through it, dig out old memories I probably shouldn't dig out. "I don't know why you are always such a jerk about my stuff."

"Be nice, Flea," Pop Pop scolds me with a yawn.

"He could have respected my stuff more, Pop Pop," I gripe about Zach. "It's all thrown in here like he tossed it from across the room."

"He probably did toss it in here." Pop Pop wiggles his hand toward the back of the garage. "But if you start digging in those boxes, you better clean it up. I'll throw it all away if I got to do it." He shakes his head. "Did you hear me about the tournament?"

I hard-sigh loudly. "Did you hear me about the mayor buying up houses for his company so the city gets more taxpayers?" He's not a big man, nor is he small, my surly (but devoted) grandpa who raised me. His name is Ray Davidson, and being my mama's father, I couldn't call him daddy even though he's always taken care of me. So I settled on Pop Pop.

"That's old news, Flea," is Pop Pop's answer. And the end of the discussion, I'm sure. He is seventy-something and had worked the Brandy Mountain coal mine from the time he was fourteen until it closed in 1977. Then, he eked a meager living renting out a few houses he got in the mining company buyout, one of which I rent on the cheap. He also works at fixing up ATVs, motorcycles, and RVs at his shop in the unattached garage behind his house where we are right now. He had seven sons and one daughter, my mama. No one's ever said aloud why I ended up on his doorstep. But it isn't a mystery that is difficult to crack open. My mama has a long history of bad boyfriends, short-lived jobs, and an inability to prioritize important things. I was one of the important things she ranked beneath staying out at the bars until three in the morning. Such, it was my Pop Pop who tucked me in at night since I was two years and three months old.

His shoulder-long, grayish hair is always tousled and his dingy blue jeans and 1970s flannel shirts, rumpled. He likes to toss in big words when he's talking just to throw people off. After each big word, he gives a wink-wink like he's passing on something slyly. He gets his big words from my great grandma, Denise, who lives with him, but gets dropped here and there a few times a week because of his work schedule. They sit in front of the TV at night and she does her crosswords, and he watches the sports channels and complains about never getting the chance to be a racecar driver or a baseball player when he was young. Because he could have done a hell of a better job than the pansy-ass idiots doing it now. He is still clinging to the 1970s as if he watched the 1960s fly past and reached out a hand in desperation to stop the years from fleeing and latched on tight to somewhere between 1974 and 1979. Such, I'm thinking that big ball is something from that time period. I'm wrong.

"Is that what you and all the old guys have been doing at the old Lost Hollow ballfields?" I ask him. Because after church on Sundays (and maybe before the last hymn is sung), the old men swagger-march out of New Grace Fellowship like over-smug rap singers parading off a stage to loud cheers, swap out their suit coats and button-ups for the t-shirts beneath, and toss the ball around like they've played pro ball for years. "Because it looks more like a game of hot potato the way you all toss and miss—" It does. They got a pitcher that hits the saggy fence more than he gets the ball over the plate and a handful of men over fifty and overweight and—

"Don't be sassy, young lady. Those ballfields are hallowed ground and that game, *big ball*, like softball and baseball was the holy sport of mining back in the day. Just a man and a ball. No glove. Just flesh to leather. It's what took walking into those dark tunnels bearable. Because any minute the roof could collapse on top of you." Uh oh. *Back in the day.* When Pop Pop starts on *back in the day* I know he's going to lecture me about something. And here we go— "My dad used to play big ball in the 1930s. He was a Spartan. That was his team. And he was an exceptional player, unparalleled." (Yeah, sometimes he tosses in two big words.) He said that just as I sashay around the truck toward the boxes. I'm trying to waylay a long lecture on sports I could really care less about. "He played right out there in the fields by the church. The company built those fields for their team down here. Kept 'em out of trouble when they weren't working, you know. The really good guys got to use the fields after work. Dad and his buddies got them from eight until dark. That they are building a complex is glorious." Glorious.

"Um." I shake my head and tug at a box on a shelf. "I've never heard of big ball nor have I heard of the Brandy Mountain Baseball *Complex*." I declare, trying to hide the chuckle beneath my breath while I dig hard through the third of five mildew-scented cardboard boxes in the darkened, stale air of his garage. "Big ball sounds like something sissy preschool kids play with plastic bats and foam balls. The *complex*, it sounds big like a stadium, and there isn't anything like that around here. The only sports facility I've seen up on the mountain is the high school's meager football field, and the almost-attached baseball field shoved up next to it for lack of flat spots to play on here."

"A sissy sport, it is not. Like I said, there ain't no glove. You caught the ball with the bare hand. You say you know everything about history and you don't know what big ball is?" Pop Pop makes an exaggerated wave of his hands, so their shadows dance on the walls. I hear his entourage on the lawn chairs laugh.

"I never said I know *everything* about history," I grunt. "Doctor Williams says there is no way to know everything about history." Doctor Williams was my favorite professor in college. He took me places I'd never been before without leaving the stuffy auditorium.

"Um." Pop Pop grunts. "Yeah, we know all about your professor—"

"The demi-god," Zach snickers. "And I can assume you dated him too—"

"Shut up! No—Zach, you are an idiot. He's as old as Pop Pop, like a hundred and ten."

"I'm not that old," he growls. "Before you dig too deep, take a look up on my worktable." I see the shadow decrease and poke toward the old, gritty wooden counter where tools are piled here and there along with little, glass baby jars filled with nails and screws. I see something round and off-tan within reaching distance. I stop long enough to balance the box with my shoulder and take the round object in my hands. I roll it around and feel the smooth, slightly malleable surface. It *looks* like a softball, but it is much lighter and almost the size of a cantaloupe. I can't wrap both my hands around it together.

"It's huge," I mumble almost transfixed. "But it doesn't weigh as much as even something as small as a bouncy ball." I like the feel of it in my palms, make a knock on it with my knuckles. It feels hollow. It is incredibly light and just a little flexible when I squeeze it. "You'd think I'd heard of this before. You're not making this up, are you?" I grunt at him and give it a couple tosses in the air. *Nice.* I want to sniff it, see if it smells like a leather baseball. I don't, knowing Zach and his buddies will laugh at me.

"No, I'm not making it up. You better know more than you act like you know after all the money I doled out of my wallet the last six years." Pop Pop sniffs. "And that's a 16-inch instead of the 12-inch softball now, Miss-know-it-all. It's filled with kapok tree fibers, like cotton yarn, wound around so the core is lightweight like cork. Back in the day, they couldn't afford gloves. The men didn't need them with big ball because of this light core."

26

The men. It is exasperating. Like women couldn't handle baseball. "Whatever," I say softly and gruffly. "And I'm sorry I didn't finish." It's another blow aimed at my ego. Pop Pop annoys me. He always takes jabs at me for going to college, an expense he feels was a waste. I'd be better off waitressing at the restaurant like my mom and not sitting in a chair with a roomful of three-hundred other nameless, faceless students listening to some dull professor talk and spending Pop Pop's hard-earned cash. I wait for him to say it aloud, that one thing that everybody knows about my mama's daughter is I'm one step away from her because I never finish anything.

"Well, for one, I wasn't tossing your inability to finish college in your face. I'm assuming, young lady, you plan on finding a suitable job after you finish—whatever that thing is called where you work at the museum."

I realize the box is sliding from my shoulder. I'm making a vain attempt to pin it with my elbow as it slips past. It is the third from the top. I just might be buried alive by my treasures.

"So—let me get back to what we were talking about before you swayed the conversation away," Pop Pop mutters with a saucy glare. "Big ball, for your information, is the kind of baseball we played in town. We used a bigger ball and had a different set of rules than the teams the coal company sponsored. The ladies club at the camp made the uniforms for us instead of some big-name company. Not many men got to play for the coal camp team. But we all wanted to play. So we improvised. We didn't strike a batter out. And the batter got to pick his pitch. We did fastpitch still, so sometimes, it might be a long game."

"It still sounds like sissy softball," I say, and I hear Zach snicker. I turn, and Pop Pop is standing not far behind me. He's not making much of a move to help me. I look up, watch the top box teetering. "Pop Pop, can you give me a—" Just then, I see it start to topple and cringe, ready for it to fall on my head. But it doesn't. A huge paw of a hand comes out of the darkness and pushes it back. It's Beck. I feel his belly against my shoulder. He's so frigging big and stealthy.

"How can you be so quiet like a mouse when you're as big as a moose?" I ask him, still in mid-wince.

"I don't know." His face is red. I embarrassed him.

"Well," Pop Pop looks a little red around the cheeks and ears too. "If that's what you think, then never mind. I thought you might want to get involved by persuading your girlfriends to help us sew some uniforms."

Silence. That was a belly punch if I've ever gotten one. Zach outright laughs. Pop Pop would never understand how insulted I was at that moment because I really thought he was going to ask me to play ball, not sew.

"Flea sewing? That's funny, Dad," Zach is chuckling with his friends.

"Shut up, Zach. I don't sew, for God's sakes, Pop Pop," I mewl. "For once in your life, could you not see past my padded bra and recognize me as a human being and not as some ignorant woman from the 1800s?"

"What the heck are you talking about, Flea?" Pop Pop rolls his head back, scrubs his chin with his fingers. "And do not say that word out loud—" He pauses. "—bra. Don't say that with young men in the room."

"Bra isn't a bad word." I sigh. "Tits, maybe. Boobs might be considered inappropriate. I've heard Aunt Rita call them tatas. Never mind." I grit my teeth, look to the ceiling. "No, I'm just going to say it. Why do you never respect me for who I am? Did you ask Zach to sew uniforms?"

"No, because he is playing for the Brandy Mountain team. I thought you would want to be involved with our team somehow. It is big ball. With grown men who know the game." Pop Pop chuckles softly beneath his breath. "Baby girl, you're like a teeny, tiny butterfly."

Zach is playing for the Brandy Mountain team? I let this sink in, and for the moment, my anger at Pop Pop is waylaid and simmering somewhere in the back of my mind. "When did you decide to do this?" I turn my attention to Zach. "Why would you play for *them*?" Zach was always good at baseball. Not being one of the coach's sons nor from wealthy roots, he did a lot of bench sitting.

"He just don't want to play with a whole bunch of old men," Pop Pop tells me for Zach and I can see in the purse of his lips, it was as much a gut-punch for him when Zach told him he was playing with the younger men as it was when he asked me to sew uniforms. But, I'm sure he doesn't see my side. "Same thing everybody else is telling us. Billy Stinger is diabetic and two-hundred pounds overweight. Me, my knees act up."

"I didn't say that, Dad." Zach shifts in his chair. "Hey, I think we're heading out." He's going to leave me with Pop Pop all mad. I can see that.

"I have you parked in," I tell Zach, stuffing the box back up to the wall quickly. "I'll come back later and clean this up. I got to go."

"Are you going out with your new friends from the city?" Pop Pop asks me. "They're nice, right?"

"Yeah," I lie. "It's just a few girls and a PG movie." I feel horribly guilty right then telling him that untruth. I'm glad it is dark in the basement. "We're going to the movies." I didn't tell him about the award ceremony tonight. He'd want to go. I don't think he owns a suit and he wouldn't fit in with all the city people.

He reaches into his back pocket, pulls out his wallet. Then he opens it and pulls out a twenty-dollar bill. "Here, this will pay for the movie, a popcorn, and soda pop." I don't want to take it. Every shred of decency in my mind begs me to push it away. Yet, my car is running on fumes, and twenty dollars would get me three days of gas to work. "Thanks, Pop Pop," I tell him while he stuffs it in my hand. Then, he tells me he loves me and that I must wear my seatbelt.

"I'm not sixteen." I give him a peck on the cheek.

"To me, you are," he says. "You'll always be a little girl in my mind. Pint-size, not inconsequential." *Wink. Wink.* "Now, clean up your mess before you leave." He points to the boxes on the ground. Then he disappears out the door to get a soda.

Ah ha. Found them. I snatch out a pair of blue-tinted sunglasses, a red bandana, a little round dangly crystal and bobble-head Hawaiian girl that dances and wiggles. Then I cram the stuff back into the box. Ew. "Of all the things you trashed that you thought belonged to me, what could possibly lead you to decide to keep this? It's not even mine." I turn to Zach and hold up, between pinched finger and thumb, what could be a ripped bathing suit bottom with an American flag on it.

"He thought you might need it at the strip club if you didn't get a job," T.J. snickers right after looking toward the door to make sure Pop Pop left. I toss it at him and he ducks. Zach gives him an elbow in the side. "Oh, God, don't give me that mental image. You're burning brain cells."

"It isn't mine. This woman dances for no man, strip club or not," I announce. "Not me. Never. It is demeaning."

"Oh, come on," Beck chuckles. "Not even if you loved him—?"

"No, and I am not discussing how disgusting it is in the first place, women standing on a table and getting paid for taking off their clothes. A man would have to be sick to like it. I mean, what does the creep do? Go out to his car afterward and jack off?"

"Stop, Harley, you've gone too far." Zach snatches up the panty-things and gives me a pursed-lip gaze. "They are mine from my twenty-first birthday. Just put them in your box for now. I didn't want Dad to see them."

"So you put your creep-trophy in my box? That's even better." He tosses the bottoms to me. "If I put them in the box, you clean up the rest of my stuff. That's the deal." I haggle with him.

"Then you have to wash my truck."

"Then you have to cook supper on Sunday." I step back and they bounce off my leg. I fake a gag and pick them up.

30

And none-the-less, I drop them into the box and lug it upwards in my arms.

"Oh, my Lord," T.J. interrupts with an exaggerated sigh. "Will somebody just pick up the crap on the floor? This could go on forever. He's not asking you to put the damn things on—" They all groan like it is the grossest thing they could imagine.

"It's how they roll." Beck chuckles. "Just be glad we're not included in the negotiations this time."

I peer upward again, then turn. Still, they didn't have to act like it would be like watching a hippo dance across a stage or something. "A little help?"

All three stare at me unmoving. Then finally, Beck's the one who gets up and takes the box from my hands. "Just so you know, not every man is like the creepy bastards sitting in those chairs," he tells me with a nod toward T.J. and Zach. He gives me a smile, so I know he's mocking me. I'm not sure what his game is. I don't always catch sexual innuendos. Pop Pop was overprotective. "It's a trust thing."

"Screw off, Beck," I grunt. "I could not love a man enough to dance naked for him. Ever. It is degrading." My face is red because he laughs, and Zach asks what he just said to me.

"He's a perv," is all I say, and stomp out of the room.

Chapter 4

I wasn't lying when I told Max I am getting an award tonight. It was just exaggerated. The award is for being a Central Independent Realty Sales Agent Trainee of the quarter. But please hold your applause. There are three others in my region who will also be announced with the same honors and getting the same cream-colored, card-stock paper shoved into a dollar store frame that I watched Theo Winters, senior associate, design from a free customized template store online eight minutes before he had me run them through the printer.

Theo's thirty-seven with a faux-orange suntan and a sixty-dollar haircut. He reminds me of the fake-looking six-o'clock newscaster on TV with a big-toothed smile that's always plastered on his face even when somebody takes the last cup of coffee. He's also snooty, probably makes a million bucks a year, and knuckles me on the arm once a day to tell me *you'll get there, kiddo.* He told me the award is meant to give the company newbies some self-confidence; this is the point new sales associates start dropping like dead flies on a windowsill. Because life *inside* Central Independent Realty Team is like being a scrawny Chihuahua somebody found on the street who is tossed into a pile of Rottweiler pups in a pen at the pound already fighting over a too-gnawed-on bone. We aren't a team as the name implies. Well, unless you are comparing it to a game of dodgeball. Then yes, we are a team. The scrawny of us all get shoved in front of the ball, so we're first out. Because it will be another three years before I see that light at the end of the tunnel of selling 1970s mobile homes and ranch houses in low-income neighborhoods. And I've got to fight my way through the Rottweilers snatching up all the single-family townhomes, condos, and mansions to get there. Still, three hours after making a bored stare at the printer running the awards, I can see the stack of self-assurance frames plopped on a podium in one of the four, mid-size conference rooms at Brandenburg Lodge and

Conference Center. Audra Metzger, salesperson of the year for the fifth year running, finishes up on her three-hour, drawn-out speech to fifty-eight sets of bored eyes during our bi-yearly seminar started this afternoon. She's ginger-haired and drove into the parking lot in a little red Porsche. She hasn't blinked once beneath her too-black and too-thick eyelashes.

"What are you doing?"

I hear a whisper next to me. It is Lexie Todd leaning into me. We've gone through six months of training together. She started out looking like a high school dweeb, but eight months in, she lost the thick glasses and exchanged them for contacts. Not surprising, her family has enough money to help her build that expensive bridge from point A to point B; she sold one of her sisters a house already. She's also become a clone of all the other rigid, fake-tanned agents in the realty club with her shoulder-length hair and makeup plastered so thick on her face, I'm beginning to believe Central Independent is an alien abduction agency hell-bent on sucking the souls out of wannabe realtors and slowly taking over the world.

"I'm timing her," I poke a finger at my cell phone next to my glass of water. "She hasn't blinked. If she goes another forty seconds, I'm calling the cops. She's an alien."

Lexie stares at me with puckered lips. "Well, just so you know, you wouldn't call the police. You'd call the Pentagon." My head tips to the side because honestly, I think she is joking. She isn't. She's being sarcastic. She used to laugh at my stupid jokes. Now that the juice has been sucked from her brain and soul, she just sighs and shakes her head. Maybe it is getting sucked from mine too.

"If you don't like doing this, why are you doing it?" Lexie barks at me. "It wouldn't hurt to conform a bit." She has to lean in more so I can hear her. There's a wedding going on in the convention room next to us. The *boom-boom* of the music is making a muffled bang on the walls.

See? The brain is sucked out. But she has a good

question. Why? Well, that's a long story that I can't whisper to her from across our elbows at the table. I can, however, sum it up in four, short sentences. Because I was a history major in college. I can't find a job in my field. I have to pay back seventy-thousand dollars in student loans. My last two jobs lasted three months each. *Boom*, there you have it.

"I don't know," But that's how I answer her. I'd rather be over at the wedding, third glass of wine in hand, and gyrating across the dance floor into the middle of a crowd of sweaty, mostly drunk people I just met, but feel like my new, beautiful best friends. Instead, I'm sitting in the back of a room full of stuffy windbags in matching black, retail store suits letting my finger loll over the condensation on the glass of ice water left over from the mediocre, boxed-lasagna dinner. Every now and then when the band takes a break, I watch the wedding goers spill out of the room and flow toward the restrooms in the lobby. They are drunk and slap-happy. It irritates me. I'm bored and feel like a caged raccoon.

"—and this is for Record of Outstanding Quarterly Performance. Harley Davidson, who is our newest associate, can you come on up and accept the award?"

And that would be me. Yes, that is my name. My Pop Pop used to be in some sort of a motorcycle club called the Specters in the 1960s and 1970s. And you can guess his favorite kind of bike. My mama wanted to name me Willow Dawn. Pop Pop said if mama, who is his only daughter, called me that, I'd end up working at the dollar store during the day and as a stripper in the club off the highway all night. *Then what about Babe Ruth?* Pop Pop told me she said with a sassy waggle of her shoulders. *Because that's all you ever talk about is baseball, baseball.* He never told me why she didn't name me after that particular baseball legend. Because I ended up named after the motorcycle.

I rise, set my sights on Lissette Baker announcing the award. It's probably the only nice thing she has ever said about me. She's more about pointing out the flaws in my performance, more about noting to everyone that I'm probably at the bottom of the barrel of anyone she would choose to work in the business. She's Barbie Doll perfect with deep brown hair that looks like a sheet of black, shiny plastic rolling to her shoulders, complete with a slight curl at the bottom. She is forced-smiling at me while I balance my weight and strut up to the stage and accept the award from her cherry red fingernails.

She hands me the mic. I say a soft *thank you* and shove it back at her like it is on fire. Lissette giggles and makes some offhand remark about me being the softest-spoken realtor she has ever known. She makes a funny drum roll like she's just told a joke. Soft chuckles are returned from the audience who have all known me for the last eight months and know she is right as far as they know. For the last eight months, that is the person I have become because, for God's sake, the other didn't work out well for me. And that's when I hear the loud, hand-slapping clap-clap-clap over the polite patter of hands from the hundred or so guests at the bi-annual meeting. *Horrors.* I let my eyes roll over the heads slowly turning to the back of the room.

I stop my gaze just short of two men and one woman standing near the open doorway. It is the sandy blonde-haired man doing the clapping. He's wearing dress pants and a white shirt with rolled-up sleeves to his elbows. I catch a flash of the expensive gold watch his dad gave him six Christmases ago he never takes off and fiddles with constantly on his wrist. I'm sure his suit coat is nestled on the back of the chair at a table at the wedding next door. It is Trevor Woods, and I know him well.

"Way to go, Harley!" He yells drunk-loud over the heads of the crowd. I feel my face burn and know my pale cheeks are the same color as the two pieces of bread I caught on fire in my dollar store toaster this morning. I watch Lissette narrow her eyes out into the misty darkness, pucker her lips. Then her wary gaze turns to me like she has no clue what to say to this strange, out-of-ordinary bleep in her usually routine and most likely, pre-programmed-to-turn-out-bland life. But the heads in the audience are wagging curiously and cautiously toward the back, necks craning while they try to piece together the puzzle of the relationship between the *unobtrusive girl who never gets a sale* to the three drunk business meeting crashers. Oh, shit, and I see him take a step and I blanch. Then I whip my hand out, snatch up the mic from Lissette's limp hand and commit social and professional suicide.

"For those who are wondering who my fan club is in the back. That's my *ex*-boyfriend—" I point to the blonde-haired, brown-eyed drunk smiling up at me with a slightly evil narrow of his eyes. Then I wave a hand at the auburn-haired, slate-gray eyed eye candy next to him wheeling around to face my opponent like he's an offensive lineman playing block for a scrawny quarterback, me. "—a*nd* my ex-boyfriend's best friend. Just because simply the two of them don't add enough drama to put a new twist on this old performance playing out on the stage, the girl that's with them both—" I wag a finger at the slightly chubby, big-boobed blonde bombshell that would be better suited for a porn flick in the higher-than-mid-thigh dress she's wearing now. "—is my ex-best friend and the one who was sleeping with them both while I was planning my wedding. To give you a timeframe, we were best friends since fourth grade in Missus Midkiff's class. Her name's Lila Chambers, and she'd been screwing my boyfriend for a year. *Ba-dum chah.*" I do a drum roll with my fingers like I just laid out a good punchline and then cock my thumb and gunpoint both my forefingers at my audience. Lissette is still staring at the three in the back with this wide-eyed gaze like a doe caught in the headlights before she tows her gaze to me with slightly parted, speechless lips. I thrust the mic back at her and humbly hug my award to my chest. Then I make the most incredibly humiliating run-walk back to my seat while Max drags Trevor out of the room.

I plop down. Lexie's eyes are wide and staring hard at me

while she makes a quick shift of her chair a couple scoots away and turns quickly, so her back is to me as not to allow anyone to think it was her fault we are sitting together. She is quietly contemplating how she can make it clear to Lissette she doesn't know me.

I clasp my hands together like a good schoolgirl at her desk and hard stare up at the podium where Lissette is fumbling around with the awards and a little paper she uses to remember what she is going to say. "Is the drama over then?" Suddenly, Taylor Dixon has bounded up the little steps to the stage. She's Lissette's sidekick and (if the office gossip is correct) her secret lover. Lissette is married with two kids, which I suppose makes big-eyed Taylor *the other woman*. I mean, I've got to be honest. If I liked girls, I'd be hightailing it towards her like a fat kid rushes into the kitchen when the timer goes off for a pan full of double hot-fudge brownies. She's long-legged and gorgeous with these huge eyes that look like one of those flying squirrels. Her hair is deep chestnut brown and shimmers down her shoulders to halfway down her back. I only know two people who are take-your-breath-away gorgeous like that. They are Taylor Dixon and Max Matthews-Branntwein, my ex-boyfriend's best friend. In fact, when she settles into the stage next to her could-be-lover, I almost hear a sigh of contentment in the crowd while she spars back and forth with Lissette leaving everybody laughing in their seats and I'm fixing the two up in my head—a match made in heaven.

"Hey, Soul Sister."

I am walking alone to my car. It is so far out in the parking lot, I had to zig-zag twice around two sections because I couldn't find it.

"Max," I say it flatly, fondling the doorknob with my fingers. That Max was able to get to my car before me makes me uneasy. On the third of June nearly five years ago, ol' Max was sitting on the couch in the living room of the apartment Trevor and I shared when I opened up the front door to slip inside. He was lounging with his tan arms folded staring at the TV. I hardly noticed him make a quick jump up. I was opening the last envelope I'd just gotten from the mailbox.

That's when I heard Max bang on the wall. It was two times loud with his fist, a slight lull for three seconds, then one slap of his hand. I jumped, startled, and looked up at the exact same time the contents of the envelope spilled out on to the floor. He laughed while I watched my life flit away with seventeen well-taken photographs of Trevor with other women.

So, *Soul Sister*, I am not. I grapple with the door handle. "If you're looking for your stuff, most of it got tossed when I left, Max," I divulge. There's a ball of tears laying in my chest and feeling like it is bouncing its way back up. To make matters worse, I see a gray Mini Cooper with the convertible top down whipping its way around the corner of the parking lot heading for the exit. It comes to a jolting stop just past me and Max, then backs up a few feet.

It is Theo's car. I try to make a quick bargain with Max to get rid of him: "Listen, do you know if Trevor—" I take in a breath, puff it out, "—tossed my stuff? I mean, like my—"

"I've got your stuff." He is flat-line gazing at me and not the car. "That necklace your mom got you and your clock. I've got a whole box of it. I got it before Lila tossed it."

"Okay, I've got your crystal and stuff in a box under my bed. I'll get it to you. We'll make an exchange."

"You sound like we're two warring countries exchanging prisoners." Max turns, takes in the car. "Who is that?" he asks. I take the moment to tug open the door, plop inside.

"People I work with. Can you please go away, Max?" Both our eyes turn toward the front seat. "My new friends don't know what the *old me* was like. I'd like to keep it that way." I see Theo push his elbow on the edge of the driver's side window, craning his neck to look from me to Max while Lissette peers at me from the passenger seat.

"Is he bothering you?" Theo asks. I feel like the backward

little kid that's getting bullied on the playground and the popular kids have come to save me.

"No," I tell him, and he tips his head to one side, narrows his eyes like he doesn't understand. I hear soft laughter in the car, and my eyes sway to the backseat. It's Taylor smiling while she scoots up and rests her chin on her wrist between the seats. Audra Metzger is beside her. Considering the four had spent the rest of the conference leaning over and appearing to whisper when they looked my direction, I'm surprised they even stopped to see if I wasn't getting kidnapped by Max in the parking lot. I'd be one less pup with whom to compete.

"She's fine," Audra sighs and waves a hand in the air.

"We're going out for some drinks." It is Lissette who is staring at me with a less than welcoming face and from the passenger side window. "You want to come?" I know if I don't take her up on the offer, I'll double my etiquette blunder from earlier on the stage. However, her face is screaming for me to say *no*. Still, there's something about wanting Max and Trevor and Lila to know I'm worth keeping around and especially with people like Lissette and Theo who have money and good jobs and clout. I set my eyes on her.

"Yeah, sure," I mutter.

I hop out of my car, ignore Max who is shaking his head with a little smile on his lips.

"See you around, Harley," he sniffs at me. And he leans in while I pass. "You can change the way you dress and even change the friends you have. You can't hide the old you. You can't keep secrets. *And* you're a nervous drinker. I know you and eventually, the shit is going to hit the fan." He stops and taps his chin reflectively. "I give it two months. And who's going to bail you out then? Them?"

Chapter 5

The shit hit the fan within twenty-four hours. I will say it was the same time my life would take a jagged twist to the left with the similar outcome a cat tries to make a sheer turn on a freshly polished wood floor while running from a dog. It turns, claws raking the floor. Sliding. Bam!

It would occur the second I sat down with my coworkers at the table at Black Jack's Club and Theo asks: "So, Harley, what's your story?" I answer: "I—I don't have a story, really, I just get up and go to work, then I come home at night." They all stared at me deadpan. But it isn't like I really know anything about them outside the confines of the workplace. They all appear just like unfamiliar faces on a stranger's framed picture hanging on a random wall to me. Somebody ordered drinks and shoved one in my hand. "I don't drink," I gripe while I stare at what Taylor Dixon called a *Mystic Whiskey.* "I'm warning you. I don't hold my alcohol well. I start thinking I'm superwoman." That got laughter. Three sips of the drink and I think the last sensible thing I remember saying was: "Okay, guys, you want my story? I'll tell it. But it plays out like a B-rated horror movie where I'm running in the darkness from a couple clowns, an ax-murderer, and the cops and I realize everybody in the audience thinks it's funny and they are laughing—"

Theo thinks this is funny. He starts laughing, and I don't think he stops snorting at every stupid attempt I make at a joke for the next hour and fourteen minutes. I tell them about stupid college pranks I did and about Pop Pop and the old guys running around like clowns trying to play ball. It is a bit of an ego-builder, I suppose. Trevor never laughed at my jokes, stupid or occasionally spot-on. Such, when Theo follows me to the dance floor and tries to buy me more drinks, I drunk-fall-in-lust with him. Then, when we're heading back to the office to get our car and even as sober starts to take over, he makes sure I'm smooshed up against him in the seat.

It isn't surprising when I find myself alone upstairs to use the bathroom, Theo is waiting for me at the door. "So, I thought there might be a little wildcat hidden underneath the pussycat. I wasn't wrong."

"What?" I'd slipped partially out the bathroom door, planning an escape down the stairs.

"Lissette's good at reading people. She culls out the meek—"

"Like a wolf picking out the juiciest sheep to eat?" I ask. I feel his finger wiggle on my right shoulder. I suppose the last three hours of dirty dancing with him across the floor has given him the opinion I'm open to anything.

"No," he snickers. "She gets rid of the weak ones, the ones who won't sell the houses or will get rolled over by the customers. She must have seen something in you. You're still around. Then, tonight, I saw it. I thought all along you were this little, quiet mouse and you're like—"

"A wildcat." I sigh inwardly. I'm just not good at being somebody else even if I want to change it up a bit.

"I'm going to kiss you. Is this going to be a problem?"

He's got the same scaredy-cat look on his face as Zach used to get when I would dive on him and start punching when we would tussle around at six or seven years old. He was like three times bigger than me and no less meek, but he always told me I scare the shit out of everybody. *Why are all the boys scared of me?* I asked Pop Pop once. He just laughed, told me I had a wild look to my eyes and a certain confidence. It made me appear bigger and badder to them than what I really was kind of like my aunt's teeny Chihuahua thinks it is a Pitbull and somehow convinces everyone in the room he is by yapping and baring his teeth.

"Just one kiss." Why did I say that? I'm not sure. It just didn't seem like an option to opt out after grinding him on the dance floor. And well, he's kind of drunk-cute. And I'm still a bit superwoman. Then, his tongue's in my mouth. We're sliding inside the bathroom door. Theo reaches under each of my thighs. He tugs me up to the sink.

"Show me something new," he whispers to me. "I haven't been with a lot of women."

I'm thinking I don't know anything *new*. I mean, I've only been with a handful of guys. I've been called a bit wild. But not that kind of wild, you know, the sleep-with-every-guy-who-walks-through-my-door kind of wild. However, I can see where my persona might have gotten misconstrued when I started screaming: *Let's close this place down!* at the dance club while I was gyrating so hard against Theo, my butt's still a little numb.

Still, in flipping through channels on the pay TV, I have been known to take a short recess on what Trevor used to call soft porn weepies—love stories with a whole lot of sex. I try to be cool before I bump my head on the mirror of the sink and say: "Let's just make it easy." I reach around my purse and pull out one of three condoms I've kept tucked in a side pocket for longer than I'd like to admit. Okay, seven months. Shit, eight. It's been eight months. "I'll drop my panties, wrap my legs around your waist—" And suddenly just saying that in the aura of still being soused enough my head didn't hurt after I bumped it on the mirror *and* after eight months of celibacy makes me horny enough to just latch on to his pants, drag Theo over and rip the condom open. "Screw it, big boy," I make a throaty whisper while I slither off the sink, wiggle my dress up and my panties down. I hop back up on the sink, motion him forward, and wrap my legs around his waist and know he's ready because he's hard against my thighs. "Just do it."

"I think I'm going to die." That's me. I'm sitting in the dark breakroom with my face flat on the fake wood of the table four hours later. It is cool on my forehead. My head is throbbing like a balloon getting filled with too much water from the sink faucet and getting ready to burst. The only light is the digital pad on the microwave by the sink. It is one o' clock in the morning.

"You're not going to die." Taylor Dixon is telling me

42

those words softly, rolling her eyes, and giving me a gentle, motherly smile. She has whisked across the room with a plastic baggie filled with ice from the freezer section of the refrigerator. She lays it on the back of my neck. I peer at her out of the corners of my eyes. "You're just going to feel like it." She pats my back, sits down beside me. "I think you threw most of it up outside Lissette's office door."

"Is she mad about that?"

Taylor eyes me cautiously, bites her lip. "She's a little upset. I'm not sure if it was that—" She is grinning at me like we have some little secret. "If you know what I mean."

"What I did with Theo?"

"Well, no, you're a consenting adult—"

"Oh, it was the kiss." I groan. The kiss. Oh, yeah, I kissed Taylor Dixon. Why? Because she's beautiful and funny and everything I want to be in a woman. Oh, and I can't handle a drink. Ugh. That's probably another reason Theo tracked me down like he was sniffing out a dog in heat. I vaguely remember dancing. I can kind of remember a lengthy conversation about baseball and Pop Pop. Then I started asking her if she wanted to sew baseball uniforms with me because that's all Pop Pop thought I could do. After that, the foggy conversation swayed to hamsters or something really weird and then just asking her what it was like kissing another girl. She said it was gentle and sweet and suddenly, the booze kicked in and my superwoman comes out. I leaned over in my chair, pushed up to meet her height and gave her a longer kiss than I'd ever given Trevor. She was right. Her lips were soft and tasted like rum and coke. She kissed me back with a gentle hand on my cheek. My face turns a deep shade of hot red. "I kissed you." I sit up long enough the ice rolls down my back. I throw back my head and groan. "I am sorry, so sorry. I warned you. I can't hold a drink worth—" The *old me* wants to say *shit*. The new me pauses and finishes with "—anything."

"It was nice. No worries." Taylor makes a quick catch of the icepack, and plops it back on my neck, balances it there with her fingers.

"It was nice." I blush. "It was the best kiss I've ever had. It still doesn't make me like girls. Is that weird?"

"No, it's kind of built-in, I think, liking men or women. Or both."

"You're not mad?"

"For getting kissed by a *hot* girl?"

My eyes dart upward to her. She is tall. I know my cheeks are probably as red as a burner on an oven turned to high. "I'm not hot. I'm somewhere in the middle."

She laughs. I cringe. I feel like the dorky thirteen-year-old girl who just got lucky and, for lack of a place to sit in the middle school lunchroom, plops down with the most popular girl who scoots over spontaneously, so I don't accidentally end up in her lap. I let my chin rest on my wrist. "You think Lissette's going to fire me?"

"Why would you say that?" Taylor asks. I look up. She is staring at me with the vigilant gaze of one who has a secret that may or may not have been leaked to the person to whom she is speaking.

"I don't know," I elude the question. Because Lissette likes Taylor. It's obvious the sensual looks they give each other. It makes the room sultry. "Because maybe it's just not appropriate behavior for the work staff, throwing up on the carpet outside your boss's office—"

Taylor laughs. "Or coaxing an entire bar full of strangers into the parking lot for a game of baseball with a lemon from the bar?"

"I did that. Ugh. I'm dead, right?"

"You did hit Lissette with the lemon in the head. But if she does fire you, Theo will probably put a stop to it. I heard him whistling the National Anthem after he came out of the bathroom." She sniffs a laugh. "Or after that kiss, *I* will stop her."

"Aw, Taylor," I groan. I scrub my face with my hand.

"Listen, Harley," Taylor reaches out, swipes the hair

from my eyes with her fingers. "You worry too much. You'll fit in with all of us. Can I make a suggestion?" she asks me, and I nod. "Okay, *you* being *you* is great. You're going to be a great salesperson. I can see it in your stature. It's your clothes that maybe hold you back; you get me? I'm not being mean. I just think you need to step it up a bit. And I wasn't kidding. I did fast-pitch softball in high school. I can show you how to pitch. Then maybe those old guys you were talking about will see the light and let you play. I'd like to get to know you better." Her words are lost to the clack-clack of high heels. Our eyes to turn to the breakroom door.

"Somebody's been trying to get you on your cell phone for an hour, Harley." It is Lissette leaning against the door, waggling her hand out toward me. She looks up at the clock. "You know it's one in the morning, right?" She's holding my cell phone in her fingers. I nod. Her face has no expression while she slips through the door and slaps my phone down a little roughly next to my elbow. "I heard it from my office. It was by the toilet in the bathroom." She looks from me and to Taylor, and then back to me again. "Where it must have fallen out of your purse. I'm assuming whatever went on tonight isn't going to disrupt our office. Don't let it happen again." Then she looks at Taylor. "I'm going home and get some sleep. Make sure she's not drunk before she takes off in her car."

I'm stuck between wanting to say *yes, ma'am* and *yeah, okay*. I choose the former and Taylor giggles, looks up at Lissette. "Can I see you in my office?" Lissette eyes Taylor coolly then and Taylor's smile fades.

"Yes, ma'am," she giggles again and pats my arm like we share a joke. Lissette doesn't join in her soft laughter. I grit my teeth and sit up, letting the ice pack skate a moist-chilly down my back. Then Taylor leans in. "Think about what I said. I'll take you shopping. We'll get you a new wardrobe, make you look like a sales rep—a sexy sales rep." I narrow my eyes at my phone. There's no caller ID. Still, I pick it up, imagining any one of the people in my family broken down on the side of the highway or worse.

"Hey, Harley. This is Harley, right? It's Trevor."

I think I'm broke. It only took hearing Trevor's voice on the other end to send my head reeling.

"Yeah, it's me. It's way past midnight, Trevor, don't call me. Especially after making me look like an idiot in front of all my co-workers tonight. What the hell were you thinking clapping like that?"

"Don't hang up. Harley, you don't have to hate me," Trevor's purring on the phone. "I'm drunk. I need a ride from Billy Youngblood's house. Max took my keys at the Main Street Bar, and then we ended up here. I need to get out of here. Max won't take me home."

"Billy Youngblood," I grunt the name. Billy's the neighborhood party house. He was that guy who was twenty-something when we were in high school and bought all the underage girls beer hoping he'd get a screw out of it. Now he's forty-one and still partying with the high school kids. "Listen, I'm an hour away. It'll be too late."

"Please."

"No, Trevor. I'm not your doormat anymore. Go find some other dumbshit girl to step all over." I hang up, wish I could hear some of that victorious girl-tells-crappy-ex-boyfriend-to-go-to-hell scores you hear in the movies at the epic point a battle has been won. I don't. It is just the clock tick-tick-ticking and then the ting of my phone again. I stare at it in my hand. BILL YO That's what the caller ID says.

I pick it up. "Hey, is this Harley?" I hear Billy Youngblood's voice on the other end. It's deep.

"Sweetie, you know the drill. Trevor's shitfaced. He's picking fights, and he's not trashing my house again."

"Tell him to get his girlfriend to give him a ride."

"Listen, I'm nobody's secretary. I'm not spending another minute on this phone trying to search up somebody he hasn't pissed off. It is either you or I'm calling the cops."

Chapter 6

It was the November 28th of this past year when I came back to Lost Hollow. I stood outside my grandpa's little paint-peeling house with the sleet pelting on the windows and the little porch and my bare shoulders. I had never felt so alone. Nothing had changed since I'd left five years and two months ago. There was still an old riding lawnmower with four blown-out tires parked on the side lawn with tufts of knee-high grass growing in an oval around it. The first wooden front step was still broken, and Pop Pop's neighbor's cat was hunkered down on the railing growling at me while he dined on the dollar store Me-Wow Kitty Chow Pop Pop still put in a lime green bowl for him. Julie McCoy, in the house next door, was still pretending to wash the dishes while she peered out the window to catch every juicy bit of gossip going on in her neighborhood. I didn't have anything but the clothes on my back—a tank top, a pair of jean shorts, and my flip-flops. Pop Pop stood there at the door, looked me up and down.

"What are you doing in your underwear in the cold, girl?" Pop Pop demanded. "And what's all that on your face anyway?"

I'd reached up, touched the earring on my nose absently. "It's just an earring, *Poppy*—"

"Not that, girl. The tears. Are you crying? Uh oh, you called me *Poppy*," he groans. "I'm always Poppy when you're in trouble. Are you in trouble?"

"You said—you said if I left," I stumbled past chattering teeth, "I couldn't come back. But I don't—I don't have any place left to go. Can I just stay a couple—maybe just a night? Pop Pop, I—" I wanted to tell him the truth, I'd been living in my car for a month. It was too cold to sleep with sleet pelting my windshield in the Park and Ride lot off the main highway. "I just need a bed for the night." I think it was the hardest thing I'd ever had to ask. By the look on the wrinkled face with prickly whiskers, he expected no less. "I stopped at Mama's, and her boyfriend's there, and there's only one room in the trailer." Mama's boyfriend is skinny and weaselly, and when he talks to me, he talks to my boobs. He creeps me out. There was no way I was sleeping on the couch only to wake up with him squirming on top and wrestling up my shirt with his dirty fingers.

"Was it all you thought it was going to be, Harley, that big world out there?" The door wasn't opening wide enough for me to come inside. I think my toes were blue. I could smell a waft of beef stew which must have been Pop Pop's supper still lingering in the oozy darkness behind him and sweeping out to the porch.

"No, it was too big, too—" I sighed. Too what? Crazy? Life outside the little town I'd been nestled in my entire life wasn't what I thought it'd be. I've fallen on my ass so many times, and in so many ways, I didn't think I could quite possibly surpass my last failure. I did. And, mind you, I'm not scared to jump in feet first. I suppose, in retrospect, that is my greatest fault. I don't think things out all the way.

"Well, this little stint didn't last long," he grumbled while I worked up one of those all-body shivers against the icy sleet coming down from the black, midnight sky above and dribbling a tiny river down my spine. "Did you find your dream out there? Did you catch up with that unicorn you were chasing?" He looked up at the dark sky above my head. "Did you finish what you started for once?"

He wiggled his fingers in the air, reminding me of those last words I screamed right before I slammed the door in his face. *If this place is what dreams are made of, why are you sitting on a couch that's twenty years old and so beat up, it has holes every three inches. Dreams. What do you know about dreams? You worked for the same damn coal company for fifty years, and you live in—this. Now all you do is sit around and watch TV. It's easy, Pop Pop, to finish stuff if what you set out to do every morning is nothing more than sitting on your old ass on the couch! I'm not going to get stuck in this hell-hole—*

But no, I didn't find my dreams out there. He didn't have to be so mean about it. I nodded. He was number four on my long list of people who had not answered the phone when I called or didn't open their door to me. "Okay." I turned. I remember the tears. They were so hot on my cheeks to the cold wind patting my face. My heater in my vehicle had gone out sometime last summer and gone unnoticed until I tried to use it in mid-September.

"All storms die down after a while," he told me. I didn't know what that meant. I turned. Pop Pop had stepped back from the door and held it open wide as if to let me through. I eyed him cautiously.

"He's trying to tell you, dumbass, that you're going to freeze out there." That was my Uncle Zach working his way up behind my grandpa. He was jabbing his spoon into stew in a bowl and digging out a carrot. "We thought you were dead in a ditch, Flea. You just disappeared off the face of the earth. Well, that's what Beck and T.J. wagered ten bucks on. I said you were way too mean. If you got into a fight with somebody, it'd be the other guy curled into a ball and crying his eyes out. It sure as hell wouldn't be you—"

"Do not curse in my house, son," Pop Pop snarled.

"—Guess you're not dead," Zach ignored him. "I'm twenty bucks richer." Zach would also be the one who dragged me back into Pop Pop's house that night. "Get your butt in here. That's just Pop's way of telling you that the last one thousand and fifty-two times you screwed up, he's picked you up off the ground. You got at least three more before he boots your sorry, scrawny butt completely out. You're broke or something; you know that, right? Something with you, it just ain't right." Still, he smiled at me. "You're like a bottle of Mountain Dew with a hole in the bottom of the aluminum can. The good stuff's all leaked out." He bounced his free knuckle on the top of my head. "Nothing but air left. But if you're coming back, I get four days to get all my junk out of your old room. I'm using it for storage."

"Two days and I'm not helping you." I think if he hadn't been there, I would have left, and my grandpa would have just let me leave.

But it's because Pop Pop's already seen me screw up those one-thousand and fifty-three times, exaggerated or not, that I pause at the stop sign at the exit ramp at Main Street where the Main Street Bar sits halfway through the town of Baker and Billy Youngblood's house is only a short drive away. It's almost like I can see into the future and know this is that one mistake out of so many I've already made tonight that I'll regret the longest. And yet, I take the step forward, push my foot to the gas. I'm stone-cold sober and feeling ugly with doubt. It is way past one or two in the morning. I'm dog-tired, have a raging headache, and an hour ago I was a good ankle-deep in disappointment in myself for getting drunk earlier in the evening. Now, that uncertainty has worked itself knee-high and mixed with the resentment that I simply can't walk away from Trevor. He's standing on the front porch of the older, two-story home. It's wood and white.

"Why's she here?"

I can hear a voice belt those words out when I pull up to the curb and roll down my window at the end of a walkway. It's Max Matthews-Branntwein. I can hear Trevor and Max barking low at each other and the next thing I know, I see the punches flying. *What?*

This is something new. I've known both since middle school. I've never seen them fight each other. I sit there in subdued disbelief for ten seconds watching them scrap it out down three concrete steps. It's like I'm watching the final scene of a seven-part miniseries play out that has gone far south of the original plot in the first six episodes. I suppose I'm a bit mesmerized by it all; those two always disagreed on everything in the same way brothers agree to disagree, but I've never seen Trevor throw a punch at Max. It's something akin to flipping on the TV and having the goriest part of a horror movie playing out on the screen, and for some reason, my finger pumping on the button to change the channel isn't working. It's that sudden and unexpected taste of disbelief mixed with the inability to stop what is going on.

And still, I try. I jerk open my car door and make a mad rush up the walkway. By the time I get there and grunt-yell at the two bodies flopping wildly half in the spring grass and half on the broken concrete sidewalk, Billy Youngblood's slamming back his screen door and trip-running down the steps.

In their melee, both the men rise, and Billy does this chest thrust at Max, who is two-sizes bigger and something of a wildcard. I know why he picked Max, though. It was a knee-jerk reaction to protect me because I've been known to jump in with fists flying and, in the past, my allegiance was with Trevor. Nobody wants to see a teeny tiny girl get hit, not that Max would hit a girl. However, I suppose in the heat of the moment, Billy assumes since Trevor had never hit me in the past, it wasn't going to happen now. Of course, that leaves me standing with a stupid gaze on my face staring at Trevor, whose loyalty I no longer have. He starts to move forward, and mini-me takes a rigid step in front of him and if for no other reason because I know he'll reach over Billy and punch Max.

"Trevor, don't," I say softly, push a hand on his shirt near his belly. I cringe inwardly because my wide eyes are looking up at him with a pleading gaze something akin to a scared, sad bunny. But when you're tiny like me, there's only so many defensive tools to utilize when you're stuffed between two grown men randomly tossing punches at each other. I'm quite proficient at it. I've had so many boy cousins and uncles growing up, I've learned by the tone of my voice and the way I carry myself at this very second when there's a turning point in a disagreement, in a twitch of an eye, I can either start World War III or end a quarrel pretty fast with what my Pop Pop calls crocodile tears. I'd even lowered myself, at age twelve, to plopping three sexually explicit magazines with naked girls sitting on ATVs on the covers I'd dug out from underneath my Uncle Nate's secret hiding place (which was his mattress). I'd plopped them in the middle of the living room floor where a battle between bigger Nate and much smaller Zach was taking place and not to Zach's advantage and hollered out: *Look, Pop Pop, come look what I just found upstairs in Nate's room!*

It can backfire like it did with Nate. I couldn't steal his stash of Slim Jims he hid in the same place anymore and blame it on somebody else. This time, I'm thinking it worked, though. I look up at Trevor who is shaking his head like a dog shakes his head after taking a dip in a creek and looking down at me. "Let's go," I add and nod toward my car. "Please."

Just like that, he steps back and I see him eye a teeth-gnashing Max with an almost confused twist to his dark eyes. "Let's go," I say it again. This time, I push a little gently on his belly. I see Trevor looking down at my fingers on his shirt, a denim blue button-up, and he bobs his head up and down.

"You're making a mistake, Harley," Max grunts to our backs. I could have killed him because Trevor flinches. His fingers ball into a fist. I have to grab a swatch of his shirt and tug him along with me to the car.

"So where have you been, Harley?" Trevor asks when he sinks into my passenger side seat. He breathes it out like he's just been waiting with bated breath to ask me those words. He's dabbing at a dribble of blood on his nose with his wrist, then wiping it on his jeans. They are light blue, and his forefinger leaves a print of red where he swiped it off. I feel a spit of rain pattering my bare forearm while I close the door. Droplets have settled on the windshield. I wait until he shuts the door. I lean over, snatch a leftover fast food napkin from the glovebox and hand it to him. He's strangely subdued for just belting it out with his best friend.

"I've been working for a realty company. Well, it's mostly training right now," I say, turning on the car and pushing my foot to the gas. I flip on the windshield wipers, watch them shove away one layer of droplets before the glass is covered again. I'm afraid to look at him. I hate him for what he did to me. And still, it's like a little piece of my heart thinks I should just let it slide. Luckily, my brain overrides with images of pictures falling to the floor, a soft porn collage of Trevor with one girl, then with another. "You obviously know that. Are you going to your house or—?"

"You know what I'm talking about," he retorts. "And yes, I'm going home." He's got a chip on his front tooth, he's had it as long as I can remember, and when he makes a sarcastic smile at me, I take it in for just a second before I turn my attention to the dark road. I always wondered why he didn't get that fixed. His family is from up on top of the mountain just like Max's. They're middle class, and his dad works for the telephone company. "You fell off the face of the earth for five years. Gone." He snaps his fingers. He's drunk, and I think he might be high on something. He's got dark cinnamon-colored eyes. The irises look almost like two big, black peas right now in the two street lights that are actually working on the corner. "You've got a boyfriend?"

Leave it to Trevor to broach that subject. "Why do you care?" I spit back. He sniffs a laugh. "Listen," I say. "I don't really want to talk to you, so let's keep it simple. Ask me the time of the day or what the weather is going to be tomorrow. Then we can have a conversation. Don't get personal." I look over, cock my chin, but I see him tuck his chin just a little like he's peering out the side view mirror at the light bobbing up and down from the car behind us. I make the turn on one street, then the next seconds after.

"My dad always called you a spitfire. He was right. But we had some good times, right?"

"*Had* is the keyword. And it sucked finding out I was sharing them with you *and* with a bunch of other women."

"I can assume you're not going to be the one I ask to hide all those porn magazines you made me pack away in my garage if I die so my mom doesn't find them. You know, *the tub of love*." He gives me a sly smile. *The tub of love.*

"It's more like the tub of lust," I retort sourly. "But no, I'm not saving your fake girlfriends from the trash."

"There might be something in it for you," he chuckles hoarsely like he's talking sexy to me. He's poking nervously at the blood on the knee of his pants. "But you'd do it, right? We had enough good times you'd do that for me?"

"When you think you're dying, you ask me again. I'll consider it." I sigh and shake my head. "Don't get weird on me." I don't even know enough about drugs to ask him what he's taken because he's antsy settled into the seat, leaning up, leaning back and shifting constantly.

"I think somebody's following us," Trevor mutters. I turn the windshield wipers on higher. The mist is turning to a steady rain. I peer into the rear-view mirror. There's a car behind us. It isn't tailgating or anything. I don't note anything strange about it. However, Trevor is jittery and jumpy like he's downed six cups of coffee.

"Trevor, there's only one way in and one way out of this old subdivision," I tell him. "It is just somebody leaving the party heading the same direction. Besides," I go on, turning out on to Main Street in town. "Who would follow me? I've got no enemies barring the guy I dropped my grape slushy on at the gas station the other day."

"I don't know," he mumbles under his breath. All three lights are green while I head through town. I burst out the other side at about thirty-five miles an hour and into the darkness of the bottomland of the mountains on my left and the river on my right.

"Listen, I just wanted to tell you I'm sorry."

After Trevor says those words, I feel my hands vibrate on the steering wheel. I listen to nothing but my little car engine grinding away on the asphalt road and a song on the radio that is so low, I can't even recognize the tune. The driver of the car behind me has the brighter, high-beam lights on. It stings my eyes. I try not to look in my rear-view mirror. It doesn't sound like Trevor. He never apologizes because he never thinks he's wrong.

"I'm just saying."

Again, I let his voice fall flat in the air. This is going to be a long forty-minute drive to Brandy Mountain.

"Lila, she's a bitch. She played me; you know that, right? As soon as you were out of the picture, she was—"

"I don't know why you're telling me this. Please, just shut up. Let the silence be awkward between us."

"Oh, God, I don't know what went wrong with me," he groans and sits back in the seat. "I threw a punch at Mateo tonight. Mateo, of all people. My life's out of control." He takes a breath, smiles a little to himself. "I can't believe he didn't kill me."

"Yeah, that wasn't the brightest thing I've seen you do." I peer over at him. "He'll forgive you. What was that all about?"

"I don't know. He's weird. He's always been weird about stuff. He gets attached, you know?"

"No," I say. "No, Trevor, I don't know."

He chuckles low. "Yeah, I think he'd rather have gone with mommy than daddy after the breakup."

"Well, he tried to go with his mommy after his parents divorced. He came home to live with his dad." I am hardly focused on the conversation. The lights in the car behind mine are flicking consistently from low beam to high beam as if the driver is signaling me to pull over so he can pass.

"No, doofy *you*. He was like a kid who got stuck with the wrong parent after a bad divorce. Our breakup."

"Yeah, he wouldn't have liked going with mommy." I flip on my right turn signal and start to pull over on the gravel brim so the idiot behind me can pass.

"What are you doing?" Trevor's head snaps upward.

"I'm letting him pass. The idiot's blinding me."

"No, don't." Trevor is looking wildly behind us. The car seems to sit there, the driver indecisive about why I'm suddenly driving along the solid yellow line on the side. I see it slip out as if to pass. But the car is going slowly, and through my windshield, I see oncoming traffic—the lights of a truck rumbling along the route.

"What the hell are you doing?" Trevor hisses as the car lights come up almost to my back-passenger door.

"There's a truck coming!" I snap back. "I don't want to kill us!" I shove my foot to the brake. I'm assuming the driver behind us doesn't have a clue what I'm doing. The car makes a jerky veer into the other lane and then, as if realizing there's a semi-truck coming head on and the vehicle *has* to pass me, the driver floors it and makes a fishtailing race to get in front of me.

The moment passes in a flurry of lights and the drawn-out howl of the semi-truck horn. I stop my car, turn to Trevor. "See, dumbass?" I throw my hand out toward the taillights disappearing in my windshield.

"He's following us. I'm telling you."

"And you're on drugs or something, Trevor," I bicker with him. "What's wrong with you?"

"You got to go, Harley. Listen to me—" And it is like suddenly, Trevor's eyes are wide, and he looks crazy-antsy. "Get out and let me drive."

"No way. You're crazy. I haven't paid off my car, and the insurance is high—" And it is just like this—I feel Trevor's hand wiggling near the buckle of my seatbelt. I feel it unlatch from my chest.

"GET OUT. LET ME DRIVE!" He bellows those words. I jump, startled.

"I said, no!" I slap his hands away. It isn't hard, but I'm yelling at him to get the hell out of my car, he's crazy. And he's yelling back and suddenly, Trevor latches on to the top of my dress, and he shoves me up against the passenger door. I'm not expecting it.

"Do you want to die?"

"Trevor, stop! What is wrong with you?" I'm just rabbit-blinking rapidly, then grunting out something about not touching me or I'll break his damn fingers. Then, unexpectedly, I feel the thump of the back of his fist to my cheek not just once, but *bam, bam, bam* three times. It's like he's incredibly mad and can't stop.

"See you won't listen!" he yells. I hear me screaming and feel the smack of his palm on my head while I hold my hands up, feign his blows. I'm stunned, outraged, and dazed all at once. It is all I can do but scrabble for the latch of my driver's seat door while one more smack of the side of his hand slams down on my shoulder. I twist awkwardly and spider-crawl out into the wet dark opening of the door while the car starts scooting forward on its own. I feel my knees smack cruelly on the wet gravel road. I bounce upward, make an awkward walk-crawl with my palms smacking the side of the car for balance. The car stops, and I see Trevor's shadow like he's coming out the driver's side door.

"Jesus Christ," he yell-whines. I cringe thinking he's coming back to hit me more. Something plops near my knee. It's my purse. That's not a good sign. I barely note it while I balance there shaking. This isn't the Trevor I know. It isn't. He wouldn't drop me in the middle of the state route on a dark, rainy night. He grunts. "Something is going to happen to me. I know it. Don't let my mom see the stuff in the garage, okay Harley? You know what I'm talking about. Get the damn thing out of there so she won't see it."

I hear him. I also hear another car far off. Then, there's the bang as he shuts the car door. I hear my own voice screaming at him about how much of a dumb, fucking shit he is. My hand stretches out. My fingertips tickle along the cool, dampness of my purse. Then, I feel the back bumper skim off the pinky finger of my left hand. I trip-walk, trying to maintain some balance to get to my feet. I feel the warmth of blood dribbling on each knee. My palms are skinned, my cheek aching. That's when I turn, blink, and see headlights bearing down on me, blinding me to the desperate squeal of tires on drenched pavement.

Chapter 7

"Hey, I didn't know who else to call—" I'm sitting on the concrete curb in front of Bakers Quickie Stop and Gas. It's in the orange glow of the storefront lights. I am also as close as possible to the front doors as I can get in case the two grungy-looking, old men, who have settled into their dented pickup trucks near the men's bathroom on the side of the building, decide to stop sexy-eyeing me and get out of their vehicles for the eighth time to feign buying a soda from the machine. I think they are vying for my affections. They have both offended me several times with catcalls out their driver's side windows.

I rise. Already, I'm feeling the pain from diving into the tall, wet grass of the ditch on the side of the state route. I rolled about three feet, came to a stop against a sapling. I walked two miles to the nearest open gas station and borrowed a cell phone. The only person I knew I could call without my grandpa finding out about my HUGE miscalculation of judgment was my ex-boyfriend's best friend. I'm looking up and into the driver's side window of the souped-up truck that just pulled into the parking spot in front of the station and staring with a humbled grind of my teeth at Max Matthews-Branntwein and a dark-haired woman shoved up next to him in the center of the seat.

"I can almost bet I was at the bottom of your list." He is giving me a shitty grin that I'm letting fall off me. Sadly, I can say this isn't rock bottom for me, having to stoop to my ex-boyfriend's moody best friend to drag my sorry ass off a dirty curb at the only gas station near the highway exit ramp.

"Are you giving me a ride or not?" I huff. I've got a Gatorade in my hand, and I sigh. "You got two bucks I can borrow, too?" I wag my head to Orv Saylor who is homeless and shoved up and sitting in the shadows of the ice machine in old blue jeans and a striped shirt. "He loaned me a couple dollars for a drink." I sat with him and talked about the time there used to be a sawmill right here where the gas station is located. He remembers all sorts of stuff about the old highway and the towns once thriving here but are now just memories. He used to work on the B & O Railroad, then he drove a truck. Now, he says he wanders around a lot.

I can see Max squinting at me before his eyes slide slowly and carefully to the man giving me a toast with a bottle of beer hidden in a soggy, brown paper bag.

"You're kidding, right?"

"You know better." I turn my head. "You got it or not? I'll pay you back on Thursday."

Max shakes his head and climbs out his door. He leans forward and tugs his wallet from his pocket. He flips it open, wiggles out two twenty-dollar bills. Then, he bypasses me, steps over to Orv Saylor. "Thanks for babysitting her." Max hands off the money to the outstretched hand and they both laugh like they share some inside joke. "She needs it."

"You got it." Orv tucks the money into his shirt.

"You sweet talk anybody else out of their last dime, Davidson?" Max scoffs at me while he passes, leans in, and lowers his voice. "Like some poor little old lady who just cashed her social security check?"

"Why did you give him that much money?" I sputter in return. "That's half my paycheck after I pay my bills."

Then his eyes drop. He takes in the bruises on my knees and the dirt on my dress that led two truck drivers and three old men in dirty compact cars to think I rub elbows with the local truck stop pimps and such made offers that I must assume were far under the going rate and were downright insulting.

"Why are you looking at me like that?" I grunt. "You want to make an offer too?"

"An offer?"

"Sweet Jesus," I sigh. I jab a thumb toward the parking lot and the two perverts in their trucks. "They offered me fifty bucks if I gave them a blowjob."

"Both of them?"

"That's more insulting than the fifty bucks they suggested."

"Geez." Max adjusts his glasses, works them up and down on the bridge of his nose. "Harley, what happened?" He's making a funny grab of my arm, looking me up and down. "Did Trevor do something to you? I just thought your car broke down—cripes, what happened?"

"Your buddy went all paranoid and shoved me out of the car. Then, he stole my car."

"*Stole* your car?"

"He flipped out and said somebody was following us. He pushed me out and took off."

"Trevor said somebody was following you?" He waves at the truck as if to tell me to hop inside. "I've got some Band-Aids in my glovebox." He veers around the bumper and he's right behind me, swings a hand out, and opens the door for me.

"I don't need any. And what's up with this?" I wiggle my hand at the door and try to tease him, but it just comes out sour like a damp, mildew washcloth slapped hard between us. He gives the woman in the seat an embarrassed shrug of his shoulders.

"I don't know. It's just being nice. Chill." He points up toward the woman who is giving me the kind of forced and nervous, big-toothed smile girls give to their new boyfriend's mom when they first meet them. He smiles softly at her. "This is Mikayla Tinsley." Then he has the audacity to turn to me and say: "Now play nice, Harley."

"Play nice? What's that mean? And you've never opened the door specifically for me before." I pause, tap my chin. "I mean, unless I'm at the long end of a line of pretty girls and it would make you look like a jerk if you didn't. And still, you have closed the door on me a couple times—"

"It wasn't my job before. It was Trevor's."

"It wasn't his job then. It isn't your job now," I counter.

"I know you are perfectly capable of opening your own

door. I just chose to do it to be—"

"—a frigging *gentleman?*"

"Yes," he says with an exaggerated roll of eyes, sweeping his arm out as if to direct me to the only seat before me. "Like a *frigging* gentleman."

I laugh right then, a bubbling ball of cackles overriding the sound of cars in the highway behind us. It leaves an odd ache in my chest and a satisfying tickle in my chest at the same time and in the same way, a glass of ice water on a hot August day swallowed too quickly gives both a quenching sensation to the belly *and* a dull ache in the forehead. I haven't belly-laughed in a long time.

"Ow." But I still must reach up and cup a palm to my bottom lip. I've got a fat lip from hitting the bumper of the car before it sped off.

"Why am I scared to close the door right now with you sitting alone with Mikayla?" He tells me. "No nipping, you hear me?"

I see Mikayla turn to me. "Grrr," I growl softly at her. She's the usual beautiful women Max dates—it's an almost boring kind of beauty because she has not a single flaw—a tiny nose, doleful eyes, and the kissable kind of full lips I missed out on. She's like a pretty, full-blooded Christmas poodle in a box with a big red bow around her neck. I'm like the tiny beagle with mud-caked paws and nicks on my too-big ears somebody found on the road that got tossed inside the box with her, all yapping and stinking.

"Harley, cool it," he sniffs at me.

"Hi," she says, and her voice is soft, sweet, and childlike. "So you're Harley?" I see her eyes roam up to my eyebrow piercing, then to the little ring on my nose. Her gaze screams small-town-girl-home-by-ten. I might as well be a seven-foot man with tattoos on my arms and a chainsaw dangling from my hands in a dark alley the way she is scared-eyeing me.

Max must have sprinted to get to the driver's side. He hops in and backs out of the lot.

"Are you going to call the cops?" he asks me when he drives off.

"Well, for one thing, my cell phone is still riding around with Trevor on the dash of my car. So probably not. And what do you think I would tell them? I was giving my ex-boyfriend a ride home, and he ditched me in my car?" I shrug. "I imagine that would give all those old cops at the Brandy Mountain Police Department a good laugh. I'm not exactly on their good girl list." I heave a sigh. "You can't, maybe, stop at Trevor's house on the way to see if he headed home?" I request with the same kind of approach I would take if I was asking him if he would like to share a bite of a cupcake with me that he was holding in his hand. Max's reaction is about what I would expect if it was the last, luscious bite and it was almost to his lips.

"Can't it wait? It's late." Max takes off in his truck, the grind of tires on the wet asphalt.

"Yeah, sure." I nod, see his reflection in the windshield, and watch his girlfriend lean into him. I don't know why it bothers me. Maybe because (although I will never admit it) Max and I got to be close friends. I mean, we had to maintain our distance, but I can't say I've ever had anybody I'd trust more than him. He knows my stupid stuff. I know his.

"Yeah, alright," Max breaks that silence in the truck. I didn't realize it had gotten so quiet in about a minute and a half following. Maybe he can read my expression I see reflecting back on me in the glass—I'm sitting there about six inches from his girl, alone and kind of huddled against the door. In a flash, I see me alone and looking beat up and sad. And I realize while I shove my hand through my hair and sit up straight, I don't want anybody to see me like that.

Chapter 8

"He's not here, Harley," Max is telling my back while I walk up the black, asphalt driveway leading to Trevor's garage. "It's black inside. The lights are out." He's got the passenger side window rolled down, and he's leaning around Mikayla who is looking from him to me. "Come on. I'll give him a call tomorrow. He's probably sleeping it off at somebody's house. We'll get your car back. It's late. Leave it until tomorrow. You need to get some ice on your eye."

"I just want to check and see if he parked my car in his garage," I call back, but not too loudly. I turn to the house. It's a 1970s brick ranch with an attached 2-car garage. It's out of place on this street with little post-World War II white wood houses shoulder to shoulder from one block to the next. Trevor inherited it from his mom and dad when his grandparents went to live at the local nursing home and his parents moved into their old house. "I've got to get to work tomorrow, Max. I'm not walking."

"Get your old jeep from your grandpa's house. I know he's still got it. I saw it in the garage the other day. Use it until Trevor returns your car."

"And then Pop Pop will wonder where my car is, and I'll have to answer too many questions," I answer. "Besides, my jeep isn't the kind of vehicle the people at my work would like sitting in the parking lot next to their luxury cars." I know Trevor leaves the side door to his garage unlocked, so I slip my hand over the knob and turn it. With a bump of my hip, I shove it open and take in the stale air mixed with a hint of motor oil. Trevor always changes his own oil in his truck. When he does, he uses an old, plastic cat pan. It has a slit in the bottom where it had fallen off the shelf, and he always spills some in the pan, and it leaks out.

It's a kind of melancholy moment leaving a pit in my chest. It's warm inside the garage. It reminds me of pulling inside in high school and making out until his mom opened the kitchen door and peered out. His truck is there now. The garage looks the same—three walls of ceiling-high shelves full of stuff like old basketballs and baseball bats, and plastic tubs filled with household cleaning supplies.

And then there is the deep blue plastic storage container holding all his girly magazines. *The tub of love.* I have to assume it is the same tub Trevor wanted me to hide from his mom. I told him long ago, it was either me or them. I can't make out the words in the flimsy glow from the plug-in nightlight by the doorway that leads into the kitchen, but I know it says: THE TUB OF LOVE—THE ONES I LEFT BEHIND in bold, black indelible marker on one side. Every time I asked Trevor if he loved me, he stumbled around the response. He would point out the tub settled in his garage and tease me about how he'd given up all those girls for me.

There's a shovel next to my foot. I trip over it when I step inside. My eyes are still lingering on the tub nearly hidden in the shadows. I hear the shovel make a bang-bang while the wooden handle bounces off the floor. I freeze, hoping nobody is inside the house. No one comes to the door. I bend over, pick up the wrong end in the darkness and feel the slimy dampness of mud on the blade. Three pats of my hand up the handle and I set it upright. I wipe my hands on my dress.

"Harley, I'll get your car for you tomorrow. Somebody in your family will give you a ride if you need one, right?"

I jump in a startled reaction to Max's voice behind me. I thought I heard his steps grinding on the cement pad outside the door. "Yeah, alright. I need to get something first."

"Don't steal anything from Trevor," Max groans. I glare at him. "I'm getting a bad feeling about bringing you here."

"It's a stupid container of my stuff." I jab a finger toward the plastic tub. Max's eyes follow.

"The tub of love? Seriously?" He sighs deeply, gives me a long look. Then Max shrugs. "I know. I'll get it. If I don't, you'll climb up there yourself in high heels and break a leg. But if he asks who stole it. I'm playing stupid."

Chapter 9

Grant Lebowski's number twelve times on my landline answering machine the next morning should have screamed WARNING! He never calls me unless he's having a near-death sickness which is never. I swallow hard, poke my finger on the button to listen to the messages. Here's what I hear: "Harley, there's been a break-in to the museum. The police need to ask you some questions."

I call Pop Pop first. I don't want to tell him what is going on, but I do. I hear wind noise on his end. He sounds far off on the phone like he's outside and his voice is muffled. "Can you cup your hand over the phone? I can't hear you." I grunt. "Where are you anyway?"

"I'm at the ballfield practicing."

"Practicing what?"

"Did you hit your head or something? What do most people do at a ballfield?"

"I don't know. I suppose they sit around and watch a game. Is that what you're doing? Because you never go out to the ballfields except on Sunday."

"No, baby, if you had been to church in the last ten Sundays, you would have heard the preacher talking about the different towns starting teams for the new league—listen, I'll talk to you later. I'm up to bat."

"Pop Pop, wait. I called you to ask you something. Last night, I went to pick up Trevor. He was drunk, and he took my car. Now there's been a break-in at the museum, and the cops want to talk to me."

There's a long pause. I know Pop Pop wants to say, *I told you so. That boy's trouble.* He doesn't. Instead, he asks: "Did you break into the history museum?"

"Of course not!"

"Well, that's a no-brainer then. Just tell them the truth. Do you need me to take you to the station?"

"No, sir. Grant said they were coming here."

Pop Pop gives me one of his deep sighs. "I will be there in fifteen minutes."

"Thank you, Poppy."

"*Poppy*. I'm always Poppy when you're in trouble."

It sounded so easy. Not so much so. Two hours later, I'm calling in late to work and trying to cancel the one credit card I had in my purse that is missing. Grant Lebowski is standing on my front porch along with a skinny, pimple-faced Brandy Mountain cop in a starched, gray uniform. To his right is my paid replacement, Beck O'Sullivan who is looking quiet and uncomfortable. Grant's nose is a puffy red, and he is spraying some kind of nasal mist into his left nostril. He is also rubbing a white tissue above his lip at a rapid pace. I see his eyes dart left to right like he's keeping an eye out for my invisible, non-existent cat. Beck is looking pale and uncomfortable like he'd rather be anywhere but here on the opposite side of Pop Pop who has been like a second father to him. He keeps chewing his bottom lip and staring at the ground like he's trying to be unobtrusive. Unfortunately, when you are as big as Beck, it is like trying to hide a bull elephant in a compact car.

Pop Pop is positioned slightly behind me, my granddaddy-cheerleader without the fake smile nor the pom poms. Still, he's managed to give me that look when he saw me—the one where his mind is screaming: *What did I do wrong with this one?* He's got his arms crossed and the same kind of somber expression on his face he usually saved for run-ins with my high school principal. One of my aunts slipped once and told me that in his twenties, he took off on a cross-country trip with his buddies on their motorcycles. He got in a fight with two off-duty cops in a bar and ended up in jail for two days. The cops, they ended up in the hospital for a week each. I'm not so sure if he's going to be of any assistance. He looks a bit surly with his chin held high, and his eyes narrowed. I wonder if the cop knows Pop Pop beat up one of his own brothers in uniform.

"I'm not pointing the finger at you, Harley, but you were working yesterday," Grant is saying. And he *is* jabbing a finger at me. "You left abruptly with those two men. We all know your reputation when you're together."

"With whom did you leave?" Pop Pop interrupts.

I turn to Pop Pop, shake my head. "He's talking about Trevor Woods and Max Matthews-Branntwein." I'm turning my head back, wide-eyed and blinking at Grant Lebowski, and the new officer they hired up on the mountain whose fake bronze nameplate on his right breast pocket says: *Lance Washington, Officer. Brandy Mt. PD.* Officer Washington is looking between the three of us, not sure which side to pick— the starched-suited man whose face is getting redder the more he pokes his finger in the air or the crazy girl with the bad reputation dragging along an old, gruff bodyguard who, with his gray ponytail and black, sleeveless vest, looks like he might be concealing either a piece of pipe from a moonshine still or snub nose .38 from his motorcycle days. "But no, I didn't leave *with* them. I left *before* they had gone. I saw Max's truck in the parking lot when I drove out."

"You were talking to one of them after you did your spiel," Grant points out. I nod.

"That doesn't make me a thief."

"Would you have reason to believe the two men would have the motive to break into the museum?" Lance Washington is the newly hired cop from the Brandy Mountain Police Department, a tall and thin man of about twenty-five or twenty-six who reeks of rookie. He doesn't know the town's dynamics well yet, although I'm sure he knows Max, considering his father is the mayor. I can almost catch a whiff of subdivision oozing through the pores of his not-so-hairy arms, the sweet scent of All American Boy who wants to save the world. I heard he came from Ohio. I can guess he grew up in some middle-class housing development with two upper-middle-class parents, a skateboard he rode on the sidewalk in front of his house, and teachers who expected him to go to state college. His parents proudly display, on their fireplace, the picture he got at graduation from whatever cop school he went to, and they quickly point out he's working his way up to detective.

He's uncomfortable speaking to me. His gaze keeps fluttering from Pop Pop to my early stages of a black eye and swollen lip, compliments of Trevor. He's not sure why I look like I've got one foot in knee-high, uncut front yard grass with three broken down riding lawnmowers, three ATVs and a banged-up truck in the driveway, and an old white house while the other foot's daring to tread on middle-class mowed lawn with a ranch house and built-in pool.

Lost Hollow doesn't have enough money to pay for a police department, so Brandy Mountain's cops cover the area. They tend to side with the mountain folks. They are the ones paying the higher percentage of his bi-weekly paychecks. He's here because someone broke into the building last night and ransacked the entire place. Although Grant had not taken an inventory of the contents of the entire building yet, he had noticed that more than three major items were missing: the dead baby trunk, a display of company scrip, and six boxes stored in a back room.

"You're kidding me, right?" I ask him. "They wouldn't steal anything from here, neither of them." But yes, my asshole ex-boyfriend stole my car. "And I wouldn't either. We haven't gotten in trouble since high school." I look at Lance. His hair is buzzed so close to his head, state-highway-patrol-style, I can't tell if it is brown or red. His dull, brown eyes tell me he's sitting on the edge of this conversation, half on Grant's side, and half on mine.

"Well, you stole the statue of Hans Branntwein from the center of town and left him in Joey Greene's old outhouse. You tore it off the base with a rope around the statue and dragged it with your jeep." Grant Lebowski comments and he looks to Beck as if for support. Beck just stares back at him. "And, Harley, you stole your principal's car in high school and parked it at the All-Nighter Strip Club along the highway. So yes, you have—"

"That was never proven." It wasn't. But I did procure it for a short amount of time. "And I'm not discussing this. This is ridiculous."

"Do you see what that young man did to my granddaughter? It was inexcusable, despicable." Oh, great. I groan inwardly. Pop Pop's trying to use my great grandma's crossword puzzle words to sound smarter. I'm hoping he doesn't throw his fist in the air and start spitting out something from Julius Caesar like *Cowards die many times before their deaths*! Her crossword plopped on the couch yesterday at his house was centered around Shakespeare. Pop Pop takes a step forward, wags a hand at my face. I cringe. "If anyone should be under scrutiny, it should be that Trevor Woods character." Now he's looking to Beck for support. Beck latches on to his collar and tugs it, wiggles his neck like it's a noose he's trying to loosen.

"Pop Pop, please don't—"

"Do you have someone who can account for your whereabouts?" Officer Washington gives my face a hard look but doesn't change his bland expression.

"Well, I've got an alibi until after midnight. I was at a company seminar." I turn to him and narrow my eyes. "Did you question Max? He and Trevor were at a wedding and then a party in Baker. A hundred people had to see them."

"Between one and three in the morning was when the robbery occurred." Grant grunts at me.

"Are we certain of that specific time? How do we know that time frame?" Beck is the one who speaks up. Everyone stops and is silent, looking at him. "I'm just—just asking," he mutters a lot more quietly.

"I was working until midnight. I turned the lights out," Grant offers. "John Matthews drove past around four in the morning going to work early. There was a water main break in town. The lights were on when he passed."

"Well, I got a call to come and pick up Trevor sometime after midnight. I drove from Charleston to Baker, and that took an hour." I find myself wondering if I would rather go to jail than have Lance Washington walk into Theo or Lissette's office to make sure my alibis pan out. "I can't believe you're pointing a finger at me on this, Grant. I've never given you any reason to doubt my integrity at the historical society. I've volunteered there since I was in high school. I've never even borrowed a pencil from your office."

"Yes, you have given me reasons to distrust your judgment. You cursed loud enough yesterday that those children heard you." He shakes his head. "And you three are always up to some kind of—what did my grandpa call them? Oh yes, monkeyshines."

"Whoa, there." Pop Pop's holding up both hands. "Carrying out a few, childish pranks does not make my granddaughter a thief." He turns to Lance. "Now, I can see where this is going. You're not going to pin this on her because you've got to point the finger at somebody and not the rich mayor's kid up on the mountain."

"We can clear this up pretty quickly, Miss Davidson," Lance has both hands on his gun belt, and he's wiggling it back and forth. I see him eye Pop Pop, then me while he rocks back and forth on his heels. "If you simply give me the name or names of the person or people you were with last night and they can vouch for you, we can focus on someone else, right? I'll need someone who can account for your whereabouts at the meeting—"

"It was a realty seminar." I cringe, hoping Pop Pop doesn't find out about the award because I didn't invite him to come. But he doesn't have a suit like everybody else. He doesn't quite fit into my work scenario in his raggedy clothes and long hair. Grant sneezes and I jump. He has the whiniest sneeze I've ever heard.

"And you said—" The officer taps his pen on the paper in his hand, "—you were partying with Trevor Woods after that. Do you know where Trevor can be found?"

"I didn't say I was partying with him. I was at my office. I picked him up because I got a call he was too drunk to drive." I open my mouth to finishing speaking. Grant holds up his hands. "He took my car. He's got my phone too. He tossed my purse out. That was all."

"He borrowed your car *after* you picked him up?" the officer asks.

I would hardly call it borrowed. I rub my face. "Well, kind of. If I say I pulled over to let somebody pass and he pushed me out of the car and took off, is that—?"

"It's called a carjacking. Is that what he did?" Officer Washington demands. "Are you willing to press charges or is this not even something we need to pursue because you were just fighting with your boyfriend—"

I feel like a snitch, so I feel like I need to minimize the situation. "He's not my boyfriend. He hasn't been my boyfriend for over five years—"

"Let me just say something first," Grant grabs our attention with a sniff. "You're done volunteering here. I took the chance allowing you to work here as an intern. You're bad news. I knew that when I hired you."

"What do you mean by that? I don't think it has anything to do with blaming me for stealing something I did not steal." I know it isn't said aloud, but most people from up on the mountain, they look down on us in the hollow. I see it for what it is—just an excuse to get rid of me and put dumbass Beck O'Sullivan (pretty, male, and hometown sports hero) in the paid position. "You just wanted to hire Beck, and you couldn't hire him and make me stay a volunteer." Grant just stares at me. "You can't do this, Grant. I have to finish this internship to graduate."

"I don't care. You're done." He makes one final swipe beneath his nose and wiggles the crumpled tissue into the breast pocket of his shirt. And it was like the light at the end of my tunnel just got doused out.

Chapter 10

Forty minutes later, I'm sitting on a red swivel barstool at the counter of Big Dee's Diner three miles outside Lost Hollow. I'm listening to scratchy country music on a vintage boombox near the cash register. I'm waiting to drown my misery in a good, old-fashioned ice-cream sundae and some uplifting advice from my mama. I'm spinning around just like I used to do when I was seven years old and visiting her after school.

Pop Pop gave me his phone. He told me a girl shouldn't be driving around without one in case of an emergency. There's a missed call on it when I sit down. I realize I had the volume turned down, and I groan. The call is from my missing cell phone. I'm wondering if it is Trevor calling. Why would he call Pop Pop? I try desperately to call it back six times. No one answers. It just goes to voicemail. I finally leave a message: *Trevor, if this is you who called, please call me back. I need my car, and I need my phone—*

"Here, baby girl, this'll make you feel better." That's my mama followed by the thick, bitter waft of smoke clinging to her blue jeans and t-shirt after just taking a cigarette break outside the back doors of the kitchen. I put my phone back down and sigh. "Ice-cream always takes away the sorrow." She's only forty-three, and she doesn't have a gray hair on her head yet or even wrinkles.

But she's got that look, the sunken cheeks and dark rings around her eyes from working too hard all her life. She doesn't look anything like me. She's got dark hair like my great grandma's and a dark complexion and she's six inches taller than me. She's plopping down a tulip sundae glass with two scoops of vanilla ice-cream topped with hot fudge and three, plump cherries on the very top. I stop, feel a little queasy from all my spinning, and she laughs her deep, smoked-since-she-was-thirteen cigarette laugh. "You ain't gonna throw up, are you?"

"No, Mama." I feel seven years old when I'm with her. It isn't like she treats me like a little kid. It's like we're both in first grade, best friends, and skipping across the playground hand in hand. The relationship is great in the respect if I swing with someone else for a while, I can always come back to her. It wasn't so great when I was seventeen and she snuck-bought me my first beer.

"And you ain't going to quit school just because of some idiot from up on the mountain."

"Mama, I don't know where else I'm going to get an internship fitting the criteria I need to graduate."

"I don't know nothing about that stuff. But I know you. Give that professor a call. Ask him." She reaches out and gently touches my cheek just below my black eye. I want to tell her it isn't that easy. I can't. She doesn't understand that I'm just another number at the college. My professor probably doesn't even know I left. "You ain't gonna turn out like me, right? Promise me. Nobody beats up my baby."

"Yeah, because it's hard to outrun a runaway train." That's Arnie O'Malley. He's fifty-something, thick-gray-haired and mid-size, except for a thick belly. He always wears a cowboy hat and has the cowboy swagger. "Shouldn't you be working or something?" I suppose he reminds me of an old, laid-back bulldog. My Pop Pop told me he used to be the star baseball player for the old high school four years running. All the girls followed him around trying to get his attention. Not so much anymore.

He's settled into the barstool two seats down with his elbows resting on the counter and yesterday's Charleston Gazette open in front of him. He's the closest thing to a mayor we've got in Lost Hollow. He clears the streets with his tractor, files all the forms for taxes, and oversees any problems we've got in our little community, with a baseball bat in hand if he has to do it. He also spends a lot of time drinking coffee and reading the newspaper at the diner.

"You're calling me a *train wreck* waiting to happen? Who are you to judge me? How many times have I seen your car at the hotel up the road, Arnie, because your wife kicked you out. Has it been like a hundred? And why are you listening to our conversation? It's private."

"Well, if it's private, you're sure talking about it out loud. Ain't nobody in here that didn't hear you whining and complaining about ol' Grant Lebowski." He shuffles the paper loudly, leans a little to the right, and peers over his shoulder to the three tables with customers. "But he's a good guy, right? He goes to church every Sunday. Do you?"

"Arnie, you shush now. My baby girl has a heart filled with gold."

"Um, and a brain filled with crazies," he grunts at Mama. Then he grumbles under his breath: "And her soul's got a certain darkness—"

"My heart is as clean and pure as a snow-white dove," I gripe at him with a smile. But when you're not looking, Arnie," I growl lightly. "I'm going to spit in your coffee."

"Clean and pure, my ass." He eyes me cautiously, takes the tip of his finger, and scoots his white coffee cup three inches away from me. He shuffles his paper, narrows his eyes at something. "They're gonna start a ball league up on The Brandy, you hear that?" *The Brandy*. That's what everybody calls it up on the mountain.

"Who cares?" I mumble, throw my hands out. "It's got nothing to do with me."

"I'm just saying. Don't be sassy. You could have some pride in your town."

"The Brandy ain't my town. They are trying to sell us out, Arnie. Did you know that?" I spat back. "The mayor is buying out all the land down here to put in a new town. He doesn't seem to think ours is pretty enough and rich people got the right to see pretty more than us."

"If I was rich, I'd think I deserved pretty more. Maybe I'll sell my house to the mayor, buy a pretty little ranch outside Charleston. He's right. It looks like shit down here."

"Well, I don't think I'd be selling us all out so quickly. I doubt you'd get enough to buy a trailer outside Wheeling for what he'd give you for your house," I insist. "The Bottoms is my town. I'm proud to be from down here. And when they start a ball league down here, call me." *The Bottoms*. And that's what we proudly nicknamed the old mining town, Lost Hollow. It's been called that for a hundred and fifty years.

"Alright, enough!" Mama scolds us both. I adore her. It isn't just for saying that. She's my superhero. She never finished high school because she got pregnant with me. Everybody tried to talk her into giving me up for adoption because they said I'd always be her black eye. She works two minimum wage jobs—one waiting tables here at the diner, and one serving beer at Maplewood Bar near the old highway. She rents an old, run-down mobile home in Lost Hollow. But her eyes sparkle like two, navy blue sapphires when I walk in the door. That's where we match, our eyes.

"Your old friend just pulled into the lot," Mama says while she pretends to scrub the counter around me with a raggedy, blue washcloth. She nods over my shoulder and toward the parking lot. I follow her gaze. Sure enough, I see Max's truck pulling on to the buckled asphalt drive. Her eyes peer back to the double doors leading to the kitchen. She's watching out for Theodore "Big Dee" Wallace who has owned the place for thirty years. He's gruff, doesn't like her socializing too much with the locals in the diner. He's also a bit deaf, and when he sees my mama talking to me, he always yowls like a grouchy Rottweiler at her. But Mama's banter is what brings them coming back, and he knows it, or he would have fired her just like he fires everybody else two weeks into working. "Max. He growed up, huh?" She asks me with a sly smile. I shrug.

"He's an ass just like Trevor." I pick up my spoon, dig into the ice-cream with gusto. "He's looking for the stuff he left in my jeep. The sooner I get it to him, the happier I'll be. They'll both be out of my life."

"You're bad luck." That's what I'm telling Max when he

walks in the door of the restaurant. "Go away." I'm poking my finger in that air above his head. "Every time you come around me, something bad happens."

He doesn't say anything at first. He's dragging that same dark-haired girl along with him. She's got huge boobs. They're the kind that are cute and stand upright without any sagging like two ripe winter cantaloupes, and you have to force the eyes away from even if you're a girl, and they make you a bit jealous. She's dressed in a skirt and blouse and has the perfect strut. She instantly makes me feel like I just walked out of Goodwill with a plastic bag recycled from the dollar store full of old jeans and t-shirts clutched in my arms. At the same time, she walks out of the little expensive clothing shop next to it clutching a bunch of pretty little boxes filled with classy dresses and topped with pretty bows.

"Well, I was good luck last night, wasn't I?" He's got a shoebox in his hand and he stops just short of me. He reaches out his knuckle and jabs it toward my eye. "Maybe a few minutes late, but I was there for you. You got a shiner, now." He must sense I'm glaring inside because he drops the knuckle and holds up his other hand. "Your stuff, princess. And what the hell happened that I get a call about you stealing stuff?" He thrusts the box at me and I reach out my hands, accept it.

"Now, I'm princess?" I grunt, roll my eyes. Mama is smiling at Max just as Big Dee yells there's an order ready. Arnie O'Malley has a curious half-smile on his lips while he looks from me to Max and then lingers way too long on the big-boobed sidekick who is wide-eyed and staring toward the kitchen where Big Dee is doing his waddle-clamber out the door with two plates in either plump hand. He's huge, bald, and nearly takes up the entire doorway. He looks like a giant, chubby two-year-old toddling to his mama.

"Do you have my stuff?" Max asks. "I think you either don't have it, or you don't want to give it up." And I think he is suggesting that, like a four-year-old exploring a treasure box from a beloved aunt, sorts through the items over and over, I am coveting his junk. It is infuriating.

"Gracie! I said order up!" Big Dee shouts before he interrupts us, stops just short of Mama, and plops the plates into Mama's outstretched hands. "This is not a social hour, and you ain't a movie star."

Mama looks embarrassed. She turns her head away. I watch her cheeks turn a bright pink while she gives me an apologetic widening of her eyes. I think Max's girlfriend is going to faint while wild-eyed blinking at Big Dee.

In the awkward five seconds following, I half-heartedly watch Mama slide past us toward a couple sitting at one of the booths. She's walking fast like her life depends on getting those plates to the customers chatting over their coffee. I suppose it does. She pays her three hundred and fifty dollars a month rent off tips she gets. If she doesn't have enough, she doesn't eat, doesn't have gas for her car.

"—so, do I need to hold *your* stuff hostage until you manage to find *my* stuff?"

I suppose I realize all those people on the mountain, they are like walls to us down in the hollows. My life is turning out much like hers. Maybe that's the way it is supposed to be because it was always like this. There are those who live in the old mining camps—The Bottoms, and eke out meager lives working for those up above in The Brandy and watching them get rich. Yeah, I don't have a kid I have to drag around. But I do have to grovel to the people up on the mountain. I'm one step away from waiting tables the rest of my life.

"No, Max, I'll have it to you by tomorrow after work. Is that good?"

"What time? I told a bunch of guys I'd be at the ballfield by five." He stops, shoves his glasses along the bridge of his nose. "Not the ones down here. My dad had his contractors build a temporary practice field at the Brandy Mountain Rec Field to use while they're building a new playing field, regulation-size." He gets a funny smirk on his face, leans in a bit. "Now we're not trespassing on you Lost Hollow folks. But your loss. It was printed in the newspaper, and we got twelve calls from Brandy Mountain High School alumni varsity ballplayers who want to play for us. Just saying. That could have been your old ballfields. It could have been your team, the winning one, I expect."

I ignore the remark. I know it would take more than a few thousand to fix up the old ballfields they used in the mining town. They are scrubby and overgrown with knee-high weeds. There's a maple tree growing through first base, and the wire fencing is buckled and six inches from the ground.

"I don't give a crap, Max, where you play. Pop Pop said he was getting a team together anyway. He probably had some sort of rights to that ballfield down here considering he owns half the town now."

"The town proper is still owned by the Branntwein heirs, Harley, which both my father and myself are among."

"Whoopy shit," I mutter. Arnie's eyes get big like I've just blasphemed by saying the Lord's name in vain in the middle of a church service. "Your kin may have owned the coal mines with their money, but we mined them with our hands, sold our souls to you devils for meager company scrip, and put our lives on the line so you could get rich up on The Brandy. A part of us down here in The Bottoms is inside that mountain. It's like our souls mingle with it—" Max starts to chuckle like he thinks what I am saying is silly. I narrow my eyes at him, dare him to interrupt. "You can sit up top of that mountain all day and count your money, but you can't take it to the grave with you."

"Your grandpa's starting a team?" Arnie interjects and seems to hang on my words. He snickers almost nervously, looking at Max like he's got his back. "That old fart and his buddies from the garage against the young guys? That ought to be entertainment. It'll be a tragedy like one of those old Shakespeare plays. Your old Grampa Ray will surely embarrass himself and take the town down with him."

"Those *old guys,* as you imply, will probably beat the fire out of the boys on the mountain. They might be over forty, but they've got guts and experience." I grind my teeth to keep from snarling at Arnie.

"They'll need more than that to beat those boys." Arnie laughs.

"Well, they aren't my fields. I could care less." I really could care less. I wanted to play softball when I was a kid. I hated when ball season rolled around. Coach Simmons told me he'd already chosen his players. He had. They were all either related to him or from The Brandy. Now it is a melancholy reminder of things I didn't get to do growing up. "You don't know crap, Arnie," I mutter, stand up to leave.

"Harley, baby, wait just a sec—" Mama's voice stops me when my hands are on the door, and I've pushed it just enough to catch the faint scent of wet, spring air. I turn so I'm only catching her in my gaze while she walks the expanse between us and holds out her hand. I know what is inside. It is five dollars of her hard-earned tips or five dollars less of her rent payment or one less package of hot dogs, dollar store potato chips and a six-liter bottle of off-brand soda pop that she doles out for lunch every day.

"Mama, you don't have to—" I hold out my hands like I'm shooing her fingers away. She shakes her head pridefully, interrupts me with: "I want to do it." And before I can do anything else, she shoves it in my pocket with her fingers. I nod and force a smile. "I don't get to give you much, baby, never could."

"Five dollars is a lot," I say softly in return. But I know even over the low drone of country music bopping out a beat on an old, red boombox at the counter, everybody can hear us. Mama pats my arm and gently pushes me to the door.

Chapter 11

It's a small town. Everybody in Lost Hollow and Brandy Mountain knows about the break-in at the historical society within two hours of Grant Lebowski wagging his knobby-knuckled finger at me. He also announces it to a reporter. They all know I volunteer there. And when he declares: *The police believe the suspect is a volunteer,* everybody deduces it is me. It's a forty-second segment on the six o'clock news in Charleston, tucked between a report on four people arrested for having a methamphetamine lab in their daycare center in Cincinnati and a recount of the high school baseball scores. I'd hoped it hadn't crept up the local highway to the town I worked in. I was not so lucky.

I hadn't been settled but five minutes into my hand-me-down, partially-ergonomically correct conference room chair (someone broke a lever, so the height is no longer adjustable. I sit with my chest equal to my computer keyboard and look like a seven-year-old sitting at a teacher's desk) when I hear the little security bell ringing to let us know a customer has entered the building.

"Hey, I'm looking for a girl called Harley. She said she worked here. You know who I'm talking about?"

I hear the deep, gritty voice from downstairs creep upward to my office on the second floor. I freeze, somewhat unsure of who could possibly be looking for me. I'm hoping it is perhaps a salesman and whoever's shoes I can hear clacking on the tile floor downstairs will deflect whatever sales pitch he has for me. Then, I hear Taylor call from the bottom of the steps. She's never done this before. It is more typical for her to come upstairs and knock on my door.

I rise and make my way to the stairway, lean on the top banister, and look down. I see Taylor's wide-eyed gaze staring up at me. She must have been surprised to see Orv Saylor, the homeless man from Bakers Quickie Stop and Gas stepping cautiously inside. He's a bit disheveled in the same dirty jeans and striped button-up shirt he wore the other day, and he looks scared-rabbit with wide eyes darting around. But he's smiling when he follows Taylor's careful eyes up to me at the top of the stairs and gives me a floppy wave of his hand.

"Hey, Orv," I'm not sure what else to say while I step down the stairway. "It's okay, Taylor," I add, shaking my head. "I know him. He's a friend." I'm wearing high heels. Since they weren't my typical attire up until Lissette pulled me aside and told me two days ago I must conform or perhaps find a more appropriate job to match my meager wardrobe (*like working for the sanitation department*), I have to think out each step so I don't collapse upon myself and take the last four or five on my butt.

"Hey," he returns. "Do you remember me? You was at the gas station, said your old boyfriend dumped you. Remember?" Taylor's got this curious peer to her eyes when I make the base of the stairs and come face to face with Orv.

"I do remember. You bought me something to drink because you said I was pale as a ghost."

"I got something for you. Look—" I drop my eyes. Orv is holding out his fist. I can see a bit of peach-colored tissue paper peeking out of his clasp. "It's okay," he coaxes me until I hold out my hand. "It's inside. He said to keep it safe." I feel it drop, the crumpled tissue into my palm. "Open it."

"Who said to keep it safe?" I answer softly, see Taylor move up beside me and peer at the tissue hesitantly. She is still careful-eyeing Orv, who does have a certain reek of BO and cigarettes clinging to him, while I peel back the tissue to expose an old copper-colored skeleton key.

"*He* did."

My eyes pop up to Orv's at the same time, I pinch the pinky-finger-size key between finger and thumb and hold it up. "You saw him? You saw Trevor Woods?"

"I know what he looks like." Orv reaches into the pants pocket and wheedles out a crumpled piece of paper. He opens it with his fingers and holds it up. Trevor's smiling face is staring at me. I recognize it as one of the little posters Trevor's mom has been leaving all over the place. "This is him. He's the man who is missing. I saw this in Logan. It was on a sign outside a pizza place. He came about two hours after you left the gas station. He asked if I'd seen you. He had a picture on his phone. I said I did. He handed me the little key and said to give it to you."

"Why would he think you'd see me?" I ask Orv, and he just shrugs. "That's just weird."

"I told him that. I mean, I'd only met you once and I'd probably never see you again. He said weirder things happen. That's exactly what he said: 'weirder things happen.'" Orv looks at Taylor and smiles. He's missing a couple teeth, and one front tooth is silver. "Then he says that he thinks I must be a good man and I'd know the right thing to do, get you the key and all. Then he just walked off and into the store." Orv nibbles his lip. "He came back out with a bottled water, smiled at me, then gives me one of those cheers where he holds up the plastic bottle. Then he gets into a little red car and drives off. There was a white truck that pulled in after him and stood out in the dark."

After he leaves, Lissette calls me into her office. She tells me to close the door behind me and waves a hand at the leather chair across from her desk. I do as she says.

"I didn't think you were here again today, didn't recognize the—" she hesitates before she goes on. "—*jeep* in the driveway." She stops, pushes back the curtains and peers out into the little, gravel lot. I know she's looking at my jeep. Pop Pop's been keeping it in his garage for me, tinkering around and trying to restore it. It's an old 1960s Willys Jeep that's military green with a ragtop. I had to drive it this morning because nobody's found Trevor or my car. "It is a jeep, right?"

"Yeah. It's old. It was sitting in a field when I found it in high school. My grandpa and I, we've been restoring it." I stop because I've said too much and she's cupping a yawn with her hand. "My friend borrowed my car."

"We can't have this, Harley," she says firmly. "Homeless people just making themselves comfortable coming into the office." The office is an older, but tastefully remodeled house on Main Street in the ritzy section of the town of Chilton. It's a twenty-minute drive south from Charleston, and the town is described at the local chamber of commerce as *offering the charm of a small town close enough to the big city to commute.* It's true. In my case, it also offers a long enough commute from deep, down in the belly of West Virginia and another forty-five more minutes from Charleston. It is far enough distance from my Pop Pop to keep him from showing up in his flannel shirt and 1970s raggedy jeans with a microwave potpie and a bag of M & Ms stuffed in a dollar store bag to make sure I got enough to eat for lunch. I just don't think my new shiny world would understand the old one. Especially, my boss. She's looking her typical perfect— her brunette hair is in a tidy bun on top of her head, and she's somehow managed to pull off making a belted business pantsuit look professional *and* slinky.

"I didn't know he was coming. Orv's a nice guy. He just lost his pension, lost his house."

She narrows her eyes at me, pokes a pen at her bangs, pushing them away. "I'm just going to nip this in the butt, Harley," she starts out. I cringe inwardly. Why does everybody say that? It isn't correct. It is *nip in the bud.* "I got a call from the Brandy Mountain Police Department. It was an officer—" She pauses long enough to make a deep sigh, drop one well-manicured fingernail to a yellow Post-it note settled next to her laptop, and poke it once. "—Lance Washington. That's his name. He was asking if I could account for your whereabouts on Friday from approximately ten o'clock at night to six in the morning. You want to elaborate *why* he needed to know this?"

"I volunteered at the museum in Lost Hollow and—"

"Lost Hollow," she repeats softly. "Is that still a place?" Lissette looks up, narrows her eyes. I think she hates me. "I thought that was listed as one of the ghost towns not far from the New River Bridge they bought up to make into parks."

"Well, they let some of us stay. And my grandpa thinks it is very much alive. He still lives there." I try to be witty. She deadpan-stares at me, so I stutter along. "Um, well, the museum got broken into the other night. It was the same day I had given some high school kids a tour. I left for the conference right after."

"That's a big thing, you know, breaking and entering. It isn't simply because it is a felony. Our customers are trusting you to show their homes to prospective buyers with their valuable possessions inside. I'm handing keys to these homes over to you. I am handing my trust over to you. If you steal something or people believe you have stolen something in the past, our credibility—our integrity is completely shattered. That is something that could break us, Harley." I see where this is going. She's leading me by my hand down that trail I've traveled far too often. It's the one I'm trying to curtail.

"I didn't steal anything. I was with you guys."

I can see her eyes roaming above my right shoulder. It's killing me. I want to turn around, crane my neck to see what's going on behind me. "Yes, until a bit after one o'clock when you got a phone call and left. Three or four hours is a lot of time I couldn't tell the police that I knew you were with us. There isn't even a fudge-factor there." She settles back in her chair, pretends to pluck lint from her sleeve. "Can I ask why they would obviously assume it was you?" she asks me straightforward. "I mean, a volunteer who left before closing would be the last person I would suspect." She takes in a breath, puffs it out of her lips. "Because we did a general background check on you when you applied. It came up squeaky-clean. But there's—" She pauses once again, looks over my shoulder. Lissette is a little hazy to read. Her jaws are churning like she's mad, but her eyes are dancing like a kid who just opened the door to a candy shop with an EVERYTHING IS FREE INSIDE sign tacked up on the door.

I desperately try not to fidget in my seat. I'm usually

good at it. I spent countless hours under the cold, hard stare of Principal Brandenburg at Brandy Mountain High School fending off accusations from toilet papering the Christmas tree in the lobby to catching the science room on fire. It was probably the best part of my education considering all the teachers had me pegged as *one of the kids from down in the hollow who'll end up either in jail or with twelve kids in foster care.* I give Lissette my same wide-eyed blink. "I've never been arrested for anything, Lissette. I don't steal." I'm not even sure she is listening to me while she rolls her eyes to the ceiling and dips her head to one side.

"Dangit!" she announces and waves a harsh hand over my head toward the door. Lissette's eyes are narrowed to someone outside the window on the door. "Listen, what I'm getting at is there's about a year's worth of time I can't account for in your background check. And if you excuse me a minute to take care of whatever is going on outside, I will be right back. It will give you time to think out your whereabouts—*carefully.*"

I feel the blood drain from my face. Who would have thought anybody would dig that deep and give a rat's ass about what I've been doing? I turn slowly and finally get to peer over my shoulder. I can see Taylor waggling her head back at Lissette through the window on the door before she gives me a silly grin. "Someone, who shall remain nameless, is trying her damn best to keep you from getting fired."

"You're going to fire me?" I feel the words make a grunty croak from my lips and not unlike the sound a frog makes when stepped upon. I watch Lissette jump up from her seat and make a quick step around the desk. I think she's going to answer, but bam! She rams her hip into the corner, and I see her wince, try to hide the pain away in tight lips. I can almost bet it isn't going to help whatever appeal I can come up with to fend off the accusations.

For about four minutes, the two have a mumble-dispute with the door opening a crack. I can see hands waving wildly while I digest the news, then realize I must have known it was coming while I mentally collect up the four things I have on my little desk in an office that is so small, it must have been the youngest child's bedroom. I mean, it's not like I was trying to beat my personal best at keeping a job for more than three months. I sigh and rise. I know the drill. I take the steps to the door, push it open, and step outside.

"—I'm not turning a blind eye—" Lissette's words fade away as she turns to see me standing there. "Can you please wait in the office, Harley? I'll be back in—"

"I'll save you the agony of firing me. I quit." I waver there long enough to look from one to the other. "Thanks for giving me a chance."

"No, no—" Taylor shakes her head at me and glares hard at Lissette. "You're not going to get fired."

"Well, yes, she is going to get fired," Lissette intervenes. "Let her quit. Taylor, this company cannot take a kick in the gut. We're barely treading water. The economy is spiraling fast downward. The competition is incredible. We can't even vie for a nominal position in smaller niches of subdivision housing there is so much competition now. Everybody's a realtor, you get it? And we certainly can't hire people who are a part of any criminal activity."

"But she hasn't done anything. She's never been convicted of a crime!" Taylor pauses, looks around Lissette to me. "You haven't, right?"

I just sigh, shake my head while the battle ensues between the two. I know they see me leave by the front door. They just stare at me like they've never seen somebody walk out on a job.

Chapter 12

I'm trying to come up with a game plan, so when Pop Pop finds out I've gotten fired from two jobs this week, I've got back up. I called my college professor at Southern Tri-State Community College, Jim Williams, to see if there are any internships nearby that I could work to finish my class. I had been avoiding the call knowing it would arise, the reason I didn't finish my internship at the Lost Hollow Historical Society. I know I was one of three or four-hundred students going through his classes. I'm probably just a vague shadow always sitting in the second seat from the left second row and stuffed between two other students.

When I called, I waited to hear his office assistant shuffle through his files to figure out which one I was. But there wasn't any shuffling, and she put me right through to his phone. He already knew what happened. His staff had done a routine call to Grant to see if I had finished my internship because I hadn't turned in my forms and, at the time, they were readying for graduation. Grant was quick to tell him what happened.

"I didn't take anything," I explain to him. "I liked working there. It's what I've always wanted to do. I'm the only one in my family who was going to graduate from college with a four-year degree. Well, I *was*. My Pop Pop, he—he busted his ass working extra jobs, so I didn't have a hard life like he does—" I don't know why I'm bothering. He's really deadpan about it so I'm assuming he doesn't believe me, nor does he care. I'm sure my files are already sitting in the community dump. "It doesn't matter," I finally say. "Nobody's going to believe me." I start to hang up.

"Why wouldn't they believe you? I don't know anything about this Grant Lebowski, but I remember you from class. You're the little blonde who sat in the second row and wrote down every word I spoke. The first day of your freshman year, I asked all the students in my class to raise their hand if they were only taking my class because it was a required course. Eighty percent raised their hands. Since then, I've lost ten-percent of those remaining to other career choices and another five-percent to quitting because they couldn't afford it. That leaves you and a handful of others. But you were the only one who raised your hand that day when I asked, of those remaining, why they chose history. And you said: *I don't know. I just like it.*"

Ugh. "That's what I said." It was embarrassing because my words somehow lit up the room with laughter like I was saying it because I didn't have another answer. "You've probably held that against me my entire college career." I force a laugh.

"I've heard lots of answers to that question over the thirty-two years I've taught. Honestly, I had never gotten that explanation before, nor have I since. It was refreshing and uncomplicated. History should be so unpretentious. I think more people would take my classes."

"Well, it seems the obvious," I defend myself.

"If you aren't doing what you like right now, what are you doing?"

"Please don't judge me. I'm learning real estate."

"And you like doing that?"

"No."

"Well, since you like history, it just seems such a shame to simply give it up. Have they found anything that would make them believe you are involved in a break-in? It just doesn't make sense to me, even after speaking to this Mister Lebowski, why they would point the finger at you and not the man who disappeared on the same night of the break-in." He sighs. "If it was me and I had spent four or five years of my life trudging through the learning so I could do what I like to do, I'd be out banging on doors trying to figure out who broke into that museum and where the articles that were stolen have ended up. You just don't seem like the real estate agent type."

"Why does everybody keep telling me that?" I groan.

"Here's a suggestion. I'm just saying this because I'm probably one of the three percent of people you know who likes history too. Don't settle. Sometimes you've just got to work a little harder to get what you want. You've heard the saying - *you've got to pay your dues*."

"I worked my butt off in class, Professor Williams. You don't understand. I worked a full-time job while I took a full course load. I wouldn't even know where to start—"

"May I suggest that you look through some historical crime books and try to come up with a game plan? I mean, have you asked around any pawn shops for the missing items or checked online auctions?"

"No. I've just been kind of waiting for Trevor to come back. I don't know what else I can do. I think everybody believes he's going to walk through the door any minute and then answer the question: did he do it or not. Then for whatever his answer is, we move on from there."

"I would assume the police are concentrating on that aspect too. They just don't have the staff to continually check the items. Historically speaking, items that are unique like the ones Mister Lebowski state were stolen are hidden and sold quietly because they are easily recognizable. Take for example, one of the thirteen handwritten copies of the Bill of Rights kept in the state house in Raleigh, North Carolina. It was taken as a souvenir by a Union soldier during William Sherman's occupation of that area in 1865. It took 138 years, but the FBI seized it during a sale in 2003. And then there's the well-known case of Leonardo da Vinci's *Mona Lisa*. It was stolen from the Louvre Museum in 1911 and found in 1913." I can hear someone saying something over his shoulder and then the squeal of his chair while he wheels around. "I've got class in five minutes. I would recommend figuring out what items were stolen, get a list. Then figure out what kind of people would be searching for each item."

Chapter 13

Our town founder, Hans Branntwein, was born in 1841. He was only seven years old when his mother and father brought him, a twelve-year-old brother, Ulrich, and his one and a half-year-old sister, Mila, from Germany to America. His mother died of diphtheria on the ship a week into the voyage. A short note is made of the end of her journey in a family bible in the historical society. His brother, Ulrich, is also mentioned in the 1850 United States Census, but in a separate part of the city. His occupation was listed as *attending school*. Then, he completely disappears from records. Little is known about his sister either. She is also shown on an 1850 Ohio census record with Hans and his father, Alfred, who is listed as: Grocery Store Merchant. After that, there are no records of her. I assume she died and was buried at an old cemetery, her name worn away and unidentifiable on the stone above her grave.

Alfred had worked his way to Ohio and amassed a small sum of money running a grocery store in the German Village section of Columbus. His name is not listed in the records after 1858. Hans vanished off the records until his misspelled name appeared in a Clarksburg, West Virginia newspaper in 1866: HAYDEN SELLS ALL COAL PROPERTIES TO BRANTWINE AND PARTNERS. BRANDY MOUNTAIN COAL MINE TO OPEN.

That is all stuff I've collected in my little file system inside the Lost Hollow Historical Society. It may not seem like a lot, but it is three years of digging and following trails of people long dead no one has bothered to preserve in one place over the last one-hundred and seventy years. It is still sitting there on a little table I used as a desk but won't be using anymore. I'm assuming Beck has already taken over my desk. He's sorted through my stuff, culled out what he needs, and is prepared to take over my spiel for his own.

"Hey, big guy. Can you do me a favor?" I corner Beck in Pop Pop's kitchen; literally, I suppose. Because when I come around the kitchen door, he moves to his left to avoid gutting me with his can of beer. Pop Pop has always given our friends full reign of his house and his kitchen, which means everybody's used to opening the refrigerator door as soon as they get to Pop Pop's and dig out a drink or a sandwich. I step forward and push one hand out and gently lay it on his belly and chest, and you would think he was a teeny mouse and I was a big tomcat trapping him to the wall. He backs up step for step with me until his rear bumps against the wall. "Are you afraid of me?" I furrow my brow, look up what seems forty stories to examine his eyes. They are wide. My voice was soft.

"No." He protests. But he's unmoving except to crane his neck a bit wildly like he's unnerved and looking for help. Zach and his army of friends are watching a soccer game at Pop Pop's. He gets the sports channel, and they don't.

"Then why are you pressing yourself against the wall like I'm going to bite you?"

"Are you?" He stutters and swallows hard, then makes a deep sigh and rolls his neck around his shoulders. "That sounded bad. But I've seen the teeth marks you left on Zach when we—"

"Seriously?" I grunt. I drop my hand. "No. of course, I'm not going to bite you." I put on my best suck-up face with a big smile and doleful gaze. "Come on, big guy, do I look like I'd hurt you?" He doesn't look like he believes me when he narrows his eyes. "Dammit, I grew out of biting when I was eight." Beck eyes me cautiously. He knows I'm up to something.

"And what did you grow into? Knives? Guns?"

"Haha." I back up, roll my eyes. "Relax. I left some stuff at my desk at the museum which is *your* desk now, and I'd like to get it back. You think you can get it for me? Please, please?" I give him wide, puppy eyes. "And, maybe, can you get me the list of the stuff that was stolen?"

"What are you going to do to me if I say *no*?" He stands up straight, and I don't ever forget how huge he is while my head rolls back to take in his face. "Hang on, let me clear the clouds from your head," I tease him, waving my hand between us. "I can't see all the way up there."

"Haha," he says blandly, rolling his eyes. "You're making fun of me, and at the same time, you're asking me to steal something for you?"

"I'm not making fun of you—" Well, I guess I am. I ponder this less than six seconds, then move on. "But steal it? *Oh*, no. I don't think *my* work belongs to the museum. It's stuff *I* collected since I was in high school about Lost Hollow."

"Well, yes, it would be stealing," Beck says. "So, no. Whatever you're going to do, do it now. Get it over with."

Did I expect anything less from Mister-never-does-wrong? He's never late, never owes a bill. He put his wife on a pedestal even when they got a divorce. He even places my dumbass uncle's needs above his own. I know. I watch Beck eating chicken nuggets from the gas station off the highway all the time, half-gagging and stuffing the little, extra crispy turdballs in his mouth. He hates them. Zach can't get enough of them and the catsup he dips them into. But when they got to pick someplace to eat, Zach says: *I want the Dusty Road Gas station nuggets.*

"Okay, I get it, stupid asshole," I growl at him. "Fine. It's all yours. Take it. Frigging six years of digging crap up and you walk in and use it for your talks this summer. I hope everybody finds out you stole it from me."

I pivot on my feet, start to stomp out, and Beck stops me with a hand on my upper arm. I freeze. I'm not normally afraid of people bigger than me, considering almost *everybody* is bigger than me, and I'm just simply used to it. His grip isn't tight, but it is firm enough to bring me to a stop. His bear paw encompasses more than half of my skin from elbow to shoulder. I take in his clasp on my arm, then glare up at him. Beck O'Sullivan's got an expression I have never seen on him, like the huge, white flash of lightning that lights up even a house with the shutters down and comes only seconds before a crackle of thunder loud enough to shake the house.

"Hey, don't call me a stupid."

"Okay. I'm sorry," I mutter. I'm standing there staring at him and my heart is pounding like drums, but I'm trying to maintain my angry scowl, so he doesn't know I'm completely and utterly terrified right now. My, how things can change fast. Now he's the tomcat. "Let me go." Now I know why when he played football, and he took a step in front of the quarterback to protect him, his opponent getting ready for a tackle would just stop before even bothering to go around him. Everybody would chuckle back then. Now, it's not so funny. I also know my eyes are getting that red and puffy look right before I cry.

He sniffs a laugh, releases my tiny arm. "I figured you'd use that stupid ploy. Knives leave blood. Bite marks leave evidence. If you punch yourself in the arm to leave a red mark, nobody's going to believe I hit you. You've drastically reduced your strategy to employing empathy on my part. Go ahead and cry. I know your game." It is demeaning at best. It doesn't hurt, but I rub my hand over my arm like it does. I feel pity for his old opponents on the football field right now. It is humiliating, and I just want to cry. Zach yells out for Beck to get his butt into the living room; they're tired of putting the game on hold. I turn, set my sights for the front door. "I'm going home," I tell Pop Pop on my way through.

"Aren't you staying for supper?" he asks me. I hope he didn't notice I came home from work early. I shake my head, trying to hurry and snatch up my purse on the coffee table in front of the TV before Beck comes out of the kitchen and starts bantering about our conversation.

"Naw, it's just been a crappy day," I lie.

"Okay, now can you shut up?" Zach grunts and waves me out from in front of the TV, leaning elbows on knees and keeling forward in an exaggerated effort for me to get out of the way. "I want to hear this."

"You should have thought about that last week when you

stood in front of it for twenty minutes whining that you were missing your favorite, stupid hillbilly ghost hunting show when I was watching my show."

Pop Pop knows something's wrong. I see him giving me an eyeful before I shut the door behind me. But he knows when to leave me alone with my misery. I don't even get to the bottom of the steps before I burst into a thousand tears. I can't get to my jeep fast enough while the hot tears stream down my eyes.

Knock, knock. I wasn't quick enough. My eyes work upward to my driver's side window just as I turn the key in the ignition. Beck.

"Go away, Beck. You've had your say."

"Roll down the window."

"No, don't tell me what to do."

"*Please*. Roll down the window."

I don't want to do it. But I do turn the window lever around and around while the glass lowers excruciatingly slow and a bit sideways. "What?"

"I didn't take the job, Flea," he tells me. "That's why it would be stealing because I don't have a desk there—your desk or anybody's desk. I told Grant I didn't want the job."

"What do you mean?" I am sniffing into my wrist.

"Because I don't believe you'd steal that stuff and I don't like that he said you did. You're Zach's sister—"

"Niece," I remind him.

"Whatever. I'm not as stupid as you think. And I'm not afraid of you."

"It was just an expression, Beast, that I pulled out of my head on the spur of the moment." And yes, he is afraid of me. I don't know why. But he is. I see it in the way he won't keep eye contact with me. I lean over toward the passenger side, open my glovebox, and tug out a tan restaurant napkin. Then I scrub it under my nose. "I don't think you're stupid. I call Zach stupid all the time when I get mad at him. *He's* not as stupid as he looks." I force a smile to hopefully smooth it over. "You're just sensitive." Beck coughs up a bland laugh.

"Oh. Okay. Don't call me Beast, alright? It sounds like I'm something I'm not."

"Whatever. It's just been a shitty day. I lost—" Oh, crap. Why'd I start to say that aloud? I scoot past it quickly. "I—I lost my purse for a while. I want to go home and climb into bed and pull the covers over my head." I start to roll the window up. I stop because he is just wavering there. "Thanks," I say to him. "You know—I mean, I don't know what to say. I appreciate that you don't think I'm a part of all of it."

"I appreciate you don't think I'm stupid. When I interviewed for the job at the mayor's office with Grant Lebowski and John Matthews, the mayor actually said that they don't need somebody smart in there. They need a pretty face to get folks to come. History is boring. A good-looking guy giving tours might just bring people in."

"You're kidding me? I don't know why you're worried. At least, you got one of the two criteria for getting the job. Because that would mean I'm neither pretty nor smart."

"Haha, that's funny." No, it isn't. I glare at him and he says: "What?"

"Nothing," I grunt and start to roll up my window. "Some men think I'm pretty and smart too."

And what does he say? "Oh, yeah. They probably do."

Chapter 14

"Pop Pop, I need to ask you a question." I'm sitting on the dilapidated stands of the old Lost Hollow ballfield the next Sunday. I'm staring at a hodgepodge of men, most of them fifty-something, trying to do anything but attend the New Grace Fellowship church picnic. And I say fifty-something, but I don't know their real ages. I just know none of them are under forty because ninety percent of the guys under forty either got the hell out of Lost Hollow as soon as they turned eighteen or once they moved out, their mamas couldn't make them go to church anymore. The youngest of the whole lot of them is four or five and rounding the bases over and over. It is the oldest, though, that I have my eyes focused on. It is the scruffy, gray hair of my grandpa who is turning and rubbing the salt-and-pepper stubble on his cheeks with one hand.

I still haven't heard from Trevor. My car is nowhere to be found. And I cannot for the life of me stop thinking about what Professor Williams advised me to do. Last night, I tossed and I turned, trying to figure out where to start like he suggested. I watched two old crime movies, one newer reality show on murders in small towns, and I perused a couple free online crime novels. Of the thirty ideas I came up with, none of them seemed the intelligent thing to do. I hadn't opened the plastic container I'd gotten from Trevor's garage other than to simply wiggle up a corner of the lid and peer cautiously and a little nauseously at two bare and big-boobed girls fondling each other on a motorcycle and staring back at me on a magazine cover. *Hey, girl, come join us.* I almost hear them trying to tempt me, and I close the lid quickly. Gross. I wonder if they know how many other bare-butted, naked girls sat on that motorcycle seat before them. I'm sure that didn't bother Trevor. They probably persuaded him in some solo fantasy in the bathroom.

I shut it tightly, pushed it up against the kitchen wall. I suppose I was going to use it as leverage when he called me from his house to come pick up my car. I knew if I opened it, he'd know. I was going to tell him if he wanted his stupid porn magazines, he'd have to bring me my car.

But at a quarter past two in the morning, my phone rang. I snapped to attention, heart racing, and jumped up from the bed. Two rings, that's all there was. Then just as I put my hand on the telephone, it stopped ringing. Wide awake and thinking either someone in my family died, or it was Trevor, I stood there waiting. I couldn't get back to sleep. I wandered around my living room, then stopped at the kitchen, staring down at Trevor's plastic porn container. Do I really want to know what I *lacked* (other than a motorcycle and a friend to join us) and the girls inside his magazines *possessed* that made him look elsewhere?

I suppose a part of me still wanted to know. Such I knelt, opened the container, and pushed past the two girls with big boobs. The box wasn't at all full of sexy magazines. Underneath, there was a large, brown paper grocery bag. When I tugged it out and delicately drew back the paper, there were six Ball Mason jars with dirt still clinging to their glass outsides and each, carefully wrapped twice in three lunch-size paper sacks. And inside each jar, there were six five-dollar bills from 1915 and seven ten-dollar gold Indian coins, dated 1910. One was full of coins, company scrip, that stated BRANDY MOUNTAIN COLLIERY. $1.

But it was what lay beneath; a square object tucked carefully in an old, dull-white t-shirt catching my attention. I tugged out the strangely wrapped package, unfolded the dingy short sleeves and the neckline to expose what appeared to be a leather-bound journal.

"Oh, for the love of God," I heard my wispy voice slit the quiet air. It was an old, deep-brown, leather-bound journal. I picked it up, caught the scent of mildewed paper and ran my fingertips across the parched leather of the cover. A puff of air from my lips blew a ball of dust into the air, and I sneezed quickly, twice. I let my forefinger roam to the top corner of the cover, and I gingerly tugged it back to expose yellowed pages beneath.

Daily Journal. Hans Branntwein. I read that and flipped through ten or so pages, stopping at a date at the top of one page. My heart took a jump. Hans Branntwein. Where did Trevor find this? I racked my brain, tried to recall if there was one of these at the museum. No, I'm sure I would have known about it; Grant Lebowski would have been all over this. He would have displayed the journal at the front door of the historical center beneath a quadruple-locked glass case.

There were pages ripped out of the front, maybe ten or fifteen. I pondered this for a moment, took a gentle-handled look front and back. I didn't see the missing pages secreted anywhere. I did see where the numbers were handwritten in the top corners of each page. I squinted, made out the first page present. It is *Page 34 —*

September 13, 1862, it said in cursive that was quite elegant, but difficult to read in its swirls and twists. *Harpers Ferry, Virginia—It was the September 9th, 1862 when we took on the prisoners in camp. The roads were bad. It must have rained buckets because short people like me and short horses like my pony were knee-deep in muck and horseshit from a thousand soldiers marching in front of us. I would have liked to have grown three inches this year. I'm not so lucky. I think I'm full-grown like the pony; this is all the bigger I'm getting. The surgeon at the last hospital we stopped at to get a bullet out of Bad Bill's foot told me it was because I don't get much to eat. He told me to go home to my mama. I was too little to fight. I didn't tell him my mama died when I was only one-year-old. My papa raised me all alone. The surgeon thought I was ten or eleven, get that! Bad Bill lied and told him my papa was some big general and he was just watching me to keep me out of trouble. He didn't tell him the truth that he dragged me and Hayward out of the barn where we were hiding last September before his boys burned the house clean down. I suppose I should be happy I'm alive. Hayward thinks we'd be dead by now if I hadn't told Bad Bill last year that the* *wagons the Union boys were hiding in the barns around Scuttle Creek and had been secreting across the state were full of gunpowder and fuses to blow up the train tracks. He asked me how I knew that, and I told him it was written on the side of the boxes. He asked me if I could read the directions on using them if somebody wrote them down, and I said that of course, I could. I wasn't stupid. The next thing I know, Bad Bill's new orders were to steal those explosives and blow up three bridges in Harpers Ferry. Papa always said I was too big for my britches. I don't want to think about that. I should have gone left that day in a dead run back to Ohio. Instead, I went right. Now, after what I've done, I can't ever go back at all—I don't like where I am, but there's got to be more sunshine where I'm heading than where I've been.*

"I can't ever go back," I repeated Hans Branntwein's words aloud. Back where? From where in Ohio did he come from? Where did he go? I'm mesmerized, eager to know more. It is Hans Branntwein's diary from the time of the Civil War and long before the coins found in the Ball Mason jars. I pulled the journal up to sniff the cover and take in the waft of leather. I sneezed three times. Something tumbled from the back of the journal when I held it aloft. I slipped my fingers down, caught a gold, square frame before it fell helplessly to the floor. Holy cow! It was a cased tintype portrait. The framing was gold-colored and almost as pliable as aluminum foil. I brought it up to my face, stared into the faded face of a boy that looked not more than ten or twelve. His hair was cut short and nearly covered by his Union hat. His eyes were glassy, almost white and his lips were heart-shaped, almost laughing. He was holding a sword in his lap, and a gun was tucked beneath one tiny arm. At his elbow, there was a violin or fiddle. Private Hans Branntwein, is etched with tiny writing beneath the image.

My heart was racing. Surely, nobody knows this exists. I can remember Grant Lebowski being asked by a student once if he had a picture of the town founder. He had clearly stated none existed even in the family archives. The only way I can think to describe my feelings last night was in the same way my Aunt Joy explained to me how she felt when she got baptized in the big bowl of bathwater at our church. *Harley, baby, when I came up from the water, I was just shaking with delight.*

I was literally shaking with delight. Yet, even as I stared into this wondrous find, my mind was racing. These artifacts couldn't have come from the same place as the jars. It wasn't covered in dirt and rotted. Because I know for a fact the jars were buried somewhere at some time. I had scrubbed the dirt from the shovel in Trevor's garage from my hands with a napkin Max had stuffed into the glovebox of his truck. There were a couple pine needles sticking to my fingers. I wouldn't have noted them except one slipped beneath the nail of my thumb and caught there like a teeny-weeny wooden spear I had to dig out later with a pair of tweezers. It hurt like hell. That dirt and the tiny pine needles on the shovel and my hands matched what I saw dried on the Ball Mason jars.

What I was wondering is this: Where did Trevor find the journal, and did it lead him to the treasure? Such, was Trevor really getting chased by somebody and was it because he'd dug up those jars and found this book? Because he obviously has not shown up in a week and his mom has called me twice and left messages asking if I know where he is. What if— what if he wasn't lying and he *was* getting chased? And what if those jars have something to do with Hans Branntwein's treasure everybody has been looking for in Lost Hollow for the last one-hundred and God knows how many years and some crazy, money-hungry fiend would do anything, including killing Trevor, to get to it? Or did he just steal the whole lot of it and dump part on me, so the cops think I did it? Crap.

I scanned the journal for clues for a hard forty minutes until my eyes felt so tired they ached. I stared at the picture like a mama stares with loving eyes at a newborn baby. I don't know why. I suppose as the door to Grant Lebowski's historical society building closed for me, it was like a new door was opening. It's an adventure. It's a mystery. I may not be where I want to be just like the boy in the journal, but if he can find the sunny side in the middle of a war, I can dig my way out of the darkness in my cozy bedroom even if my utilities are three weeks past due. It is somewhere to go to save me from falling into the depths of the realty job I don't want to do and past-due bills and feeling like a failure. Like Hans said on one of the pages, and I turned back the pages, tasted the words again: *I don't like where I am, but there's got to be more sunshine where I'm heading than where I've been.* I wished I was that profound.

I am desperate for some key that will unlock the mystery of Trevor's disappearance. Maybe that particular key goes hand in hand with the location of the hidden treasure. And maybe the journal holds some clues to *where* it is hidden, and such finding it will lead me to my ex-boyfriend. Such, I dug into the journal. The handwriting at times was nothing more than a scribble and too difficult to decipher. There were pages that had gotten wet and stuck together. There were hundreds of entries for almost three years. Most of it was day-to-day activities: *I got stuck again putting up the tents* or *It snowed, and I need new socks.* Then there's stuff like: *George Queen and six other boys died today. I played my fiddle where we buried them. Not one of them was over seventeen. A soldier looked like he was just sleeping, and another boy tried to wake him up until they pulled him off screaming.* I ended up closing the book, falling into a restless sleep.

Then I thought I'd try a different angle the next day, making my way to the ballfields when I knew church had ended.

"Shit on a stick! Are you trying to kill me?"

That bellow was heralded right after a sickening smack of softball to chubby knee and a few curse words. It's Billy Armstrong yelling. He owns the Dusty Road/Lost Hollow Grocery and Gas just outside town. He's one of Pop Pop's long-time buddies along with skinny, buggy-eyed Jay Short who just made one of many wild pitches of the ball. If the sound of softball smacking flesh alone had not ripped me from my thoughts, Billy's angry holler did. He's making a funny hop-skip around in circles and waving a fist toward Jay who is standing on the pitcher's mound looking guilty.

"That's it. I quit. I lived through Afghanistan and marrying that witch-wife of mine. I ain't dying on a stupid baseball field—we got nobody that can run or pitch—"

It wasn't the first man to walk off the field this afternoon. Even when Pop Pop offered up a beer to rub on his knee, Billy just mumbled something about having to get to work at the store anyway. They all watch Billy limp toward the benches. He's still griping when he snatches up his cooler and winds his way to his car in the New Grace Fellowship parking lot.

"Pop Pop," I wait for the men to assemble again and Jay Short is juggling the ball while another man is wincing at the batter's plate before I call out to my grandpa. "Hey, when did they stop using company scrip in the Brandy Mountain mines?" The ballfield stands with wood board seats are uncomfortable, at best. I pucker my lips forcing myself not to move, so a splinter doesn't ease its way past my panties and jean shorts to the delicate flesh of my bottom. Everybody's been to the Sunday morning service, and everybody's eaten. Now, it's time to gossip and clean up, something the older men avoid except to drag the folding tables and chairs into the shed behind the church. Shortly thereafter, I watched them leave one by one with a vague excuse and a knowing nod to each other like it's a big, top-secret operation they've got going to sneak out of the picnic and head to the ballfields. If you can still call them ballfields. There aren't any real bases anymore, barring the use of a well-worn ballcap that is first base. Third plate is a baby blue NFL jacket, and home plate is an empty box of cigarettes. I can't see second base because the sparse, knee-high grass and a small sapling are hiding it.

Pop Pop narrows his eyes at me. I swear, he is still giving me that tip of head gaze every time I walk into a room that screams GUILTY! "I don't know. Maybe the 1940s?"

"What did they do with all the money leftover? Did they just throw it away? I mean, there had to be a lot that didn't get used."

"You're the one who went to college to learn history. You should be telling me when we used it." He shrugs. "At least four years of college wouldn't be going to waste, then. What's got you so curious?"

"Ouch, that hurt," I grunt, and he rolls his eyes at me. I don't tell him the truth. I know if anybody knows the diary and jars of money exist, it would get plucked out of my fingers in less than two seconds and with a lot of questions as to how I got my hands on it. "Some stuff isn't found in the books, Pop Pop," I answer. "Hearing it from you old farts is where I get my facts and not from some dumbbutt who collected his information in 1960 and copied it from another dumbbutt who got it in the 1950s."

"You know how Lost Hollow got its name?" T.J. Atkinson is skinny, tall and standing with his arms crossed looking out over the field. He's taken off his Sunday best jacket and skinned himself down to a sleeveless t-shirt. He stops long enough to turn his head back toward me.

"Yeah, T.J.," I wave him away with my hand. I notice he even has those big freckles on his shoulders. "Everybody knows how it got its name. They started a tunnel through the mountain, but it never got finished. End of story. Grant Lebowski wrote a booklet on the town history."

"Yeah, that's the dead-end story *he* tells. But the story I'm talking about plays out more like a Grimms' Fairy Tale and has a curse with it. The Straightline Railroad Company decided to build a section of tracks from the ones that run parallel to the river and right up through the hollow here." He stops, blows out a puff of air. "I think that was back in the 1870s. The rail company realizes that it must put a hole through the side of Brandy Mountain to get to the other side.

And every time they try to dig one out, it caves in and men die. They got through about six deaths when those railroad workers quit. But the railroad company was putting pressure on the Branntweins to get the tracks completed. They had a contract and said they'd shut the whole place down if they didn't get it done in two weeks. Somebody contacted a few county jails. The wardens sent out twelve prisoners at a time to cut through the mountain." T.J. stops for a moment, holds up a finger. "You notice I said *at a time?* Because they figured most of those boys wouldn't come back alive, right? And who cares? They were murderers and thieves. Now they are ghosts. They say they come back and chase Hans Branntwein's ghost through the cave for leaving them there."

"Ghosts. You're a dumbass, T.J. This is hearsay, you know that, right?" Buddy Peterson had just walked up carrying a bag full of bats. He drops them and rolls his eyes. He's barrel-chested with buggy eyes and a limping walk.

"Well, you can say what you want. I only know what I was told. But there are dead men in there. *Mad* dead men because they got left in there. A week into cutting a hole in the mountain, it collapsed. There were prisoners and miners inside, and one of them was a woman."

"A woman?" I ask, curiously.

"Yeah, her name was Minnie Bean. But every time they tried to get them out, more rock would fall. They left them to rot, no burial, no stone to show they died there. It got its nickname then, Lost Tunnel." T. J. tells me. "And where you're standing right now, Lost Hollow. The story wasn't written up nowhere. It was just told. That's why they say this place is cursed, you know. Because those men are still buried there. My great grandpa was one of the men who was sent in to get them out. He told my grandpa that he heard them yelling." I'm not sure if I believe him. I wonder why I've never heard this story. Grant told me Lost Hollow got its name because everybody overlooked Brandy Mountain when they were running to see who could buy up the most profitable places to mine the coal.

"It ain't cursed." Pop Pop scoffs at T. J. Then he looks at me. "And there ain't no ghosts. I got some old mining scrip, though, in my drawer at the house. Take a look-see. And if you're gonna interrupt our game, you're gonna have to come out here and hit us some balls," he grumbles while the youngest of the players, a four-year-old with a buzz cut makes his fourth round of the bases screaming like a plane coming in for a landing. Pop Pop points to a pink, plastic Easter bucket filled with baseballs and softballs. "We're using baseballs and softballs most of the time or at least until closer to the games. The big balls are expensive."

I shrug. "As long as you don't make fun of me," I grumble and make my way down to the field. "I know you think girls can't play ball." But I know they will tease me while I snatch up a bent and banged-up bat from the mangled remains of what used to be the backstop with one hand and dig out the cleanest baseball I can find with the other. "You all practicing for the big leagues, Grandpop?" I tease him gently and point to the odd assortment of his buddies on the field. "Because I got five bucks that says you all missed the tryouts." I toss the ball in the air with my left hand and use my right to swing the bat. I miss. I'm not very good at batting with a single hand.

"You just got fired from your job. You ain't got a cent on that scrawny body of yours to wager." It's Jacob who says that while I chase the ball down. He's one of my uncles and I know he sees my eyes go wide. How'd they find out so fast? Jacob's in the ten percent of men who were dumb enough to stick around Lost Hollow. He's two years older than me and quick to trounce me in a battle of *who-is-Pop Pop's favorite-kid.*

"That's what Zach told me," He snitches. I glare at Jacob, then let my eyes follow the path of deceit to Zach.

"How'd you know?"

"I heard your jeep's been in the driveway during the day. I wouldn't have told him if you would have been nice and gotten me that beer off the table in the garage the other day,"

Zach says smugly.

"There's a big difference there, dumbbutt," I remind him. Next time we swap something, I'm going to get him back. Because, crap, my grandpa doesn't know about the latest little blip in my life.

"What do you mean you got fired?" Pop Pop groans loudly. I try to ignore him and toss the ball. I miss again. "You got fired from your job selling houses?"

"It's not a big deal, Pop Pop," I mutter and slam Jacob with a glare before I bend down to pick the ball up in my fingers. "You're such a frigging tattletale, Jake. What are you, twelve years old?"

"So that's a *yes?*" Pop Pop tells me. "It is a big deal. You got rent to pay. What's wrong with you, girl?"

"She's broke, Dad," Zach yells that from left field. "I've been telling everybody that forever, isn't that right, Beck?" He yells that second half over to the third baseman who isn't difficult to see even from my vantage. Beck just laughs in agreement. "She's broke like those toys that people put in the donation boxes at church. She just don't work right." He makes this loud moan, then plops down on his butt on the field and shakes his head. "She can't pitch to herself and get it one foot, much less out here. Can't you pitch to us?"

"No, she needs to do something other than sitting in the stands all her life. She ain't broke, just—" my grandpa stops and seems to contemplate an answer, rubs his chin, and shakes his head. "She's just cracked a little."

I pull back the bat, feign a practice swing. "Mama says I'm just like you. Meaner than snot and stubborn."

"Speaking of losers, Flea, you find the car and the boyfriend who stole it?" Roy Adkins is forty-something and a hundred pounds overweight. He glares hard at me through his thick glasses, spits on first base where his left foot is planted, then uses one hand to wiggle his pants up a couple inches. Then, he turns his attention to Pop Pop. "Does your grandbaby always sass you like that?" he sniffs.

"I thought you said you weren't dating that boy anymore." Pop Pop ignores him. His shoulders drop. "What made you decide to start hanging with that boy again? What are you thinking with that goofy, little head, girl? You're too old to be boy-crazy. You've gone all waggy-whoop!" He wiggles his hand over his head. Pop Pop's always making up words and sayings. Waggy-whoop is one of them.

"No, Pop Pop. I just went to pick him up because he was drunk. I couldn't leave him—"

"Yeah, baby, you could!" Pop Pop groans and everybody thinks this is funny and laughs. "He isn't your job anymore." Then his voice drops. "Don't you see what that Matthews's boy is doing?" I know he is referring to Max. "He's hanging around you to get you to talk everybody into signing off our houses the easy way without going to court."

I can't believe he said that in front of everybody. My face burns beet red. "I'm not friends with him anymore." I toss up the ball and imagine I'm mad enough to hit it to Japan, but I don't. The bat completely misses the ball and falls to the ground. I just growl at them when they groan because I know it's not going to be the last one I miss.

One ball. Two balls. Three balls. I miss them all. I wish I could just leave. Beck finally throws down his glove. He tugs out a Little League bat from his bag and tells me to *try this on for size* because it's not as long or heavy. It is belittling. He comes up and wiggles the ballcap on his head twice, then dives in with his arms around me and everybody hooting he has to ask me out on a date now.

"Stop!" I hiss-whisper to him while he's holding me like a rutting bull on a horny cow. He ignores me and shows me how to hold the bat a little better. "You're a little girl. You need a smaller bat." I can't help but think he's putting on a sex show for the ball boys. Zach is laughing so loud, he is rolling in the dirt. "Choke up on it," he tells me gruffly, softly and moves his hands up the wooden shaft and pushes mine with them. "This is how you hold it."

"*Your* bat, Beast?" I grunt softly and angrily to him.

"Because it is true—even little girls like big bats. *I* like bigger bats."

"My bat's too big for you." It suddenly occurs to him I'm not talking about bats at all. He's red-faced, and his jaw is set hard. "See," he says, "this is why I'm scared of you."

"And if you don't stop," I hiss. "Pop Pop is going to be at your front door tonight with a shotgun and a wedding ring and dragging me kicking and screaming up the steps."

Pop Pop finally calls it a day. I try to slink off before everybody else, but I don't quite make it past the stands because Pop Pop hands me a plastic grocery bag and tells me to pick up the empty bottles. Beck's lingering there ready to help Pop Pop carry equipment to his truck. "I'll make a deal with you," Pop Pop says. "You get my boys in some kind of shape, like let's say taking off ten pounds each and we'll talk."

"Well, I can do that!" I pipe up a little too energetically. What is wrong with me? "Can I be on the team if I do? I mean, like actually be something?" Then I pause and think out his words. *We'll talk.* Hmmm, sounds fishy to me. He either doesn't think I can do it or he's just trying to keep me so busy, I'll forget I want to play. In other words, this is my new job instead of sewing or hitting to them. "Okay, Pop Pop," I inquire, "is that like when you used to say *We'll see* when I asked you for something, and you actually meant *no*? Or do you think I don't have enough competency to get the job done?" He doesn't answer.

Chapter 15

"I used to pitch in college, did I tell you that?"

I didn't see Taylor settled into the old wooden stands until I pass her while I am tossing the last of the empty plastic bottled waters Pop Pop's team had left strewn near the benches. My eyes are on Beck who is following along behind Pop Pop with two bat bags slung over his shoulder and the pink Easter bucket full of balls in his hand. He said something. I'm not sure what, then he had looked up over my shoulder to the stands and then back to me with a goofy grin on his face. I follow his gaze. That's when I see Taylor. I should have known. Her beauty doesn't just suck out women's brains; I suppose men get thrown off by it too.

I probably wouldn't have recognized her even if I did look up earlier. She's wearing jeans and a blouse, and her hair is in a ponytail. I've only seen her wear dresses. And usually, she's two inches of caked makeup with hair a sleek shine down her shoulders. "You were pretty deep in Mystic Whiskeys when I told you I pitched," she goes on. "I don't know if you remember the conversation. You told me your grandpa hurt your feelings by asking you to sew instead of playing ball."

I peer up at her through the setting sunshine. It's strange seeing her in this environment—my stomping grounds of the old town and beat up ballfield. "I guess I'm the batgirl and cleanup crew." I hold up the yellow plastic grocery bag filled with candy bar wrappers and empty bottles. "Oh, and personal trainer for eight old, fat guys now, too."

"That's a step up, isn't it?" she laughs softly. "Better than sitting in the stands. And he's not so old and fat." She wags a finger in the direction of Pop Pop and Beck. He's still turning and grinning at her and then at me.

I follow her gaze and scrunch up my face. "No, he's not. And if you decide you like boys, he's single and has his stupid-in-lust face on now for you." I roll my eyes bitterly.

"Men really need to take a look in the mirror and see how dumb they look when a pretty woman walks past." I wave the conversation away and turn my attention to Taylor. "Regardless, once the games start, I'll be back to picking up water bottles." I toss the bag into the metal, lidless garbage can the church placed out here. It says: GRACE on it.

"Um, maybe. Maybe not. I saw them out there. I'm thinking if you're good at something, they'll realize how stupid they are for thinking girls can't compete."

"I'm doomed then. I'm finally realizing the only thing I'm good at is getting myself fired."

"You quit. You weren't fired."

"Listen, whatever." I shrug and push my hands into my jean short pockets. "Regardless, I can't even hit the damn ball when *I'm* tossing it up to hit."

"If you come back to work, I'll show you how to pitch and even hit the ball." She stands up. "Listen, all you have to do is apologize and kiss ass for a couple weeks. Lissette has a lot of time and money invested in you."

"Why do you care?" I ask while she steps down the warped bleachers. I reach out my hand, help her balance on the last.

"I like you. You've got je ne sais quoi." She leans in. "And now I'm the one with the stupid-in-lust face."

She is giving me that goofy grin. I shrug it off. "I'm assuming *je ne sais quoi* means the one who walks straight into poles to make everybody laugh?"

"No, it is French. It translates into: *I don't know what.* It's that something you can't quite put into words but draws people to you—um, charm."

"Charming. You saw me dance, right?"

"Exactly. You were funny and cute." She's facing me. I think she's prettier without makeup, but I don't say that.

"So how did you know I'd be here?"

"Lost Hollow isn't that big. You weren't at the address I pulled out of your files. You weren't at the playground or the restaurant or the gas station."

"Makes sense."

"Why don't you let me show you a few things about throwing and hitting. Except for the use of a glove, the size of the ball won't make much of a difference in getting the skill down. We'll practice with the fast pitch 12-inch ball because that's what I've got. In return, you'll think about coming back to work, Harley. Please. For me."

For me? She acts like we've been best buddies since grade school and not just two people who sit at separate tables in the breakroom—she at the cool kids' table surrounded by laughter and most of the staff. On the other hand, I'm alone poking at my cell phone for company, watching the clock, and mentally begging for my lunch break to end.

But she's staring at me with these big, bunny eyes and I think if I say no, it will be like purposely kicking the gas in my jeep to hit that bunny stunned and unmoving on the roadway. "Yeah, okay, you can show me. And I'll *think* about it. I don't know if Lissette wants me back, okay?" I sound like Lissette is some lover I shunned when I say that. Taylor giggles.

"She doesn't want you to come back, Harley?" Taylor eyes me. "Or you don't want to come back?"

"Why do you say that?"

"Because your heart doesn't seem into it." Taylor is trying to read me. Her eyes are going back and forth between mine. "I get the feeling selling real estate wasn't your first choice of jobs. Lissette says you have a degree in art or something."

"History. I almost do. I was working as an intern at the historical society for my final paper. It doesn't matter. I was well aware my degree was based on something I *wanted* to do and not necessarily where I would make my money. I figured if I made enough selling houses, I'd have enough money to explore the thing I wanted to do."

"You better start selling houses, huh?" Taylor nudges me in the arm. But she does spend the next few hours playing ball with me like a dedicated mama patiently walking me through difficult homework.

It is nearly six-thirty when she just stops and says that okay, she's done. I get it. I'm clumsy. There are seven different pitches, and each one requires a hand that isn't tiny like mine. There's a certain stance with fast pitching where you take a stride forward and your body rotates while you make a windmill wind of the arm and release the ball. It is incredibly intricate, almost like dancing with a partner. But the partner is a ball. My dancing is like a crazy gyrating ostrich. I don't usually care. I just like the dance. But when someone is scrutinizing it with a professional eye, I feel a bit inept.

"We'll do this three times a week, alright? There's a ballfield down the street from work. We can meet there."

"I'm supposed to meet after work at the ballfields to help my grandpa—"

"We can do it from three-thirty to five and tell Lissette I'm training you."

"You're serious about this? That's your bait to get me back to work, make your side of the bet close to the office? But why? I see Lissette's loss in spending all that money on my training. But you, Taylor, I'm not sure of your motives." I pretend to hold a fishing pole in my hand and cast it out. I'm reeling, reeling, reeling, waiting for her answer.

"Why do I need one? You've grown on us. Our office is boring. We just need someone like you."

I sniff a laugh. "That's pretty lame." But I reel some more and then tug my line like I've got something on the hook before I pretend to hold up a fake fish. "Oh, look, it's Harley on the hook."

"So, you're in?"

"Maybe. Give me a day. I'll let you know."

I pretend to check my phone when I get into my jeep. I

wait for Taylor to drive off then turn the ignition to start. Sometimes I've got to open the hood and wiggle a few wires to get it to start. I'm embarrassed enough she saw our meager ballfield. She drove a loaded, white SUV complete with what Pop Pop calls a deer killer—metal grill guards above the bumper. I know she drives a couple cars and SUVs from expensive compacts (so she can flash her money to higher selling buyers) and more lowkey SUVs for everybody else.

As soon as she disappears down the street, I hop out and pop the hood. The bar to hold the hood up is bent, so I have to use one hand to balance the hood open and the other to pat and bang every wire I can see. It is a matter of elimination. I don't know which one is not working properly. I'm focusing on the darkness inside with my eyes, and in my mind, I'm working through my conversation with Taylor.

"You need help?"

The voice is incredibly deep, and I jump in a startled reaction so hard my arm bends, and I have to make a knee-jerk retreat before the hood falls on my head. BAM! It shuts. I take a step back, pivot, and I'm standing there with my hand on my heart staring up at Beck. "Did no one ever tell you *not* to sneak up on a woman like that?" I snap at him loudly. "If I had a gun, I'd shoot you; you know that, right?"

"I was just trying to help." He tips his head. "Would you really shoot me?"

"Just don't sneak up on me." I sigh, my cheeks now red. "I'm fine." I look over his shoulder to see if Zach is with him. No, the parking lot is empty except for an old truck at one end. "I thought you left."

"I did. I helped your grandpa take stuff to his house, had a bologna sandwich, and was heading back to get some gas. When I passed, I saw you down here. I thought you were having car problems."

Oh, I get it. He came back through to check out Taylor. We don't get many women her age in Lost Hollow. "Um," I follow up. "Her name is Taylor. She openly likes girls more than guys. And she has her sights on one particular girl. I'll save you the heartache." He rubs the fuzz on his chin, then reaches into the breast pocket of his shirt and brings out a folded piece of white paper. "Thanks, I guess. But, here." I take it in my fingers, look up at him.

"What is it?"

"Just open it."

"Is it a love letter?" I tease him, wiggle my eyebrows. "I mean, I don't mind delivering professions of love on recycled copy paper, but just so you know for future reference, it'd probably take more than that to get her to change teams and lovers."

His cheeks turn a rosy red, and he shakes his head. "Harley," he huffs. "Just read it."

I grin at him and turn my attention back to the paper, unfold each flap and open it wide. I'm staring at a list two lines long. I scan a few - 2 suitcases with 1870s military uniform - $160.00 each, 1862 top hat - $120.00, set of silverware—Ames - $1270.00—

"It's the list from the museum of the things stolen. It is an account of everything in the museum, straight down to the number of paperclips in Grant's desk." He reaches out and pokes it with his finger. "Grant had a girl come in and do an inventory of the intake forms. I guess she had to go through a bunch of boxes."

"How did you get it."

"I'm *pretty*, right? At least, that's what she said."

"You flirted her up, and she gave you this?" I'm not used to carrying on long conversations with Beck. Our encounters are usually while he's with Zach and his pack of friends, so I'm addressing my uncle in what most would consider typical brother-sister banter while his friends stand politely nearby or heckle one or the other. I do know him well enough he really doesn't think he's pretty. Yes, he was the most popular guy, the biggest athlete all the way through February of his senior year. Then he got drunk one night with a couple guys from the basketball team and flipped his car. He never regained the full use of his leg. He lost a sports scholarship and walks with a slight limp still.

"Yeah, kind of. I went in to pick up my stuff from my desk, and she was working. She made me a copy."

"My history professor told me that if I could figure out what items got stolen, then maybe I could figure out what kind of people would be searching for each item," I divulge. "He thinks I might be able to find them at online auctions or something. Then I could trace them back to whoever stole them."

"Can I say something?" Beck doesn't let me answer before he goes on. "Grant Lebowski was pointing his finger way too hard at you, don't you think? I mean, why suggest it was the one person who has worked her ass off for the last ten years for free for him, right?"

"I agree."

He nods his head up and down. "That's why I stepped up to bat for you." He feigns tossing up a fake ball with one hand and hitting it with a fake bat with the other. "Get it? Haha."

"It was bad. I kind of want to kick you in the shins and hug you at the same time." I say flatly. Then I smile. "But thanks."

"No problem." Beck shoves his hands in his pockets. "T.J. was talking about a sign up on the mountain where they tried to dig the tunnel. You ever see it? Were you serious you'd never heard about it?"

I rock back and forth on my heels. "God's honest truth, I haven't. You would think somebody would have told us kids."

"It's like this. My sister's living with me with her three kids. She lost her job. Zach probably told you. It's like crazy town there from dawn to dusk. I'd rather be anywhere else right now. You want to go for a hike, check it out?"

Chapter 16

When I was six years old, Zach and I were wrestling on the top of our bunk bed. It was about nine o'clock on a school night, and Pop Pop had already trudged up the stairway and come into the room once with a warning purse to his lips. He waved a forefinger in the air and told us to get to sleep or we'd get a whooping we wouldn't forget. Still, a half hour later, we were laughing and kicking and putting each other in headlocks when I heard Pop Pop's footsteps on the stairs once again. I remember giggling and slapping my hand to my lips. My wide eyes locked with Zach's wide eyes and I burst from the bed like a butterfly taking flight, my skinny arms in the air and my knees bent in a quick, but not well thought out, retreat to my lower bed. Regrettably, the toe of my right foot caught on Zach's bedsheet. I keeled forward instead of soaring and made a headlong dive to the hard, wooden floor.

Zach says he still remembers the THUNK sound my head made when it hit the floor. I laid there while he peered over the top bunk. He says my eyes were wide open and I was staring at nothing but the ceiling. He thought I was dead. I remember one thing. My grandma, Pop Pop's wife and Zach's mom, had died six months earlier. While I was laying there, I recall seeing her in the blackness of my mind. *Grandma*! I called her. I remember reaching out my hand. But she turned and started away. I followed her in whatever dark dream state I was in, down strange hallways until I heard Pop Pop's voice and he was saying over and over to wake up, baby, wake up.

I had an almost identical dream last night. Except it wasn't my grandma I was chasing in an endless maze of Pop Pop's hallways. It was Trevor. And I was following him through the dark trails of Lost Hollow. He was always just far enough away, he almost blended with the oozy darkness of the passageway made by the full moon lighting a path between trees on either side of the trail. It was like the horizon was a drain and he was being sucked into its dark depths, and I could not stop him. And then, suddenly, he just vanished. I stopped, out of breath, and before me was the old, lost tunnel.

"You know you drive like a sissy, Beck," I tell him. He's driving twenty miles-per-hour in his truck along the mud-gravel road. To avoid potholes, he is weaving in and out. Then through the worst where there are deep puddles from the rain, he is riding one tire down the center. The farther along the road we travel outside of the newer town and into the old, the more ramshackle the old homes become until they're nothing but collapsed rooftops laying atop foundation stones. Where we are driving now, any signs of life have been gobbled up by thick-trunked trees and lush undergrowth. What thin carriage road that once led to the half-finished tunnel is but a faint path.

"Listen," he mutters, narrowing his eyes at my bare feet propped up on his dash. I took off my tennis shoes to feel the wind on my toes. His eyes work upward to my bare calves, then my thighs and all the way to the dangly fringe of pale blue jean shorts. "I don't know what you're used to driving back here—brand new stuff and ATVs, but my old truck is fifteen years old, and the whole, entire engine might drop out if I hit another ditch." He realizes I just caught him rubbernecking my position, shakes his head, and turns his gaze back to the windshield. His cheeks suddenly have two cherry-red patches on them. I don't want to look down to see if my panties are showing and make it obvious, so I'm stuck in the position while I try to figure out a graceful escape.

"I could have driven my jeep," I remind him. He ignores me because there was a bit of an argument over who would drive. I ended up parking my jeep at my house, and he picked me up in my driveway. I told him if he drives, I get to kick my feet up to his dashboard and play my kind of music on the radio and not the crappy heavy metal crap he and Zach listen to in Pop Pop's garage. That was the deal.

"Yeah, that is so much better," he grumbles. "I can see that playing out like a horror movie at dusk when the engine doesn't start again and we're ready to leave halfway up the mountain. Besides, you wouldn't get to bounce around like a tennis ball dancing in your seat and sing loud enough over the bad muffler on my truck to scare away the crows if you did, would you?" he utters and adds a smartass waggle of shoulders. "Or drag those dirty feet up on my dash."

I look at my bare feet. They are pink and slightly sunburnt on top and not dirty at all. "It was your muffler that scared those crows. Pop Pop says I sing like an angel," I huff. There's my excuse. I slide my feet off a little perturbed and start to sit up. Trevor wouldn't let me put my feet on his dash either. He said I left toe smudges.

"I've never heard Pop Pop say that."

I don't know why Beck's so sensitive about everything. He giggled like a twelve-year-old girl when a rap song came on, and I lip-synced the guy's part. "Regardless, I'd still do it. Everything but putting my feet on the dash. If you didn't want my feet up here, you should have just offered up some other proposition." Beck swoops out his right hand and pushes my calf, so my feet go back up.

"Just put your feet on the dash. It was part of the deal." Just as I let my heels rest above the glovebox, there's a big bump and the truck makes a sickening bang when it comes back down. I can hear the shocks scream-grinding out in pain. "Okay," Beck says, pushing on the brake and putting the truck in park. "We're walking from here."

Twenty minutes later, I am standing with my arms crossed on the far side of a swinging bridge that runs across a raggedy break in the mountain about thirty feet deep and where Long Creek makes a sharp descent downward. It is the only thing standing between Beck and the tunnel just a stone's throw away. It is big, this section, with full-size dead trees laying atop man-size boulders. The trace of sunbaked moss is sweet in the air mixed with the thick scent of pine. The sound of water running through rocks below is not quite deafening, but loud enough to drown out the chirping of birds and occasional tweets, chirps, and trills of summer insects that had followed us from the truck. "Are you coming or not?"

"Not."

"You are the personification of the term *big baby.*" I taunt him. In Beck's defense, though, it is a rickety, sagging bridge made of wooden planks and metal-fiber rope, including the railing that wiggled like crazy when I walked across. "You watched me cross. It didn't even waggle."

"You weigh like a hundred pounds soaking wet. I'm way too heavy for that. I think this whole thing is a setup to kill me for telling Zach you got fired the other day."

"You were the one who told him? How'd you know?" I give him what Pop Pop calls *mean eyes,* a narrowing of my eyes and a cock of my chin.

"Because you tried to cover it up by saying you lost your purse. Then your car was in your driveway in the morning when I went past."

"Seriously, Beck. You can't tell Zach anything. He's a tattletale. And anything you tell him that's secret about me becomes a tool I have to negotiate in an exchange that is akin to haggling over the fate of my soul with the devil."

"I had no clue you were keeping it a secret. And it was the right thing to do."

"The right thing to do," I repeat and roll my eyes. "Yeah, right. You boys run in packs like a bunch of frigging wolves just waiting to cut me off and take me down for Zach to chew on." I look down to the creek below. I suppose if we add another hour on to our hike, we can find a way to get him across via jumping the boulders over the water.

"Alright." I start to slide down the hillside toward the boulders. The incline is steep, but it is almost layered like a stairway.

"What are you doing?" Beck leans on the railing, gives it a little wiggle while he peers down at me on the other side.

I look up. "I'm finding a way to get you over to this side

without *killing you*."

"Naw, just go ahead." He flaps a hand at me. "I'll just sit here and wait. You go check it out and come back and tell me about it."

I stare at him like my fourth-grade teacher, Missus Murphy, used to glower at me impatiently outside the classroom in the hallway when I came sauntering in after a twenty-five-minute bathroom break. I was really strolling around the hallways and doing anything to stay out of sitting in the hard chairs in her room for the last half-hour.

He laughs. "What, Harley?"

"Well, for one, Beck, you give up too easily. Two, it's no fun by myself. And three, it is not you or me, it is *we*. You quit your job defending me. You're my friend now whether you like it or not and I don't leave my friends behind." I pause to take a breath. "Just don't tell Zach you're my friend. He gets a little spicy about stuff like me allegedly stealing his friends or something. I don't think you're a negotiable part of any of his packages."

I'm almost to the bottom, shimmying here, hopping there when Beck parallels me on the opposite side. I see where two boulders are just a close enough together, with a good jump, he can—

"No," Beck declares while I point at it. He's got this down in the dumps expression, almost like he's giving up. I see him glance up the hillside where he just came down like he's going to buck and clamber back up.

"You can do it," I start to chant. He holds up his hands for me to stop. Then just when I think he's going to shimmy back up that hill, he just takes this running jump and lands with two feet on the boulder with me.

"Holy shit!" he gasps and does this bull-waggle of his head. "That was crazy!" It really wasn't that crazy. If he missed the boulder, he would have probably just hit a few rocks and rode the stream a few minutes. But I don't tell him that while he holds his hands on his head and looks down to the creek below. "I can't believe I did that."

He's like high on himself for the next twenty minutes of climbing up the other side, rehashing every moment over and over. You would have thought Beck had done a skydive off the Eiffel Tower or something. Then for the next five minutes, he's already worrying how he's going to get back over again. We make a steady pace to where a seventy-foot high gouge lay in the side of the earth and ends abruptly in piles of moss-covered boulders against the side of the mountain.

"This is it," I say. I feel almost let down. It isn't anything, but a break in the mountain like a huge bowling ball was rolled through the valley and stopped when it hit the wall.

"It's not much, is it?" Beck looks it up and down. "No wonder nobody ever talks about it." But within minutes of both of us clambering up on the rocks, he calls out to me with a flash of excitement in his eyes. "Look, look, look," he says, pointing to a bit of off-white beneath years of pine needles, soft loam, and leaves. He wiggles his fingers overtop while I slip up beside him. I squat down next to him. We both sweep away damp leaves and dirt to unearth words on an archaic metal sign:

"On January 22, 1872, an explosion in the Brandy Mountain Tunnel killed sixteen miners." Beck reads. "The bodies were never recovered, and the tunnel became a mass burial for those who had died within. Hans Branntwein, founder of the mine, was among the dead."

We're both quiet for a moment. "Did you know Hans Branntwein got killed in the explosion?" he asks me softly.

"Nope." I am staring at the sign like I expect it to change. "I was always told by Grant that he simply disappeared. There was no record of him after a certain point. He wouldn't let me tell the kids what he thought and that was he ran off with some miner's wife and got shot."

"Okay, that's odd. You would think he would know this."

"Maybe not. I couldn't find it in anything I looked up,

Beck." I'm going to have to rethink the whole process now with this new piece of information. "I don't know if I feel like I've found some piece of a puzzle that was missing, or if I'm just thinking this isn't correct." Still, it is sobering to know that men still lay beneath the mountain, forever gone, mostly forgotten. My eyes roll to the base of the sign. Curiously, it looks like someone purposely pulled it out of the ground and laid it flat. There's a ball of concrete around the base and a huge hole that is filled with grown grass, cluing me in that it was jerked out a long time ago.

My head is swimming. "You think somebody knocked the sign down because they didn't want people to know?" I ask Beck.

"I don't know," he answers with a shrug. "It is odd nobody talks about it, right? I don't remember anybody talking about it in school. It's the same with you, right?"

"Yeah. I mean, why would the town purposely deny the accident even happened? Or in the least, why not tell about it in the history books?"

Beck shakes his head. He tries to pick up the sign. I trudge a little farther up the mountain and notice the sound of water splashing is becoming less and less distinct while the sounds of the forest become louder. I can see Beck trying to wiggle the signpost from the dirt, trying to restore it to its original position. He glances up at me, looks away. I'm still within eyeshot of Beck, but far enough away that I can barely see him through the trees. I'm twisting slightly to my right, untangling a long strand of thorny brier fusing to the seat of my shorts when I hear a wispy whistle. A warm summer breeze is blowing across the canopy above me, and it nudges away much of the birds singing. The whistle is distinct. My eyes dart upward, snap to the moss-covered boulders to my left and then, to the thick forest surrounding. I see nothing, no sign of life along the dark pathway leading upward and above the tunnel.

I stand, scan the surroundings for movement. Above, a little bird hops around on the branches. Below the thick shade of tree trunks and brush, a brown squirrel scampers along the remnants of last year's leaves. It is a deep, oozy brown beneath the thick canopy that lays like a thousand black umbrellas blocking the sun's rays to the ground. My head tips upwards toward the dusky trail beyond. I freeze, momentarily stiff with the jolting realization I'm not alone. Because within the darkness of the land working its way upward over the stones and along a faded trail, I see a shadow hovering there. Is it a man? I blink, thinking maybe it is my imagination and nothing more than the shadows of some shrubs, but my rapidly beating heart tells me differently. I can make out the figure—slightly taller than me and wiggling back and forth, walking away at a fast pace.

"Trevor?" I call out. I veer around one boulder and work my way along a worn deer path. "Stop! Who is that?" I follow the form, quickening my steps up the hill, hearing my breaths while I come to a near run scrambling around one turn in the path and then another. It occurs to me it could be anyone including Willy Dunn's dad who rents property near here. He's known to be scary-angry and known to carry a gun.

And then, the shadow is gone. I toss my hands into the air, grunt, and snap my neck left to right. Gone? How can someone completely disappear even in this brush? But the shadow has vanished and even as I follow the trail upward for another twenty minutes, stopping to look around often, there is no sign of human life.

"Harley!"

I can hear Beck calling out my name not far behind me. I give the path ahead of me one more glance, see nothing, and turn back the way I came. I make my way back down, focusing on the place the shadow had disappeared. I shuffle through the leaves and feel a coolness coming from the earth. I roll my hand in the air, feeling it. The scent of old earth and stone seeps from somewhere, and I follow it to a small cleft in the earth.

"Hey, why'd you disappear?" Beck is huffing when he

stops not far away, resting one foot on a thick, moss-covered limb on the ground and his hands lying on a knee. He reminds me of a cartoon caricature of Paul Bunyan on an old frontier tales book Pop Pop used to read to me and Zach at bedtime. The only thing Beck needs is an ax and an ox. "I got the sign up. Come look."

"I thought I saw Trevor." I don't know why I blurt it out. Beck looks over my shoulder.

"You saw him—*here*?" he says slowly, carefully. I see the disbelief in his eyes. He probably thinks I'm crazy.

"I don't know," I backtrack. "Maybe it was just shadows or something. I heard whistling and—" I sigh. "Forget it. It sounds crazy when I say it out loud."

"It's no crazier than him just vanishing off the face of the earth." He lumbers over the log and holds a cupped palm over his eyes. Then Beck scans what little horizon we can see in the trees. "I've got no problem hiking up farther to check it out, but it's going to get dark soon. And if he didn't stop for you five minutes ago, I don't think he's going to turn around and show himself to you now."

He's right. I tell him that and still look over my shoulder one more time.

"It's getting late. We should probably head back," Beck reminds me. I could kind of guess he knew it was going to take a while to work himself up to cross the creek again. He takes his time strolling along the trail, stopping to tug up logs and look underneath. He marches off the trail a couple times to climb up a big stone. He keeps telling me he hasn't done this kind of stuff since he was a kid. Still, he's laid back about it almost like he's bored. I follow along with him, tossing rocks and once, even trying to hang on a thick grapevine that breaks from a limb and nearly hits me on my head. I land flat on my butt.

I suppose I enjoy his company because when he drops me at my house, I kind of wish I didn't have to go inside alone. But I do. I spend the evening popping words into the search engines trying to find anything about the tunnel I can.

I find it sadly lacking in the depth of death that must have clung to the air after so many died here. Because to those who lived, there must have been so much more. Around ten o'clock, I came across a website about mining and railroad accidents. I found that the tunnel collapse occurred in Lost Hollow at 10:12 in the morning of January 22, 1872, under Brandy Mountain. Prison workers and contractors from Ohio and West Virginia were a quarter mile in and using picks and nitroglycerin to barge their way through another three-quarters of the mountain. They were blasting out huge sections, picking at the walls with axes to bring pieces of the roof and sides down.

The reason I know is because of a name: Minnie Bean was listed as one of the dead. T.J. was right. It occurred to me that Hans' name had been misspelled in other newspaper articles I had seen in the files at the museum—Brentwine, Brentwein, and probably three other variations in the written archives. I wrote down the ones I remembered and bingo! Then, I found an old Written Express Newspaper from Atlanta, Georgia that stated the following with the misspelling of *Brendwine* and an incorrect first name: *TRAGEDY IN THE MOUNTAINS OF WEST VIRGINIA. 20 Workers Die in Tunnel Collapse. JOHN BRENDWINE, OWNER MISSING. ONE VICTIM A WOMAN. Minnie Bean, colored, consort of prisoner working in the tunnel was helping lift rock when she vanished inside tunnel before last of three explosions—*

The closest other newspaper article I found was a Fairmont, West Virginia report that there were ten men killed in a rock collapse sixty miles from Charleston. How vague could they get? I had to pull an old book offline about mining accidents in 1870 through 1890. Curiously, the book lists those who died as such: Fifteen men—six prison workers, four contractors, two prison guards, one mining personnel, and two rescue workers. The book does not mention Minnie Bean as being the sixteenth person who died. Fourteen hours later, they could still hear the voices of the workers inside. Twenty-four hours passed and there was only silence. But as I dug deeper using the misspelled name, I found that unceremoniously, the rescue was abandoned after the bodies of the guards were discovered. A total of thirteen men and one woman were buried there, six of them prisoners. Alive or dead, they did not know. Within a few days of the incident, the news faded away; there was no more mention of the tragedy.

I get a text message while I'm sliding into bed. It's Beck. I know he knows Pop Pop's cell phone number because it is his emergency contact. It's an image of a male ballet dancer superimposed over the Rocky Mountains, so it appears he is making a jump across the peaks. Below, it just says. *Thanks for not laughing*. I laugh softly now, though. On the way back, he jumped the rocks and did this funny pirouette, accidentally, of course. His cheeks had been red. I send him back an image of a cartoon duck flattened by a rock. *You didn't laugh when the grapevine broke on me.*

Yeah, I did. You just didn't see—all the way home after I dropped you off. Haha. The look on your face was priceless when you landed on your butt—

Chapter 17

"Guess what I found out," I say to Billy Stinger while I plop down next to him. I'm holding a bottled water and a bag of carrots. "If you lose weight and eat right, you probably won't have to shoot up with insulin anymore."

"I ain't eating those nasty things. Do I look like a damn rabbit? Aw, hell, no," He's sitting there with his legs splayed on the dugout bench.

"No," I spat back. "But you're going to look dead in a year if you don't." I've got back up anyway. I dig out a dollar store chocolate diet milkshake from a plastic bag I've got. "How about this—my Aunt Ruth is a dietitian at the nursing home. She can show you how to portion for free." I wiggle the milkshake in front of him. "And they have good stuff like this and protein bars and—"

"Baby, nothing works for me."

I've got double backup. "Okay," I say and wave a hand behind me where his daughter has his five-year-old grandson, Joshy coming along the walkway toward us. "Come and tell your grampy something," I say to Joshy.

"What are those two doing here?" Billy looks at them, then looks at me with realization sinking into his eyes. "Aw, no, don't do that."

"Grampy, I want you to be around forever. Will you drink Miss Harley's milkshake and be Superman for me?" He recited that exactly how we practiced. Billy's daughter is laughing. I know I lip-synced what Joshy said. "He drew you a picture, too," I tell Billy. "It's you and him playing baseball someday. *Someday*. Like five years from now. Because you lost weight and you're still alive."

"I'll think about it."

Roy Adkins walks up right at the end of my speech. "Oh, hey!" I call out to him. I see him stop and his already buggy eyes get twice as buggy while he swings one leg around in a half-arc, makes a ninety-degree turn, and tries to make a quick retreat the opposite direction.

"Crud! I heard you were on the rampage. You left six messages on my phone. You stuck a nicotine patch on Buddy, that's what I heard—" He's huffing and puffing while I jump up and come up beside him. He's right. I did. "Why are you trying to kill all of us, little girl?"

"Kill you? I'm stopping you from being killed."

"Didn't anybody ever tell you we was doing this for fun?" He stops, mostly because he's out of breath. I almost bump into him. "Look here." He jabs a finger at me. "Ain't no way I'm changing my ways for a stupid ballgame. I just want to hit the balls. If you're going to make it hard, I quit. I'll do it in my backyard by myself."

"I was going to offer you two bucks for every pound you shed," I sigh, shrug. "And Pop Pop said your TV died. I got you an exercise bike and a TV to set in front of it. Ride the bike, watch the TV. Lose weight, get paid for it."

"You ain't got that kind of money."

"Maybe I do. Maybe I don't." I don't. But I got both the TV and exercise bike at a yard sale for twenty bucks.

"What if I don't lose weight, then what happens?"

"Oh, you will," I say. "You will."

Beck has been watching what is going on from a seat on the bench while he puts on a sock. "What about me?" he asks, standing up and stretching his arms over his head. He makes an exaggerated show of his muscles.

"You've got a bit of an inflated ego," I tell him and walk over, tickle his belly with my fingers. He grunts and brings his arms down. Roy laughs. "Ain't that right," he says. "Why aren't you up playing with ol' Matthews's team?"

"It's not as fun, and they aren't practicing until six."

I see Pop Pop eyeing me. Then his gaze works slowly and carefully to Beck. Back and forth, he goes before I see him get a funny twist to his lips. "Enough of that. Let's get to work."

Chapter 18

I think it started with a splinter, my stupid crush on Beck. It was on the back of my thigh and from the broken baseball bleachers. I usually have my anti-flirt shield up when I'm around my uncle's friends. They are off-limits. Period. It's easy. I wouldn't even think about dating guys like his friends anyway. They are just too *oh-lets-watch-football-all-day-long* for me. They tend to lack ambition, for the most part, except when it comes to hunting season, baseball season, or trying to use their awkward sexual prowess to pick up a girl for a one-night stand.

"Get a grip on yourself, woman." Beck is kneeling and two inches from my bottom, wheedling the teeny bit of wood from my skin. I can't stop my leg from shaking. He is chuckling. Okay, there's nothing sexy about calling me woman like that in his husky, deep voice. I'm lying. There is.

"Quit laughing," I groan.

"I can't help it, you're like a mouse who caught its tail in one of my live traps." Live traps for mice? Who does that? That should have been a big red flag to hold up the shield. But I'm letting it down, down, down. I catch the scent of Beck, try to toss it aside. "I had to calm him down by rubbing his little back. Do you want me to rub your back first?" He's trying to shame me into acting like an adult. But he reaches up with his free hand and pats me on the back. Such I catch his scent. It is like the classic masculine old-school aftershave scent—with a little bit of sandalwood and shea butter. Yummy. Oh, no. None of that chocolate chip cookie shit I associate with Max and Pop Pop and Zach, if you know what I mean. He flashes me a smile. My stomach jumps. He's got a sexy twinkle in his eyes. I know I'm taking this one step too far. I suppose because he is off-limits is only making it worse. "Be easy, Harley, this won't hurt if you just spread your leg a little farther and just let me do it."

Does he not realize what he is saying? "Beck, listen to

yourself. I kind of feel like this is my first time doing it, you know?" I clear my throat. "Oh, baby, this is going to hurt just a little the first time—"

"Huh?"

He can't be that naïve. I guess he is that naïve. "Nothing, Beck," I tell him. "This is awkward." And it is awkward in Pop Pop's dimly lit kitchen. "Your hand is—" His hand is back to holding my thigh and less than an inch from my girl parts. I am literally starting to sweat. I look down. He looks up. "For somebody who likes danger so much, who prides herself on jumping feet first into any circumstance without worrying about the risk, you are sure a wimp when you get hurt. And I don't understand how you could possibly get a splinter on the inside of your leg. Were you straddling the bench?" He looks up. I look down. Straddling the bench. I'm imagining I'm straddling him right now. We're lying on the floor. He's naked. I'm naked. I'm sitting on his waist, legs splayed on either side, knees banging the floor, him banging me— "Why are your eyes so big. You look scared to death. I've seen you jump off your grandpa's roof without blinking an eye."

"It's a little too sexy for me, Beck," I stutter-tease-mewl at him, trying to pull off being cool. It isn't working. Oh-my-God-his hands are firm on my inner thigh and I'm wondering what it would be like if he just moved it up that teeny-weeny inch and touched my girl parts. *He's not my type. He's not my type.*

"You know, you were my first scent of a woman. It was cocoanut sunscreen and Sweet Baby perfume." Ow, I feel him digging the tweezers into my flesh. "It was ninth grade. You'd been laying out on your grandpa's back porch, and you came in to answer the phone. You were standing in your grandpa's kitchen with your back to me and leaning on the counter in that teeny tiny pink bikini talking to Kylie Hensley on the phone. You were rolling your hair around one finger, and you were kind of balancing on one foot and tippy-toeing with the other." I'm trying not to look at him while he talks.

"Sunscreen and baby-powder scented perfume. Perfect shoulders. Perfect back. Legs to die for. Sexy as hell. I'll never forget that moment, and every time I catch the scent of sunscreen, I think of that moment. But it plays out differently than you hanging up the phone and calling me a pervert and walking out. Every time. Man, that was one sweet memory."

What does that mean? I'm just staring at him while he stands up. He holds out his hand, palm up to expose the tiny splinter. "All that over something as small as a rose thorn." I'm not looking at his hand. I'm staring at his face. "Do you want a band-aid and some antibiotic cream?" I am thunderstruck to the point my lips won't move. "I take it that's a negative." He says that, turns and walks out of the kitchen. And me, I've got a dribble of sweat running down my back, my heart is racing like I've just run a mile in forty seconds, and my tummy is upset.

Chapter 19

"Okay, so if there were nine deaf, dumb and blind old ladies in wheelchairs, on oxygen, and with six cats in their laps and cold sores on their lips," I pause for dramatic effect, "and then there was me, who would you pick first in a game of dodgeball?"

"Are we still playing this game?" That's Max eluding my question two people up from me in the line for the register at Harkin's Hometown Grocery. He's got a six-pack of beer, a bag of expensive dark chocolate candy bars, a hot water bottle, and a mega box of tampons. I don't think he knew I was behind him until I poked him in the arm and said that. It wasn't easy getting his attention. I'm juggling generic brand toilet paper, a half-gallon of two percent milk, a twelve pack of bottled water, and a magnifying glass. The first two items, I suppose you can guess why I'm buying them. The third is for Pop Pop's baseball practice today because I think he has given up on making me sew uniforms and has persuaded himself I'd make a good bat boy (or bat girl?). The last, which was difficult to find, but in a clearance bin by the school supplies in the back, is what I am going to use to decipher the old-fashioned cursive of Hans Branntwein's diary.

It is mind-numbing at best, trying to read the light ink and piece together a sentence from words I can't make out. Most of the entries are unremarkable, little more than daily activities in the camps and endless marches from one place to the other. I suppose I could just skip them. Of course, being the history addict I am, I want to decipher every word, suck in every detail because maybe they are code to some great historical event everyone else has missed. I follow Hans from camp to camp, pulling out my computer and use the online maps to figure out his destinations, his journeys, and at which battles he fought. And there is one entry that stuck in my head last night and is probably the reason I didn't even see Max Matthews-Branntwein until I ended up in line behind him a few people back. It went like this: *From the*

Journal of Hans Branntwein, September 15, 1862

My feet got blisters all over them. They hurt so bad; I just think of numbers in my head to forget them. Numbers, numbers, numbers, they are always bouncing around my brain. We couldn't ride most of the day. My pony has a bad leg. We're going back to Harpers Ferry well over a year since I blew up my first bridge there. I don't mind so much. It's pretty even if everybody complains the roads are bad. The horses were too tired marching in the muck. I think I've walked five-hundred miles since we left Richmond and it's all uphill. The bottoms of my feet have so many blisters, it hurts to wiggle them. My only consolation is knowing that everybody else is suffering too. Some far worse. Some of the boys don't even have shoes, and it's way down in the fall. We just got here in Harpers Ferry followed by a few hundred Virginia militia troops in Maryland Heights and everybody coming in was tired and on edge getting ready for another battle. But our boys set up guns and just walked right into Harpers Ferry like fleas marching on a toothless dog's back. There wasn't anybody there to guard the firearms at the arsenal!

There were seven of John Grey's Union boys, whipped and all with head lice and torn up clothes riding horses right in the middle of that big old puddle of the Shenandoah River that first day knowing they were easy targets. They were just looking like a red-haired boy named Asa I knew from home, and I was in a poor mood that day missing home and such. I think every time I run into a troop of Irish prisoners, I ask if anybody has seen him or anybody else I knew. Not that anybody'd recognize me. Nobody's heard of him yet. But a couple guards had the Yanks corralled in the river and everybody was in a high mood from the march and ready to fight anything that was blue and moving.

Our Confederate boys were just riding circles around them, taking pot shots and missing like Widow Vaughn's cats used to pat around a mouse with their paws until one finally jumped from the pack and killed it. So I said to one of the soldiers: "Can I play them a song with my fiddle, share a smoke. One might be my brother or might be yours." He just stared at me and shook his head while I walked out onto the water and told them to drop their guns. I said what I always used to say to my brother when he kept pinching me. I'd make a line with the toe of my shoe on the ground between us, tell him not to cross it. Such, I did with the red-haired man in front of me: "I'm gonna draw a line," I told him. "If you stay on the other side of the line, I'm alright with it. If you cross it, we're gonna have words."

"What's that mean?" he asked me in such a deep accent, another one of his soldiers had to translate for me.

I say: "What's that mean? It means, don't cross the damn line because it means trouble! Hand me over your guns, and I'm going to take you prisoner. Everybody's just too tired today to fight. Drop those guns, boys, you're my very first prisoners. I'm tired of being a private. I'm ready to be general." Everybody had a hoot out of it because most of them think I'm just a little drummer. My gray-coated brothers patted me on the back when the blue-coated boys followed me in. They didn't have much of a choice, but I don't think most of us Rebels wanted them dead either. Killing gets old when all the enemies look like your next-door neighbor. Those boys weren't in any hurry at all to get away. I guess they knew their asses were going to get whipped. Everybody says it was them who burned the arsenal buildings so none of us Rebels could take them. I figure they must be important. Still not one of them had boots. The tall, handsome lad (the one I took prisoner first) with a scar beneath his right eye, red hair, and a deep Irish brogue was wearing one sock. He told us a couple privates took their boots for lack of their own. He begged them to leave one sock so he had something to gnaw on when he got hungry. He also said that what goes 'round comes 'round because all his boys, they had foot rot. We laughed. Sometimes just the littlest things can be funny and take us away from this hell. He reminded me of the boys back *home, full of piss and vinegar and the colonel in charge hooped it up with them around the fire. I didn't see them for three days before some guards gave them to Bad Bill to guard. Sadly, that's bad news for them. If Bad Bill's got them, those boys are going to be hanged. I think Hayward's going to miss them. They were nice to him, which doesn't come much with Bad Bill, and I heard the red-haired one (I call him Irish because he sounds straight off the boat and hard to understand) teasing Hayward asking him if he recognizes he was on the wrong side being black and all? I hope he's not putting crazy stuff in that boy's head. I told him not to believe him. But Hayward says the man's name is John Grey, and he's a big man for the guerrilla fighters. That's why he's getting hanged. But he doesn't know Hayward is mostly white in his head and he'd never leave me because we're family and all. I keep telling him not to get attached. Don't call him Johnny or smile at him. Bad Bill said the Yanks are the lowest of the low and fight dirty.*

All of Grey's boys wear a tattoo on their wrists. It's a vine that runs all the way around with J.G. initials by the thumb. Irish let me look at his. He's got a heart on his shoulder. I'll miss Irish just because I'm sour on Bad Bill. I keep losing my glasses and Irish keeps picking them up before Bad Bill steps on them and he gets whipped for it. He says they make me look smart, those little, wire glasses. I told him I am smart, but my papa told me not to parade it around because it makes everybody else think they are dumb. And dumb people do dumb things. He said nobody's that smart. I told him to give me two big numbers, and I'd multiply them for him. He did, and so I did. He said that yeah, I'm smart. It's my birthday today. I'm fourteen. I don't tell anybody that. I'm saving it for one of Bad Bill's bad beatings, so maybe he won't hurt me so bad. They processed out twelve-thousand Union prisoners. I must go. I got to set the fuses. I will write more later—

"Hey, are you in there?" I blink past the man in front of

me in line. Max is staring at me.

"I was daydreaming," I say. "Okay, you're not going to pick me or one of the old ladies? Would you rather play a game of truth or dare?" I ask. "Because here's the question: How sucky is it being a guy in a store full of guys and being the only one buying a box of tampons?" I lean in while the two guys between us snicker. "And here's the dare: I dare you to come home without the tampons and the sweet, little box of chocolates, and instead, grab one of the soft porns behind the counter. Keep the beer. You'll need it."

"I'd choose any of those old ladies. Just pick one for me." He turns around and looks past the first guy who is now trying to size up my expression after Max's mean remark. He doesn't know the game. "I'm beginning to think you're stalking me. Are you? You don't change. But then again, that's probably why Trevor kept that porn on the top shelf of his bathroom closet under the towels and got one every time he went to the store. It was too high for a five-inch midget like you to see. Just so you know, it was never in that container you took from the garage the other day. He duped you for three years with that stupid container."

"Bam!" I nod my head, give Max a wink and a shot with the fake pistol I make with forefinger and thumb. "You're on fire today." Then it is like it really sinks in, what he said. I suppose it is because it is Max who said it, it hurts the most. I mean, he's getting his stupid girlfriend tampons, chocolates, and a damn tummy warmer for her cramps. The only thing Trevor ever did for me was stay out of my way when I got period-bitchy. I feel like Max just shot me right through the heart with a hundred rounds of bullets filled with old stuff I don't want to deal with and exploding in my chest. Because for some reason, the guys I choose always end up being jerks.

I just turn slowly and quietly set my toilet paper, magnifying glass, bottled water, and milk down at the base of the nearest candy bar shelf. Then I take in a soft intake of breath and start to sniffle-sob while making a brisk walk of escape toward the automatic doors that don't open quickly enough. I smash right into the center of them with a loud BOOM! It sends a searing pain across my forehead.

"—she knocked herself out, that's all. You're alright, sweetie, right?" The girl from the register is squatting next to me, patting my shoulder, and smiling at me way too hard. I'm shoving away the tears and her hand. "Leave me alone, I'm fine." I didn't completely knock myself out. I just saw a little bit of gray and speckles of light and ended up on the floor on my butt. I'm telling them that while I push myself up from the linoleum floor. Three faces are staring down at me. One is Max who looks a bit shaken up. I'm not sure if it is because one of the two men who was in front of me in line is glaring at him right now and confronting him with a hand on his shoulder.

"You always go around making little girls cry, dude?" he'd just asked Max.

"She used to be my friend. I mean, my friend dated her. I was just kidding, right?" Max is stumbling around his words really screwing up trying to explain the strange relationship he has with his best friend's ex-girlfriend. I push them all away. I stand an excruciating amount of time in front of the doors, about six seconds, waiting for them to open so I don't make the same mistake again.

"Harley, wait up," Max is calling out behind me. I take a second to look back at him. He's tall, so I have to look up at him which, now, makes me feel inferior.

"What?" I spat at him. "Leave me alone." I'm grumbling to myself knowing I'm too embarrassed to walk back inside and pay for the stuff. Now I'm going to have to go down and pay double at the gas station convenience store for bottled water for Pop Pop's ballplayers.

"That was funny, right?" He whips up a smile. "I mean, from my perspective. You mouth off at me and boom! You run into the doors. I should be laughing."

I glare at him. I know he has no clue that within a one-week span, my life went from boring normal to completely crazy lopsided. It is like I was balancing myself on a curb minding my own business and simply trying to get from Point A to Point B when somebody just came and gave me a shove with two hands and knocked me off.

I keep walking. He catches up and grabs my arm. "Hey, the cops questioned me again. Did they question you?"

They did. I spent six grueling hours in the police station telling them over and over about that stupid night. I went to the seminar. I went to the office. I picked up Trevor. He dumped me on the highway. Max and his girlfriend picked me up and took me home.

"Yeah," I stop and turn. "What do you think? They told me they have a list of people of interest. I'm one of them. They told me they always examine the people closest to someone who might have been a victim of a crime first to eliminate them from the suspect list."

"You're *not* a suspect, then?" Max stares down at me. I can't read his eyes. He's lost expression on his face. "I mean, that's good. Suspects are the ones they think did it. People of interest are just people they want to question because they think they might have information—"

"No. I mean, I don't know. Do you interrogate someone for six hours that isn't a suspect?" I hold up my hand. I can still smell the scent of lemon disinfectant they had sprayed in this little brick-walled room of the police station on the main street in Brandy Mountain. The room was tiny and dark, and they made me sit there for an hour and a half before anybody even came in. Then it was the same questions over and over. *Do you know where Trevor Woods is? Did you kill him? Do you know anyone who would hurt him? Now, go through it one more time for us. What happened that night?*

"They came to the house and talked to me and Mikayla. I told them he was acting crazy that night."

"They also talked to the guy in the gas station and the homeless guy to check my story. I get this sneaking feeling they are reenacting the statement piece by piece to see if I could rob the museum, kill Trevor, hide the car, and then get to the gas station in a forty-minute span. The cop at the station tried to trip up my story a hundred times. He got me so confused, I'm not sure *you* even picked me up."

"You don't know anything, do you?"

That makes me a little angry. Why is everyone pointing the finger at me? "He's your best friend, Max. I should be asking you that. You two were fighting it out when I got there. What was up with that? I, on the other hand, have moved on from him. I didn't give a rat's ass if he has ten girlfriends. I don't date assholes who ask me to marry them, then sleep with three of my friends. There's no crime of passion or whatever they want to pin on me. I just don't like the guy. I just made the second stupidest mistake of my life picking up his sorry ass so he didn't drive home drunk and kill somebody." I narrow my eyes suspiciously.

"He threw the first punch that night, not me," Max states. "He was crazy acting. You know that."

I rub tears away from my eyes, push back the desire to cry. "Just leave me alone. I want to forget—"

"Because you don't get a call from his mom every twenty minutes asking if I've seen him yet," Max grumbles. "Yeah, that's not so easy to forget, Harley. Every time, she's like really cool about it, then starts sobbing. I don't know what to say to her. You haven't sat up for the last five nights trying to rack your brain thinking you missed something—some hint he gave of where he might be. Or that maybe the car he was driving went off the road into a ditch or over a cliff or into a lake and he's lying there hurt or dying. You haven't been up and down every backroad knowing that the last thing you might have said to your friend was *you're the biggest, fucking idiot I've ever met.*"

"Leave me alone, Max, you don't get it." I fumble with my purse, dig out the wadded-up ten-dollar bill Pop Pop gave me for the toilet paper, and I stuff it into his fist along with three quarters and a dime I've got mixed in with the lint at the bottom of my purse. "Here's ten dollars and eighty-five cents of the forty I owe you that you paid the homeless guy for the Gatorade." Then I turn and walk fast toward my jeep.

"I'll get you the rest this week."

"You don't have to pay me back, Harley, you know that. It's only forty bucks." Max, he's not done. He's staring at the money, holding it back out at me. I see his shadow overlapping mine when I stop an inch from my jeep door. "Take the damn money; I don't want it."

"No, there's no way in hell I'm going to owe anybody anything, especially you."

"Especially me? What does that mean? You know what? You suck," he hisses low and like a growl. "You suck as a friend, you get that, right?" His voice gets louder while I stare at my fingers on the doorknob. "I wasn't hanging around you because I was friends with him, I hung around him because of you. I wasn't *your ex-boyfriend's best friend.* I was *your* friend. It obviously wasn't mutual so go hang out with your new friends that are suckier than you. Because you suck, Harley Davidson. You suck as a friend."

I guess I could have just told Max Matthews-Branntwein he sucked too right then. I could have flipped him off, gotten into my jeep, and driven away. That's the usual way I deal with situations. Everybody who knows me knows I'm good at all those things, especially walking away. But this little image of Max sitting on Trevor's couch one night with me pops into my head. I was at one end, he was at the other. We were watching some dumb sitcom. We had this little Nerf football we were lazily tossing back and forth between us during the commercials. It was about eleven-thirty at night. Trevor had stomped out two hours earlier, mad over something stupid I can't even remember. *You don't have to stick around waiting for Trevor to come back, Mateo,* I'd said to him. *He's mad at me, not you. He's probably out at the bar right now, getting a drink and wondering where you are. Go have fun.* Max had just snickered and said. *I am having fun.*

"I think I saw Trevor in the woods last night," I gasp the words.

"What?"

"I was hiking, and I saw him. Then he disappeared."

140

"He disappeared." Max rubs his chin, looks up at the sky. "You mean he like just vanished into thin air?"

"Well, kind of—"

"You saw his face and everything? You could clearly define—"

"No, it was like a shadow." I hear my words tossed into the air and realize how silly they must sound. Trevor's not in the woods, running just out of reach.

"I don't want to tell you, Harley, that it probably wasn't him. It could have been someone with the electric company checking the right of way or one of the Dunns out walking around. I mean, I would bet a hundred bucks against it. What would he be doing up there, hiding? Naw, if Trevor's decided to go off the grid and start a new life or something, he's not going to be living in a tent in the woods or someplace like that. He'd be in Mexico or New York. But if you want me to go back up there with you, I'll do it. We can look for footprints—"

"Footprints," I exhale the word. Why didn't I think to look at the ground for footprints? "Naw, you're right. I didn't notice anything. I would have." Maybe. "Maybe it was just the light coming through the trees, playing with my head," I shrug. "So how do I stop sucking at being a friend, Max?" I ask him. "How do I get from being the last in line of a bunch of old ladies on oxygen, when you're picking a team for dodgeball, and to the front?"

Chapter 20

I'm standing in a patchy stretch of lime-green grass just off a two-laner outside East Bank, West Virginia listening to Max's newest girl chatter on in a pointless conversation, mostly with herself, about whatever seems to come to her mind at the moment. I think she's talking about some cooking show on TV. I can't really tell. I honestly don't care about how hot Chef Olivier is when he *gets going hard on the grill,* as she calls it. The traffic has been non-stop, and the squeaky, high-pitched splash of tires on wet asphalt seems to blend far too well with her high-pitched voice underneath the polka-dot umbrella she is holding over her head while my own head is getting drenched.

Max says she's just nervous around me because she wants to impress his friends. I'm not so sure. When I walked up, she looked me up and down and said: "I've got a garbage bag of old clothes that have been sitting in my garage waiting to go to Goodwill for a year. You'd look cute in them. I'll give them to Max, and he can drop them on your porch." I blanched because what I wanted to say was she was way too fat for me to fit into her old, outdated clothes. But Max made a quick step in front of me and tried to shove the missing posters in her hand. She wouldn't accept them, just wiggled too-perfect nails at him. "Can't. I got nails." She gave my hands a patronizing snap of her eyes like I don't. And I don't. Mine are nervously bitten down to the nub.

Now I'm the who can't juggle a cute umbrella so I can press a single eight and a half by eleven sheet of paper with MISSING—TREVOR WOODS written on top to the eroded wood of the telephone pole. It is no mere feat. The pole is spongy from spring rain. And I'm trying to juggle three more damp sheets between ribs and elbow so I can press it against the wood and Max can attach it with the staples in the staple gun in his hand. There is a constant line of cars and RVs dragging ATVs in their trailers passing us by. There have been two semi-trucks barreling past and barely missing me, tossing little bits of pebbles at our feet.

It is poster number forty-two Max, Mikayla, and I have tacked to poles or taped to gas station windows up and down the main highway from Charleston to Brandy Mountain. Trevor's picture, his height, weight and the police phone number are underneath. I'd much rather be sitting at my kitchen table, running page by page through the old journal so I can unearth any connection the diary has with Trevor's disappearance. But that isn't happening.

"Nobody is going to see it because there's a sign hiding it, Mateo," I complain. I have to nod behind me at the sign that states ROUGH ROAD—35 MPH. My hands are full. Drivers would have to crane their necks to get an eyeful of the small, wet paper dangling there. Besides that, we are in the opposite direction from the last ping off a cell phone tower that the police got from my cell phone records. It was somewhere near the New River Gorge Bridge and almost fifty miles away.

"Were you always this whiny?" he gripes back. "I don't remember all this whiny shit. What else are you going to be doing in this rain?"

"Playing baseball with Pop Pop," I grunt. Even though I don't think my grandpa is taking me seriously, he's decided to let me hit the balls for them every night. And he lets me stand out behind first base and catch the extras when my arm gets too tired. I think, although I'm not sure, I'm Zach's replacement since he's been practicing up on The Brandy.

"Yeah, how's that going for you?" he asks and I look up, think he's making fun of me. But his expression is just blank before he smiles. "I'm teasing. Zach and I sit on the bench a lot. We talk about you. Quit being whiny." I also heard that from Zach. He says it's like high school all over again. They've got way too many men signed up to play on the team, and it is the same family names who are getting the most practice in—his old coach, Niles Gates and the old coach that never let me on his team, Coach Simmons.

I'm grumpy. But I know Max is trying to make light of

things. Trevor's mom met us with a handful of flyers to put up three hours ago and right before she got an interview with the local TV stations asking for help in finding her son. She's forty-two, short, and slightly plump. She was dressed in running clothes and stared at me with suspicious eyes. And she confronted me in front of everyone and came an inch close to accusing me of murdering him. Now, with Pam Woods's words still searing my brain, I'm feeling queasy and angry both at once.

"Why can't *she* do anything?" I ask, jabbing my thumb at Mikayla. "Other than waving at people while they pass."

"She's not waving. She is the one thing keeping us alive. Mikayla's actually standing there so people see us."

I'm not so sure. But God forbid his girlfriend does any hard labor. She's acting more like she's the prom queen sitting on a parade car and waving at the crowd than some super girl traffic cop fighting off cars. I don't make a comment; he thinks she's Supergirl because Max has this sweet little smirk on his lips whenever she turns around.

"You're not going to attack me like you were going to attack Trevor's mom, are you?" He is trying to be funny. I groan, give him a punch with my knuckle.

"Oh, don't hurt him!" Mikayla mewls while Max sucks it in like a puppy bounding for a meaty bone. She latches on to his arm, gives him a knowing smile like they share a secret, then leans into him hard. "Because you're my big ol' bear, right?" I get the distinct feeling if she was a pup right now, she would be lifting her leg to mark her territory.

I'm in mid-stare at them both, doling out the kind of gaze people who aren't in love and don't plan on being in love for a good amount of time give newlyweds fawning over each other. "I'd rather be doing anything but watching you two idiots google-eye each other."

"You need to find somebody to google-eye," Max gives me a brotherly smile. "Some guy with lots of money."

"I'd rather be ghost hunting," I tell him with a searing glare of my eyes. I suppose it isn't that searing. He rolls his own eyes. "No, really. T.J. told me there's a tunnel under the mountain that sits up against Brandy Mountain with dead men inside." I start to tell him Beck and I went looking for it and were on the cusp of perhaps discovering some secret door or something before it got dark and we left. I stop. If he's hanging out with Zach in the dugout, he might mention I'd gone hiking with Beck. No use getting my uncle-brother mad at me for *borrowing* a friend for a bit. We've never seen eye to eye on the fine line between borrowing and stealing.

"There is." Max pokes me with his finger, grins. I can't tell if he's lying or not.

"How come everybody seemed to know this but me until a couple days ago?"

"That's funny because you're the history geek." He pretends to shoot me with the staple gun. "Damn, I know more than Harley about the town history." But I'm not thinking about that. Max sees me staring off a second. He reaches out and knuckles the top of my head. "What are you thinking?" he asks.

"He was never going to marry me, was he?" I ask. I suppose if anyone knows, Max does. Trevor probably laughed about me thinking I was good enough for him. They probably thought it was some big joke. He shrugs. "I don't know. Who cares? It's done. You've got a whole world of guys out there just waiting to get to know Harley." It was a gentle way of saying that no, Trevor was just using me.

"Hey!" That's when I hear a familiar voice. But it's out of place, distinctly not what I'm expecting to hear along a state route and connected to my personal life. I turn my head, catch the faint hint of black hair.

"Shit," I curse beneath my breath. It's Lissette Baker. She looks out of place standing in the gravel in her high heels and pricey dress. "What is she doing here?" I ask no one in particular while I stare out across the roadway and past three or four cars flying past. She's standing on the far edges of the parking lot and waving a hand over at me.

"Who is that?" Max asks while I sigh.

"It's the woman who runs the place I used to work at—Central Independent Realty."

"Oh, yeah—" Max's voice trails away while I snatch up the papers I'm holding between arm and ribs and dodge a semi-truck and car to get across.

I stop just short of her unsure if she was just waving a hello to me or if she was trying to catch my attention. I find out quickly enough. "I was watching TV and saw the Channel 13 News segment of the guy who came up missing." She has to yell over the traffic. "You were in the background tacking up signs. I kind of followed the path of the posters and stopped and asked which direction you were heading and it led, um, here." She pauses like she is waiting for me to say something. I don't, so she continues. "Taylor was worried about you. She couldn't get you on your cell phone."

"The guy who is missing stole my car and my phone."

"I didn't think about that. You are kind of elusive. I didn't have another number." We stare at each other awkwardly. "So, you're fine. Okay, I'll let her know."

I'm strangely fascinated that she has driven all the way here to tell me that. I know she's lying because Taylor knows where to find me. "Okay," I say. "I'm fine."

Lissette looks like she's going to turn and go back to her car. I see her eyeing it like this is her chance to escape. She hovers here a moment. "She's mad because she says I fired you."

"You kind of *did* fire me."

"No, you quit."

"Are we going to fight about this?" I ask her. "Because I've got better things to do than hash out a bad memory of quitting before I got fired. You get where I'm coming from, Lissette?"

She looks over my shoulder to Max and Mikayla staring across the expanse to us. "Yes, better things." She says. I'm not sure what she means. Still, I toss out my hands. "What do you want from me?"

"You're her *type*, you know?"

"Excuse me?" I ask, feeling uncomfortable in the shoes I think she is making me wear.

"Taylor. She likes the tough girls. The strong ones, the dangerous type. The ones that don't take crap and have, you know—" she hard-sighs. "You've got swagger."

"What are you talking about?" I ask her. The dangerous type? That's a joke. "I don't have swagger. I don't know what you're implying, but I cried like a two-year-old after I walked out—"

Lissette interrupts me with a sniffy laugh. "Yes, that makes it so much better—a tough girl with a heart." She looks back to me and shrugs. "I guess you're all the things that I'm *not*, okay?"

"And that leads you to—East Bank, why?"

"I don't know." She looks at the gas station behind her and throws up her hands. And I don't think Lissette Baker really knows why she has left work in the middle of the day and chased down a girl she thinks is a loser and, quite possibly, a murderer and a thief. I have to imagine she saw Taylor watching the TV in the breakroom from the vantage point of her own office. She saw something in Taylor that showed maybe, just maybe, I'm not a felon, and Lissette was wrong in concluding I am a criminal. She probably made an excuse to leave because of her kids (they are always sick or need some homework paper taken to school they forgot at home). And she drove wildly down here wrestling with her sense of sanity—

"Listen, if you come back, we'll forget about the other day, just let it—slide." She stops, again, like she is waiting for me to pounce on that tidbit. I don't. "Just think about it over the weekend. If you want to come back, I'll see you on Monday like nothing happened."

"Why—?"

"I want Taylor to be happy, Harley. Why do you think? Don't be stupid and don't make me spell it out for you."

Chapter 21

"Hey, it's been nice spending time with you today." Max follows me inside, and his voice sounds a bit too cordial. It's six-thirty, and he's got a half-gallon of milk hooked on his forefinger and a yellow, plastic bag in the other. He sets both on the counter next to my refrigerator.

"Well, thanks for stopping at the store on the way back, so I didn't have to make another trip," I return. I see his eyes roaming around.

"This is nice," he says. "Did you buy it?"

"No, it's one of Pop Pop's rentals. When folks started moving out, he started buying a few houses. He got them cheap." I smile, shake my head. "I don't think he makes much renting them. Half the time, people can't pay the full rent, and he lets them do upkeep instead. I pretend all the time my toilet is broken just so I can pretend fixing it and get a few bucks off my rent," I divulge with a sly smile. "I think Pop Pop sees through my deception. But it's rough right out of college. Hard to find a job."

"Tell me about it." Max steps back, leans against the doorframe of my kitchen. "I don't know what I'd do if my dad didn't have my back." I see his eyes stop at my refrigerator. His gaze narrows, eyes to fine slits before he takes a step forward and leans in front of the door. "You still have this?" He is staring at an old picture he drew for me the summer of eleventh grade. It is just a regular 8 1/2 by 11 sheet of copy paper. What was white has turned a shabby shade of gray and two corners are curled from being stuffed in suitcases and backpacks and once, even knocked off the refrigerator by a roommate and danced on during a party. The middle is wrinkled from being folded once accidentally, and the bottom corner is crimped. There's scrawled writing at the bottom that has been erased and is illegible. But it's been through a lot with me, traveled the paths I traveled from high school to now. On the paper is a pair of incredibly realistic looking hands with palm upwards and just barely clasping a tiny, chubby wren. The teeny bird is intricately drawn, so much so, on a whim, I had picked up a magnifying glass once to hone in on the detail.

I'm kind of shy at the moment, realizing it is strangely personal, Max knowing I kept that picture. It was like having a little bit of him with me although I'd never say it out loud. He was just a friend. He wasn't ever a boyfriend, not a cousin, not just the guy who sat in front of me in Algebra. To me, he was my best friend. To him, I wasn't sure back then how he classified me. We never really hashed it out. It just *was,* what we had—no grand expectations, no worries, no doubts. But when he looks up at me, I feel my cheeks blush. He knows that too. But he doesn't say it. It just appears to roll over him and he's quiet for a moment.

"She was but a wild, little thing. I wanted to keep her in the clasp of my hands and pretend her wings were broken. But they weren't. So I let her fly."

"That's beautiful. Where'd you hear that?"

He shrugs with a sudden boredom, stands erect again. "I thought it up myself. I had a lot of time to do that before I met you. I was the shy-fat-kid with shy-fat-kid friends which meant I hung around with a kid who picked his nose and ate the buggers and one who always smelled like pee. Then, I met you, not a shy-fat-kid kind of friend."

"Were you really that fat?" I ask seriously. He reaches out and knuckles me in the arm and laughs like I'm kidding. I'm not. "And I wasn't popular."

"Yes, Harley, I was really that unpopular and fat and incredibly aware of it. And you with your goofy clowning around and getting in trouble even made the teachers laugh most of the time. Let me remind you of the time you tried to steal the Algebra teacher's cigarettes from his desk drawer as a joke, and you crawled underneath to get them out of the back of the drawer and your arm got stuck."

"That hurt. They had to get the gym teachers and the custodian to flip the desk with me still attached."

"Oh, but it was funny when the whole class funneled in and your feet were sticking out the back." He ponders something a moment, shakes his head and gives me a wane smile. "And my girlfriend obviously thinks I should be that way again, chubby. I am getting fat again."

"So stop eating and sitting around so much."

"You make it sound easy."

"You did it before."

"Hanging with you was non-stop running. Hanging with everybody else is sitting and playing video games."

I roll my eyes, give him a lame shove with my hand. "What happened with your artsy stuff? You still do it?"

"Not much. Real world. Real job."

"And lots of video games." Crap. Why did I say that? It just popped out. It's like I called him fat. And he really isn't. I just think he worries about it so much, he sees himself like that in the mirror. I think his girlfriend preys on that because she is insecure she's not good enough for him. "You're not fat, dumbass. You're just right. Don't let other people tell you differently." It's awkward right then. I don't know why. I can almost feel like there's something Max isn't telling me, he's hiding. Or maybe he's just bored with the conversation. He's different now, grown up, and reminds me more of his snobby family than the boy who used to hang around with me everyplace I went. I quickly turn the attention away, and I wiggle a finger at the wren. "She never looked like she wanted to fly much. She looks pretty content in those hands." She does. The little bird is settled in with half-closed eyes and feathers fluffed up like she's happily dozing and a bit pleased about something. Then I realize what I'm saying because I realize those are Max's hands and maybe, that wren is me.

"Yeah, that was the idea," Max says and looks at the gold watch on his wrist. Then he adjusts his glasses. "Well, Mikayla's waiting. I better go. Let's not be strangers."

"Like we could be strangers," I mumble-lie, realizing

we're really kind of strangers. "You didn't get to talk to your dad about not buying up the properties, did you?" I don't know this man at all. He's a bit pompous. By the look in Max's eyes, he recognizes it too. Still, I reach out like I always used to do when Max got hoity-toity, and I poke him in the side with a little tickle of fingers. I really expect him to try to act all grown up like Zach does now when I do it to him. He gives me a grunt from pursed, irritated-daddy lips, narrows his eyes like he's snapping at a two-year-old, and pushes me away with his hands. *Grow up, Flea,* he growls.

"Yeah, of course. He's thinking about it." Max, he sniffs this funny laugh like suddenly, he remembers who I am and who he is and what we used to be a long time ago. He reaches out and pokes me back. I suppose for the first time since we ran into each other, I see a flicker of the old Max in his eyes. I honestly didn't notice anything missing until right at that moment, and it hits me; he's different. But it's a certain sparkle, a shine in those gray eyes that escapes right now. He reaches out and nails me with tickles in my belly ending in me screeching a witchy laugh.

"Oh, I didn't miss that," he says, and he's close right then, really close. He's so close, I feel the warmth of his skin and catch the waft of Max-scent—something I can only define as a mixture of the pricey aftershave and cologne that sits on the luxury department store shelves boxed together with a real bow, sterling silver keychain, and a price tag of a few hundred bucks. It's an outdoorsy, musky smell and right up my alley. Couple that with my fingers banging against his belly trying to get a tickle in and hearing him laugh—it happens.

I look up. He looks down. I think for just a second, I see this fear in his eyes like a chipmunk that just jumped out of its little hole in the forest floor and suddenly realizes there's a full-grown mountain lion staring him down. Why do I do that to men, scare them? I realize, I've moved both of my hands up, and I'm letting them rest on either side of his neck, cupping his jawline. He's leaning in, and I'm not even tugging him. Max rolls his head back for just a mere fraction of a second, then he slams his lips on mine. And he whispers almost like it's the punchline of a joke: "I waited forever for this."

What? I'm not ready for this—the feel of his chin stubble tickling my chin, his cool lips touching mine and his tongue parting my lips. And I'm certainly not ready for the explosion when the kiss goes straight too hard, and Max leans in and smooshes us together like the kind of kiss that only happens at the end of old movies before the credits block the lovers out.

The sound of a truck door slamming ends it. Am I glad? I don't know. Max jerks away. I take a step back. "Holy shit." That's what he says and pats the counter. "Didn't see that coming, Harley." Did I initiate that kiss? Oh, crap, I did. The image of my hands on his neck, now the coolness between us.

"I'm sorry," I say that, and it sounds stupid enough he tips his head to one side. Then Max pivots on his feet and bumps his shoulder into the wall. "That's Mikayla. I got to go. See you around." He almost makes it to the door, and I'm just standing there with my arms akimbo and watching him go, speechless. And Max turns and says: "Can we get past this? We can get past this, right?" He's got no expression in his gaze, no glint in his eyes anymore. And the only thing I can do is bob my head slowly up and down. I mean, who says stuff like that?

Chapter 22

"Doctor Williams, I'd like to pick your brain if I could—" I'm so nervous talking to my professor on my phone via video. Zach's right. I do have a demi-god-type crush on him. I keep stopping myself from giggling like I'm a kindergartner and he's the fifth-grader at the playground who gave up his swing for me.

"Oh, you again."

I wince, and he smiles. He looks kind of long and thin in the frame. "Yeah, me."

"Any news on who robbed the museum?"

"I got a list of things. It's nothing uncommon. Everything on the list is probably less than a couple hundred dollars apiece." I searched every auction online and read every antique and collectible price guide I could dig up. Comparable items were common. Any I didn't know, I called an appraiser who was kind enough to give me a ballpark on a few. "There are a couple Victorian dresses, 1920s bottles, Kewpie dolls, vintage toys and some random silverware that was not even a full set."

"Did you happen to contact an antique appraiser?"

"Yes, on anything that had a price range," I answer, then give him a big smile. "I still have my textbook from your class. I followed the outline in it on how to find the price of early historic items." He's rolling his eyes and smiling back.

"Well, at least one of you read the book."

I give him a thumbs up in front of the phone. Man, why did I do that? He probably thinks I'm geeky. "Do you get what I mean? It was all in storage because they already had enough on display. I love antique shops. I've seen everything on that list in antique shops for cheap."

"Maybe whoever stole the items wasn't an antique collector, per se, but just saw a chance to rob a place that might have something expensive. He or she could dump whatever was worthless. Desperate people will do anything for money." He rubs his hands together. "You didn't find any of it for sale online?"

"None of it."

"It could be anywhere—a pawn shop in Cleveland, a storage unit in Nashville. Maybe you'll need to go another route until an item sells and shows up. Keep looking. If you want to send the list, I'll check randomly too."

"Thanks. A friend of mine gave me an old Civil War journal to borrow."

"Really? Now that's worth something."

"More than you know. It belonged to our town founder, Hans Branntwein. He started the coal mine here. It's interesting. I'm trying to dig up history for lack of being able to actually work history."

"Find anything good?"

"There's an old story about a dead baby in a chest. It was supposed to have a curse on it. A couple people came up missing in the 1930s including the town cop. They never found them. Have you heard of Missus Cora's Cure of Women's Diseases?"

"Like the medicinals and herbs sold in newspapers?"

"Yes, sir," I say. "One of the people who sold those was an actual doctor in this town. He got rich from it. They called him Ol' Doc Brown. His whole name was Bobby Brown, but most folks only knew him by the fake medicinals he sold them. He was one of the people who was around when the dead baby in the trunk was found."

"Fascinating. I love local history. Did he die too?"

"Hmm," I say and tap my chin. "No. When people started getting sick from an outbreak of TB, he survived. My great grandma told me there were four or five people who had fevers of one-hundred and four degrees. He had probably been around so many sick people, he built up a resistance."

"Well, Miss Davidson, keep digging until you find something. When you do, call me back."

Chapter 23

I did go back to work on Monday with little fanfare. The only person who questioned my attendance after watching me walk out was Lexie Todd who shares my teeny office with me. "I thought you got fired." She'd said that sitting at her desk. She didn't even look up, just stared at her computer like she was working. "Does Lissette know you came back or are you just hoping everybody forgot?"

"I begged and pleaded, and she took me back." I was just kidding, but Theo took just the wrong moment to walk past my door. He put on the brakes just a step past, then backed up with this funny pumping of his arms. He's a big guy, a bit chubby but funny. Barring him drunk-screwing me in the bathroom, I think Pop Pop would like him. "I thought you got fired."

"She begged and pleaded, and Lissette took her back," Lexie answered for me in a weepy voice. "And surprise, surprise, she's back." He looked at Lexie with a bland face, then winked at me. Then Lexie gave me a scathing glare when Theo returned twenty minutes later and gave me a stack of papers to go over. On top, he'd put a little baby blue Post-It Note: *Will you go out with me for dinner Friday?* The letters got smaller and smaller as I went down the tiny paper and I had to squint. Then I'd blinked at him and in all likelihood, I would have said *no*. My lips started to part, and I look up to see Lissette standing at the door with her commanding frown.

"Just say *yes*." Then she looks me up and down. "If you are going to be a part of this business, you will need to revamp your business attire, Harley. You look like one of those girls in middle school who picks her nose and sits in the back chair." She stops, seems to think this out. "I'm going to have Taylor take you shopping. If you don't have the cash, I will give you an allowance on a credit card and take it out in bi-monthly increments."

"Okay."

At three o'clock, Taylor takes me shopping and to get my hair done. But we really don't go shopping for the first hour. She drives me to the town rec league baseball fields and we change in her car. "This is a good time to practice. Everybody's at work still. We're limited on time getting you ready." Then she runs me through a rigorous program and makes me promise I'll practice the pitching rotation for at least an hour. She has high hopes for me, but I think I'm screwed. Pop Pop isn't going to let me pitch even he doesn't have a pitcher. He'll just do it himself.

For the next two weeks, I practice, practice, practice and I swear I throw a thousand balls. Taylor even brings in backup from what she calls her *old friends from her softball days,* a few women who I think want to still embrace their glory days playing ball. They are patient and funny, though, and we slip in a sandwich and beer at the local bar most nights before I excuse myself to head for the ballfield at The Bottoms. Yet, I can't take the step, rotate, and windmill that ball hard and fast instead of stepping on my own two feet and tripping. And when I'm at the ballfield with Pop Pop, I'm not doing anything but tossing up the ball and banging it out to them.

If I'm not trying to stand in front of the mirror and practice pitching, I am wandering around the house thinking about Max's kiss. It is still as fresh on my lips as if Max had kissed them two seconds ago. I've kissed a few people in the last few weeks—Taylor, Theo, and Max. But it's Max's kiss that lingers. My fingers play on my belly, and each time I touch my lips, I think of Max. I'm strangely subdued about it all. I suppose years of gently goading back sexy feelings for him have made it a reflex, like programming a computer to have a virus scan run automatically each time I download a file from the internet. All of that overrides the place where my mind starts weaving different trails Trevor could be journeying right now.

I find myself plopping Hans Branntwein's journal in my

156

lap on Thursday and sifting through the entries. It's the only thing that seems to take my mind off Trevor's disappearance and losing my job at the historical society.

September 21, 1862

It's September 21st or 22nd. I can't remember which day it is. Bad Bill was given orders to come to Maryland so I can set up explosives on a bridge. He hasn't killed the Yank prisoners yet. He had to wait for direct orders from General Jackson, and when the paper came in, I was the only one who could read. I said: "It says not to kill them yet." It really said: "Hang the prisoners noon September 18. Let's show the Yanks we mean business." I hope we don't see the old muckety-muck general because he'll be fit to be tied. I hope these Yanks appreciate my southern hospitality, me keeping them alive and all.

We've been in Maryland. The fighting is bad here, worse than I've ever seen it since Bad Bill took me in from the farm. Men are stacked up like corn in a silo. It has been eight months since I was taken from my Virginia family. I miss them only a little because they were better than this war, but I still got Hayward Jackson. He's the only one who doesn't think I'm strange for all the stuff I read and know and the numbers going through my head. Because I taught him how to read when I taught Benjamin Jackson's sons. He didn't want to learn at first. He was scared he'd get caught. Then I started putting papers up on the wall and door and horses and saying the words out loud when we passed just like I did for the boys. I watched him look at them and mouth the words. Now Hayward says it makes him feel at home when I multiply big numbers in my sleep and say them out loud.

I had a shell shatter over my head three nights ago while we were near the Potomac River at Sharpsburg. I slept right through it. Bad Bill made us boys stay back away from Antietam Creek with all the explosives. I wanted to watch the boys fight, cheer them on. Half the town showed up. But he says if we get killed, then those boys don't have a chance.

I told him I was sick of blowing up bridges. I wanted to shoot a gun. He told me with his fist that I was just plain dumb. Then he broke my fiddle by banging it on a tree. It's the only thing I got left that was my mama's. In all rights, though, it wasn't really passed on to me in the same way the beloved watch my Papa got from his Papa was passed on to him, entrusted after death. Where it is now, I don't know. Probably buried six feet under with him. I got the fiddle because there was no one else to take it. Not by rights, but just because I could take it. Papa never wanted to look at it after Mama died.

That day was the first time I've cried since I left home because I climbed up in a tree and hid so nobody knew. I think Irish knew where I was. But I think he thought I was crying because Bad Bill beat me and ruined my fiddle. I wasn't. I snuck out of camp late evening. They said by last afternoon, so many boys died there along an old farm lane at the battlefield, blood turned the dirt on the road to a red soup of blood and dead soldiers—a bloody lane. I couldn't see it in my mind, so I wanted to see it with my eyes. I walked among the dead and dying feeling dizzy with all of it. Still, if I closed my eyes and pushed my hands over my ears, the sun on my cheeks and the breeze reminded me of warm, late summer days when I was little. One man called out to me, "Boy, bring me water." I did, but when I got there, he was already dead. Nobody knew I was a Rebel soldier in my old torn clothes. They just thought I was a boy from town coming to see the bodies.

Now I can't un-see them from my head just like I can't stop the numbers from rolling through or the words to books always tumbling into my brain. I was glad for the beating, I suppose, and Bad Bill calling me stupid for running off. There are so many men deserting, he thought I'd headed home too. We're moving onward at a fast pace.

Irish told me later that wasn't true, me being dumb. I was the smartest boy he'd ever known. He's never listened to somebody read a whole book from heart like I did with

Charles Dickens' A Tale of Two Cities. I didn't tell him I skipped a lot. He says half the time he can't understand what I'm saying with my German brogue, but he likes hearing me talk. He likes my accent. I'm not the one who talks all the time. He is. And he's the one with the thick Irish accent that sounds like ice thawing on a creek. And the book was about the French Revolution, so it has nothing to do with both of us other than take our minds off dying another day. Now he keeps making me say a quote from the book over and over— "It was the best of times, it was the worst of times—" He says it reminds him there are good days and bad in our war. He says I'm the first part today if I don't keep bugging him.

It's probably because I saved Irish's butt another day. But Bad Bill has John Grey's boys down digging their graves. Bad Bill sent me to Sharpsburg hospital to check for news, and they made me help while I was there. He beat the fire out of me when I got back, said he thought I was dead. I am his bread and butter. I told him I found out that the Union boys are pissed that they let our troops head back to Virginia and we better get our butts moving that way. They're just going to sit here for a while.

"Sharpsburg," I repeat the words and cup a yawn to my palm, reach for my phone to follow the newest battle playing out in Hans' life. It was the Battle of Antietam and one of the bloodiest battles of the war. 22,000 men lay wounded or dead there. It says there was a road, Bloody Lane, so covered with dead and dying soldiers, it was red with blood. And Hans got to see it firsthand, or at least, the aftermath. I realize he talks about his fiddle being ruined and I tug out the tin-type and stare at the picture. Sure enough, there is a fiddle there.

Chapter 24

I don't understand how a grown man and a red car can simply fall off the face of the earth. Funny thing, I never noticed how many little red cars there are until Trevor stole mine. I don't understand why he wanted me to get the plastic container with the Ball Mason jars and the journal which is probably worth a lot of money. Nor do I know how he got them. I am wondering, however, if it has something to do with the legend of Hans Branntwein's treasure. I'm divulging this to Max who is leaning against my jeep a mile and a half from my house and deep in the forest. We are off an old dirt road that is thick with ruts and overgrown brush and hardly passable. Most people don't know that just a mile down from where we live, the oldest section of the mining town even existed. It's like a lost city, a ghost town in the middle of nowhere with huge trees and overgrown brush cloaking the past to those without a keen eye. There are nothing but old foundations and collapsed buildings beneath years of abandonment, and dead autumn leaves in the forest that grew around it when the company closed.

It's just Max and me on a cool Sunday afternoon. He saw me getting gas after church, said Mikayla went shopping for the day with her sister. Max asked if we could just forget the kiss like it didn't happen. Could I please never mention it to Mikayla? *What kiss?* I had asked him. He sighed in relief and asked me if I was mad about it. I didn't like him or anything, did I? I laughed and probably a little too loudly. I can't stop thinking about the kiss.

I'd asked him if he wanted to ride along on a little treasure hunt and look for the lost tunnel T.J. mentioned. He said he'd rather be helping Trevor's mom put up more posters. I told him for the tenth time, nobody saw Trevor, so putting up stupid posters isn't helping. I went into the bathroom and sloughed off my dress, exchanged it for a pair of jean shorts and a ribbed, pink tank. I figured he'd left when I came back out, but he was still parked next to me. So,

I showed him a copy of an old map of Lost Hollow. My Aunt Rita works at the county engineer's office and didn't mind sitting in the dark, dusty confines of the records room last night for two hours while I dug around the old county archives. Sure enough, I found a map showing a tracing of railroad tracks that went right into the south side of Brandy Mountain. It stated: PROPOSED BRANDY GAP RAILWAY.

"What's next?" He doesn't even bother to look up from his phone that he's tapping and cursing because there's no service here. He's wearing a beanie hat, and he adjusts it absently with his fingers. He looks so out of place here, this city boy plopped in the middle of backwoods. I suppose it's in my nature to entice him into my beloved world of history. Such, I take a chance and toss something out to him. "I came across a diary belonging to Hans Branntwein, your—" I know when I divulge I have the journal, Max may confiscate it. Maybe, he will tell his dad who will lay claim to it. Or someone will believe I stole it.

"—my great, great, great grandfather. I think I know who he is," Max tells me blandly, if not with a tinge of sarcasm attached by a narrowing of his eyes. "When you say you came across this item, was it at the library or online?"

"Do you remember your dad having stuff in a safe?"

"Why would I know that?" Max doesn't seem to care. He keeps trying to hold his phone up toward the tree canopy to get service. "Since you mentioned it might have been in a safe, I'm assuming it is valuable. Since you are weaselly about it, I should also ask how you came into possession of said journal. And please don't tell me you stole it from the museum, Harley." Max drags his eyes away from his phone for a second and lets his head roll back.

"No, of course not. I'm offended you even say that."

"But you expected it. You've got a history of taking things that aren't yours like a serial killer saves something from each of his murder victims as a souvenir."

"Max, I don't steal—"

"I'm sure the Zodiac Killer said the same thing," Max

mutters. "You are like a packrat, Harley," he scoffs at me. "You've got a thing about collecting stuff, sometimes not belonging to you, to remind you of certain people or things. For example, my crystal and my sunglasses. You still haven't returned them." He goes back to his phone. "Can I have the journal or are you going to drag that away to your den, too?"

"You can have it when I'm done if you don't piss me off any more than you have right now for calling me a weasel, serial killer, and thief. And you aren't going to get cell phone service here. You're down too deep in the valley which is funny because now you know how we feel in the hollow while you guys up on the mountain get service."

"You suck," he says, then grunts something about Mikayla getting upset when he doesn't call.

"*You* suck," I return. Max chuckles softly. I look up. He is eyeing me with a soft smile on his lips. As soon as our eyes meet, he snaps his gaze away. It screams, *you ain't gonna try to kiss me again, are you?* He focuses once again on his phone with another pucker of his lips: "Why do we have to live in this hellhole of poverty and desolation?" he groans.

"You don't have to live here. Move to the city. You are free. But for now, put down your leash and listen to me, Mateo." I reach out my hand, push his arm down. Then, he turns his head slowly to stare down at me. "You haven't heard a damn word I've said," I huff. "You've been too busy poking your fingers on the phone. You told me you were bored. I'm trying to make you *un*-bored. I'm holding out a frigging treasure hunt for you that also might lead us to Trevor, and you're more worried your girlfriend is going to make you sleep on the couch tonight because you didn't check in every ten minutes."

"Stop right there. History is boring. And still," he pauses to look hard at me, "I listened. This used to be the center of the town of Lost Hollow. See? You think you can solve the reason Trevor disappeared by finding out if he was digging here. And you didn't steal a family heirloom from us, but you're just *borrowing* it—" he holds up both his hands with fingers bent in air quotes. "—temporarily."

"Oh. Well, I didn't steal it necessarily. It was in the container Trevor wanted me to take."

"Which you *stole* from his garage."

"It isn't stolen, Max. He told me to take it so his mom didn't see the porn. Except it wasn't porn. It was this book." I open the door to the jeep, reach under my seat, and tug out the journal. "Can I read you something from it?"

"You're kidding me, right? Because I'm thinking that *take the container so my mom doesn't see the porn* was code for: *get the container out so the cops don't know I stole it*," he gripes. "You need to take the journal to the police, let them sort this mess out. The longer you hold on to it, the more you're going to look guilty for stealing it."

"Did you know your grandpa fought in the Civil War? He was at a battle at Harpers Ferry." I don't look up, start to open the journal. "He was only like fourteen and I think he was captured from his house a year before it and made to be like a servant to a guy called Bad Bill with the Rebel guerillas. The Rebels burned down his house."

"Are you listening to me?" Max sighs.

"How about this—your grandpa was super smart and he blew up bridges. He knew how to do the calculations for the explosives. I think he was using nitroglycerin they were sneaking into the United States because he talks about mixing chemicals. Nobody had hardly used it then. There isn't any record of nitroglycerin being used for another four years. And how many fourteen-year-olds can do that, right?"

"I don't know, Harley."

"None. That's how many. He must have been a genius. I was reading last night where he captured a bunch of Federal soldiers and stopped them from being killed before a battle. One of them, he calls Irish. He's got a bunch of entries where he and another boy named Hayward are sneaking them their rations, these little flour biscuits called hardtack. I think Hayward's a slave from the place where Hans was living in

Virginia. I think Hans might have gotten sent there when his dad died, maybe started working for someone—" Max is blinking at me dumbly, but I have his attention, so I don't want to stop. "Okay, so I kind of got obsessed last night deciphering his cursive in the journal. It's hard to read, and the journal looks like it has been through a rainstorm, it's so dirty. But I was also piecing together the people in his life— John Grey, that's—"

"Wait a minute, please." Max holds out both his hands, stopping me from going farther. He rubs his forehead, bites his lower lip. "Just give me a second to think this out, okay? I get you're excited about this. I've just got to figure out where I'm standing on this." He pushes from the jeep, turns, and plants both hands on it. I see him looking down to the ground, focused somewhere between the tire and his feet. "We're not kids anymore. We can't get in trouble like we used to, you know? You're always walking that fine line between—" he stops there. The fine line between what? Good and evil, fun and not so fun? He must know I'm getting ready to ask what line I walk, because Max looks up, gives me a doleful stare. "You're always standing on the edge of the cliff ready to jump, Harley. I don't know if I can jump anymore. We don't get sent to our rooms or get detention—we go to jail or die." I see him stop, look up to the sky. Then he pivots on his feet, gives me a hard stare. "This stuff that you're finding out about my grandpa might help figure out what's going on with Trevor and the stolen stuff from the museum? Because he's disappeared off the face of the earth, won't answer my calls. I feel like I should be like driving up and down the road looking for him. I know that's like looking for a needle in a haystack."

"Max, I didn't steal this. I haven't done anything wrong. Walk away if you want. I'll take you back to your truck." He looks defeated for a second. I see him patting his pocket, his phone. "You won't be mad? I really should drive up the road and call Mikayla."

"Nope." I lie with a forced smile. "Not at all."

Later, when I get to the ballfields to practice with Pop Pop's team, my grandpa hands me a note. "You know a man named Theo Winters? He called twenty times this afternoon." I take the paper warily in my fingertips and peer at it. "That's his number. He wanted your cell phone number. I told him I didn't give it out without asking."

I take a few minutes while I'm watching them play to return Theo's call. I'm thinking I'm in trouble for something at work. I don't know what. Theo answers before the second ring and says he's going to get right to the point. He said he was thinking we should meet somewhere tonight. He has a few houses I can work on with him, get some experience and we can grab a bite to eat. I can see Pop Pop eyeing me from the pitcher's mound. He's got a funny smile on his lips. I'm thinking although my heart's not in it, I probably should. I think it might be more than work stuff, maybe a sloppy way of asking me out on a date. Such, I agree.

"Hey, fallen off any good vines lately?" Beck's voice comes up behind me, and I give him an absent wave while Theo looks up the address for the house he's selling, tells me to meet him there. I wait patiently, half-heartedly watching Beck. He is just getting to the practice and drops his ballbag on the rickety stands. His voice was low, so nobody else hears. He's got a silly grin tweaking his lips.

I hold my hands out to my sides and pretend I'm doing a ballet leap before I bring the phone back up to my ear. He knows I'm teasing him about his jump across the creek. It's not a typical interaction I have with him. Honestly, I pay little heed to him like I ignore or small-talk all my uncle's ten or so friends always dipping their heads into Pop Pop's refrigerator or flopping their butts on his couch. If I do have more than a three-minute conversation, Zach embarrasses me with something like: *You trying to steal another one of my friends, Harley, like you did Trevor? How'd that work for you?* Ugh. Like a train wreck.

This is the first time in a couple weeks since we walked

the trail, I've been near him without anybody else around, culled from Zach's herd. If he's not attached to Zach's left hip, he's parked in Pop Pop's garage on a lawn chair jawing with him. Zach told me after Beck's accident and after he lost the college scholarship, Beck and his dad just kind of stopped talking. That's about the time Beck became a daily fixture at Pop Pop's house and settled in Pop Pop's garage listening to him grunt and growl underneath cars and motorcycles while he worked on them.

"Haha." Beck laughs low, "At least mine was graceful." He's wearing a suit coat and button-up shirt. He slips out of the suit coat and hangs it on a metal fence post, then proceeds to unbutton his shirt down to a white t-shirt.

"Everything alright?"

Oh, I'm not sure. He smells like sweat and wintergreen breath mints and looks like he's just stepped off the cover of some hot guy workout magazine. Beck's built like a brand new semi-truck fresh off the showroom floor. He's got fireman muscles, the kind of biceps that come from working out. He's downright buff. I really don't like buff guys. They're always so full of themselves, more interested in poking at their muscles in the mirror than really using them for something. Or do I? I must, because I'm googly-eyeing him like a shy and chubby, pimpled high-schooler drooling over the boys on the cover of a teen magazine.

"Um, fine. Ph—phone call." What the hell? *Phone call?* What does that mean, stuttered from my lips? Shit. I forgot about Theo on the phone. I can't even think straight, he's so *hot*. No. No, I'm not one of those giggly-crap women who push out their boobs and give men flirty come-hither gazes. I find myself waving my hand in front of my face like I can wipe away the warmth in my cheeks. I realize I'm staring at him with my hand holding my phone two inches from my face. I think there is something wrong with me lately. Guys I'd never take a second look in their direction, I'm soaking in the same way an old lady laying by the pool slurps up the young men in swim trunks with her eyes. I've seen Beck and

Zach's buddies take off their shirts hundreds of times to jump in the creek for a swim or to play some sport in Pop Pop's backyard. Nothing. Not so right now.

"He does that to women."

"Huh?" I turn and bump into T.J. who must have snuck around to snatch a bottled water from his bag.

"Oh, oh—" Oh, hell. "No, it's the phone." I wave it again like an idiot. "I'm on the phone with—my boyfriend—"

"I'm your boyfriend." That's Theo on the phone. "Did you just call me your boyfriend?"

Now my face is burning red. I wheel around, do a trip-dance over a piece of cardboard laying on the ground. "No, Theo, sorry," I say, far enough away I think no one can hear me. "Creepy guy in a parking lot. I was just using you as an excuse—"

"Oh, wait. Can you hold a sec? I think that's Lissette on the other line."

"Okay." I hold there in silence for at least thirty seconds before Theo comes back on the phone and mutters something about Lissette needing him to run across town for a client. He says he'll have to hold off on tonight's lessons, but we'll get together and do it soon. Hmmm. I'm kicking myself for calling him my boyfriend. I think he's just ducking out on a date.

"So I'm the creepy guy in the parking lot?" That's Beck leaning into the window while I pump my foot to the gas in my jeep. *Ptt-tut-tut.* My jeep's out of gas. "I'm putting a whole new twist to it then, right now, aren't I?"

"Huh?"

"You're out of gas in an empty parking lot. It's getting dark. I'm the creep. You know, like a horror movie."

"Oh, Beck, it was the first thing that came to my mouth," I bumble. "You've been there. Some guy from work was asking me out. You all weren't making it easy on me."

"Yeah, right, you need a lift to get some gas?"

"Please."

"I'm starving. You want to go get something to eat?"

"I don't care. Sure. Your treat. I mean it's not like a date, right?" I tease him. "We can go halfsies, but you'll have to pay a bigger half because I'm broke."

He rolls his eyes, shakes his head. "It's not a date. Zach went to the gas station to get chicken nuggets. That boy could eat the rust off a bumper. I can't even look at those things without gaining ten pounds," he says, pats his belly. "We could get a pizza and run up the mountain again, have a picnic off my bumper and look around up there."

"That sounds like a date."

"It's not a date."

I snatch the milk jug I keep in the back to fill up with gas for just these occasions that Beck knows probably happen way too much. I see him grimace. "You're not getting gas in that, are you? It's not safe."

"It's safer than using my hands."

It's funny, I suppose. Beck's got this nice truck. But he drives like a little old lady. "Drive faster," I tell him coming out of the parking lot. "Let's see some dust fly."

"No."

"Then, let me drive."

"You're kidding me, right?" Beck asks me. "You're not covered under my insurance and—" He must see my bored detachment. He gets the same sickly look in his eyes as Zach used to get five minutes before he got carsick. I'm suddenly bored. I don't really like Beck that much to hang out with him. "It's not that I don't trust you. I just don't like to—" *Break the law.* I know that's what he wants to say and doesn't. He's just too by-the-book and humdrum for me. I don't go around robbing banks or anything, but a girl's gotta have some fun. "You just can't be too careful, Harley."

"Yeah, you're probably right." I reach down and tug my phone from my pocket. BORED. It's screaming in my head. I suppose it isn't surprising. He did pick the tedious job of teaching kids day after day. It's safe. It's full of monotonous tasks like grading papers and staring at bored kids staring back at him. Enough said. "Whoa, it's later than I thought. I've got a bunch of work to do. How about we go get a milk jug worth of gas, and we call it a day, alright?" He nods his head. I know he knows I'm lying.

We stop at the gas station and Max pulls up while I'm filling the milk jug with gasoline. He looks at Beck in the driver's seat, then back to the milk jug. "You know that's illegal."

"I've been told that."

"If you blow Beck's truck up, they'll know who got the can." He pokes a finger at the surveillance camera. "I got a real gas can in the bed of my truck and an empty passenger seat. Want to hang?" Max asks. I know Beck can hear him. "Why are you riding around with that dork?"

"I'm not. I'm out of gas, and he gave me a ride."

"Jump in. I'll make you legal. We can get a beer." I'm finished pumping. I let his words lay there while I put the pump back and screw on the lid. "You said I was boring."

"Just when you don't stop talking about history."

"Hang on." I walk around to the driver's side of Beck's truck and lean in.

"Do you think I'm boring?" I ask softly.

"No."

"So, if you talk to me like you did the other day," I say. "You know, the splinter thing. Maybe we can hang."

"You're serious? *With the dork?*" he asks me, and he looks hurt. "I heard him. Did he tell you to say that?"

"What?"

"Did you tell him what I said about you? About you and the bathing suit?" He pats his steering wheel. "Are we back in high school again and it's okay to be mean to me? Forget it. Just go. I just said that to get you back for calling me a pervert then, you know that, right? It wasn't true."

169

"Seriously?" I ask him curtly. "Because I didn't tell him anything. I promise. I don't—" *I don't want to go with him.* I stop and let my shoulders fall. Beck looks at me, swings his head back to the steering wheel. "Thanks for the ride." I pat the window and start to turn. I feel like crying because, yes, I can't get his words out of my head. They make me feel sexy and beautiful and not boring like I feel when I'm with Max. Now they aren't real. And never were. And I feel stupid for believing them.

"No, Harley," Beck slaps his hand down on mine. "I was speaking from the heart. I wasn't lying. Let me give you a ride back to your car."

Max isn't happy when I tell him I just want to go home. Beck gets out of the truck and leans his arms on the hood while I snatch up the milk jug full of gas. It makes Max antsy, and he postures a moment, hovering over me like he's helping. Beck pushes up some junk in the back to hold it and we make a steady, but slow, drive back to my jeep where I put the gas in the tank.

"I thought you and Max were like—let's see, what do the girls in my class call it? Oh, yeah, besties."

I laugh and close the lid to the milk jug. "I wish. He's changed. I've changed. We've grown apart. When I hang with him, he's always on his phone, can't wait to leave. I guess I grew up and got boring."

"Hardly."

I flash him a smile. I can't figure out if I like that I like being near Beck. He gets a text and jumps to get it. I'm sure it's Zach the way he answers. "That's your brother—"

"Uncle."

"He was wondering where I was. You good?"

Do you want to hang? That's what I want to ask. I don't. I just nod my head. He's Zach's. Beck's not mine. Doesn't make me want him any less.

Chapter 25

I'm thinking about Max. My mind rolls to the gas station. I think of him looking up to the surveillance camera. It occurs to me that the Bakers Quickie Stop and Gas probably had a surveillance camera that would show where I was for an hour of the time that the museum was getting broken into. And maybe, the one in Lost Hollow would have some videos of cars going past to show who was up at the same time. I call Officer Washington with the Brandy Mountain police and offer up my advice. He thwarts my handy detective work by telling me there just isn't enough time in the day for him to run through hours and hours of videos. Still, he tells me, if he gets a chance, he will.

My great grandma, Denise, is 94 years old. We call her Nana Nisee. She's Pop Pop's mother and can't stay home by herself anymore because sometimes she does stuff like trying to fry her chicken noodles on the toilet seat in the bathroom and using the stovetop as a—well, you can guess. Up until a few months ago, a bus used to pick her up for an adult day care and senior center in the next town over, but she kept wandering off with an old man named Ned. So, we all take turns staying with her now.

I usually try to sidestep my turn by simply not answering my phone. Especially today because I wanted to see if Beck was still up for that pizza picnic. He didn't say much after he dropped me off. We kind of lingered until it got too quiet, then we both mumbled an excuse to part ways. And text each other. So far, no texts. However, I've got Pop Pop's cell phone. When my Aunt Rita called two days after Max bailed on me, I automatically picked it up and such, Nana Nisee's with me today. I can't help but wonder if she isn't actually babysitting me to keep me out of whatever trouble Pop Pop thinks I'll get into. He must be quite pleased with himself getting Aunt Rita to call me.

"We're going up the side of the mountain above the old

mining town, Nana Nisee, okay?" I tell her impatiently and loudly while I help her get into the car. Her thin, gray hair is tied up on the top of her head in a lazy bun. And she's skinny and full of wrinkles like a big balloon that's lost all its air. "I'm going to pull all the way up to almost the top of the mountain on the old logging roads where Hans Branntwein's house was located. You can sit in the car. I'm going to look for something. It won't take a half hour."

I'm not so sure she's all there in the head. It isn't because it is seventy-eight degrees and she's wearing a thick, crochet cardigan and long slacks. "That's fine, Jenny. Whatever you want to do," she sighs, settling herself in my passenger side seat smiling at me. I open my mouth to remind her I'm not Jenny while I help her tug the seatbelt over her thin waist. I blow a puff of air instead that makes my long bangs ride upward with the current of breath.

She always calls me Jenny, though, just like she calls Aunt Rita, Bessie. Jenny was her sister who died when she was young. Pop Pop tells me that it's rude for me to correct her like she's a child. So, I don't. I nod, knowing that everything's fine with Nana Nisee, at least that's all I ever really hear her say. She's quiet, always tagging along behind one of my relatives with bored, cataract-ridden gray eyes that brighten up a little when she sees me. For that, I feel guilty I always dodge taking care of her. I think sometimes she knows I'm not her dead sister, but wishes I *was* her.

Forty minutes later, I'm trying to avoid potholes the size of large mixing bowls dotting the old dirt road and driving about ten miles an hour, so I don't jostle her too much. She has her window down, and her skinny arm resting on the frame. The warm spring-summer wind is blowing her hair and she has her eyes closed like she might be asleep. Or dead. It'd be my luck I'd be the one who killed fragile Nana Nisee. In the least, I'm hoping she doesn't report back to anybody that I dragged her out four-wheeling on the old roads that are probably closer to game trails the deer have made with their tiny cloven hooves. Her typical day is sitting in front of the TV with a blanket on her knees, her remote set on back-to-back 1980s game shows and her nose pressed to a crossword puzzle booklet.

"I've got to be kind of sneaky about this," I have to yell over the grind of tires while I cross a rocky section of a creek. "The Dunns rent the property up here where the old house was, and they've got dogs. I want to see if there's a foundation or an old chimney or something. It will only take me a few minutes because, well you know, I don't want to trespass." What I really mean to say is that I don't want to get chased out of here with a shotgun. I'm curious to see if there are holes where Trevor could have dug out those jars.

However, Lester Dunn's got a bit of a reputation. Every town has folks like the Dunns who don't get along with anybody else. Lester Dunn's six feet and probably eight inches of what Zach calls *enormous white trash redneck*. He doesn't have a job. The only time he comes to town is to get drunk. And he's a mean drunk. He always crosses the yellow line on the main road outside of town. At least once a month, he runs me off the road coming around a curve. I think he does it on purpose. His family hates my family. According to Zach, it goes back as far as when Pop Pop was working in the mines as a blast hole driller. This was long after the Brandy Mountain Colliery expanded to more areas in the region and he got a promotion as mine foreman over Lester's great uncle. Lester's dad then cornered Pop Pop behind the gas station and tried to punch him out. Pop Pop knocked him flat, then somebody at the corporate office heard about the fight and fired Lester's uncle. Lester's uncle owned a bunch of land on the hill that he let the rest of the family live on. When he got fired, he lost the land. The Armstrongs, who own a nearby gas and grocery, bought it up. They let Lester Dunn and his uncle keep living at their old homes. But now the Dunns must rent what they used to reside in for free.

"If we get caught, I'll take the fall," I joke with my grandma. She just smiles at me. "Or maybe I'll tell them you're the one who made me trespass. They wouldn't send someone over ninety to jail, would they?" Or shoot them and bury the body up here? I sigh. I could have probably said the last part. It isn't like Nana Nisee even understands what I'm saying. "Oh well, whatever. You know, Nana Nisee, I've kissed three people in the last three weeks. Two, I just kissed because they were there. One was—" I scratch my head in thought. "—an old friend. I was hoping his kiss would leave butterflies in my belly. It didn't. I kind of wish it had."

"Butterflies are nice."

"They are," I agree. "But butterflies scare me. Is that strange?" I stare at the windshield. "I'm more scared of butterflies in my belly than Lester Dunn murdering me up here and burying my body in an old well."

There's a plateau three-quarters of the way up that held a couple homes and yards. They are two, tiny black squares on the 1897 township map. I stop short beneath a copse of trees where the road just fades away into overgrown shrubs. I reach over Nana Nisee's knees and to the glovebox, where I tug out the map Aunt Rita helped me dig up. With it, comes a handful of pictures of the old mining camp I pulled offline last night and copied to sheets of paper so I can try to match the background behind the homes to the location now.

I unfold the map and study it, turning it left to right to try to synchronize the road on the map to the one we are settled on. Then I fiddle with a paperclip and picture. It's cool here, and the sweet scent of pines tickles my nostrils. It must be catching in Nana Nisee's nose, too. She sits back, lets her head roll to the seat behind her, and drinks it in with a huge inhalation of air. "Oh, this reminds me of home." Then, she starts to sing an old song, *In the Pines*, I remember she sang to me when I was little.

I get out of the jeep and look around. Three times, I make passes of the landscape, following the little outline of square boxes on the old 1897 plat map. I can hear dogs barking far off and pray they are tied to some tree on the Dunn's property and not wandering feral to eat us. There's simply nothing left but a stack of old sandstone foundation stones to one side. I see the ground isn't upturned.

"Well, so much for that bright idea," I mutter when I get back into the jeep. "If Hans Branntwein lived up here, there's no trace of the house." If Trevor was digging, it wasn't here. I feel like I'm looking for a needle in a haystack. Nana Nisee smiles at me. She's holding the copies of the old pictures in her lap and patting them with wrinkled fingers.

"What are you looking for, Jenny?"

I start the jeep, thinking at first she isn't talking to me, but the ghost of her sister in her mind. Then, when I glance over at her, Nana Nisee is staring at me. "Oh," I say, turning the key in the ignition. "I'm trying to find Hans Branntwein's old house. In one of the books I read, it said his family lived up on the hill overlooking the coal camp and away from all the smoke. But if it existed, there's nothing left. I suppose that's why nobody ever found any treasure."

"Are you looking for treasure?" She's still eyeing me solidly. I tap my fingers on the steering wheel.

"Not necessarily. You're not going to tell Pop Pop or Aunt Rita, are you? I mean, it'd be nice to find that treasure they say is buried here, but—" I pause. I suppose I'm just using Trevor as an excuse, really. I'm more interested in unearthing old stuff about the town. It intrigues me. "I don't know, Nana Nisee. I want to do what I went to school for, and it's history stuff, learning it and teaching it. But there aren't any jobs. I'm dead broke, so I guess I'm just trying to make do with what I've got and it's—this." I wave a hand around me. "Sometimes I wish I could jump in a time machine and see what it was really like to live in a place."

"But looking for a treasure would be fun."

"Yeah," I chuckle. "Finding it would be even better."

"I miss Ned," she tells me. I nod and ask her if Ned was the guy with whom she snuck out of the senior center.

"Yes. He was sweet on me. We went for ice cream."

"I could take you to see him sometime if you want."

"And I could help you find treasure," she answers.

"Because the Branntweins never lived up here." She's furrowing her brow. "Hannah rocked me when I was just a wee thing on their front porch and used to carry me around like a baby doll. Katie Lynn used to sing to me. And it was down in the holler where everybody lived and right next door to my mama's house. Katie Lynn and Hannah, they was two of the Branntwein girls. There was lots of girls in that house, there was." This is the most I've ever heard her chatter on, my quiet grandmother. She's usually just sitting and watching the world go by. Now, she has a soft smile playing on her lips. "They was such good folk."

"Wait, stop." I tip my head curiously. "Every pamphlet I've read, everything I've seen online says they lived up on the mountain just like the rich people do now."

"Well, back then, they was just like everybody else, sweetie. They didn't care so much about being away from the community. Nobody wanted to be alone. We was like a big family, rich or poor." She cranes her neck. "I think Owen Dunn's family had a house up here. Or maybe it was the Armstrongs. Both them families had sawmills."

I'm not sure if I believe her or not. "Do you remember where the Branntweins lived?"

"Down in the holler."

"If I drove down there, Nana Nisee, could you maybe show me?"

"I suppose my old head could remember. Jenny used to have a jeep, you know that?"

I sigh. "No, I didn't." I put on my seatbelt, look at the time on the cell phone. I'm not getting anywhere with this idea that Trevor found the treasure. "Is your seatbelt buckled so we can head back home? I'll make us some supper." I push my foot on the clutch and smile at her. But she's not looking at me anymore. "Alright, time to—"

"They're watching us."

"Watching us?" I ask, follow her gaze that is slowly working toward the roadway ahead of us. "What? Who?"

"That man—and them." Nana Nisee doesn't move except to sweep her eyes toward the darkness of trees.

Oh, no. I see him as clear as day standing in the roadway. It's Lester Dunn, and he's got some kind of mixed Rottweiler-shepherd on a rope beside him and three hound dogs loping up behind. My heart takes a soaring leap of alarm. He's hauling a shotgun over his right shoulder. He takes a step closer to the jeep and works the shotgun downward, making a quick pump to chamber a new shell.

"Oh, no, the Dunns," I grumble. "Nana Nisee, you're going to have to hang on, alright?" I say to the windshield, see a soft reflection of my own face before my vision focuses on Lester Dunn's body a stone's throw away. Strangely, I don't look terrified. I take a quick glimpse over his head and about ten feet up in a tree, I can make out his daughter, Willy. She is hanging on to a branch and peering at us through the leaves.

"That's fine, sweetie. Let's bust out of here."

I make a hasty shove of my foot into the clutch, start to push the gear shift back and into reverse. The jeep gear always gives me grief, and I hear them make a screaming grind while I shove it back three times, not once catching. I can't get it into reverse. But I never can when I'm in a hurry. Twice, again, I shove my foot to the clutch, drag the gearshift back. Finally, the jeep makes a hearty heave backward, tires spitting dirt and pebbles. I back up into the grass just as he lets loose the Rottweiler-shepherd, its head held low and his body launching toward the jeep. The pack of hounds makes a mad dash after the lead dog, baying and scuffling to be in front. I feel the passenger rear wheel dip down, and I panic, snapping my neck to the right to see a small, grassy ditch hidden in the scrubby knee-high grass.

KA-BOOM! The sound of shotgun rings out in my ears. Not three seconds after, I can hear the spatter of pellets ripping through my roof.

"Shit!" I screech and hit the accelerator. Nothing. It isn't moving. I can make out Lester Dunn long-stepping forward just as the first of his dogs makes a leap at my open driver's side window with a thump of a head and long-nailed paws grabbing on to the sill. I've got no choice but keel to the right while it jumps a second time, splattering me with saliva. I can hear its bottom feet scraping like it is climbing to get inside. There's a pack of dogs barking at my tires, running around the back and nipping and growling at each other like they're fighting for their meal.

"Roll up your window!" I scream at Nana Nisee, realizing the dogs are rounding the vehicle, a one-legged hound loping up and getting close enough to leave a slimy spittle splashed on the passenger side sill. My grandma has the rolled up pictures and tries slapping the muzzle.

"You drive, little girl. I'll get these damn hounds!" my great grandma growls like she's got a .22 caliber rifle and not flimsy paper in her fist she's using to swat a nose.

I jam my foot down on the clutch, jerk the jeep into 4-wheel drive, and hit the gas. It makes a shuddering wrench forward. The sound of rubber tire begging to catch firm earth makes a whirring hum before the tire grabs it. The entire vehicle heaves forward and into mid-air.

We crash down on the road. I wheel the car around to the sound of the shotgun and howling dogs and—the thumpity-thump of my tire grazing something I am praying isn't one of Lester Dunn's stupid mutts. *God damn you!* I heard Lester Dunn yowl. When I peer into the rear-view mirror, he's holding his arm above his face while the dusty remnants of roadway flying off my tires spray his body from head to boots. As I tear down the old dirt road, banging and crashing over rocks and mounds of dirt as fast as I can down the mountainside, I look over at Nana Nisee and she is laughing so hard tears are running down her cheeks. "Ride, Jenny, ride!" she's yelling while her stringy arms and hands cling to the window and the dash. "Ride, Jenny Ride!"

Chapter 26

I'm standing inside a gas station squinting up at the old plastic sign above the counter—*Hurricane Hollow Carry Out and Gas—Fill Your Tank. Fill Your Belly.* It's not directly off the main highway. It's on one of those roads commuters take who have four-wheel drive and know they can dodge the rush hour traffic going the back broken-asphalt roads their grandparents took sixty years ago and before the highways were built. It's a warm eighty-two degrees, the sun is blazing a pretty yellow-orange, and a breeze is sifting through the mountains. I took the route home tonight just to roll down the windows of my jeep and let the air run through my hair, feel the sunshine on my bare arm with my elbow settled on the window. I stopped in to get a bottled water and ten bucks worth of gas.

There's too much drama in my life right now. I need some me-time. I was two hours late getting Nana Nisee back yesterday, and Pop Pop and Aunt Rita were pacing back and forth in my driveway. Pop Pop started yelling at me when he saw Nana Nisee all windblown and with pink sunburned cheeks. She was sound asleep in the car when we rolled in. I think they thought I left her in there for hours with nothing but the windows rolled down while I went shopping at the mall or something. Zach and Beck were standing on the front porch like they just couldn't wait to hear Pop Pop yell at me because I didn't call. Aunt Rita was wagging her head back and forth, adding a few words here and there to Pop Pop's rant while she helped my sleepy great grandma from the jeep. "Harley, I'm ashamed of you," she finally said about six minutes into the chastising.

I didn't say anything. I've learned it's much better to just keep my mouth shut than try to make peace with excuses. Finally, Nana Nisee wagged a finger in the air. She whipped up a flat-lined gaze at Pop Pop and told him to shut up. "Now see what you've done?" she said to him. "That little girl was trying to keep a secret for me. You've gone and spoiled it. I wet my dress, and she took me home to change. Now everybody knows. The whole street knows." Nana Nisee burst into tears and I was blinking wildly at her until Aunt Rita started crying because she believed her. I was thunderstruck and thought Nana Nisee had gone completely off her rocker until Aunt Rita came over and gave me a big hug like I was some superhero. Nana Nisee winked at me from behind Aunt Rita's back.

I'm thinking about Nana Nisee and my new alliance with her when I pull out my wallet from my purse to pay for my water. I owe her a trip to see Ned. While I'm tugging out my money from a little pocket, the gas station attendant starts to put my candy bar and bottle in a brown paper bag. I shake my head, stop her with my hand in the air. "I don't need a bag." But my wallet's laying open, and an old picture of me and Max and Trevor sitting on the bumper of Max's truck is staring back at me. The attendant is about sixteen or seventeen with a round face, hair in a lazy bun on her head, and a soft, southern drawl more likely from Alabama than where we are standing right now. She's craning her head to look at the picture and pokes at it. "That you? Are you from around here?"

"Naw."

"He looks familiar." She pokes Trevor's forever-smiling face. Then she takes the fifteen dollars I set on the counter and starts to ring me up on an old-fashioned register.

I'm mesmerized. I look at the little homemade nametag on the right breast of her shirt. HALEY. "Hey, Haley," I ask her. "You haven't seen that guy, have you?" I turn my wallet around, offer up the little picture so she can get a better look. I'm reluctant to pull it out, ask random people if they have seen Trevor Woods. I don't know the reason. I suppose I think he's still alive and probably hiding somewhere behind me, laughing that I still care enough to ask. "I mean, you may have seen his picture on the news. There are signs of him along the highway. He's missing."

She leans in. "Isn't that the dead guy they found?"

"Dead guy?"

"Yeah, on the tracks." She points a finger toward the doors. I'm slightly numb, follow her finger and stare at nothing but the door. "Well, about a mile down the road next to Walsh's house. You know the Walshes?" I shake my head. "They found a dead guy—or what was left of him. Well, my cousin, Robby, he found it first walking down here from his trailer to get cigarettes. So he went to flag somebody down on the highway, but it was like six in the morning and just getting light and nobody was going to stop for him. He saw Joe Walsh up on the hill. He was out looking for his little Pomeranian. It gets out and comes down here all the time. But he flagged him down, and while Joe stood there in case another train came through, Robby came down here and called the cops. He was all messed up. That's what Robby said. Got hit a couple times. Are you a cop?"

"A cop?"

"I mean, you look like the detective who questioned my boss. All dressed up and stuff."

"Oh, no, I'm not a cop." I look down at my dress. "The guy's name was Trevor Woods."

"Yeah, I remember that name. That's him. When they heard somebody was dead on the tracks, they had the fire department out there and the ambulance and the cops. There were lights and sirens everywhere—hey, you forgot your candy bar and water."

I don't even remember wandering toward the door. Trevor's dead? It is sinking in. Trevor's dead. "I don't need it."

"You alright, sweetie?"

No, I'm not.

Chapter 27

"Is it true? Did they find Trevor in Hurricane Hollow?" I'm standing on the small, wooden front porch of a mobile home just outside the city proper of Lost Hollow. I've got a raggedy fast-food restaurant napkin with TACO TIMS embossed on the front still dabbing at my nose because I had a damn good cry getting from the police station that was empty save Dispatch Carla who was washing her car in the parking lot, to here. My knuckles made six sharp bangs on the front door before it was answered by a blinking Lance Washington who is making a wild scramble to button up his shirt while he slides between the front door and porch.

"How did you hear that?" He looks over my shoulder with a rash twist of his head to my jeep and then quickly back at me. I honestly can't help but think he's afraid of me in the same way Pop Pop is afraid of Nana Nisee. She looks as crumbly as a cracker in a week-old open bag and probably barely over five feet tall. But she's got a way of giving him mean-eye and Pop Pop goes into *yes, ma'am* mode. "Nobody knows anything—how do you know where I live? You shouldn't be here."

"Why not? Everybody knows where everybody lives in Lost Hollow, Officer Washington—or do I call you Lance if you're not wearing a uniform?"

"I don't know."

"You don't know if Trevor's dead or if I call you Lance?" I take in a heaving breath, and it ends in an after-sob. "Or—or the reason why I can't be here. Because I don't care. That's not important." Sniff-sniff. "Dispatch Carla at the police station won't answer me—that's what I call her, Dispatch Carla, but she said she was going to call somebody if I didn't leave her alone, somebody like a cop. In retrospect, she probably would have called you and saved me some gas. But I wasn't thinking right when she said it and regardless, she kept saying; *no comment*. I called my Aunt Ruth and she said to stop by here, and I would have known that sooner if I'd go to church more often because you go to her church. You were—what did she call you? Oh, *a nice young fellah.* What does that mean?"

"What does a nice young fellah mean?"

"No, don't be stupid." I put out a hand at his suddenly cop-life expression which is expressionless. "I'm saying that because you *aren't* wearing your cop uniform. It kind of means you're not off-bounds to say how I feel if you're being stupid because you can't arrest me."

"I can arrest you even if I'm not wearing my uniform. But if I arrested every person I meet based on simply being stupid, I would be arresting ninety percent of people." He hard-sighs. "Never mind. If you're asking why she won't tell you if the body is Trevor or not, it's because we do not have enough evidence—" His body suddenly becomes cop-rigid. I can almost feel a wall go up between us. "Let's stop right there. What do you know? And how do you know it?"

"I stopped at the gas station, and the girl told me they found a dead body up the road. I was taking a drive along Hurricane Hollow heading home. It's a longcut home instead of driving the highway and having all that city traffic. She said they thought it was Trevor."

"Okay." He looks left to right as if, due to my spoken declaration, he's expecting the local TV reporters to come dashing down the dirt road he lives on to report it. "You had no clue and just happened to be in Hurricane Hollow?"

"Like I said, it is the long way home, the backroad." I know my eyes are red and puffy. I sniff and heave an after-cry yawn. "I'm sorry. The second I heard, I got into my car and drove home. I couldn't stop crying, and I didn't have any tissues but a napkin from a fast-food restaurant. Taco Tims. And it is stiff like rubbing paper on my eyes." I hold out the napkin, displaying it. Officer Washington drops his eyes only momentarily, drags his gaze back up cautiously. I think he actually believes I'm trying to divert his attention so I can pull out a shotgun from somewhere inside my dress and murder him. "Regardless, everybody who lives in Lost Hollow knows it's another way to go north instead of the highway. Is it him or not?"

It's like suddenly, Officer Washington's guard drops when he lets out a long breath. He leans back, holds the door open, and steps aside. "Listen, just come inside. I'll get you another tissue. I'll tell you what I can as long as you don't go running to the nearest newspaper—"

"The Brandy Mountain Herald?" I push out a soft laugh past the miserable still clinging to my chest. "It comes out once a month if we're lucky we've got any news above somebody shooting their foot during hunting season."

"You know what I mean."

I do. I sit down, and Officer Washington grabs about twenty squares of toilet paper from his bathroom for me to use as a giant tissue. I bunch it up, and it is almost too big for my fist, so I tear it in half and mumble something about saving half for later while I sit on his flowered couch and he sits on an old olive-green recliner with the faux leather peeling off the armrests.

"We don't have enough evidence to say it is Trevor or not," Officer Washington begins, then hesitates. "Uh, the body had been hit by several trains and perhaps, dragged by neighborhood dogs." I feel the blood run from my face. Trevor. Shit. "I probably shouldn't have told you that."

"No, I'm just freaking out. You would think I wouldn't be freaking out since he stole my car and my phone and ditched me for another girlfriend. But I mean, if he's dead—you know, we were close. You know—"

"Of course." The way he says that I know he doesn't understand. "And we aren't sure of that yet," Officer Washington reminds me with the same upswing of voice Pop Pop used to console me when my tomcat would disappear, reminding me Tom Kitty vanished quite often when a female cat was strutting around our neighborhood. "The family has asked that an autopsy not be done for religious reasons, nor that a DNA test performed simply because they just want to give him a burial. It was his clothing on the body. They believe it might be suicide."

"Suicide? Trevor?"

"They state he's been acting strangely. From the erratic behavior with you that night, that only makes this conclusion seem more plausible. I mean, you did say he had never hit you before, hadn't called you recently."

"Well, yeah, but—"

"But—" He stops my words with his hand. "It isn't up to me. The medical examiner has the final say. He usually requires an autopsy. It is just that even with an autopsy, there wasn't much left of his body. I saw the clothing and personal effects before they were handed over to one of the family members, an uncle, I think."

"You aren't keeping his stuff for evidence? He said somebody was chasing him. I think—" I think he might have found that treasure and somebody else wanted it. But I don't say it aloud and finish with a shrug. "I don't know what I think. Maybe you're right. Did they find my car?"

"No, we still have not found your car. Searching for it has been on my radar. I figured if we found the car, we could find evidence within that might give us some hints where he was—or if someone was with him—fingerprints, bloodstains, anything else we could identify was not his. But it could be anywhere—in a parking lot at the airport, in the river, in someone's barn back in the woods. Can I be blunt?" Lance asks me. I nod a bit guardedly. "The case is closed—"

"But what about my car?"

"Let me finish. John Matthews has good reason to believe Trevor Woods was probably involved in drugs—"

"John Matthews is the mayor, not a cop. What does *he* have to do with this?"

"Cop or not, he's a part of a task force they have put together to stop the drug problem in The Bottoms and various parts—"

"Drug problem?" I ask. "Hold on. I think weed is

probably the worst thing anybody does down there. Besides, beer is easier to get at the local store."

"Well, John doesn't think so. They've had a huge task force around the towns of Baker, Thomas, and Fort Hill. He's involved, in part, to stop the flow into Brandy Mountain. It's not a secret. They just arrested Lester Dunn and a whole lot of people in a police sting at Damon's Bar and Grille. If you use your imagination, you can figure out that maybe someone believed Trevor was an informant. I think that is the general perception and the reason the family just wants to make a quiet escape."

"Was he an informant? Wouldn't you know?"

"No, it was out of my jurisdiction. Miss Davidson, I'm just a part-time cop in a town the size of a thimble. I might as well be a security guard at a flea market for all the crime I get to see. I'm sorry your loss. I would contact your insurance company about the car. I don't think it is going to show up anytime soon."

"I really don't care about the car. If he drove off the face of the earth with the damn thing and he was still alive, I'd be elated. It pisses me off I have to make the payment, but honestly, I'm trying to wrap my head around Trevor actually being dead. I thought he'd just show up and tell me it was a big joke, you know?"

"I'm sure—" he sighs. "Listen, I went to school with a guy who was killed in Iraq. I was in two classes with him and played baseball with him my junior and senior year in high school. I barely spoke two words to him all through school. I probably wouldn't have thought much of him until he got killed by a bomb while on military duty. Now it lingers, and I think of him all the time. So whatever loss you're feeling, I'm sure it is overwhelming. Do you need me to call somebody to come get you?"

"No." I look around his bare, little trailer. I see a few family pictures sharing a glass console table with one of the old TVs with the big tube in back. There's a couch with a single can of soda on a coffee table. It's bare and lonely enough I note it even as I wonder if Max knows about Trevor yet or not. Officer Washington's gaze follows mine, and it's almost like he can read what I'm thinking while he holds out one hand toward the door.

"What I've told you is public information at this point. However, I ask that you keep it to yourself." He stands, and I follow suit, pressing down my dress. "I've only been working this job a few months. I'd rather not get canned just yet. My mom is banking on it—" He must have seen my head twist questioningly because he chuckles low on his breath. "She's a bit overprotective, would rather I do anything but work for the police department. She has a job all lined up for me at the local newspaper in Gavinsville, Ohio—the Gavinsville Weekly Press. You ever heard of it?"

"Uh no."

"Yeah, exactly."

Chapter 28

I'm leaning against my jeep on the grassy dirt road of the Brandy Mountain Cemetery. It's raining a soft mist that is getting ready to turn into a downpour. I see the black clouds pushing away the gray on the horizon. Nana Nisee is sitting in the passenger seat behind me. She was working on a crossword puzzle, and now she's singing loud enough I can hear her. I think she is trying to annoy me like a four-year-old jumps up and down to get his mom's attention when he gets bored at church. I sigh at her antics and stare down at the funeral below. Most of the town is there mourning Trevor's passing—well, everybody but Nana Nisee and me. Pop Pop didn't want her standing in the rain. He didn't know I was going to sneak-come to the funeral. I'm parked rather well-hidden between a couple huge SUVs and a truck. The little dirt road isn't that big, so we're all packed into the cemetery side by side.

It wouldn't be like she would fit in with this crowd anyway with her little housedress draped over her and fluorescent pink garden clogs on her feet. I can see mostly Brandy Mountain townspeople in the front. Anybody from the older part in The Bottoms is settled to the outside. Already, the mayor has built a wall between The Brandy and The Bottoms, easily distinguished by class. I wasn't allowed to be there. Max told me that. I'd called him halfway home from meeting with Officer Washington. Max met me at my house, came in, and plopped himself right down on my couch. I guess Max had heard the same news only hours before I took the drive to Hurricane Hollow. "Listen," he'd said, poking me in the arm a little too hard. "I don't know how to say this, but Trevor's mom asked that you don't come to the funeral. It's on Saturday."

"I don't understand. I mean, I know she didn't like me. Does she still blame me for this?"

"I don't know, Harley. I suppose so. I get it that you were his girlfriend, but he treated you like crap. I'd just let it go. It was suicide. He hadn't shown up for work a couple days before he came up missing. He's been acting strange for a few weeks. Did you know he was on anti-depressants?"

"No. How would I know that?" I ask him hotly while I hover over him still standing. "I hadn't seen him since I ran into you guys at the wedding. I would have avoided him for the rest of my life if he hadn't called me." He's not telling me the truth. I know the lying Max, the one who pats his leg and won't look me in the eyes.

"I thought so. It's just the day we stopped at the historical society, he acted like he knew you were there."

"Where else would I be?"

"I don't know. His mom found your number on his cell phone he left in his truck. He still had your pictures in it, still had your number as his emergency contact."

"Trevor had like a million different phones. He always lost his phone, then found it after he bought a new one. It was probably an old one, Max."

"Yeah, I know. I just want you to know the question came up. You weren't with him, were you?"

"No."

"I told his mom you hadn't been. But she's probably kicking herself for all those things people look back on and wish they'd done or should have seen. I think it's easier to blame stuff on somebody else to make the hurt go away. Letting her do that is probably more helpful than all the food people are bringing over from the church."

"Taking the blame for somebody dying is a good thing?" I wolfed down his words and felt them already coming back up in a big, ball of feeling like I'm being left out simply because a finger is being pointed at me as a suspect in Trevor's death. "I can't swallow that without wanting to vomit it back up."

"The doctor who looked him over said Trevor has been dead since the night he left the party. I think the general consensus is that he took too many anti-depressants with alcohol and drove off the road. Then he just started walking the tracks until he got hit."

"So, where's my car?"

"I don't know."

I plopped down on the couch next to Max grumpily. We were sitting there, and I reached out my hand and latched on to his. He was resting his elbows on his knees, but he wasn't responding to my sisterly affection, just gave me this funny, guilty smile. "You okay? You just lost your best friend."

"I suppose I saw it coming."

I gave him a short kiss on the cheek. Then I lifted my knee, started to slide it along the couch next to him. Max, he just wiggled his hand from mine and held out a hand in front of him, gave me a gentle push back.

"I wasn't trying to make out with you," I lied. "I thought you might need a hug or something." We both knew better. I snatched up the TV remote and fumbled awkwardly finding a show.

"There's this guy I met in college. He called me the other day, wants me to do the artwork for a comic book series. I mean, he wants me to do a comic book series for him."

"That's cool," I muttered. My voice was flat though, and I yawn. I didn't really feel like having Max around. I just wanted to be alone, cry Trevor tears into my hands. He was quiet. I was embarrassed and wished he'd leave. Then my landline phone rang. I'm so not used to it ringing, I jumped. I got up and answered it.

"Hi, this is Officer Washington, but I'm calling as Lance—"

"How'd you get my number?" I asked.

"I called *Dispatch Carla*—" he stressed my name for her with almost a chuckle, "—who gave me your Aunt Ruth's number. Aunt Ruth proceeded to tell me all about how you're playing ball with your grandpa, and you're such a good girl." He said that, and it made me laugh a little. "You went to Tri-State Community College and you're a wild one, but you mean well. I think at some point she was trying to fix us up on a date and I told her that I had a girlfriend. I was just concerned—I don't know why I'm telling you this. My point is that I just wanted to make sure you made it home okay. You were upset."

"Yeah, I'm here. Thanks, Officer Washington—"

"It's Lance right now."

"Well, thanks, Lance."

Max got up mid-conversation and gave me a half-hearted wave while he poked a finger at his wristwatch. Then he gave me the I'll-call-you gesture with his fist and pinky finger to his cheek and his thumb sticking out towards his ear. I'm a bit perturbed. Who leaves like that when somebody finds out an ex-boyfriend just died?

He's weirdly quiet the next two days and doesn't call me before the funeral. He says he has to work a job with his dad in Kentucky. I don't see him until he stops in on Saturday night. By then, I had already trudged around knee-deep in watching old videos on my phone of me and Trevor.

"Jenny? I have to use the little girl's room."

"Huh? Oh," I wheel my head around, realize Nana Nisee isn't in the passenger seat. I had to weave my way through a few trucks to watch the funeral. I blanch. I am making a quick retreat into my jeep only two seconds after the crowd at the funeral disperses. I'm sure it was made quick by the oncoming storm. I see Trevor's mom and sister and his dad. They aren't crying the same kind of weepy-eyed tears I've been dropping for the last few days. His dad is just wagging a hand toward their SUVs, and they are piling inside.

"I'm back here." She gives me a little wave from the back seat and my heart slows that rapid beat it was making because I was sure I was going to have to search her out in the cemetery, start weaving through the crowd screaming I can't find my crazy grandma.

"When did you climb into the back?" I ask her. I hope

nobody saw Nana Nisee with her butt in the air baby-crawling over the seat and belly-flopping into the back because that's how I imagine she did it.

"There was a man looking at your jeep."

"What?" I snap to attention. "Who?"

"I couldn't see him well. I was asleep back here. I just heard him snap his umbrella and woke up. Here." She hands me up a yellow tissue. "You need this." I take it, swipe it across my nose. "He threw something in the window and on to the floor. Pop, pop, pop."

I look at Nana Nisee. Then I keel over to the right and peer to the darkness of the dirty floor of the passenger side of the jeep. Something shines copper-colored on the floor. I reach down, scoop up three empty spent ammo shells in my palm. They are identical to the shells I pick out of Pop Pops .38 caliber gun when we target practice behind his house.

"You don't know who it was?"

"No."

"He just tossed these in the window?"

"Then he walked away."

"Was he big or little?"

"I don't know. I told you that, Jenny. I have to pee."

I wiggle the shells in my hand, then open my purse, toss them inside. Why would someone throw empty gun shells in my jeep? I don't know. I only know I'm reeling over Trevor and I wish I wasn't. How can I detest him so much and miss him so much at the same time?

Chapter 29

It's warm in Pop Pop's kitchen while I rub the water off the last dish from the sink with a raggedy, polka-dot dishtowel and set it in the wooden cabinet. It's six o'clock Friday evening. I just changed into one of the outfits Taylor picked out for me at the mall, a slinky black dress that barely makes it halfway down my thighs, but she says will sell houses like *all get out* and get me laid on a date if I want. And I've got a date with Theo. I'll be sneaking out soon. He's picking me up at *my* house. I hadn't wanted my two worlds to collide. I suppose they are whether I want them to or not. I'm hoping the dim light of evening will hide the paint chipping off my porch and the railing that's broken. I'm going to park my jeep so it hides the dead lawnmower sitting in the driveway with knee-high grass growing around it.

I suppose I'm a bit nervous about the date. I'm not really excited. It's not like I'm looking for a husband or anything, but Theo's been avoiding me since I called him my boyfriend at the ballfields. I don't even think Lissette asked him to do anything that day. It was just an excuse to untangle me from any relationship he thought I might believe we were working on. He reminds me too much of the bland reporter on the six o'clock news. But I'm thinking bland is better than bad boy which is what I usually gravitate toward. That certainly hasn't worked for me. Never-the-less, with a bit of anxiety, I curled my hair. Then I straightened it. I put on makeup, then I put it on thicker. Red lipstick to peach and back to red again. I got dressed a half hour early, so I am puttering around anxiously doing stuff I don't usually do like washing and drying tonight's supper dishes. But it's the only room not full of grandparents, aunts, uncles, and cousins. Even the back porch beside the kitchen is full of my aunts playing a loud game of cards on one of Pop Pop's foldup poker tables.

I suppose worrying about a date is better than thinking about Trevor being dead. It's all I can think of, that empty space that was still kind-of there for the last five years and now it's back and gone in a different way. It's like stuck in my brain like whatever is stuck in my window air-conditioner that goes around and around in the fan and makes a droning *bang-ponk-bang-ponk* hum all night until my head whirs.

I turn, take a breath and try to *not* think about Trevor. But I also don't want to listen to the chatter in the living room about rumors the mayor has been offering money for a couple of my uncle's houses. I eye Nana Nisee sitting just outside the kitchen in the living room watching TV with some of my cousins. She happens to turn my direction, looks at me. I look at her. We share a smile.

Today is Pop Pop's birthday so I have to do something other than sit around and stare at the TV and pretend I'm watching it because I can't help but wonder—is Trevor really dead? Pop Pop's birthday was a good excuse to have everybody over and as my Uncle Zach says: *get my sorry ass out of the house and do something to help somebody out because Pop Pop's done nothing but help me.* I know everybody's tiptoeing around the whole thing and then this thing with Nana Nisee because they think I'm a good girl for once in my life. I'm not sure if I am or not if it was Nana Nisee who lied. There was no way in hell I was going to step up and call her a liar.

Coffee is brewing, and the scent passes me by. There's an overhead light on the ceiling with a thick layer of bugs in the lopsided light fixture. One of the three bulbs is burned out, and the two left leaves a yellow-orange glow to the room. I think it makes it cozy, especially with the window over the sink open. A warm breeze wafts inside carrying the voices of my family. It's after supper, and the lawn chairs come out—a hodgepodge of rusted metal gliders and wrought iron chairs with paint peeling off to ten or so bold, green folding lawn chairs from the 1970s with webbed backs and bottoms.

"Do you think he committed suicide?" Zach sneaks into the kitchen with Beck in tow. He eyes me up and down with a scathing, disproving glare. With almost meticulous precision he sweeps his arm to the refrigerator door and feigns snatching a soda while his huge counterpart leans against the doorframe with a beer in his fist looking back and forth between us like those kitty cat wall clocks with swinging tails and big beady eyes that roll back and forth.

"You didn't kill him or anything, right?" Zach rambles on. "Because I couldn't blame you. That was wrong what he did to you." This youngest uncle of mine has this thing about throwing his questions at whomever he is speaking to all at once when he gets more than one soda in him, so I know to wait until he's finished because I won't get a word in edgewise. "Don't you miss him or anything?" He's like a mad blue jay on steroids. I can imagine him hopping branch to branch, squawking at me. "I figured you would be crying like crazy. Dad says you're acting too quiet. What happens to your car? You got insurance, right? Man, that would be sick if you got stuck with payments on a car that you didn't own anymore." I've gotten used to sorting them out. Sometimes I cull out the most important question and answer it just out of spite so he has to ask the others again.

"The girl who works at the gas station down the street from where Trevor's body was found said he'd been hit by a few trains coming through over the night," I tell him. "He could have been laying there a day or two. It was thirty miles from where he ditched me."

"The cops think you did it, don't they?" The talk of the night has been the newest rumors winding their way from one end of our town to the other about Trevor. "If you stop doing weed, I'll go in and tell them you didn't kill him."

"You're kidding me, right? I'm not haggling over something I don't do in the first place. It would imply I *did* smoke weed." I snap at him. I know he's been dying all night to ask me this. But he thinks I'll lie about stuff if Pop Pop and my aunts ask me about it. I won't lie to him. Pop Pop used to tell us we were like *two peas in a pod,* which means we were always alike. And we are. Most people, they think we're twins we look so much alike and are so close in age. I look over and he's peering over the refrigerator door at me, and for a

195

moment, I do see so much of him in me and me in him.

"Yeah, I'm kidding." He smiles for just a second. "Dad said you got your job back. And you've got a date."

"I did. And I do."

"Are you going out with somebody I know?"

"Nope."

"It's probably a good thing, going out instead of staying around here and listening to everybody talk about Trevor. Does Dad know you're wearing that?" He waves a forefinger at my dress.

"I don't know. I don't care. God, Zach, stop!"

"Can you afford that or did some guy buy it for you?"

"You're calling me a whore; you know that, right?"

"What is up with you?" Zach retorts. I zone him out for at least a minute and a half while I walk around the table and use my palm to swat a kitchen cabinet closed. "Dad's right. You're acting weird. Are you okay to drive? Did you hear what I asked you?"

I didn't. But I sifted through his questions and came up with: "I don't have a clue where Trevor went just like I've told everybody else, Zach. He dumped me and the next thing I know, I stop for gas and the girl at the station tells me they found him dead on the tracks. The guy on the six o'clock news said they checked the surveillance tapes at the gas stations up and down the highway and there's no sign of him getting gas. I know I only had five bucks in the tank and told the police that. I can't sleep at night because it's freaking me out. Now you're freaking me out because I'm sick of talking about it." That's true. I get up and wander the wooden floors up and down, up and down, a restless wreck.

"You don't have to be such a witch about it," Zach sniffs and closes the refrigerator. He starts to leave the kitchen, wags a hand at Beck like he's shooing a dog back out into the living room. "I was just asking. But just so you know, that stupid girl you used to call your best friend—"

"Lila Chambers?" I ask his back.

"Yeah, Lila, the one you caught with Trevor. She was telling Amber Graham at the gas station that after you and Trevor left that party, you went to buy weed at Damon's Bar and Grille off the highway. Somebody saw your car there."

"What?" I ask him. "Somebody saw my car there?"

"You're not buying weed, are you Harley?"

"Get the hell out of here," I hiss at him. "Would you believe the girl who'd been sneak-sexing my boyfriend behind my back for a year over me?" I grit my teeth. "And think about it. It was three in the morning. It was closed."

"There's a hotel next door," Beck announces. "People take their parties to a room. Just saying." Zach passes him. Beck says he's going to grab some chips from the cabinet. "He just cares about you, Harley," Beck apologizes for my uncle whose shadow has left the room. I know that. That's why I didn't show him the three spent shells I put in the drawer of my bedside stand that were dumped in my jeep at Trevor's funeral.

"He cares about his reputation," I correct him. "And don't say it, Beck, that *my reputation precedes me*. I heard that enough from my teachers in high school before they even knew me. I was bagged and tagged the second I sat down in their classroom. I'm not a complete train wreck."

"I wasn't going to say that." He pushes away from the wall and makes his way to the cupboard and opens the door. "Don't put words in my mouth. He does care about you." He grabs an entire family-size bag of potato chips in his hand and closes the door behind him. Beck is facing me, looking down while I look up. "Now, did you find out anything else about the tunnel?"

"No."

"That was fun the other day." He starts to turn, and I roll my head back.

"Wait. I did." I wait for him to stop and turn back around. "I found a newspaper article that related there were fifteen men killed in the tunnel and they only pulled the guards out dead. They spelled his name wrong in the paper. It was B-R-E-N-D-W-I-N-E," I spell out for him. "The sixteenth person was a woman."

"Minnie Bean?"

"Yes. I'm not sure the reason she was in there. Hans Branntwein was killed in the tunnel like the sign said."

"Amazing." He's got a twinkle in his eye like Pop Pop's cat gets when he wiggles a piece of tuna fish above his head. Now I know why Pop Pop likes to spoil his cats.

"You think so?"

"Yeah, I keep wondering what else we don't know." *We.* Does he mean *him* and *me?* He wiggles the potato chips, peers over his shoulder. The canned laughter on the TV is followed by the laughter of my family. "Why are you looking at me like that?"

"Nobody else ever wants to hear this stuff. I can't tell if you're really yawning inside and just trying to be polite."

"Test me."

"Test you?"

"Tell me something more."

"Okay," I say slowly as if he is actually doing the testing. "I know Hans Branntwein was living in Virginia when he was thirteen or fourteen. Confederate guerillas burned the house he was living in. He was what we call gifted, I think now. He was figuring out formulas for using nitroglycerin to blow up bridges for the southern troops. I found where nitroglycerin wasn't used much in the U.S. until a couple years after the war."

"This was in the newspaper?"

"No." I'm mentally kicking myself for divulging the information. "Just books and stuff."

Zach yells at him from the backyard. It echoes through the kitchen window. "See, I didn't yawn. I want to know more. Don't keep me in the dark." He walks over to the sink, leans over and yells to Zach he'll be out in a second. Then he turns to me. "That guy you're going out with tonight, he's nice, right?”

"No, he's a serial killer," I say matter-of-factly. "Girls mostly with blonde hair and blue eyes. He cuts them up into little pieces and feeds them to his dogs. Like Zach says, I date crappy guys. And dating's getting boring because, well, you can only date so many craps. I thought I'd spice it up a bit, take it to the next level."

"That's not funny, you know that, right?"

"And it isn't any of your business, Beck," I say, "who I date. Unless, of course, you want a piece of this—" I wave my hands in front of me. "Then we'll talk."

"I'll pass." He just turns and steps through the metal doorway between kitchen and back porch. I hear my aunts greet him. He flirts them up a second, then his voice fades away. I'm standing there staring at the empty space where Beck was and feeling like I just got snubbed by the popular girl at her birthday party. He hurt my feelings. I'm insulted. Then the waft of cigarette smoke slips to my nostrils along with the hint of freshly mowed lawn as he leaves.

I hear crickets and laughter and the sound of someone opening a bottle of beer. I take this all in with an appreciation that I know surpasses most of the people my age because they never left *home* and didn't have a point of no return. Most of them are sitting around complaining about how boring it is right now and making excuses to leave because their kids are tired, or they've got to work in the morning. I just want to put the scene on hold and let it sit in front of me like one of the Norman Rockwell paintings in Pop Pop's book he has for reading material sitting in a little basket by the toilet in the bathroom. Maybe it isn't the typical, middle-class family displayed in his art, but it's my family, eclectic and probably a little backward in most people's eyes, but that's good enough for me.

I hear Pop Pop laugh, and it makes my tummy jump. I love him so much. I suppose life will go on without Trevor. It already is. My grandpa has this idea he's going to get a team together for something the regional tourism has put together—the Brandy Mountain Classic Big Ball Tournament. I can hear him trying to talk a couple old guys into playing just outside the window while they sit in the evening sunshine and sip beers and smoke cigarettes like old ladies at a country club swimming pool. They are chuckling and joking while I lean into the window to listen.

"You're an old man. You've just got to get that in your head, boy," one of the old guys says to Pop Pop. "Look in the mirror. You ain't twenty no more." I just imagine a bunch of old guys hobbling around the bases and the score on the board being like a hundred and twenty to one and certainly not in their favor. I guess the old men with Pop Pop are thinking the same thing too. I peer out the window, see Pop Pop with this funny twist to his lips like he's hurt they think he's an old man. He doesn't see the score on the board being so lopsided in his own mind.

"Do you have a boyfriend yet, sweetie?"

I jump, startled, and turn. I didn't realize the door between kitchen and back porch stayed open. I sigh and walk toward it, stop at the doorway facing the card table. I take in the faces looking up at me curiously. I've got three aunts and a couple cousins settling down to play cards. They spend more time gossiping than playing cards. While I was washing dishes, I heard Josie King, the 24-year-old wife of 54-year-old Ted Blessing who owns Blessings Grocery and Quick Gas in Baker is pregnant with twins. Ralph Edmonton is going to open a flea market in the abandoned used–car sales parking lot across the street. Gabe's Pizza is going to start carrying beer, which is pissing off my Aunt Rita who is Presbyterian.

"No, I—"

"She don't need no man around, Kimmy," My Aunt Penny rolls her eyes, reaches up and adjusts the bun on her head. "She's a college girl. She don't need no man around. What would she need a man around for? You heard what that Trevor boy did to her, right? No wonder he's dead. Probably ticked off some girl."

"Hush now," another aunt scolds them. "Let's not speak

ill of the dead."

"She needs a man around, just not that kind of man."

I groan inwardly while my gaze goes from one head of hair to the next, all dyed different shades of blonde to cover the grays and they discuss my critically flawed love life. Then I hear footsteps and look behind me to see my Pop Pop giving me a hard stare from the opening between kitchen and living room. He's got on his signature flannel shirt, faded blue jeans and brown, leather boots. His thick, gray hair is askew which can only mean he has been rolling his hand through it recently, a nervous gesture he uses when he is going to confront someone. I assume it is me right now because Zach mentioned my outfit to him.

"Phone's for you, Harley." Even he calls me Flea most of the time. I blink at him, tip my head. He only calls me Harley when he's irritated at me.

"Who is it, Pop?" I furrow my brow. He doesn't answer, just shakes his head.

"Baby, don't make no more mistakes."

When I push the phone to my ear, all I hear is a dial tone. "There's nobody on the phone. Who was it?" I ask Pop Pop's back while I ease around the corner of the kitchen. He is already almost out the door to the back porch.

"It was that boy."

"What boy? Max?"

"I think it was the other one." He is stepping out of the back-porch door. I follow him, round the card table, and catch the door almost closing in my face.

There are six or seven of my family sitting at a picnic table. "Dad," Zach is settled in a foldup chair. He leans over and pushes his elbows on knees. His voice is low. "The other one would be Trevor, and he's kind of dead."

Pop Pop stops there halfway down the three steps and looks up like he's thinking about the question. Then he shrugs his shoulders and holds his hands out to his sides. "Don't know. I could never tell those two boys apart."

Chapter 30

"You're quiet. Are you having fun?"

Theo and I are settled into a shadowy corner at Jose Mina's. It is a small table with a window view overlooking the mountains. It is THE MOST EXPENSIVE restaurant in a three-hundred-mile radius. I know this because I looked it up on my phone in a stall of the women's restroom when we got there. The reviews had five stars. The price range had five dollar signs. I about died trying to figure out how I am going to make a hundred bucks to pay for my meal.

Pop Pop slipped a twenty-dollar bill into my hand when I left his house. Well, he gave it to Beck to give to me because Nana Nisee needed help getting to the upstairs bathroom because someone was in the downstairs bathroom. He'd stopped me getting out of the driveway by patting the hood, then shoving the twenty dollars at me. "Your Pop Pop sent this. He said to be careful—" Beck had stopped. "No, I lied. I'm saying be careful." He drummed the window when I started to back up again. I was still a little saucy over his snubbing *I'll pass* remark. "You're like a sister to me." He stopped once more. "No, I didn't mean that."

"Like a niece?" I'd corrected him like I always did when he called Zach my brother.

"No, not that either. I don't know. You look pretty tonight. I mean, you look pretty all the time." I'd brushed his words away with a roll of my eyes. "Even when you're wearing those fuzzy pajama pants things. Not all women do, you know."

"I don't know if it is more insulting that you feel like you have to tell me I'm pretty to apologize or—" He's an ass. I hate buff guys. "—I don't know. You just rub me the wrong way. Get your hands off my jeep."

I still snatched the money from his fingers. It was at the stop sign I paused long enough to shove the twenty in my purse. Beck had also slipped me a dollar next to Pop Pop's twenty, and I thought it was one of my uncle's friends' weird jokes I don't understand. But he'd scribbled: *If the guy's a jerk, here's my number.* And he'd put his cell phone number on it like Pop Pop didn't already have it on his phone that I'm borrowing.

I drove off, though, feeling a lot less pretty and self-confident than I started. And it wasn't like I was at an all-time high on the pretty and poised chart before I left. It isn't getting better sitting across the table from Theo. I've got twenty-nine dollars and fifteen cents that I owed Max stuffed in an envelope in the front of my purse. I don't even think I can buy a water here for that much.

"You know, I don't do that usually," Theo pipes up while we're staring at our menus.

"You don't ask women out?"

"No, um, what we did in the bathroom at the office."

"Well, I don't either. We were drunk." I try to focus on his face. This is an awkward conversation. "You didn't ask me out because you felt obligated to do it, did you?"

"Of course not. You're beautiful. I'm surprised somebody hasn't snatched you up and put a ring on that finger." He stops, and his eyes get wide. "Oh, yeah, I guess they did. You mentioned that in your speech at the seminar." He swallows hard, looks at the ceiling. "Sorry, I shouldn't have brought that up. Do I say that I'm sorry for your loss if you haven't gone out with him in five years? I don't know. I'm rambling."

"No, that's fine. It isn't a big deal. I'm trying to move on." I think I would have sunk into the floor if Theo hadn't bumped his water with his elbow and spilled it all over the table. He jumps up, and I jump up as it spills over the edges. Then we both laugh right then.

"Maybe we could call it a clean slate," he says, waving his fingers over the white linen tablecloth that is now soaked in water. "We'll start fresh and pretend you didn't tell the entire regional realty association that your best friend didn't steal your boyfriend. And I just didn't show how much of a klutz I am. You're absolutely gorgeous in that dress."

While the waiter sops up the water and I soak up Theo's compliment, I feel Pop Pop's phone vibrate in the purse in my lap. I ignore it while Theo orders us each a glass of wine and they reissue dry menus. I want to assume it is one of my aunts calling Pop Pop, but I'm not sure they call him much. He hates talking on the phone.

"You mind if I get this?" I ask Theo by the fifth round of calls, and I snatch it out to the bobbing of his head.

"Is this Harley Davidson?" The desperate voice on the other end sounds just like Max's sister, Ashley. I work up an *uh huh* knowing she has to recognize my voice and she says: "We can't find Max. I called your grandfather's house in Lost Hollow, and he gave me this number. You're not with him, right? You haven't seen him, right?"

Ashley and I have a bit of a history. She's one year and one month older than me and Max, and now, she's a third-grade teacher at Brandy Mountain Elementary School. But back when we were younger, she did everything she could to keep me away from him. She said it wasn't normal for a guy to have a girl*friend*. But it really goes back to middle school, and I cracked a joke in the lunchroom about how stuck up she was. I pretty much wrote myself off as being popular that day. It was probably enough punishment that she bawled her eyes out and I got sent to the office. But, no. She spent the rest of our school years together finding small, but scorching, ways to burn me in return.

"I haven't seen him in a week. The last I saw him, we passed out flyers about Trevor. I didn't even see him at the funeral."

"Oh, God, he's in a bad way right now. He's not been right since they found Trevor—you know, um, dead. You're not lying, are you?"

"I've got no reason to lie."

"Yeah, that's not what I heard."

"Are you suggesting I did something to Trevor and now, your brother? You're nuts. Whatever rumors you've heard flying around, I can scatter to the wind in less than four words—*I didn't do anything*. And let me give you a bit of advice, Ashley. As my Pop Pop always tells me: it is easier to catch flies with honey than swatting at them. Get it? If not—" I hang up the phone, shove it back into my purse. When I look up, Theo's got a lopsided grin on his face.

"Lissette's right," he says. "You don't take crap from anybody. You've got a good thing going there. You look soft and sweet and vulnerable on the outside. And in here—" He reaches out, pokes my head with his finger. "You're one tough cookie."

Tough cookie. Damn, he sounds like Pop Pop. I tug my eyes away to the sound of my phone again. "I wish that was true," I give him a half-smile. "If it was, I wouldn't be answering my phone again."

This time, Ashley is blubbering. I can hardly understand her. "Harley, please. I'm so scared something happened to him just like it happened to Trevor. If you know where he is, please tell me. Just tell me he's alright if he doesn't want to talk to me. He was acting weird and stuff tonight—"

When Max was thirteen, his mom left one Sunday afternoon with Max in tow. Nobody knew what happened for the next three weeks until they landed for a short time in Lansing, Michigan. I remember our preacher told us to pray for the family at church. It was only a week after, we found out Annie Matthews-Branntwein, his mom, had fallen out of love with Max's dad. She'd fallen in love with a guy she met online. Only a week into her sabbatical, Max's mom called his dad and said Max had run away. She had no clue where he'd gone.

He'd come home. I didn't know Max that well then. He was the new kid, wore expensive jeans, and had city kid looks. But Zach and I were riding bikes from the rundown park at dusk and up along some old ATV trails winding through Lost Hollow. I heard Max had run away or something and there he was sitting on an old park bench. It was almost dark, and I'd circled him twice, then stopped three feet away. "Well, look here. You're a regular Godsend," I'd said in my smart-alecky way with a twist of my shoulders. "At least that's what my Aunt Ruth said." She did. She said it would be a Godsend if he'd come home. Preacher Oakley is the same minister for the Brandy Mountain Holy Community Church. He'd have a service at ten o'clock up on the mountain and come down to Lost Hollow for an eleven o'clock service at New Grace. When Max and his mom left, he asked us to pray for them.

"What?" He'd looked up at me, and I'd blinked in shock as I took in his beat-up face in what was left of the sunshine peeping over the mountain. "I can't go home like this. I left. My dad probably doesn't want me home." I'd never seen a kid beat up before; I lacked for words. Pop Pop didn't even whip Zach when he almost caught the kitchen on fire with a bottle rocket. But Max Matthews-Branntwein had two black eyes, a fat lip, and was holding his arm hard at his waist.

"Well, of course, he does," I had told him. "He came to our church Sunday with the preacher and asked us to pray you'd come home. Just so you know, he didn't ask for your mom to come home." For some reason, Max thought that was funny. He'd laughed out loud. I'd laughed with him, then let my bike drop and walked up to him. I started to reach my hand out. I don't know why. It was just the kind of thing I always did to Zach when he was upset, put a hand on his shoulder. But Max slid just slightly to the right. "You think my dad's mad?"

"He didn't look mad at church." I'd shrugged and stepped forward and tried to push my hand on him again. "He just looked sad." And I don't know why, but he let my hand alight on his upper arm. I just laid it there for the longest time, then let my arm slide across his shoulders like we were best buddies forever.

"Don't leave me," he said.

I didn't leave him that evening. I sent Zach to get Pop Pop and then Max's dad drove like a bat out of hell to get him about twenty minutes later.

I suppose that's how Theo drives for me now, taking me to the place I know Max will be—the old Lost Hollow school playground full of a well-worn tornado slide, a lopsided merry-go-round, a couple teeter-totters and a swing set. Sure enough, Max is sitting alone on a raggedy bench. I make a slow push of my door, walk the expanse and plop down next to him. "Can I tame the wild puppy?" I ask him. He doesn't look right. It's the same kind of stance he had the night he came home nearly fifteen years ago.

"Who's that?"

I follow his gaze to Theo trying to appear he's texting someone in his car. He's not. There isn't service here. "My date. Can you hang on? I'm going to tell him I'm fine. He can go. You can give me a ride home later." He tries to stop me, send me on my way. I walk to Theo's car and give him a weird punch on the arm when he rolls down the window.

"I don't know why I did that," I apologize, feel my face turn red. "You mind if I cut out? He was Trevor's best friend. He doesn't need to be alone. It's kind of hitting him hard."

"I get it."

"Can I pay you back by treating you to that cute little restaurant a block down from the office? You know, the one on the corner that smells like steak when we pass?"

He chuckles. "Bud's Hamburgers?"

"That's the one."

"Okay, it's a date. And maybe I can still show you some tips on selling houses, right? Let's plan on it."

Chapter 31

Max tells me that if it isn't enough Trevor is dead, Mikayla wiped out two of his credit cards and tried to buy a living room suite with a third one. The bank called him in the middle of the funeral because the credit card monitoring service said they thought someone had stolen the card.

I think Max is going to cry. He doesn't look right. He's antsy but good at wiping sadness away with a grin like a magician performing a magic trick uses a simple sleight of hand to hide a card in his sleeve, fool the crowd.

"You think Trevor's in heaven sipping a Tequila on the beach with a bunch of hot angels?" Max asks suddenly.

"If he managed to get to Damon's bar off the highway with five dollars of gas in my almost empty car tank," I sigh, "he and his dark soul could make it at least above the clouds to bribe some cute cherub to get him the rest of the way there. Lila told Zach that's where he went that night."

"I think Lila's lying."

"There's one way we might be able to find out." I'm still sitting there with my hand on his shoulder. "You want to go for a drive?"

I know why we're pulling into the buckled asphalt parking lot of the bar. I suppose Max knows it too. Trevor's death is like a mystery locked in a suitcase. Someone must have a key to open the latch, expose the truth. Murder or suicide, either seems too unreal. But he's dead, and I want to know how and why and who—maybe if I sweep my hand in the air enough times, I'll catch a bit of the truth in my fingertips and solve the mystery. I tell Max that. He says: "I know, right?" We share a gaze, and then his eyes drop to my dress. He reaches out two fingers and pokes me in the shoulder. "You're dressed too nice for Damon's."

I stop and stare at him. For just a moment in time, I feel that year-old, stale animosity come out toward him. "Tell me something, Max. How many women did Trevor—"

"Don't ask me that." He looks away. "Dammit, Harley, why do you ask me stuff like that?"

"Because I trusted you. Why didn't you tell me?" I make a throaty whisper, stare at the windshield of his truck. I see my reflection. It's a stranger who stares back at me with too-thick makeup, dark eyelashes gunked-up with mascara and cherry red lipstick. Still, my hand is on the doorknob and my heart is laying there between us. "You say I was your best friend. And still, you covered for him. Let me be honest. This is what I'd call a game changer. For the last five years, I've felt betrayed by him and betrayed by you."

"Would you have told *me*?" He says in the quiet air inside the truck. "If you knew it'd kill me to find out some girl had gone out on me—" He stops, looks at the ceiling. "—every frigging weekend. And she said it'd only been once and then it was twice and then you got stuck in that big lie and knew I'd hate you when you found out." He comes to a complete standstill with his words. "My mom left me, Harley," he tells me softly. "You know why? Because I told her the guy she'd left my dad for was a friggin' creep. He was still married when we got to his house. He beat the shit out of me. And still, she picked him over me."

"Is that what this is all about? Your mom again?" I huff and sit back in the seat. "This isn't about you and me and Trevor. Right now, you're talking about every relationship you've sabotaged for no other reason."

"Every good adventure ends when two lovers come together." Max looks at me smugly. "Isn't that what you told me once at the end of one of those stupid, sappy movies you made me watch? You said you kind of hated that part of the movie because all the fun was over and now they ride off into the sunset, have kids, and lead boring lives going to work, coming home, paying bills."

"You're manipulating my words." I snap my head over to Max and push my hand on the knob of the door. I wiggle my foot out, feel it hit the gritty concrete. I scoot out but push my head back in because Max is still inside the truck. "Get your butt out here. I'm not going into this bar dressed like Friday Night at the Trailer Park Barbie by myself." I jab my thumb to a long line of ATVs settled into the curb.

"You don't look trailer park," he grunts, then hops out while I fiddle with the strap on my shoe.

Lester Dunn is leaning on his pool stick at the far end of one of three pool tables in the dingy light of Damon's Bar and Grille. My heart sinks. He lets it swing before he stops it only two inches from my next step.

"Move it, Lester." I hold out my hand, lay it on the pool stick. "I've got no beef with you." I turn my head and watch him lean a little on the stick toward me. He's got a scraggly, brown beard. He's shaved his head, so the lights bounce off the shiny top.

"You hit my dog, almost killed it." He lowers his gaze to me. I see his eyes narrow. He's got bulging muscles with a tattoo of a snake making its round from elbow to thick shoulder. It says: NEVER SURENDER. "Ain't nothing on my property you need. Stay out. Next time, it'll be you that I shoot and not that damn jeep."

"Let her through," Max was stuck in the shadows. Now he's not. Lester takes him in and gets a sudden look of revelation that washes away to wariness. He leans in, gets an inch from my face and growls low on his breath, "That be trouble."

I'm not sure if Lester means me or Max, so I step around the pool stick. "What'd he say?" Max leans forward.

"Nothing." Knowing Max, he thinks my womanly honor is at stake. He's no knight-errant; he lacks an adventurous side for that. But he is what Pop Pop would call a gentleman. He probably believes he must defend me from the evil knight like I'm some pansy princess.

"Just so you know, you should have gotten spellcheck before you had that tattoo drawn on your arm. You do realize the word *surrender* has two 'rs', right?" Lester's leaning hard forward with a snarky twist to his lips and almost falls over when his balance is offset. I see him blink and look at his arm.

I drop my eyes and watch his hand slowly, carefully ball into a fist while he comes close to falling on top of me, I feel the warmth of his shoulder against my left arm.

"You going to hit a little girl in a dress, Dunn?" I hiss in his ear as he leans back to gain some stability. Because I see him arching his elbow, pulling back his arm, and coming just seven inches from my ribs. "In front of all these people?"

Lester Dunn lets a shiver shake his body. He unclasps his fingers. His lip twitches while he stands erect. "You better be watching your back, little girl. There be bad people out there."

Max uses the knuckle of the forefinger on his right hand to launch me forward. I take two steps and feel him nudging until I'm out of the zone of Lester Dunn and nearly pressed up against the counter of the bar.

"Drink?" He grunts into my ear. I don't get to answer before Jake Ringgold, bartender, plops a glass of something slightly brown in front of me. He's only like five feet and three inches, and he almost has to reach to slide the drink across the counter to me. I get the odd feeling they are trying to focus my attention on something else.

"Rum and Coke. Isn't that the usual?"

The usual. "Um. Sure." But I don't pick it up. Instead, I let my fingers play on the glass, lean in, and focus my attention elsewhere. "Was Trevor in here the night he came up missing? That's the only reason I'm here."

"I wasn't working. He's dead. Just let it rest."

"Jake, I've known you since I was in sixth grade." He tried to kiss me on the slide. I pushed him down the little ladder, and he cried. "I let you copy my math test questions." I sigh, look over my shoulder. Lester's talking to someone and his eyes keep straying up to the counter. He keeps

211

rubbing his stupid tattoo. I'm thinking perhaps I shouldn't have pointed out the misspelling.

"You pushed me off the slide. I got a concussion."

"Oh, you remember that?" I give him a playful grin.

"Yeah, Harley," he says. He lifts the hair on his forehead exposing a tiny scar there. "I had to get stitches. Yes, I remember." Now he is looking over my shoulder. "I suggest you and your date go to that upscale bar downtown. This isn't the place for you. We don't want any fights."

"He's not my date." I eye Max who is tugging at the collar of his button up shirt uncomfortably. I'm sure he's wishing he wasn't here with me either. Folks talk. I know he's thinking if word gets around he's downgraded his standards to girls like me, he'll have a whole new pack of women knocking on his door. "I'm not leaving until you tell me. Somebody said Trevor was here. They saw my car."

He knocks over my drink with his hand, pretends to apologize, and then turns around to the sink and snatches up a raggedy, blue towel. This he uses to swipe up the drink while he leans into me, his eyes roaming over my right shoulder. "It's like this. You tell anybody I told you this, I'll deny it. Trevor comes in, and his face is like this deep shade of red, you hear me?" I do. Even over a round of cackling laughter behind me and the music from a bad band. "He was on something. He says: *Where's that dick, Paul Davis? He was supposed to meet me here.* And I have no clue who Paul Davis is, so I'm just staring at him in shock that he's even in here. I'm thinking he's going to pull a gun and rob us or something. He doesn't. Instead, he just starts pacing back and forth. I tell him to get the hell out of here because the bar's closed—" Jake stops. It's almost like he thinks someone is listening or homing in on our conversation. "He stands there for just a second and then completely turns around and walks right out the door. I heard the doors open and close. I rounded the bar quickly to follow up behind him, and I locked the doors. I didn't look outside. I figure he's looking for somebody to buy weed. I don't want the whole lot of them coming in here and busting the place up. I had my music on and didn't hear a thing. Then a few days later, I see he's missing on the news." He eyes me hard. "Now he's dead. I don't want the cops asking about this Paul Davis. If I mention that name and he's some drug dealer or worse, I'm dead."

"I won't tell anybody." I turn to Max. I don't have any money in my purse, save a handful of change. "Max, can you spot me fifty bucks for the drinks?"

"Fifty bucks for a rum and coke?" He's looking around the counter to the empty space in front of me. I glare at him, roll my eyes. "Please. Just give him fifty, we should get out of here."

Max doesn't question me again, instead pulls out his wallet and slaps a handful of ten-dollar bills on the counter. Jake snatches it up in his fist and is tucking it into a breast pocket while we bicker heading toward the doors.

"You don't have to act like I'm some kind of stupid sidekick," Max grumbles when the bar door closes behind us. The music fades away to a low beat and his voice seems loud in the air. "Because honestly, you could have gotten out of there without slipping him cash. Well, *I* gave him money. Besides, everybody was watching. Jake knocked over your drink and didn't even bother to get you another. They knew you were giving him money for something. Who gets a fifty-buck tip for bad service?" I just stare at him, and he shakes his head, nods to his truck. It's parked in front of ATVs that are smooshed in all the way to the corner.

"You know I'll pay you back."

"In nickels and quarters and the other spare change you've got at the bottom of your purse? Don't bother." He starts to follow, and I hold out my hand. "No, don't, Max. I'll get my own door."

He is muttering something when he slides into the seat. I ignore him. He hurt my feelings with his remark about the spare change. He starts the truck, and it makes a throaty grumble. I'm sliding my seatbelt around my waist when I look up to the windshield and the flash of bright lights spraying across the glass.

"What the hell?" I hear Max mutter. His truck is idling, and I can see a glimpse of the big, black and banged-up truck behind the lights blinding us while it eases in reverse and slides beneath a street light. One front headlight is halfway out and makes the truck look like a cat with an eye in half-wink. I remember passing him with Pop Pop when we were going to the store the other night. Pop Pop had said: *That good-for-nothing Dunn boy ain't fixed that light in three years. Take a looky-look, it's half broke. How do you do that?*

"Oh, crap, that's Lester's truck."

"What's he doing?"

Lester pops his head and his left arm out of the driver's side window and flips his middle finger into the air toward us. While I blink, he slides back inside, a smile pursing his lips. Then, he pushes his foot to the gas gently and starts to ease forward around the last of six ATVs parked along the curb and out on to the road. "You shouldn't have ticked him off, Harley," Max says. I turn my head toward him.

"You're kidding me, right?" I hiss. "I just pointed out that he had a misspelling in his tattoo."

"Yeah, right. You know, you act like I'm pointing out that you're all feisty like my aunt's little Pomeranian that prances into a room and growls and carries on. Everybody laughs at it. Nobody's afraid," he tells me while he eyes the ATVs to his right to make sure he's got a good, clear distance. "But you like have swagger. You're two inches high like a Pomeranian, but you've got the bluster of a huge Rottweiler."

"What's your point?"

"You need a frigging bodyguard. Because you're like that stupid Pomeranian that thinks he's this big dog. If you're not careful, one day, you're going to get torn up. Because I think guys like Lester see you as a damn Rottweiler, get it?"

"Holy shit." I choke those two words out. I don't get to

defend myself. I look over at Max with a heated stare just as Lester Dunn hits his gas and I watch his front bumper heading straight for us. I suppose the moment I see that old truck lurch forward, I know what he's going to do. He's going to smash into us in that dented, ancient truck that's probably got more metal on it than a coat of armor. It's got a black grille guard on the front that has taken out a dozen deer standing stupidly in the middle of the highway so one more dent when he bashes into Max's truck couldn't be noticed from the rest. And he's going to push us straight into all those ATVs. Then he's going to take off and make it look like Max just rammed into them—

"GO! D—D—DRIVE!" That's what I get to spit out, a half-stutter that ends up with Max tipping his head while I poke my finger into the air above his chest. "Hit the gas!"

There's no time. I know Max, in his harmonious, pampered-pup world, doesn't believe anybody would ever purposely hit somebody with the intent to hurt them. I let the seatbelt slip from my fingers. It slides across my chest in a slow motion while I shove myself over into the center of the seat. I latch on to the steering wheel with both hands, then I tippy-toe to stretch my foot down and press it hard on the accelerator. We screech forward so fast, both of us smash into the back of the seat. But I've still got my foot on the gas, and we make a funky fishtail out into the road until I feel a bump-bump while we bounce across a gentle median rise between the two street lanes.

I hear the crash and crunch behind us, a deep explosion of metal to metal. I snap my neck backward just as the ripping scream of Lester's bumper bursts into the night air while his truck grinds overtop the handlebars of the first ATV and shoves the next three awkwardly sideways into the side of the building.

Max is strangely quiet when he drives me home. Still, he asked if I wanted him to come over and watch some TV together like we used to do. I told him I could for an hour or so. About five minutes before he gets to my house and with a gentle beat of country music playing on his radio, his right hand slips off the steering wheel. He reaches out and lets it settle on my left hand lazily laying on the seat between us. There's this long lull of silence on the radio between songs. I'm self-conscious, and I don't know why. It is clumsy, the air between us like we're two pimpled, usually-dateless, middle-schoolers on a blind date. His fingers are cool against the warmth of my limp hand that doesn't know how to react to him. Then I snatch my hand away, thinking that maybe Max didn't mean to drop his hand there, but he did, and he's not sure if he should leave it or drag it away.

"Were you trying to hold my hand?" I ask him.

"No, I—um, I don't know. Why can't you just be like normal girls and let it go or move over in the seat, Harley?"

I'm not sure what that means. Does he want to hold my hand? And why am I afraid to ask? Oh, because I don't want him to laugh and tell me it was a joke. Because, maybe, I wouldn't mind holding his hand so much. Maybe after a few minutes, I could sidle up next to him, and we could drive around. And what? I'd end up being the next girl on Max's list? All I can think of is to throw the kiss back at him. "You told me to just forget about the kiss. I don't want—"

"Well, the problem is, Harley, I can't forget about the kiss," he almost growls those words while he pulls up to my driveway. "I can't. It won't go away." I am letting them sink in just as he turns into the gravel patch of my driveway. His headlights splash on the back of a car. But it isn't my jeep. It is Mikayla's little SUV. And Mikayla is waiting for him on the front porch, pacing, bouncing up and down and looking sorry and relieved.

We sit there in the truck, silent. I'm not sure what to do. Get out? Stay in?

"I shouldn't have said that. I'm sorry." Max finally breaks the silence. Then he just gets out quickly, walks up to the porch. I do the same, but incredibly slow. I can hear them talking, low voices while I shuffle around and pretend to adjust my dress, pretend to check the back seat of my jeep for something. The low mumblings stop while I'm poking my head through the door. I see a shadow approaching from behind. I lean back, close the door to the jeep. It's Max.

"I guess she wants to *talk it out—*"

I just stand there staring at him, staring at me. I want to tell him we can climb back in his truck, and I'll frigging hold his hand and we don't have to think about the complications, the consequences of that action right now. We'll take it one day at a time. I don't. I see Mikayla prancing off the porch steps like Zach has this happy stride after he's got a buck on opening day of deer season. She's all happy because she's bagged her own deer for the season, Max.

So instead, I nod and try not to think about my lonely laughter bouncing off the walls of my living room, blending with the canned 1980s sitcom laughter. "I know the drill." I force a laugh. I don't know why it sounds almost sad. But I'd watched Max do this a hundred times for me and Trevor. I listen to them drive off when I push the door open wishing he'd just patted my arm and said: *Oh, screw it. She's just using me like the rest of them. I'd rather be hanging out with you and watching old, stupid shows. Hell, I'll even watch something on the history station with you.* But he doesn't. I step inside and walk into the kitchen. My eyes catch on the drawing of the wren on my refrigerator. I walk over and snatch it off, fold it, and carefully place it in the drawer of my bedroom bureau. And I go to bed.

Chapter 32

"Hot damn, that one burned." Taylor stands up and worms her fingers out of her glove, then shakes her hand in the air. "She struck you out, girl. Boom! One, two, three," she tells the girl who is letting the bat swing in front of her legs right now like she is getting ready to putt a golf ball at her feet. "She's either really getting good, or you spend more time sitting on your butt in your office than chasing down bad guys." The batter is giving me a heavy glare. Her name is Tatum, and she's got at least fifty pounds on me, if not more. I didn't really want to get on her bad side because as Taylor implied, she's a probation officer and she is also in the National Guard. But Taylor gave me a wink while she played catcher behind her. I think she knew I was scared of her. She's also being extra nice to me because she heard on the news about Trevor being dead.

"Baby," Taylor goes on. "I think you've got the slider down." *Baby*? She says it like a husband of thirty years sexy-talks his wife into bringing him a beer. "You're halfway there." She tosses the ball over my head to another girl in the outfield. I think her name is Arianna. There are three more just like her that showed up today to *toss the ball around* with us. Every time we come to the field, there are a couple more girls added to the practice field.

"Halfway?" I huff, wagging my shoulder up and down. We're two hours into *tossing the ball around*. I'm sore. "How many damn pitches are there in this game?"

"There are seven," Paula (I don't know her last name) tells me. She used to play softball and soccer with Taylor in high school. Now, she's a high school basketball coach and runs the recreational league basketball for elementary kids. "You know how I know?"

"Because old Coach Dickerson pounded it in our heads," Taylor answers. I look back and forth between the two. I always feel a little like an outsider, even though I know they don't mean to make me feel that way. It's like they have this bond they share from the past, like Pop Pop's old army buddies sit around at the VFW and share and rehash old war stories over and over again. It's like a secret club. Me, I'm the one who hasn't contributed to their memory fund yet.

"She needs to learn the drop pitch," Paula informs us.

"What's that?" I furrow my brow at her.

"You take a shorter stride and the ball kind of drops right before it gets to the batter."

"Okay," I say. "Who wants to get hit first?" They all know what I mean. Because I do a lot of high throws and fence hits and balls that fall flat when I first learn the pitch. They laugh a little and Tatum steps up again to the plate. "I'll do it. I'll make you a deal though. If I hit the ball because you finally did it right, I'll buy a round of drinks downtown. If you hit me, I'll beat the snot out of you, and then you buy the rounds—"

I hit her once. For a probation officer, she's a big baby, and I told her that while she stomped toward the plate like a male gorilla advancing toward another male gorilla who got too close to the first one's mate. I think she expected me to run because she stopped just short of my right tennis shoe and thrust out her chest.

"I'm warning you. I grew up with six boys in my house. *Big* boys." I eye her boldly, stop her with one hand held between us. "I bite. I groin kick. I've got no problems with fighting dirty as hell to get my point across even if it takes wiping a booger on you. I have a signature martial arts strike with the toe of my right foot and then my fist that I learned in one of three Taekwondo classes I took before I quit in middle school. And if I have to, I'll pinch myself and cry to the nearest adult and show them the bruise *you* gave me and who will come to save me because well, I'm small and I have this look—" I stop long enough to work up my other signature move, the *Pop-Pop,-Zach-just-called-me-a bad-word* soppy-eyed gaze, complete with trembling lip. "And I'm not one bit ashamed to use it."

"Jesus!" She hisses loudly and turns to Taylor who is laughing hard at home plate. "Where the hell did you find this little psycho?"

When we get to the bar on the main street of town, Taylor's still giggling about how I managed to *not* get my ass kicked by Tatum Morris. Of course, I'm still buying the drinks, and when a stupid 1970s song comes on the loudspeaker that we both know, Taylor feigns a duet with me. I still almost get my ass kicked. Approximately two minutes into the song, Taylor is leaning hard on me with her arm over my shoulder. We're both being goofy, and I had no clue that Lissette Baker had been standing just within the doorway. I suppose, in retrospect, she'd been giving me more of an evil eye and cold shoulder in passing in the office in the last few weeks.

I had relayed my observation to Taylor who just said Lissette was having problems at home. But if so, when she weaves her way through the tables with great, deliberate strides and her eyes dead set on me hitting a horribly-dog-howling high note, I should have known there was more to the story than what Taylor divulged. Because one second, I am sitting on a rickety wooden barstool/chair, and the next moment, I am laying on the floor in a heap after she rams both her hands into my chest and shoves me over.

"You think you're cute. You're not. I know what you're doing, Harley. I'm going to have your ass."

"Alright, don't know what the hell's going on between you two, but lady, your ass is out of here." That was Tatum who came up and stood atop me like some valiant warrior ready to take on the dark knight Lissette. She didn't need to. Lissette stormed off in a flood of tears, and I sat there on the floor while Taylor helped me up. "She'll get over it."

Chapter 33

I leave not long after with a tissue to a skinny elbow from skidding along the floor. I skip practice with Pop Pop, tell him I feel like I'm getting a cold. I don't. I promised Nana Nisee I'd take her to see Ned. Aunt Rita is watching her at Pop Pop's house, and I just pop in and tell her that Pop Pop said it was my turn tonight. Aunt Rita was more than happy to snatch up her purse and glide out the door before she thought I found out it was a mistake.

"Pretty yourself up, Nana Nisee, we're going to find Ned." Honestly, I'm thinking she's going to give me directions to the cemetery in Guysville because that's where he lives now. Then she'll stand by his headstone and chatter to his ghost because he's probably not real and long-dead. "We've got two hours, give or take, before it gets too dark to play without lights on the field and Pop Pop gets back." Her eyes light up.

But when I park across the street from the little house where he lives in an upscale subdivision, it doesn't look like anybody is home. "Go knock on the door." That's what she tells me, and I'm looking at her in the passenger seat.

"No, *you* go knock on the door."

"No, *you* do it. His family doesn't like me. They'll call the police."

I start to protest. Then I decide I don't want to know what she could have possibly done to make his family shun her. I think she's making it up. "And it's not going to look peculiar for *me* to go up to the door, knock on it, and ask Ned to come out to play?"

"He's probably in bed anyway. He goes to bed early." She looks so glum then, I let my head fall back, then hop out of the car, walk around to her door and open it. "Grandma, you're ninety-five years-old. What could the cops possibly do to you?"

I shamed her enough to get out. She walks up and down

by the car, then we quarrel a little bit before she tells me I'm too headstrong, and she gets back into the jeep. I hop back in too. The squabble continues until I finally hear a rap on the passenger side window. It's partially rolled down, and Nana Nisee is turning her head to look up at the man looking down at her.

"You beautiful ladies lost?" He asks into the tiny frame of space that is open.

"No," I mumble. I lean over Nana Nisee's lap and roll the window down completely. I'm staring up at a gray-haired man, lanky and wearing a nice wind jacket and khaki pants. He's wrinkled and smiling big white teeth. "I mean, no. We're leaving."

"Jenny," my grandma announces, "this is Ned."

Ten minutes later, we're sitting in a pharmacy/grocery store with an ice cream shop dipping spoons into mint chocolate chip ice cream. Ned is retired from the military, fought in Vietnam, and was a medic. He likes to chat. Boy, does he like to talk. Nana Nisee likes to listen. And she hangs on every word he says. They both smile lovingly at each other like two flirty teenagers in a Norman Rockwell soda shop picture.

They also tease me like they are going to kiss over their ice cream and laugh when I say: Please don't do that. Please don't do that—Then as quickly as our fun starts, it must end. Ned has a phone in his pocket, and he pulls it out. "Well, my son realized I'm not there. I'm going to have to bid you two sweet adieus." He kisses Nana Nisee's hand and just stands up and walks out. We watch him go and Nana Nisee smiles softly while he vanishes out the door.

I get Nana Nisee back by nine-thirty and lie to Pop Pop, telling him Aunt Rita had something to do and had to leave. I go home to a quiet house and I dig up the journal. With a cup of hot chocolate, I hunker down on my bed hoping at least Max's Grandpa Hans will keep me company even if he is long dead. I don't want to think about Max's fingers playing on my fingers, push it a bit farther and watch myself sliding over next to him and having things different. I think about Nana Nisee and her Ned, and how she hummed all the way back to Pop Pop's. Then, I sadly fixate on Max's grandpa's life. I think he's lonely and terrified most of the time just like me. I'm not downgrading his involvement in the war. I think he'd have the same feeling of doubts whether he was farming a field or blowing up a bridge.

September 24, 1862

I want to go home. I'm just tired. I'm alone. I've never been by myself. When I was four and scared of the storms, Papa told me to use the numbers in my head to count. Maybe it'd make me feel better. I still count when I'm scared and make up big equations. Sometimes, I pick a number and multiply over and over. Like eight. That's the number today. Eight. Because I did something bad, real, real bad. If the Rebs find out, I'm a dead man. Bad Bill made them boys dig five holes, seven feet deep, and just wide enough for a man to stand inside with arms at his side. He said they were for privies. But we all knew he was going to shoot them. They knew because I heard a couple of them praying and Bad Bill had me cleaning the guns and loading them up on a rotten log.

I asked Irish if he was scared. He gave me a quote straight from the Bible that he said his mama used to tell him: "But those who hope in the Lord will renew their strength. They will soar on wings like eagles; they will run and not grow weary, they will walk and not be faint." I thought about it a moment and said: "Isaiah 40:31" He asked me how I knew that off the top of my head. I said I told you I was smart. Everything I read sticks in my head like ice to a tin bucket full of water in January. He said if I was so smart, maybe I could find a way to keep them from dying. I was all snotty and told him I'd already been doing that. I'm tired of it.

Hayward was begging me to do something, hopping up and down from foot to foot and rubbing his arms. He always gets goosebumps when something bad is going to happen. He said his mama used to tell him that goosebumps meant someone was walking over your grave. I don't know so much about that, but I had a bad feeling too. Bad Bill got drunk and had Hayward tie kerchiefs around the prisoners' eyes. There were five of them: My Irish (I call him that because he's my first Irish prisoner), Teddy Murphy who is chubby and has one eye that's white like a boiled egg, a boy they called BoBo who is tall and skinny, Sully (Callen O'Sullivan is his name and he's meaner than hell to me).

"Callen O'Sullivan," I whisper. I wondered if he was related to Beck in some way. I suppose the name isn't uncommon. The odds would be slim. I read on, letting that lay in the back of my mind, thinking I might text Beck and ask him if he knew if he was related to Callen O'Sullivan. Of course, after our last conversation, maybe not.

He looks like Irish with red hair and freckles all over his arms and face, and Sean Kelly (they call him Preacher like it's his name. He's part black and part white like Hayward. He's real quiet and wants to be a preacher). Hayward was crying outright, and it was only making Bad Bill more pissed. I told him that he was seventeen and was being a baby, and he better shut up or we'd all get killed. I told him not to get attached to the Yanks. They all had lice anyway. But even while they were digging their graves, Sean Kelly and My Irish were talking to him, being nice, and telling him it was going to be okay. Then Bad Bill got mad about something and started shooting at those Bluebellies like he was shooting rats in the barn and shot one in the hand. Hayward was jumping up and down and I told him Bad Bill was going to shoot him too.

Hayward's gotten attached to them like one of the chickens he had at the farm, mostly the one called Preacher. He's been feeding the boys his ration of hardtack. Then he made me feel guilty, so I gave them half of mine. Bad Bill just laughed while he was shooting. He said Hayward was just dirt and he'd shoot him too. I think he was just lucky he got a shot at all at Bobo he was so drunk.

I'm not so big on grown men crying, but that boy he shot, he started crying for his mama. I could hear Irish telling him that old bible verse over and over like it'd been stuck in his head since he told me it. Bobo's only sixteen with orange peach fuzz cheeks and still can't grow a beard, I think. I can hear him saying he wants to soar with the eagles, but he's still scared and he ain't going to be able to because he's going to die today. And Irish says, just keep thinking about the eagles. It made me feel bad. I stood up and drew a line in front of me, pointed at it with my finger. I said to Bad Bill: "I'm gonna draw a line. If you stay on the other side of the line, I'm alright with it. If you cross it, we're gonna have words." He just laughed and kicked me down with his boot. I rose up, told him. "If that's what you want, trouble, then you got trouble."

I held out my arms in front of Bad Bill. I told him he wasn't going to shoot any more of the boys because the general said he couldn't, and besides, they were my prisoners because I caught them, and I had a say in when they'd die. He'd have to shoot right through me if he was going to shoot them. And if he shot through me, General Lee would shoot through him. I'm the only one who can read the sheets on how to mix the explosives and I'm the smartest one in a thousand-mile radius, so good luck finding some other like me amongst all these pie eaters. He hit me once in the chin, almost knocked me out, and I got up. He hit me six more times when I got up each time and held my arms out and until I was lying in a ball on the ground with blood spurting out my nose and mouth and my glasses broke to pieces. I thought of my papa and when I looked up at Bad Bill, all I could see through my anger and my eyes was this big brown thing that looked like a giant turd. I just wanted to die. I knew if I did, nobody'd miss me really. Nobody knew I was alive. Papa was dead, and I had nobody at all. I had nothing to lose.

I could hear all the Yanks yelling and giving him hell. Bad Bill says: "You get up one more time, boy, and you're dead." I pushed myself up on my knees, then dragged myself to my feet. I kind of wavered there like skinny maple sapling in a *hard wind. I did it again with my middle finger waving in the air. This time each time he hit me, I placed myself so I was getting closer to the guns I was cleaning. I hated Bad Bill. I hated that brown turd so bad. The eighth time I went down, I came up with a gun and shot him underneath the chin. His arms just flapped out to his sides, and he fell straight back dead. Then the eight other men in Bad Bill's irregulars started yelling at me and trying to shoot me with their guns that weren't loaded. If it wasn't for Hayward telling me what directions to shoot, I'd be dead. But I killed all Bad Bill's men too. I just stood there when I was done and made a circle looking around at all the bodies, and I told Irish: "Why'd you put that stuff in my head about soaring with eagles, for God's sake?" They started laughing it up like it was the funniest thing on earth. I hear Hayward say: "Oh, no, Pony's gonna swoon." And he was right. Everything went black and oozy. I just fainted and fell flat on my face like I was deader than a doornail. Now, they are dead. Eight men dead—Lemuel Price, William Wykoff, Ellis Thomas. I don't know the last names of the rest. I killed them. But Irish, maybe now he can go back to soaring with the eagles.*

"Cripes," I whisper to myself while I stare at a website I pulled up on my phone a few minutes later that holds a federal database of soldiers during the Civil War and displays the names of the men Hans listed. Sure enough, they are all listed as starting out in an Alabama Infantry and were among the dead around September 26th, 1862. "He really killed them. God, and he's only fourteen." I'm laying propped up in bed with knees bent and the journal resting between belly and legs. I'm thinking when I was fourteen, the worst thing I did was get caught skipping school to go sledding on Potters Hill at the cemetery.

But I'm more hooked on the journal than I am on my favorite new show on TV. Page by page, I take in the life of Hans Branntwein. I found out that Hayward was the son of a slave named Clarissa and a man named Benjamin Jackson, who owned the farm where Hans worked. It was a place called Scuttle Creek in Wythe County, Virginia. They were close like Zach and me, like brothers. Benjamin Jackson had left to fight with Confederate forces in July 1861, the 4th Virginia Volunteer Infantry Regiment. Only two months later, the battle would be in his backyard and his home burned to the ground. It wouldn't have mattered to Lieutenant Benjamin Jackson. He had died from an infection just two inches above his left knee only two weeks after leaving home and from a bullet that had barely grazed his skin two-hundred miles away at the Battle of Bull Run.

I look at the clock on my wall. It is eleven-thirty. I am not going to sleep. I sigh, turn the page, and read on—

September 30, 1862

I'm sitting in a tree writing this. Irish showed me how to climb up and hold on with my arms and legs so I don't fall. He said he thinks it's funny that a kid has never climbed a tree. He didn't know any boys that didn't know how to clamber up by the time they were three or four. (I think that's what he said. He's difficult to understand with his heavy drawl). Irish told me I could climb any tree I wanted. He said boys should be climbing trees anyway and not juggling black powder and lighting fuses to break up bridges. Bad Bill wouldn't let me climb trees. Or write in my journal. He'd always say: "What are you writing about me?" And I would say: "There is a man named Bill. He was a great, great man." I don't think he believed me. One time I hid in the brush, he was going to whip me with a willow twig. I stayed there for most of the day, and he whipped Hayward with a willow twig until I came out. Then, he whipped my legs until they bled rivulets down my shins. I still have the scars between my knees and ankles. My Irish said I could do anything I wanted if I followed two rules— don't make him mad and stay out of his way when he was drunk. Then he asked me if I was staying or going. I said I was going. I wasn't sure what side I was on.

I'm a Yank now, at least for the time being. I don't reckon I want to be. But I don't want to be a Rebel either. I want to be between. After I killed Bad Bill, I thought I'd go back home. Hayward didn't want to go with me. My Irish convinced him that although he's black, he can be a soldier with the Yanks and fight and such. They have special troops for colored people, and he could help him find one. He wouldn't just be stuck getting buckets of water for the horses. He could have a real gun and shoot the Rebels. I said I was going to leave thinking Hayward would follow, but he didn't. He wanted to fight, so he didn't have to spend his life like his mama did, kowtowing to some man. I got halfway down the road, and I don't even know which way is north or south. I couldn't find home for nothing. I was alone, and I cried. I killed so many men, ain't nobody going to take me in, not even God into heaven. I went back to the place where I killed Bad Bill and I told My Irish's boys to get and go. I was going to lay out the men and all the explosives and blow them to the sky, so nobody knew what I did. And I did. We weren't five minutes into talking when a bunch of Rebels came riding past to see what all the explosions were. They thought there was another battle. Then they saw My Irish and his men and got all funny, took out their guns. I handed them a paper with my directions on setting up a fuse for the gunpowder explosives and hoped none of them could read. "These are my orders to take these men to the proper place. You boys got to understand that if I don't get them there, they ain't the only ones gonna get hanged." I told them these boys were prisoners and I was escorting them to General Hiram Bentley in Packton per his orders right there. I just stopped to pee. Three of them passed the paper back and forth and stuck it under noses. Then one said. "It sure does say that."

After they left, I said: "I'm spending an awful lot of time keeping you alive, Irish. Can't you do it yourself for a while?"

"I don't think so, Pony. Why don't you ride with us for a

while? I'll watch over you. You can burn more stuff up if you want. I'll even put one of our tattoos on your wrist. You can be one of us." I told him I didn't believe in tattoos and I asked him why he calls me Pony, and he says because I ride a pony. Them Irish boys, they've got no imagination.

October 5th, 1862
I got to burn up more bridges. Sully is Irish's best friend. He says they grew up together on the same island and their families came here together just like Papa brought me. He's got ginger-colored hair like Irish and has freckles. He's always wrestling with Irish and playing jokes on him like putting snakes in his blanket and such. Sully says I like to blow things up too much and I look like an ugly, baby frog with the glasses Irish pulled off a dead Rebel for me to replace my broken ones. They are way too big, he's right. He gives me angry eyes if I sit within an arms-length of Irish. Sully comes and sits down between me and Irish and shoves me on the ground. Irish just laughs. I got mad and put a worm in Sully's coffee. He doesn't like me much. He's always pointing to the horizon and telling me to go back to being a Rebel so he can shoot me the right way instead of when I turn on them all and kill them in their sleep. Two times in the last week, Irish has sent me and him out to find some food and Sully tells me to sit somewhere and watch for a rabbit to come and he leaves me. I do sit there like he says because I don't know if they're going to start beating me like Bad Bill. Then Preacher comes to find me about dark and walks me back to camp. It was cold tonight. I need something more than a cotton shirt and a pair of shoes that are three sizes too big that I took off a dead Yankee. I wish my papa was alive to take care of me.

October 15th, 1862
We ended up tagging along with the volunteer infantry. Bobo got a fever, so we stopped long enough to rest. We were somewhere near Richmond, Virginia. I got bored

sitting at the fire and followed a couple soldiers who were sneaking out to town. There was a big house along the main road, and it looked like the folks who lived there left in a hurry, so we went inside, and everybody started rooting through all the drawers and cabinets for stuff to steal. I watched one soldier walk out with a whole bread bag full of silverware. There was a fiddle on the wall, and I wanted it so bad. It was like the one my papa showed me how to play. I climbed up on the piano and got it down. Just as I slid off the keys, this man as big as a bear took it right out of my arms because I was holding it so tight. I wouldn't let it go and he picked me up and just dashed me to the floor. The next thing I know, Irish is picking me up by the collar of my shirt and said: "Where the hell have you been? You don't run off like that." I told him I could do whatever the hell I wanted to do. He wasn't my papa. He didn't say anything and got this look in his eyes like my papa did when I talked back to him. Then the man with the fiddle said something and Irish got mad. Then he said to me: "You leave now, Pony. I'll take care of this." I didn't want to go because I knew he was going to get beat up by that bear. But I nodded, and I left and hid for a while because I thought he'd beat me like Bad Bill used to hit me. Then I went back to the fire like Irish told me to do and sat down. Everybody said: Irish is looking for you and he's mad. Where'd you go? When the moon was just sliding across the sky, I look up from the fire and Irish comes out of the shadows, and he's beat to hell. But he hands me the fiddle and says: "So you wanted it so bad, you know how to play the damn thing?"

And I said, "Yeah, I know how to play it." I played songs way into the night. Everybody sang. Some boys got on drums. And Irish, he smiled for the first time. I decided I'm not going back home so it won't matter if I have a tattoo or not so Irish is putting one on my wrist in the morning. He wants to make a big thing out of it, I suspect.

I skim through a bunch of pages and six or seven months of entries:

When I came back this time, Hayward was gone for good. He said he's joining up with a new infantry starting: the 5th Regiment United States Colored Troops. As soon as Lincoln said the slaves in the north were free last September, he's been trying to get recruited in the new colored regiments. He says they are recruiting black soldiers and starting their own troops to fight. He'd be sitting with me and watching them march past and some of them wearing uniforms and looking important. I saw the look in his eyes, all dreamy and imagining he was one of them. Then I'd nudged him with my elbow. "You know, when the Rebels catch them men, they just kill them. It's not like the white soldiers." He just nods at me and says he knows and it doesn't matter. He said I wouldn't understand because even if the war ends and the Rebels win, I can just walk off and do what I've always done. Not so for him and all the blacks. I told him he was wrong. I could never go back to being who I was—a nothing and a nobody. Hayward didn't listen. He said I'm spoiled and would always be spoiled. He said I needed to be with my own kind and I was safe with Irish. He needed to be with his own kind. I told him I'd rather be with him and not be safe. But Hayward shook his head and told me I'd stick out like a white dot in a sea of brown just like he stuck out now. It just can't be anymore. He wanted to be a part of them. It was right after the 1st Kansas Infantry at the Battle of Island Mound helped the Union win the battle. That's all he'd talk about. I know he's wanting me to say: "Go, I don't need you anymore. Everybody that's tied us together is dead. You don't have to protect me like you think you have to protect me." I don't. So, he sticks with me, and I stick with Irish. Maybe that's a little selfish on my part. But I don't care. I'm not good at losing people. I still ask if anybody knows Asa. I didn't realize until the day I almost died that I wasn't just holding back Hayward. I was holding back his spirit. Then, Minnie Bean came along, and it all went to hell.

March 8, 1863

I have been sick with fever. Irish was gone and left me with Sully. He came back and brought me a present. It was a little wooden box with two marbles and a couple soldiers inside. I wrapped them in a piece of blanket to keep them from banging around—

June 1863

Yesterday I had to go get Irish because he went home to see his wife's grave. She died of yellow fever three months ago, and he didn't find out until two weeks ago. He didn't want to come back, and I had to make him—

When the cell phone rings, I nearly jump out of bed, startled. I'd fallen asleep to the sound of Han's fiddle playing in my head and a mound of comforters plopped on top of me. It is a quarter after twelve, and my heart is racing when I blink around my white-walled room. My hand fumbles across the dresser next to my bed and I pick up the cell phone. It says: PRIVATE CALLER. I press the button and mumble a *hello.*

"Is this Harley Davidson?" The voice is deep and gravelly like Pop Pop's hoarse tone when he gets up in the morning and before his first cup of coffee. I don't recognize it, and it holds a bit of a twang at the end of that sentence and unlike our gentle drawl here.

"Who's asking?"

"Listen, if you're going to play games with me, I'm not going to give you what I got. I'll just hang up—"

"What do you mean? What do you have?"

"Something from that man who was missing. Now, do you know what I mean?"

"Yes, Trevor Woods."

"You know where Tunnel Green is in Wheeling?" He doesn't wait for me to answer. "There's a park there. There's an old tunnel. Meet me there at three-thirty. On the east side."

Chapter 34

Tunnel Green in Wheeling is three hours and twenty-four minutes from home. Every second, I am questioning my sanity for meeting with this mysterious man. I added another six minutes to stop to fill up my tank once at a gas station and eight minutes to go back for one of Pop Pop's tiny snub nose .38 caliber pistols and five bullets from the locked, Deshler five-drawer tool chest he keeps in my basement. I added the gun to a small butt-pack I'll wear at my waist that also has an eight ounce can of Running Bear Maximum Strength and Maximum Range Assault Spray.

Halfway there, I decide to call Beck and see if he's got any ancestors with the name Callen O'Sullivan. He's like completely standoffish until he hears the name and the reason I ask. "Okay, so after Hans Branntwein was with the Confederates for a while," I say, "he saved the lives of these five Federal soldiers who were prisoners, kills this guy that had basically kidnapped him from his home because they were getting ready to hang them."

"Yeah."

"I found out last night that one of the Federal soldiers who he saved was an O'Sullivan like you. Callen O'Sullivan, to be exact."

"Really."

"Yes. How common is your last name, Beck?" I ask him. "I mean, I don't know anybody else around here with a name like that. Maybe you're related."

"I'll ask my mom. She did that genealogy family tree stuff a few years ago. I'll let you know. You do understand it is two o'clock in the morning."

"Oh, that would be the reason you sound a bit cold."

"Yeah." He yawns loudly. "Where are you at two in the morning?"

"I'm heading to Wheeling. I'm meeting a client."

"Is he a vampire?"

I laugh. "I hope not. See what you can find."

It isn't my typical attire that I would take on a walk in a park. But I don't usually get an anonymous call from someone who may or may not have murdered my ex-boyfriend, so I'm thinking better safe than sorry. I mean, it has creepy written all over it. I pull in and sit in the lot, taking in a shelter house and the darkness eating up the city-light horizon. There are two cars parked at the far end. Both have lights on facing away from me. My heart is already pumping. It's clean and well-kept, but it took me twelve minutes of lost-driving up and down the highway to find the little dead-end drive where I'm parked. It is a lonely and desolate spot. Why the hell am I here?

I get out and walk across the grass and up to a stairway with my cell phone for a flashlight. Then I walk across the trestle over the Wheeling Creek along a scantly lit path to the tip of the tunnel. It is just me and a tunnel that, when searching online, has been known to host more than a couple ghosts, all of which are skittering around waiting to take out their wrath inside the brick walls as far as my imagination is concerned.

The tunnel is only about four-hundred and fifty feet long. But it is dimly lit and there are dark manholes on either side of the path. Nearby, the sound of cars rolling along the highway is funneled into the tunnel and drown out any sounds that might give me a hint someone is waiting in the depths to murder me. Each step I take, I'm fiddling with the gun at my waist and wondering how Hans Branntwein took each step during the war, never knowing who to trust around every dark corner.

He lacked basic common sense. I can't help but wonder if that's the reason Irish kept him so close. There are two and a half years of entries in the journal, and sometimes he'd go months without writing a word. Other times, there was an entry every day. He even said once he wasn't going to write much for a few weeks because he thought the war was going to last ten years and he only had one journal.

I found where he was talking about playing his fiddle while they marched to bide the time. Then a Lieutenant Colonel heard him and plucked him out of John Grey's men and made him march with his band. But it didn't sound like Hans minded so much when it was all said and done. The date was in November of 1864. The last words I read on that date were: *I told Irish I didn't want to go with that colonel, but Irish said I'd be safer with him. Everybody's always on edge because they know who I am and they've got men sent just to kill me. I got shot in the shoulder, but it only grazed the skin. I don't want to go. The numbers were pounding in my head which isn't good because it's my brain's way of telling me I'm making the wrong decision. I felt safe with Irish's John Grey men even though we do dangerous stuff and everybody was trying to kill me. But Irish walked me to their tents. And I kept telling him I wouldn't go. I'd keep coming back. And he pushed me down on the ground and said: "I knew you could blow up bridges before you came to Harpers Ferry. The Federal Government sent me to kill you. Blowing up forty-two trestles and God knows how many bridges and towns was making them a bit antsy. So that's why we got caught in that river. Then I couldn't do it, shoot you, you know. I could have. You stick out. I could have got you and been out of there, but I faltered. You being ten or eleven and just a little bugger. Me and the boys riding around in the Shenandoah River, it was me not being able to take you out. We'd been waiting for two weeks for you to get there. I had it all up in my head how I was going to do it. I've killed so many, but I couldn't kill you. And then, you came out and poked me in the leg and stopped them boys from killing us. Well, I just got stuck on it. Now you know."*

I didn't want to believe him. But it made sense. I told him I hated him, and then Irish left in the middle of the night—I can't find him anywhere. He's just like Hayward and Asa. They just disappeared into the fog of people I'll never see again. It was the first time I ever felt like somebody thought I was smart and worth listening—

I hard-sigh when I get to the far side of the tunnel. It is dark here, and my stomach is bouncing like those colored plastic bouncy balls they put in ball pits for kids to jump in. I stand in the shadows of a half moon and the tepid air coming up from the creek nearby, and nobody comes or goes for ten minutes, then twenty. I look at my phone and dread I'm going to have to walk back through the tunnel. But no one has shown, and I'm sure someone is sitting somewhere laughing at the idiot girl who took the bait and drove three and a half hours to stand in a dark, empty tunnel.

I think the walk back through was harder than the initial one, but I break through the other entrance and walk the trestle over the creek feeling a bit relieved. Maybe I didn't want to know something else about Trevor anyway. The two cars in the lot along the far end are still there. I quickly get in my jeep, start the engine, and—

"Okay, so just drive out of here—"

I gasp, gulping in an intake of air. *Someone is in the car with me!* I'm frozen, heart pounding hard and deep while I waggle my head and try to peer into the back seat from where the voice is coming. I can't see more than a shadow, hunched over. "What do you want?" I grunt-hiss. It is nothing more than a whistle of air seeping out between my teeth with the leftover air from my lungs.

"Don't look back here!" The voice is not the same as the one from the phone call. "Dammit, don't be such an idiot. Just look at the windshield." I straighten myself out, blink at the windshield. "Don't do anything but drive. Make it look like you just went for a little walk. People do it all the time here, alright?"

"Okay," I answer. I don't remind him it is past four in the morning. My face feels warm, flushed while I start the vehicle, begin to back up.

"You see those cars over there? They were waiting for me. Don't back up so they can see you—or me. Just pretend like this is something you do every night."

I wiggle the car around, then drive it along the skinny one-lane road toward the main road into town.

"Who is in the cars?" I ask.

"I don't know. They were watching everybody going in with night vision binoculars."

"Why would they be looking for you? You know he's dead, right?" I ask softly. My voice doesn't sound like me. It is tight and forced.

"Okay, stop here."

I think I'm going to die right here. "Do you know what happened to him—to Trevor?" I ask. "I really, really don't want to be involved in whatever is going on. How—how did you get my number?" I suppose it is going through my head that Pop Pop is going to have some expressionless-faced cop knock on his front door tomorrow morning. He's going to tell him that they found my vehicle in a dark alley in Wheeling and I was dead inside. I had a pistol on a belt at my waist, and they assume it was a drug deal gone bad—

"It was the first number on the phone."

"My phone?" But my dark carjacker just opens the door and slips out into the night. Bang. My back door closes and I'm thinking I'm the butt of some big joke—until fourteen minutes later when I stop at a little gas station outside the city. I look over at the floor of the passenger side of the vehicle and there's a wallet laying there along with my phone. I lean over, snatch both up in my fingers. I turn the cell phone over. It is dead, and the cover is scratched. Inside the wallet are Trevor's driver's license and two credit cards. There are also two worn pictures tucked into clear sleeves. I close my eyes. One is me.

Chapter 35

"Let me get this straight—he was a stranger? And he handed the phone right over to you, and you didn't ask him where he'd gotten it?"

I'm standing in the lobby of the Brandy Mountain Police Department the next morning. I called in late for work. Lissette had hesitated when she heard my voice on the phone. She doesn't apologize. She just said: "Does this have something to do with last night?" And I wanted to lie to her and say I think she broke my arm so I'm going to the hospital or something so I had an excuse and she felt guilty. But I don't. I just say: "No. I met with some creepy mystery man in Wheeling who had Trevor's wallet and my phone. He held me at gunpoint making me drive around for a half hour before he jumped out. I have to take it to the police station." And she said: "Really, you're lying, right?" And I said: "I don't know if he really had a gun, but I figure he did. Other than that, no." Then there was this long silence, and Lissette says: "How the hell do I compete with that?" And she hung up.

So now I'm at the police station wondering if I'm excused for my tardiness to work or not. It is in a small, refurbished 1970s ranch house on the part of Main Street that leads out of The Bottoms and winds its way upwards to the top of Brandy Mountain. The main street, itself, plays out like a city building simulation game. There are three new structures in the process of being built next to the police station and five empty blocks of nothing but roadway and commercial-property-for-sale signs. The fifteen mobile homes and older dwellings once lining the streets have been bought up by the city and demolished. They will be replaced by more modern homes and businesses, including a dollar store. The police station is the first building on the right when you reach the top. Outside, there is a sign that states: BRANDY MOUNTAIN POLICE DEPARTMENT AND CITY OFFICES. JOHN MATTHEWS, MAYOR.

The city offices can be accessed by parking in the side lot and entering through what used to be the built-in garage of the refurbished house. The entrance to the police station is facing Main Street and through the front doors. It is just beyond a concrete pad that was once the front porch. The old living room has been blocked off to make the lobby, and a partition is placed there with a bullet-proof window and a tiny hole to talk with the dispatcher on the other side. The dispatcher today is Carla Walters, a chubby older woman with an outside tomcat attitude. I call her Dispatch Carla. That's who is addressing me at this point in a gruff, condescending tone. She has yet to pick up the wallet that is laying on the little ledge sticking out from beneath the window, so it is settled there like a dog's turd on the sidewalk it appears neither of us wants to touch. She's blunt, cheeky, and to the point. She's got thick, dark gray hair tied at the back of her head in a ball and she keeps picking at it with her ballpoint pen and looking over her shoulder at the police officer on duty who is Lance Washington.

"Like I said—" I stare into the gloomy window and barely make out the shadows there. "I got a call. I was told to walk to a destination and meet an unidentified person in a park in Wheeling. I took the walk and they never showed up. When I returned to my jeep, there was a man inside. I found the wallet and my phone on the floor after I drove the man downtown and he got out. I didn't see him. I didn't know the stuff was there until I was a few exits away to get gas."

"This happened last night?" Officer Washington leans over so I can hear him through the slot. "Did it not occur to you to call the police first? If someone murdered Trevor Woods, he or she is certainly capable of murdering you."

I stare hard at the glass. "I'm telling you now." I watch him shuffle around for a moment, then disappear only to reappear through the opening of the doorway. I can hear Dispatch Carla saying: "—and you should probably go get John Matthews. He's the one overseeing this case. I'm just saying."

Officer Washington steps out the door. He's straight-faced and unexpressive. I can't help but wonder if he saw Dispatch Carla waggle her shoulders with a smart-alecky roll like I saw her. His back was to her. If he did, he doesn't let on. He's wearing baby blue rubber gloves, and he's holding a plastic baggie in his hands. "We've gotten a hundred calls from people wanting to give leads." He picks up the wallet, plops it in the baggie. "Ten or fifteen say they have seen Trevor. We've followed up on each one, and we've gotten nothing, Haley. You don't have a clue as to what happened to him? Why'd they call you—?"

"Harley," I say. "My name's Harley. But the man in my jeep didn't talk except to tell me he called me because it was the first number on the phone. It's my grandpa's phone number and my emergency number. I left my phone in my vehicle between the seats. I had this other phone because my grandpa's letting me borrow it until I can afford a new one to replace the one in the car. I was kind of hoping it would show up with Trevor before I had to shell out another couple hundred bucks."

"Do you have the phone on your person?"

I groan outwardly, let my head drop. "Really? You're not going to take it, are you? It doesn't have anything on it."

"It is evidence of a possible murder."

"I heard they are calling it suicide," I say suspiciously.

"Until I get word from the coroner, I am treating this as a homicide." Officer Washington lowers his voice. "Such, your phone can offer clues. Every time a cell phone gets close to a tower, it connects with that carrier's network. The cell phone company will have records of it. We can find out the last place it pinged off a cell phone tower and maybe find out Trevor's last location. Your phone may have messages to or from Trevor that may show he met someone. Now, we know he didn't have his wallet. It escalates the situation. Mister Woods had the right to leave. He's an adult. But he probably would not take off somewhere without his wallet."

I reach into my purse, tug out my phone, and slap it down on the little shelf. "I'd give a thousand bucks to turn back time and not answer my phone when he called that night," I grumble. "Please don't look at the pictures. There are some on there that are private." Like me and a couple guys I might have had the chance to get lucky with in college. I turn my head slightly, see Dispatch Carla with her head up to the window like she's listening. I shake my head. "You know, his mom kept calling my grandpa's house until a week before the funeral. It's like she thought I murdered him. But for what benefit would it be to me? I hadn't seen him in five years until I ran into him at Brandenburg Conference Center that night. It was like he had me in his sights, decided to use me for whatever mess he got into."

"He was at the Brandenburg Conference Center on the night you picked him up?"

"Yeah, he was at a wedding reception in the room next to the one I was in for a realty seminar. You aren't going to look at the pictures, are you?"

Officer Washington scratches his chin. I see his eyes roam over my shoulder and toward Dispatch Carla's window. "Let me walk you to your car, Harley. It might not hurt, under the circumstances, that you have someone with you when you travel now until we get more information."

I start to question him. He has already nudged my elbow and is pointing to the doorway. I follow his lead, step out into the warm sunshine creeping across the sidewalk.

"Okay, so tell me about Trevor," he says about three steps outside the door and after it closes behind us. He sighs. "I didn't know him." He holds up a hand when I start to open my mouth. "Tell me the truth, please. You'd think by the way his family talks about him, he sat around turning water to wine all day by the hot tub. I go to the post office and ask about him, and I get the same thing. Nobody wants me to investigate it as a murder. It's like they just want to move on, forget about it. It's the same all over town from the grocery to the police station. Here's what I get: *He was a good guy, a nice guy*. But nice guys don't punch girls in the face, shove them out of cars, and then steal the car. You dated him for a while—"

"Off and on for three years," I answer. "More off than on, I mean, as far as he was concerned. I was always *on*. I was that girl who thought she was the only one and ended up finding out he had about six or seven girls just like me. I kick *myself* more than feel angry at him."

"You think he would have stolen something from the museum?" Lance Washington asks. "It just seems everyone wants to point fingers at the folks in The Bottoms—I think that's what you call it down here, right? That's not derogatory me calling it that since I'm living halfway up, right? I didn't mean—"

"No, it's not," I answer him. "Okay, let's go this route. I know what Grant Lebowski must have told you about the theft at the museum. But ask me if I think there was anything worth stealing in that place," I say. "I'll tell you this. What I saw in inventory, the most expensive thing in there was a collection of old bottles from the doctor who lived in the town during the early mining years. There's a small display of it next to a display of mining tools. They called him Doc Brown. He sold medicine in the newspapers during the 1860s and 1870s—Doc Brown Anti-Fat Medicinals, Missus Cora's Cure of Women's Diseases, Hannah J. Coffman's Herbal Remedy for Baldness, Vegetable Compounds for a Weak Mind and Women's Complaints. He had a bunch of aliases. Still, the collection is probably only worth a few hundred dollars selling bottle by bottle on an online auction. The Trevor I knew wouldn't do that. He's too lazy to set up an account to sell."

He adjusts his badge, stops just short of my jeep. "If you hear anything, you'll let me know, I'm hoping. Anything at all even if it sounds like it's not important."

"I will."

Chapter 36

I've got a date with Hans again tonight. It's raining, and we can't play ball. I snuck Nana Nisee out to see her Ned again and she cried on the way home. It made me feel sad for her. Strangely, my dates with Hans are filling some kind of void, including the dark ones, in my life and now I miss it badly. He seems to be my go-to guy now when I'm upset. Why do I find his world seems to reflect my own in some odd way? I suppose I just want to know there's somebody else out there, even in the past, that's had cruddy days too, had people leave them without coming back. It's a crummy kind of bond akin to my Aunt Rita fixating herself to the TV and the reality shows where normal people make idiots of themselves. It makes her feel less an idiot, I expect.

I also expect I identify with Hans. It's like I'm holding Zach back by being mad at him for playing ball for Brandy Mountain like Hans held Hayward back from being recruited and fighting with the 5th Regiment United States Colored Troops. I've taken our negotiating relationship a little too far in my head. I'm feeling left out because everybody at work is just plain quiet around me. I walked in after dropping the wallet and phone, and I just get these strange gazes all day. Such, I dig up the journal and start turning the pages—

November 4th, 1864

I've got it good with the band. I sleep in The Colonel's tent in a little extra room and get a meal every day. Life's much better than digging up roots with The Greys for the last couple years. The Colonel is tall and skinny like a cornstalk, and his shoulders are bent, so he looks like a cornstalk getting beaten by the wind. He's from some rich family in Ohio and what most folks call a dandy. He doesn't know a thing about battles, just likes to look pretty in a uniform so I think his papa probably had him placed as far away from battle as he could and close enough he could call himself a colonel. He collects pretty soldiers around him like a little girl collects up dolls. I think he thinks we're all just something to play with because he doesn't treat us like soldiers, but instead, toys on a shelf. Somebody came looking for me to mix the chemicals for the explosives and he told them he'd never seen me at all. I must have run off.

My first week, I got a brand-new uniform and socks and shoes. One of the soldiers (who in his real life beyond being a soldier, is a tailor in Toledo, Ohio) made it small for me from a uniform The Colonel had sent from Cincinnati. I play the fiddle soft and low while he eats and when he's trying to sleep. If there's a battle and he doesn't want to hear it, I play the fiddle loud and bounce my feet on the floor while I do it. He laughs when I sing because he says I have an Irish drawl. I told him I'm straight from Germany, although my papa worked with a bunch of Irish building a road in New Orleans and I spent a lot of time playing the fiddle while they worked and listened to their songs. That's where I met a sweetheart. He told me I'm too young to have a sweetheart, and I told him I wasn't any such thing.

He's got a drummer in there with us and the boy is always trying to pick fights with me and put rat shit in my meal, which has been lots of chicken lately. His name is Wallace Dolittle, I made up the Doolittle part. I don't know his last name. He's just fat and lazy and speaks with a lisp. The first time I met him, he said: "My name is Walleth." Such, I thought his name was Walleth and not Wallace and he got mad because I kept calling him Walleth and said I was making fun of him and The Colonel told a soldier to switch my legs. But the soldier took me behind the tent and said: "That little drummer is about as stupid as they get. Just yell, and I'll whip the ground." I did what the man said. I hate Wallace. And now he's trying to read what I write and saying: "Whath you writing, Pony? Whath your real name?" He's General Hancock's great-nephew by marriage or something of the likes, and his mama didn't want him to get shot at, so he got stuck like me here.

Wallace oversees The Colonel's racehorse. It's big and mean, the racehorse. But it is fast and worth lots of money. Just *out of spite, I've started to feed the horse pieces of rock candy I make in a jar for The Colonel who gives me packets of sugar he has with him all the time so I make it. Right before I do it, I give a little whistle and the horse nickers and grumbles with delight when I walk past him now which really pisses off Wallace. I tell him: "Some people are just more likable than others, Walleth." My new way to piss off Wallace is to walk across the camp when he's walking the horse down and give a little whistle. He always breaks free and drags the little shit about ten feet to get to me. I miss Irish and the boys. I wonder if they miss me.*

November 12th, 1864

Imagine my surprise when I saw Hayward two days ago. I yelled at him and his eyes got big, and he looked antsy when he ducked behind a couple tents. I thought it was strange and maybe he didn't see me. I chased him down, and he just stands there with his other soldier friends and acts like he hardly knew me. It's been two years. I didn't recognize him at all. He's grown up. He found me later and he was alone and when I was washing plates and snuck up behind me and poked me in the back. One of The Colonel's guards looked startled, then wary like he was going to shoot him. I laughed so hard, I almost peed my pants. I asked him if he's seen Irish and he said Irish was there somewhere, but he didn't know where. He just heard a rumor. I think he's lying because he blinks his eyes hard when he's not telling the truth. I asked him if he ever wrote his mama and he told me that he didn't. He said we should just forget them. He didn't know where she was and would probably never see her again. I told him I sent her to my uncle's house. He said she probably never got there. She probably died because she couldn't find herself out of a pisspot.

So now I'm sad. I'm hoping the war goes on forever because I got nowhere to go after this. Hayward told me I'm stupid for saying that because I'm still spoiled and still only think of myself. He asked me if I ever decided which side I was on and I told him it was whatever side paid me and fed me. I still have a Yankee hat in my bag, and I have a Rebel hat in my bag. I said I used whichever one comes in handy. He said that while I'm sitting around playing a fiddle for some dumbass colonel, his troop is on a secret mission escorting a train of colored women and children that evacuated from Georgia because they don't have any food and are starving. Some little church is paying for them to get there. They are taking them to Ohio or as close as they can get them of what train tracks are left and they'll walk the rest of the way. He asked me if I wanted to ride with them and find my family in Ohio. I told him the only family I had left was my Uncle Otto, and he was in West Virginia somewhere. He said maybe there's a woman on the train he wants to marry. Come to find out later when I'm sitting in the tent and The Colonel's having a meeting with his staff that some colored troop was helping sneak people on the train across Nashville. Hayward wasn't on some great mission like he said. The Colonel didn't know I knew Hayward and I about shit my pants. I should have known he was up to trouble and I can almost bet he was with Irish. And I would have to bail them out again. Just when my life was going good, too.

November 16, 1864

The doctor says I'm dying. I suppose if somebody reads this, I'm dead and gone. But I'll just tell you that it isn't Hayward's or Irish's fault, so they don't feel bad forever. I've got secrets and I guess only the doctor knows them because he does what he does. I figured I could go on and on in this war and maybe it'd never end. But it's ending for me. I should have known when I heard the train that night, I also heard an owl hoot, and my papa used to tell me that no good ever came from hearing an owl call out at night. It means someone is dying.

I sat at the campfire two nights last and stared at all the faces staring into the flames. I've gotten to know a few of them at arms-length. Everybody's wanting to get in good with The Colonel's fiddler, and that's me, because they think I've got his left ear and his right. But it's not just that. I've also got access to all the crates he has specially dispatched to him by his rich family in Ohio. He gets fresh food, tobacco, and the best wines to name just a few. The crates are piled up inside his tent so high, it pushes up the canvas so he doesn't even need the wood reinforcements to hold it up. Sometimes, I pilfer a thing or two and trade it off for smokes or some trinket I want. I don't worry so much about getting caught. The Colonel has so much; he never knows if anything is missing.

There's always different faces around the fire because the old ones get killed and replaced with new. I remember telling Irish that one time. When Hayward left, I didn't have anybody to sleep next to, to hold on to a fist of his shirt. I tried to sidle up next to Irish and grab his shirt. He pushed me away the first couple times. Then I just waited until he went to sleep and did it anyway. I figured he never knew I did that for two years, hung on to him hard like that at night. Then right before he made me leave, he asked me one day why I did it. I told him the truth. I was afraid he'd leave me in the middle of the night. I wouldn't know where to go, what to do. I said Hayward was always going to leave. I knew that the first day I met him. He was always looking for something. He just didn't know what it was until he found the colored troops, found he had a job to do and people he wanted to do it with. Then I told Irish I didn't want him to leave me and I knew it was coming because we were winning more battles than losing and folks were tired, just plain tired of being cold in the winter and starving in the summer and fighting. Numb. I'm numb. We all just wanted to go home.

We were all in anticipation of the battle coming and tired from all the marching. I could feel it in the air. I heard they threw a bunch of colored troops in the little prisoner camp and they might hang them for treason. I asked The Colonel the reason for the hanging. He said they disobeyed orders and were sneaking Rebels across the battle lines. Well, I could guess who was going to get hanged.

I set off across the camp, and it's a big one. Tent after tent, and barricade after barricade. I stop just short of a bunch of raggedy tents on the outskirts. There are a couple guards there smoking and talking. It's like a little town of tents outside the big city of tents.

"They're gonna die tonight, right?" And the guard shrugs and says: "I reckon some night."

"I'm The Colonel's fiddler. He said to come and get some prisoners to help load the dead from the hospital. He needs six men." I gave them both one of my smokes. They seemed to like that. "One might be my brother or might be yours. You want me to decide which ones?"

"Yeah, take six."

I walk among the ragged tents. Here and there, I go, and I think I'm not going to find the men I'm searching for. But I finally see one, tall and skinny and with red hair. I stop. "You, soldier, what's your name?"

"I'm Sean O'Malley."

"Sean O'Malley, I need seven men to load a wagon from the hospital to bury the dead." He just looks at me long and hard. I don't act like I know him like I've fought by his side for almost four years. "I'll be back at dusk."

So, at dusk, I take the men to the surgeon, and we load them on the wagon and then I watch as Irish and Sully climb on top. Then goes Teddy Murphy and Bobo and Hayward and Preacher and a man who I don't know. I walk them outside the camp and set them up with horses.

"Did you finally choose a side, Pony?" Irish asks me. I tell him I don't know. But later, when I hear the train whistle far off and I hear The Colonel laugh and tell the men at his fire that he has a way of turning the tide of war. He says he's taking out the bridge just as the train goes past in the evening. He's got his boys making it look like the Rebel troops are blowing up the bridge and taking the train full of escaping colored families with it. Surely, that is the way to make the Rebels look bad, I suppose that is when I chose my side. It was with Hayward and Irish. I didn't know where

they were or where they went, but I slipped out from the fire and snatched up the maps laid out for the morrows battle right in front of The Colonel's eyes. And I ran off into the night to the sound of him screaming that I was a spy and trumpets blaring and guns firing and then my whistle for his horse. And he came, the horse did, and I jumped on his back and rode off toward the train to warn them. I clung to that horse's mane for my dear life.

But it was too late. They were on a route and couldn't stop. I saw Hayward tossing coal into the engine and he waved to me, not knowing he was going to die. I couldn't let him die, so I kicked the fire out of the horse and rode like hell to the trestle they were blowing. I shot the two men who were planting the explosives. That's when the train came. I just stood there while the sparks were flying, and I knew I couldn't stop it, couldn't stop the train, couldn't stop the explosion, couldn't stop Irish from dying like I couldn't stop Papa from dying. I've been shot before, just a graze. It's strange. It knocks you over and it doesn't hurt for just a second. Then it's like searing pain. That's what I felt on my shoulder when I jumped down on the trestle and held on with my legs and arms to keep from falling just like Irish taught me to hang from the tree. I felt the lifeblood running out. I just couldn't—stop Sean O'Malley from dying—and I hated Minnie Bean right then for taking away Hayward and getting us in the trouble and killing all of them. And me, for hiding my secret so long.

"Hey, Beck, you're not going to believe this."

"That you're calling me in the middle of the night again?"

I look up at the clock radio I've got by my bed, then nibble on my lip. Oh, it is midnight. "I'm sorry. I don't sleep. I'll call you back in the morning. Hope I didn't interrupt something with—a lady friend." I can't remember the name of the last girl Beck dated. Maybe he isn't going out with her anymore. I don't know. "Sorry." I start to hang up. He grunts and ends with a flat voice: "Well, I'm awake now, Harley, just say. I'm waiting with bated breath."

"You're being sarcastic, right?"

"Do I sound sarcastic?"

"I don't—know." I don't. His voice was flat, but he's not hanging up the phone. "Can you keep a secret?"

"Is that a trick question?" he asks. I tell him I don't know what he means. He says: "To be quite honest, I'm worried you're going to tell me you're a vampire now because the guy you met in Wheeling last night bit you."

"Haha. Funny. Yes or no? You can't tell anybody. Not Zach or Pop Pop or the police—"

"Oh, boy. Here we go."

"You're out, right?" I sigh. I just want to share this with somebody who cares. "It's okay. My reputation precedes me. No big deal. I know everybody thinks I drag people into stuff—trouble. You're a teacher. I get it. You've got a certain reputation to maintain. Sorry to wake you up."

I hang up. I flop my phone on my bed and reach up to turn the light off that's sitting on my bed stand. I hear my phone buzzing. I follow its light and pick it up. It's Beck.

"I didn't say I was out. I didn't say I was in," Beck's voice is soft and low. "But I've had the good fortune of being entertained for the last fifteen-plus years by your pranks, antics, and what your Pop Pop calls *Oh-God-another-of-Flea's shenanigans*. Heck, I remember when you were in third grade and glued Missus Reynold's homework papers to her desk with bubble gum and Elmer's Glue. The only thing that has kept you from getting into major trouble with any one of these antics is that, even at your age, everybody thinks you're eventually going to grow out of it. But the point is—it's like sitting in front of the TV and watching one of those reality dance shows. I don't have to worry about getting hurt. I mean, why bother? I've got a front row seat."

"I don't know how hurt you'd get dancing—"

"In a show, maybe not. But with you? I'm not sure."

"Okay. For one, I'm not that bad of a dancer—"

"We aren't referring to dancing, are we really?"

"No." I throw up my hands. "Then you understand my point—don't you ever get tired of sitting in the audience *observing* instead of being a part of the real thing or the dance or whatever—because sitting in the audience is so much less exciting than—"

"—getting marched to the principal's office with three detentions? That's better?"

"I lived. You watched."

"You got a spanking when you got home. I remember. You didn't cry until your Pop Pop told you that it hurt him more than it would ever hurt you to do it. I know. I was there with Zach and Mike Wells and—"

"Trevor," I finish for him. "Well, aren't you like a little girl, you know like in the nursery rhyme—sugar and spice and everything nice," I grunt sarcastically. "Plus, a little scaredy-cat and—"

"And you're like snakes and snails and puppy dog tails *and* maybe all the stuff, dark and dangerous and rebellious, that kind of scares the shit out of me."

Maybe it is a bad idea calling up Beck and sharing this stuff with him. He's a watcher, not a dancer. He sits back and thinks things out. We're opposite, he and I. I jump. He weighs the consequences and walks the easy route. "Listen, I'll dance. You watch. Later, dude."

Chapter 37

The next morning I'm telling Theo about my trip to Wheeling. "You're just making that up," he tells me. He's leaning over the counter and tapping the filter funnel of the coffee pot in a vain attempt to hurry up the brewing. He's under the impression the grounds inside need to be jiggled because they get caught in the filter and slow the flow. "Stuff like that doesn't really happen to people." He turns, cranes his neck to give me a chiding gaze reminding me of Pop Pop when I got up from the dinner table last Sunday to answer my cell phone. "Just suck it up and tell the truth. You slept in, and that's why you were late."

"I'm not lying," I mutter and look to Lexie Todd for support. I don't know why. Maybe because she is leaning on the counter right next to Theo. However, she's just peering at Taylor out of the corner of her eyes. Taylor is settled across from me and staring at me without expression. I feel self-conscious. I'm not comfortable quite yet in high heel shoes and a two-piece skirt-suit, although I did get a *hey, hot thing* yelled out at me in the convenience store parking lot. Thus, Taylor eyeing me circumspectly makes me wonder if her little dress up doll dressed like she was supposed to today. Do my shoes match correctly? Is there some pattern or code to certain colors on certain days?

She has a little section of her chestnut hair, and she's winding it around a forefinger over and over. Crap, should I have put my hair up instead of curling it at the bottom? I'm going to go nuts with this while I watch everyone watching me. I would assume Lexie is trying to read Taylor's facial expressions so she can hop on board whatever side of the boat she's on relating to my conversation. From the vacant hint in her eyes, she was already copying Theo's response. Whatever reaction Taylor has will sway Lexie's own view.

I don't tell them I can't sleep. As my eyes start to close, just as the oozy gray of sleep wraps its warm blanket around me, I have this half-awake-half-asleep dream. I'm walking through some foggy woods and it is dark. But the moon is shining through a copse of trees just ahead. In that little bit of light, the leafless limbs are allowing the moonshine to creep through, I can make out a shadow darker than the woodland, and it is walking away. Always, it is walking away. Even if I try to follow, I can never catch up to that shadow. I know it is Trevor. I know he must have been hiding some secret. I need to find out what it is. I *have* to figure out what happened to him. Then I can clear up the situation with stolen items at the historical society and maybe, just maybe, Grant will let me work there again.

"I did go. I had to do it. Wouldn't you?" I ask them and get a resounding NO!

"If you spent as much time digging through old newspapers online as you did trying to sell a house, you might make more money." Lissette pipes up. Her coffee mugs always match her lipstick. Today it is burgundy. She is holding back the urge to tell us all to get our butts to work. However, Taylor's telling her all the time it is good for morale to let us talk over the coffee machine. Still, Lissette's all about making money. She shoves Theo out of the way and snatches up the coffee pot, pours a quick cup while it is still brewing and manages to set the pot back before a puddle forms at the base. "Enough chit-chat. Coffee break is over."

They all file out, probably glad to be out of the uncomfortable air, except Theo who lingers and eyes the doorway until it closes behind them. "I'd like to spend some time with you. Is that good with you?" he asks. He's got this sweet smile, kind of crooked and like a mischievous boy.

"Yeah, I'd like that." I'm not sure if I'm telling the truth. But I need an ally in the office.

"How about I take you through some of the houses I'm selling, show you how I set them up? We can get to know each other." He stops, looks up at the ceiling and lets his shoulders drop. "Let me throw myself out here." He looks so eager, a kid wanting that last cookie in the bag I'm holding. "I think about you all the time. I know girls like you don't usually go for dweebs like me. Can you give me a chance—?"

"Alright." I nod. He gets this silly grin on his face like I gave him that cookie, points a finger at me. "You won't be sorry, sweetheart. I promise you. You won't be sorry."

Later, Taylor takes me with her to a house showing. I follow her around like a little chick follows a mama hen. Except, it is a little brick house in the historic district. I slurp up the door framing and the architecture like I'm sucking out the last bit of sweet juice in a cherry slushy. She's all business, not saying anything about what happened the other night. Taylor's hopeful buyer is not as smitten with the house as me. He's thirty-something and more a condo-style buyer. He keeps turning the water in the sinks off and on and grouching how much work the place would be to fix up.

"You're selling to the wrong customer," I tell Taylor while she watches the man leave out the front door. She does her usual walk-through to make sure everything is still in order. She stops and pivots slowly on her heels to face me.

"*What*?" She looks at me hotly. "*You're* going to tell *me* how to sell a house? You know how many houses I've sold?"

"No, I don't know." I shrug. "I've personally seen you sell a lot of homes. But they are big ones and brand, new ones—"

"And now we're selling old ones because nobody wants to sell or nobody *can* sell them. But Lissette believes we need to venture out to new horizons or we'll be belly up. Sometimes, it takes a whole lot of showings to find the right homebuyer, Harley. This is only the third showing. You need to consider the price might be too high or it needs home improvements the seller can't afford. Don't automatically put on your unqualified gloves and point a finger at my ability."

"Okay, you're right. I should shut up." I should. She's the only one who's got my back in the office right now.

"Bullshit. Don't start saying something then stop. What is it?"

I wince, grit my teeth and take the plunge knowing I might be making a mistake obeying her and being blunt.

"Okay, yes, this house is old. Still, there's a demand for places like this. It has a history. The guy is young, divorced, and looking for women to look at him. He had a new condo with a pool and exercise room written all over his face."

"Single people like old houses. The mortgage is cheap."

"Not necessarily. Young people with families want to live in neighborhoods where their kids are safe. Look at the neighborhood. There were kids riding their bikes up and down the street and moms jogging alone. Safe. Who doesn't want safe right now? And this house isn't listed as historic, but the rest of the neighborhood is—" I hold up my phone. "I looked it up while you were showing him the bathroom. If this house gets historic recognition, the home value rises for the entire neighborhood. Regardless, you know it was once a pretty famous inn and restaurant?"

"What?" She is digesting what I just tossed at her. I hold up my cell phone. It is Pop Pop's cell phone I've borrowed still and old and cracked, but she narrows her eyes and tips her head to one side to look at the picture.

"It would be *who*?" I sniff. "John Quincy Adams, Martin Van Buren, and James A. Garfield. Oh, and Charles Dickens and Mark Twain."

"No, you're lying," Taylor tosses her hands into the air. She won't believe me. But it is true.

I get halfway home and hear a tinging sound for a text. When I stop for gas, I take a look. It's from Beck. *Mom says her great uncle's name was Callen Aiden O'Sullivan. He was in the Civil War, volunteered in his hometown of Three Bridge Creek and worked at Dillon Mining Camp, an Irish camp that moved from town to town. That's all she has found. She said thanks for the info.*

I stare at the phone. Callen O'Sullivan (Sully) must have come to Brandy Mountain with Sean O'Malley. I mean, it doesn't seem like a huge piece to any puzzle, but it does show how the O'Sullivans ended up here. I send him a thumbs up and drive on.

Chapter 38

It is a knee-jerk reaction, suddenly flipping on my right turn signal and sliding off the highway at the exit ramp. A car honks to direct my attention to the discourtesy I showed by snaking across the median line a little late and in front of the vehicle just as the white line ended.

I regret my decision the closer I get to Hurricane Hollow. I feel I am reliving the smack in the face when I learned about Trevor's death. It plays over and over in my head more often than not. Still, when I see the Hurricane Hollow Carry Out and Gas, I know I'm going to veer into the gritty asphalt parking lot. Such I do, slipping out of my vehicle and going inside.

I pretend to look for a bag of potato chips while Haley takes care of an elderly lady who is checking out with three large paper sacks of grocery shopping. There's a tall and skinny guy with pimples and greasy hair hanging around the back and peering into the refrigerators poking at the pops. I wait and wait. He doesn't look like he's going anywhere soon. I don't have all day. Such, I listen to my high heels clack to the counter before I drop the bag of barbecue chips by the register. Haley looks up, my face must register because I see her eyes take me in. "I remember you."

"Can I ask you a question?" I drop my voice, check to make sure the guy in the back isn't within hearing range. I poke the bag of chips and set a can of soda next to it. She nods. "That guy whose body they found up at the tracks, Trevor Woods, did your cousin see anything weird about it."

"Robby? I don't know. Other than he was smashed to smithereens?"

I bob my head up and down. "Yeah, I know that. It's just that he was an old boyfriend of mine. They say it might be suicide. I—I don't ever remember him being depressed. I just wondered—I don't know. If I say this to anybody else, they'll say I just don't want to believe he's dead because I miss him.

256

But that's not it at all." She's just staring at me, so I pull out my wallet from my purse. "You said your cousin or someone saw him. Did they get a good look? Because I'm willing to hand him twenty bucks just for telling me so I can let the whole thing rest."

"I can call him. He's probably at work. I can get your number and have him call you. There have been a few people here asking about it."

I'm thinking he's not ever going to call. I tap my finger on the counter. "Listen, have you ever gotten blamed for something bad that you didn't do, and you see this funny look in your mom or dad's eyes because you let them down?"

"Yeah, all the time. I got pregnant when I was sixteen."

"Okay, so you'll get where I'm coming from," I toss out while I pay for the chips and soda pop. "It's like this. I'm getting ready to leave a work party the night Trevor disappeared. His buddy calls me to pick him up because he's drunk. I'm not sure if I just fell under his radar because he'd seen me that night or if there's more to the story and I was an easy scapegoat in whatever went on with him. Because I picked him up. He dumped me out of my car on a backroad. The next day, I'm getting blamed for stealing stuff from the museum I worked at. My grandpa who raised me keeps giving me this look like he did something wrong raising me. He tips his head to the side and shakes it. I'm trying to figure out what happened to Trevor, why he's dead. I can't keep walking into a room my grandpa's in and see that look."

Haley takes my money, rings it on the register. I see the man who had been eyeing the refrigerator in the back. He's made his way up the aisle and is standing there staring at us. I tug one of my Central Independent Realty business cards with my cell phone number on it from my purse. I scratch out the cell phone number of the phone Lance Washington is using for evidence and scratch in the number of Pop Pop's cell phone I'm using.

I push it over toward Haley. "I work at Central Independent Realty in Chilton. If you can ask him, I'd appreciate it."

I almost bump into the man who steps out from the grocery shelves. I smile. He eyes Haley. Then as I pass, he says: "You're not a cop or anything?"

"No, why?" I ask. I see his gaze flash at Haley and they exchange a look like they know each other well enough he can be added to our conversation. "I mean, I've spent more than a few hours in the last few weeks in the police station getting harassed for stuff. Does that count for *anything*?"

He sniffs a laugh. "Are you a suspect?"

"I am told I am *a person of interest*," I mutter. "It's the thanks I get for picking up an old boyfriend that was dead drunk. Instead of getting a pat on the back for being a designated driver, everybody's poking fingers at me. It sucks. I lost a job over it—"

"And she gets that same look from her grandpa that Dad gives me when I walk into the house with my kid," Haley adds, chewing on the lid of a pen in her hand.

"I got pictures of him if you want to see them," the young man tells me. "They're pretty gross."

"Really gross," Haley screws up her face.

"Pictures?"

"I took some while we were waiting for the cops to get there."

I look at the man. "You're Robby, the one who found him?"

"Yeah. Robby Pierson. I've been hanging out down here to make sure Haley's safe. Everybody's freaking out about that guy showing up dead. You see this stuff on the TV all the time. Didn't ever think I'd see it." He tugs his phone from his back jean pocket and holds it in his palm. "You sure you want to look? They got blood and stuff." I suppose my stomach is making that gurgling nervous sound. I don't want to see dead, beat-to-hell and smashed-by-a-train Trevor. But I've got to know.

Blood and stuff is an understatement. Robby holds up

the phone. I see a picture of a railroad track settled on an upgrade of land. There are railroad ties with crushed stones beneath and atop, the steel rails. Flopping stuffed between the train rails, like an old, ripped teddy bear with stuffing pulled out and long-ago tossed past a garbage can and on to some dark corner forgotten, is a man's body in black-smudged blue jeans and a button up, striped shirt. He looks almost like someone has sucked the air out of him. His body is misshapen, one arm is awkwardly bent above his head, and one leg is severed and lying next to his side.

"I was told he died the night I picked him up from the party," I say, reaching out and using my fingers to enlarge the picture. I feel dizzy and like I've got prickers sticking my face. "But he was wearing a dark blue button up and stone-washed jeans. I remember. He got into a fight with another man at the party. He had a bloody nose, and he wiped it on his pants." I can't make out much more, so I shake my head. But he has more, and he slides his finger along the cell phone screen, displaying about twenty more images. I stop him on one, enlarge it. I see the head. It is smashed like someone punched a soggy white pumpkin after it had sat on a porch long after Halloween ended. In the crevices, there are pools of deep red blood coursing through like a bloody creek running down a mountain. There is hair intermingled, a deep brown almost six inches in length. "Uh, Trevor's hair wasn't long. And it was blonde." I look up at the two. "You're sure this was the guy they said was Trevor Woods?"

"Yeah, they held it long enough for some cop or coroner to come and identify him. He was from his hometown. I was there while they uncovered him."

"What'd the guy look like who identified him?"

"He was tall and had glasses," Robby says. "Maybe a friend of the family. Or maybe not. There were so many cops and police in plain clothes or suits there by the time they started taking my information."

"Does anybody know you've got these pictures?"

"Just a few friends."

"Robby, I don't think that's Trevor," I look at him, and I look at Haley. "I wouldn't show them to anybody else just yet. I don't know what's going on. I had some guy carjack me the other day in Wheeling, drove me around town, then jumped out. He left Trevor's wallet and my phone on the floor."

"The cops did stop at my house and knocked on the door, asked a lot of questions."

"Can you give me a copy of the pics?" I ask him. "I swear I won't tell anybody where I got them. I'm not planning on telling anybody about them—here—" I reach into my purse, pull out what I've got left of gas money for the week—forty dollars. "Here. It's all I've got to pay for a copy of the pictures—"

Chapter 39

The new ballfields up on The Brandy are almost completed. They've got the ball diamonds and fencing up and the sand laid. They've even got the expensive metal bleachers ready to be set up on either side of the fields. I can see all of this with my own eyes today while I'm leaning with my elbows on the fence and my chin resting on my wrists watching Zach practice with the new club. I'm dressed in my work clothes because I was on my way home and stopped. I'm getting some strange eyeballing. I'm not sure what people are thinking. And it is out of my realm because usually, I don't care what people think.

Zach said he was getting his truck worked on at Sefton's Garage, and he needed someone to pick him up after practice. I honestly think he did it just to rub it in that he's playing ball. I'm more than happy to oblige. I'm avoiding Beck's texts. There have been about six telling me to please call him. Nope. Delete. And I'm avoiding Theo's texts. He's a little more difficult to avoid and delete because he's my direct supervisor. I'm just not feeling it so much. And, I'm a bit surly because for the fourth night last night, I *met* with Theo. He says he's got a vacant home he's showing on Tuesday and he says he wants to run through a few things, show me some tips on staging a home for a sale.

That's good, right? I'm getting free real estate lessons from one of the top three salesmen in the tri-state region. Well, not so much unless you call rolling around on the floors of different homes *training*. He's on his phone the entire time, talking to me and talking to some client here or there. He starts off showing me the decorations and furniture he put in the home he's selling and he keeps saying *Harley, this, baby is the key to high returns.*

We're halfway through the house, and for the first time, he puts his cell phone in his breast pocket. He leads me upstairs, and then he says: *So, baby, there's also another key to high returns if you know what I mean.* Then he starts slapping my butt and calling me his naughty girl and asking me what kind of naughty place I'd like to do him this time. I decide every guy's different; every guy likes different things occasionally. I can put up with a spanking. Then eight minutes after we end up in the bathtub, he's whistling the National Anthem and already hopping out and yakking with someone on the phone.

The next three evenings are about the same, but at different houses and each with another set of Theo's fantasies. I tried to joke with him and tell him he needs to at least treat me to dinner for all the sex he's getting. And he returns: "If I pay you, wouldn't that make you a whore?"

Who says that to a woman? I'm standing there with my mouth agape. I tell him to go to hell. Then leave. But he's got my cell phone number and he calls me thirty times apologizing for saying what he said. He was just nervous. I didn't return the calls. And I'm not now while I catch Zach's attention and bob my head toward the parking lot, so he knows I'm here and heading to my jeep. "I'll meet you there," he says. He's talking to another man, and they seem deep in conversation. I absently shove the phone back into my purse after making sure it isn't Pop Pop trying to call me. I see the guys walking off the field. I head toward my jeep.

"Who was that guy you were talking about—John Grey?"

I had already started turning when I felt the knuckle to my shoulder about the time I'd crossed the threshold of the area the shiny metal ball stands are stacked and ready to assemble. Max is always knuckle-nudging me, so I knew who it was long before I find myself blinking stupidly at his bare chest and starting-to-replace-fat-with-muscle arms. He's half in and half out of a t-shirt, exchanging his practice shirt with a fresh one. I should have stopped walking, but I was still in mid-step partially backward. That's why I ran into the post of the fence, smashing my shoulder and hip. It's loud.

"Ow, dammit." I stop long enough to right myself, tearing my gaze away from where it had ended before my crash—his bare belly slightly dappled with downy, dark hair.

262

"Oh, good that is Harley inside that makeup and hottie-tottie dress," Max mumbles, tugging the dirty shirt off his head. "For a minute, I thought I'd run into the wrong woman."

"What are you talking about?" I snap at him. Now he's completely shirtless. He has been working out, and it is noticeable even to me who has always been quick to put on the brakes for the boyfriend's-best-friend-crush thing.

"It's not my fault." He's outright chuckling at my bumble while he wiggles his head through the clean shirt, stopping so it is half-on and half-off. "You backed right into it. Boom!" He shakes his head. "You look different with your hair all up and stuff and dressed up." Max waves a hand at me, nods toward the parking lot as if he's goading me to walk. "Aw come on, it was funny. You're not still mad, are you?" he keeps going. "I was going to text you or—whatever. I just didn't want your new boyfriend to think there was something going on."

New boyfriend? What's he talking about? Oh, my date with Theo. I start to hold up a hand, deny my newest bad relationship oozing with nothing more than meaningless, bad sex. I halt. As far as I'm concerned, he can believe it is wonderful romance. How could it possibly be more demoralizing divulging the truth that I'm still floundering out here to the man who knows the ugly truth about Trevor sleeping with every girl when he was with me because I was so bad, at well, being me?

"Can you put your shirt on or something?" Is all I can spat out instead, tossing a hand at him. He comes up beside me, takes a step on past, and I move forward to come up beside him in step. "Cover up. It's a public place." He looks down at his chest absently like he can't figure out he's oozing with enough sexy to rouse a cemetery full of dead, old women.

He makes a flippant remark about me needing to grow up and does a lazy toss of his shirt over his shoulders, wiggling erotically to pull it over baby biceps. Damn him.

"Who was he, that John Grey dude you were so interested in? I should have listened. I was kind of caught up in Mikayla stuff."

"It's just the name of the man your great, great grandpa captured at Harpers Ferry."

"Oh, that's interesting." Max makes a too-big nod of his head and wiggles his hand as if to coax me further. "Tell me more while we walk."

"Max, stop." I put on the brakes, turn long enough to shake my head. Max stops momentarily, looks back, then moves on so I have to catch up, then pass him. "You don't have to be interested. I get it—we've gone in different directions." A couple girls walking toward the ballfield stop and make a point of waving at him. I think they'd like to have him stop, but he doesn't. He continues to follow me while I wind my way through cars.

"Tell me the story. I was a dick then. I regret it."

"You're always a dick," I remind him. But I smile when he knuckles me on the shoulder again. "Alright." I stop and wheel around, and he almost smashes into me. "Your grandpa writes in his journal that he'd been with this Rebel guerilla band run by a man he called Bad Bill for almost a year fighting before they even got to Harpers Ferry. They are in Harpers Ferry getting ready for a battle, and the Union soldiers are all leaving because they are outnumbered. Some of the Rebels were surrounding this guy called John Grey and his men in the river and taking shots at them. I don't think they knew who they were, just thought that they were enemy soldiers lagging behind. Hans walked right into the Shenandoah River and made a big deal of capturing them, so they didn't get killed."

"Why would he do that?"

"I don't know," I shrug and continue walking. "What were we doing when we were thirteen?" I ask him. "I was still riding my bike and playing on my game station. I don't think he wanted to be a part of the fighting. He was just forced into it by this bad soldier who spent more time raping, killing, and pillaging than actually fighting a war," I offer. "He was probably afraid to leave. He mentions he doesn't have any place else to go. I looked up the Rebel soldier's name that he mentions, Bad Bill. Hans said he had piggy eyes popping out of his head and a scar running along his cheek from right eye to chin. I went through a bunch of old Civil War pictures and found a Confederate Guerilla leader named Savage Bill. He had a scar and buggy eyes. He was a real shit and bloodthirsty, liked to torture northern supporters. He would surround cabins and nail the doors and windows shut and toss in torches and burn entire families inside."

"So, you're telling me my grandpa was a part of all that? Well, don't tell my sister." I keep turning to address him as we walk. Now, Max has a funny twist to his lips. The sun has left a dappling of freckles on the bridge of his nose. *Why the hell am I noticing this?* "She'll freak out. She's been doing genealogy on our family."

"No, Max, he wasn't." The sun is warm on my cheeks. The scent of fresh asphalt burning in my nostrils. Max's eyes are rapt on mine when I look back. "Your grandpa, Hans, freaked out when this Savage Bill made the Yankee prisoners dig their graves and started to execute them. He stood up for them and shot Savage Bill and his men. One of the prisoners was a man your grandpa called Irish. His real name was Sean O'Malley. I found where historians first thought that John Grey was a single entity, one person. But it was discovered that the man they thought was one of the most successful Partisan rangers or guerilla warfare leaders along the eastern front was many men who carried on the name. The original John Grey died of cholera in October of 1861. His band disbanded in February of 1862. However, small factions of his men were still being paid by the Federal government throughout the war and continued to be called John Grey's Men. The principal organizer for each group was nicknamed John Grey and, upon receiving wages, disbursed all payments directly to his men. *This* was the Sean O'Malley he saved. Hans became one of them."

"Well, that's good, right?" Max laughs.

"I suppose, depending upon which side you're on." I sigh, push forward again along the hot asphalt. I duck beneath a truck rear-view mirror and Max is right behind me, making a sharp veer around it before continuing too. "Your grandpa was pretty badass for a little kid. He spent the war burning bridges and sabotaging railway systems used by the Confederate Army."

"I'm lost. I'm not sure how this all fits together. Why are you wanting to find the tunnel, and what does it have to do with Trevor?"

"Trevor had the journal. He also had some old company scrip with it. Maybe he found, in the journal, where Hans hid the money, and somebody really was chasing him to get it."

"So, can me and Mikayla help you look?" Max pats his legs with his fingers. I note that just as we reach my jeep and I open the door, plop down inside. I don't get to answer. Zach walks up with Beck and T.J., gives Max a cordial nod. Max nods back.

"You mind giving these guys a ride too, Flea?" Zach interrupts us, and I wave them inside. Then Max turns to Zach, wags a forefinger at him. "I won't forget. I'll ask Mikayla about her."

"Who is *her*?" I ask a moment later while I continue pulling out.

"Oh, just some girl Mikayla was with today. They stopped by to bring us some drinks. She was hot. I asked Max if he could find out if she's going out with anybody."

"You better be prepared to buy her stuff if she's friends with Mikayla. That girl can spend money now."

"Yeah, really?" Zach reaches into the backseat and snatches up an old towel I've got laying there. He doesn't even ask what I used it for, just swipes it on his face and then, rubs it on each armpit.

"Aw, come on, Zach," I moan. "See, most girls don't get to see the gross stuff you guys do when they're not around."

"You're a girl?" Zach thinks he's funny and laughs. His entourage in the back laugh along. "I'm making good money now, Flea. I can afford a girlfriend that likes the nicer stuff. Max's dad pays well. He says I've got potential."

"Potential for what?"

"I don't know," Zach shrugs. "That's just what he said. Potential." He digs his phone out of his back pocket and holds it up. "Take a look. These are the posters they're putting up." I lean over and watch him flip through the phone showing someone holding up flyers so he could get a shot. Almost all of them show Zach with a couple of Brandy alumni—now doctors or lawyers or teachers who are also on the new baseball team, with arms lazily slung over his shoulder. They look like the anti-bullying billboard up on the highway with a huge kid in designer clothes buddying up to a tiny one in a dingy t-shirt and thick glasses. Both are fake-beaming like they are best friends. You just know when those two kids walked away from the photo shoot, the big kid reared back his arm and shoved the little guy on to the floor. Zach isn't tiny, but he isn't clean-cut like his pretend buddies in the shot. I'm hoping he doesn't end up skidding on his butt on the floor after they play.

"You realize they are using you as the poster child for kids who are descendants of miners and grew up in the camps, don't you? It's racist or something."

"How is that racist, Harley," Beck asks from the back. I mean-eye him through the rear-view mirror.

"Are you saying I'm not as good as them?" Zach adds. "God, you make up the stupidest things."

"I don't. But Max's dad thinks he's better than us. It's insulting. They are using you to make it look like the guys on the team come from the old mining town."

"Can you drop me off last, Harley?" Beck calls out from the back seat. "My sister's making supper. I'd like to avoid burnt grilled cheese again."

Zach turns around in the seat, shakes his head hard. "You can just come home with me. I've got frozen burgers."

"What'll it be?" I ask Beck, eyes on him in the rearview mirror. I see his gaze in return. It is strangely settled hard on me. "My house," Zach answers for him, turns back. I don't say anything, just flip on the radio. But I can't help wondering how long Max's dad will say Zach has potential—if it will last longer than the ball season or not.

Chapter 40

There are lived-in houses running randomly along the buckled asphalt and gravel of our main street through town. It's called Lost Hollow Road, and it ambles along its meager path for about a quarter mile. After, it makes a raggedy veer to the right and turns to dirt with a spattering of grass and gravel. There's a big, lopsided DEAD-END sign at the turn with a pull-off for folks who realized too late, there's not much town thereafter. Then, there are seven rundown and abandoned two-story homes with NO TRESPASSING signs posted on all the porches and grass growing hip-high in yards long gone.

Finally, the road ends in a path hardly wide enough for an ATV before the forest swallows up the rest of the town in its murky green and brown grasp like a huge monster with mouth agape ready to eat up anyone crossing its path. There is a darkness in that direction beneath the thick canopy of hickories and pines. It is an oozy gray with tendrils of fog always seeming to creep up from the twisting Long Creek working its way with huge boulders, old logs, and waterfalls until it drains into the New River.

I've always avoided that darkness where the oldest part of the town once stood. Pop Pop told us not to play there as kids with a certain cautioning narrow of his eyes. *There are things down there that ain't for little kids—hobos, booger men, and the likes. And if you get lost down there, there ain't no coming back.* Hobos. I conjured up the image of a raggedy man that ate little kids and the booger man, well, he was no less scary. I assumed he was green and just wrapped his arms around kids and smothered them in soupy snot. It wasn't just the uncovered remnants of wells, outhouse holes, and old mine shafts we could fall into that made him wag a finger at us. There was something more down there, something wicked. The puff of a cool, foul-smelling wind, like that monster exhaling its stale breath with a wheezing gasp, always seemed to sift from the dark hollow even in the

269

hundred-degree heat of August. It smelled of old dead things and—fear.

And yet, I'm standing on the edge of that darkness right now while I am leaning against my ATV with a map held in both my hands. I'm trying not to think about that hollow where I followed the shadow until it vanished. Instead, my focus is an old abandoned home, the last one in line with a roof that has not collapsed and has not completely fallen down upon itself.

"So, if Nana Nisee's directions are right, this was Hans Branntwein's main house in the 1870s and actually, until he died somewhere around that time," I announce to the odd collection of three different all-terrain vehicles behind me with the same lack of zest I've heard Theo wearily describe a house to potential buyers whom he knows can't afford the high price.

T. J. Atkinson is on a side-by-side UTV with three other guys I don't know well but live a few miles outside of town. T. J. just happened to drive past when I was pulling out my ATV. He told me they were heading the same direction as me to look for signs of wild boar in the hollow. His buddies are more intent on looking for places to hunt in the fall and keep pointing out the perfect spots for tree stands. I just wanted to be alone.

My goofy, brother-uncle, Zach, is settled in front on a four-seater UTV with blonde-haired, blue-eyed Angel Ferguson. In the back is Beck with a cherry slushy in his fist and a girl named Tara Lane near his elbow, who is almost an exact duplicate of Angel. Zach's opening the top to a bottled water which he sucks down with six deep and nervous gulps. I would like to think he's listening intently to what I'm saying. He's not. Instead, he's trying to look cool and still side-peer at Angel, then Mikayla (who is settled in behind Max on the third ATV) while he fake drinks the remaining droplets from the bottled water. She has donned a camo tank top, shorts, and ballcap for the ride and keeps announcing on whatever social network she's been sending off pictures that she's *redneck for a day* because *I'm riding ATVs with the locals!!!!!!* She has no clue that's insulting to me. Obviously, it is being overlooked by T. J. and his crew because they were all staring at her like she's a cherry lollipop they'd like to lick. Me, not so. When they pulled into my drive, Max got out and plunked two white, plastic garbage bags of Mikayla's old clothes on my porch. They had: HOMELESS SHELTER written on the front.

Still, this is the most woman Zach has hung out with in three months and the only reason I'm here out of pity for him. Well, and my end of the bargain which entails Zach cleaning the PVC pipe underneath my sink. I've got a toothpaste lid stuck in there. Pulling out the waxy pieces of hair and green-brown glop to unclog the sink makes me gag. Besides, he literally begged me to come. He said he got a call from Max and they wanted to go riding and Mikayla's two friends, Angel and Tara, were coming along. Angel wanted to meet him and Tara, well, she obviously wanted to meet Beck because she is twenty giggles in trying to flirt him up in the back seat. How I got brought up in the mix is that Max suggested I show all of them where the old ghost town was located because I can imagine it looks like some big, awkward triple blind date without me. Then, they want to take the girls up to the old abandoned tunnel so they can get their knight-in-shining-armor ego boost with three scaredy-cat girls clinging to them for protection from whatever lurks there other than squirrels, chipmunks, and an occasional shadow figure that ran away from little me.

So, Zach is here because of Angel. Angel is here because of Max. Tara is here because Angel is here, and Beck is here for moral support of Zach. It's all some tactical maneuver Max will deny employing—pimping out his girlfriend's friends to my uncle and Beck because he needs them bad on the Brandy Mountain team. I saw all the old Brandy Mountain High School alumni trying to relive their glory years the other day. Most of them were only ten years out of high school and already put on fifty pounds of dead weight.

Max, Zach, Beck, and maybe three others were the only ones who could beat the ball to first base.

Even if I am the one keeping this little social event from becoming too sexy, I am incredibly uncomfortable. When we first met at my house, Max said something like: *Whoa, that's more like it. You're wearing jean shorts, boots, and camo. That's the girl I know after that dress thingy you were wearing the other day.* After that remark, Mikayla is doing just about everything including tease-groping Max hugging her arms around his waist on his ATV.

The sun is setting. It's a huge, bloodshot red basketball barely peering over the side of Brandy Mountain enough to slip the last of its rays through the thick, early summer tree canopy and leave an eerie glow on the red-brown carpet of last autumn's leaves. I'm standing at the last house, a paint-peeling, pink and white two-story gingerbread home with heart-shaped trim dripping off the rooftop and a huge front porch held up by thick foundation stones. It has a rickety second-level deck. It's got three broken stained-glass windows on the front porch. Raymond O'Malley was the last one to own the house. Pop Pop said he used to sit outside with a shotgun and pretend to shoot at non-locals riding along the old dirt road to get to the state hunting areas. Now, he just sits down at the Goose Hill Nursing and Rehab Center throwing his coffee cups at the nurse's aides.

"Nana Nisee told me Hans was maybe in his early twenties when he built this. It was right before he got killed in the explosion. Then his business partner moved in and raised a family here," I go on, poking my finger at a tiny black square on the plat map I'd copied on to a white eight and a half-by-eleven sheet of paper.

I'd read up on the Branntwein family last night on a genealogy website. But there was a lot I had to dig a little deeper from some forums and a phone call to my Aunt Joy who told me she still prays for me every night even though I haven't been going to church regularly and who also has the dirt on everybody in this town for the last ninety years.

Honestly, most of the time, what I find in local history books isn't much more than a shallow picture of people, showing their good side and not their quirks, bad habits, and faults. "From what I've read, Sean O'Malley took over Hans' company. There was some talk he murdered Hans for rights to the coal business. Hans had willed his home and business to him only a few months before he died."

I look up, see Zach puffing out his cheeks, giving his little crowd a look like he's afraid they're bored to death. I cut it short. "Sean O'Malley married a girl a few months later. She was probably only fifteen. The house, here, was actually fashioned for her to look like a fairy castle complete with turret." I point up to the little tower on the rooftop. "Aunt Joy said her great-grandma used to see her looking out the window for hours at a time. She wore these pretty dresses that came from Paris, so they had to build a wooden walkway through town so she didn't get the hems dirty. There were twelve rooms, two bathrooms, and five servants to take care of the place." They are all chattering and not listening to me, so I let the map fall and rub my cheek with my palm. "His new wife was related to Hans. Does that catch your attention?" It didn't.

"We care," Max pipes up with a half-laugh between his words. Mikayla presses her boobs to his side while she hugs him around the shoulders. "I do, at least." I know he doesn't. He's titty-dumb right now, just thinking about those big boobs rubbing up against him. He keeps making a sad excuse for a swat of gentle fingers on Mikayla's hands disappearing somewhere under his belt.

I sigh. Zach shrugs. "You found what you're looking for. Let's ride. I want to go see this hole in the mountain where you thought you saw a ghost. Let's go stir them up."

"Yeah, let's ride!" Mikayla chirps up.

"You guys go. I'm trying to figure something out."

"If you're a geek?" Zach sniffs while he plugs up his water bottle with the top and shoves it into a camo pocket near his right leg. "Because we already know you are. I've found your answer. Let's go."

"Seriously, go," I tell him.

"I'll stay with her, and we'll catch up in a minute." Beck doesn't hesitate. He lumbers out of the back of Zach's side-by-side, rights himself and stands back. Zach gives him this mad gaze, "What about Tara? She doesn't want to ride by herself."

"You guys go scare each other. We'll check out the house. Five minutes and we'll catch up."

Tara looks like a pit-bull pup that just got its bone taken away. Her lips are set. She and Angel are exchanging questioning frowns that slide over and plop dead flat on Beck. Zach opens his mouth to protest. I let my eyes sway toward Max. Zach sees it. It's code for shut-the-hell-up and let this go. Zach knows there is something up and I don't want to be here alone with those two. Negotiations or not, he's my blood first. Getting laid by some dumb chick comes second. Usually. This time, at least.

"Alright." Zach takes off. I hear Mikayla telling Max to follow Zach when he takes off to the right down a deer trail. I've been trying to ignore Mikayla's exaggerated flirting with Max and her subtle sexy gazes to Zach since we followed the old main road from the newer part of Lost Hollow to the defunct side of town. She comes off as being silly and ditzy and loves to take selfies approximately every forty seconds of her face at different angles and with different purses of her too-pink lips. This, of course, is like hanging a tangy piece of steak over Max's nose. Because empty-headed bombshells (as Pop Pop calls voluptuous women with killer looks), that suck in air to their brain like a vacuum instead of filling it with viable information are right up my ex-boyfriend's best friend's alley. And obviously my uncle, too, who has vanished into the forest.

"Let's go, baby. Angel and Tara will kill me if I don't follow. Beck is staying. She won't be alone." I'm hoping in the least, those two will move on with the rest of them taking off into the dusky, evening air. Beck's just staring at me and I guess I don't mind him so much. But while I fan the dust away from my face, I see Max still sitting on his ride and staring at me.

"What? You're not going with them?" I ask with a slight bit of resentment written in the nibbling of my bottom lip.

"No," I swear he gives Beck an almost untrusting gaze, then he turns off his ATV and hops out. "We'll stay."

Chapter 41

I'd like to say I don't believe in ghosts. However, there is a little part of me that, when awakened in the middle of the night by a bang, pop, or groan from an undetermined source, I peer over the blankets I've got clutched hard between my fists and hope it is an intruder stealing my TV instead of dead people pissed off from something I'd done to them when they were alive. Still, that seems to only happen in the dead of night or when I'm alone. It rarely happens in the evening air when I've got two, annoying twenty-somethings acting like kindergarteners attached to my hip, giggling and tickling each other. Mikayla has poked and prodded Max all the way up the porch steps and on to the porch while I shove the door open with my shoulder.

"You know how unmanly that sounds when you giggle like a two-year-old girl?" I grunt to Max when I stop at the end of a long, narrow foyer. With each step, thick clouds of dust waft into the air, and no wagging of my hand in front of me will stop the haze tickling my nose. There are no windows in here, and it is dim barring the far end where another door is opened and dull, ambient light trickles inside from the next, larger room.

"I'm ticklish." Max is feigning Mikayla's chubby finger jabbing into his side with both his hands up like shields. "I can't help it. Stop, Mikayla. It hurts."

"Tickling hurts?" I mock him. I can see Beck's shadow behind them. He's quiet, almost silent following.

"It doesn't hurt. And you like it when I tickle you," Mikayla chuckles and pokes him in the ribs again. "At least you did last night." I'm not so sure about that. I don't think he does. He is gritting his teeth when she says those words. She almost bumps into me when I take in the room in front of me. It's huge and open, an old sitting room that would have also been used for a ballroom. I rub the toe of my tennis shoe on the wooden floor, scraping away the grime. *Thump-*

thump. Crap, I think I hear something. However, Mikayla and Max are bickering softly and I can't quite pinpoint if it is in front of us or behind us.

"Oh, my God, this is like one of those haunted houses on TV," Mikayla exclaims in a suddenly hushed voice. I know she's soaking in the furniture draped in dust-covered sheets while I get out my cell phone and turn the flashlight on. I scan the area. There are settees and loveseats pressed up against the walls and rolled up carpets settled into the corners upright. That's when I hear another *thump-thump*. My eyes dart upward along a spiral staircase and to a balcony above. Max, he looks behind us. I only see murky shadows. "Did that come from upstairs or behind us?" I ask him.

"What do you mean, behind us?" Mikayla is behind Max, and I hear feet skitter.

"You know, I can't remember if it is the last person in line in a horror movie that gets murdered first or the first one in line," I remark, poking my chin as if I'm contemplating the answer. I know she must be working her way between us.

"Maybe there are ghosts," Beck chuckles and makes a spooky waver of his voice. Mikayla yelps and digs her nails into my ribs. *Thump-thump*.

"Thanks, Beck," I crane my neck around to see him. He's now behind Max. *Thump-thump*. Then I stop, turn my attention in front of me and hold up a hand. "Shush, I really do hear something." I wiggle-shove Mikayla's fingers off.

"Come on, let's go. It's probably a raccoon or something with rabies." Max reaches over Mikayla and takes a snatch of my tank top strap in his fingers and gives it a gentle tug backward, so I'm dancing on Mikayla's feet. "Come on. It's getting dark. We'll go catch up with Zach and T.J. I'll buy us all something to eat."

I take a step backward with his tugging. I twist my head around and lock my feet. "God, Max, are you actually bribing me with food? You're the biggest frigging baby."

"I'm not a baby. I just don't want to die here."

"From a little raccoon—?" I roll my eyes at him.

"With rabies," Beck adds, and I can't help but offer up a smile. "Or a ghost."

I probably should have listened to Max and Mikayla when I went bounding with a cocky twist of my shoulders across the floor toward the stairway. Pop Pop always says I jump in feet first and ask how deep the water is after. But of all the things I would have guessed the thump-thump to be, I really didn't think it was human *or* something dead set on killing Max.

I hit the last step and grab hold of the balcony railing at the top for balance. I'm kind of dangling there, leaning back, so my head is almost upside-down. "Are you coming, bitches?" I goad them, looking down at the three shadows behind me making slow, delicate steps. But they do, Max gently prodding his girlfriend forward. Beck is pushing his foot on the bottom step.

"I don't think we should do this," Mikayla whispers and tests each one with the tip of her toe before she leans forward. Max keeps shaking the stairway railing to see if it is going to provide any support should he fall. It wiggles each time and each time, he shakes his head and adjusts the glasses along the bridge of his nose. "This is not safe." It isn't. And it isn't just the dilapidated banister posing a danger at the open airway on the second floor where I am impatiently waiting, one foot on the top step and one on the second. It is the dark figure lurking in the shadows of a doorway just behind. Until the moment I feel Max nudge my shoulder and I turn my attention back to the upstairs, my eyes have yet to adjust to the bland darkness of the upstairs. And when they do, I see her.

"Oh-my-God." Mikayla's whisper is like a sword cutting the air. She's got no clue there's someone brandishing a weapon. Her exclamation is not scared at all, but as if she is taking in the hallways on either side with beautiful woodwork and framed artwork still hanging on the walls. However, I see the threat. It is Willy, Lester Dunn's fifteen-year-old daughter. She's a teeny thing with short hair she dyes pitch black and hides beneath a hoodie.

She is shy and quiet, though, somewhat of an introvert. She's not the cute kind of timid. She's the creepy kind of silent until something sets her off, then she's cheeky, vulgar, and rude. I know. I've been the brunt of her wrath when her classes come to the historical society. She would tell me I was boring and ugly, and she would ultimately find a way to knock some display over with a quick sleight of hand or elbow and make it look like another kid did it. The other students avoid her to the extent if she is standing next to them, they slide as far away as they can. She is also one of Trevor's second cousins, and Trevor's mom would take her in whenever Lester was in jail. When I was around, she'd dole out glares to everybody but Trevor.

"You made my daddy go to jail."

I cannot describe how jolted I am when her voice comes out of the darkness at the top of the steps. I feel dizzy with shock. I was tugging myself upward, turning away from Max who had almost caught up and was merely one step below me. I look up, make out the outline of a tiny frame and let the echo of the voice sink into my brain until it freezes there. Willy Dunn. But she's not looking at me when I blink upward into the shadows. She's scrutinizing someone behind me who, I must assume, is Max.

"She's got a gun!" Mikayla screams that. I mean, if I wasn't jolted enough after the surprise of seeing the figure at the top of the stairs, Mikayla's shriek sends me over the edge. She doesn't stop even when Beck starts tugging her shoulder like he's trying to get her behind him to protect her. "Hush. Stop," he is telling her. It's like this long, horribly drawn-out sound of a baby bird being murdered. She nearly knocks Beck over the railing to get around him and her feet make this pounding dash back down the stairs. Right at the moment her wail peaks, Willy Dunn decides to make her move. She lifts her foot at the top of the stairway and boots it right into my face.

I see the shadow right before her heel busts into my right cheek. It is long enough to latch on to the rickety banister with both hands, although it throws me off-balance and I fall to my knees on the second to the top step.

"You made my daddy go to jail—!"

"I get it. I get it—" Max is trying to console her while my butt hits his knee. He half-heartedly stops me from falling farther with a hand on my side.

"No, I don't think you get it at all! He's going to die in that jail because of you! He's—"

"I'm sorry. I'm sorry. But the police came. I just told them the truth. Your dad tried to hit us with his truck in the parking lot of the bar. I told them—" Max sounds like he's out of breath. I didn't have a clue he called the cops so I'm sucking in this newsflash and it puts a whole new twist to the position we're in. "Just hear me out—" He is frozen behind me. *Don't move, Max.* I'm thinking in my mind. *Please, just shut up.* I don't know at what point he lets his hand drop to my waist. I just feel it there right when Willy eases her arm up. *Click-Click.* Shit on a stick. That's the sound of a shotgun trigger. Then I feel his other hand drop to my other side, and I think he might be getting ready to jerk me out of the way. *No, don't do that.*

"Willie, it's Mister O'Sullivan from school." Now Beck is trying to intercede. He's got one hand on Max's shoulder like he's trying to go around him. "It's alright. I don't know what's going on, but—"

"Because of him Trevor's gone, and my daddy's gone. And I know why he's doing it! He's going to take our house! I hate him! I hate his guts!"

"Hey, we can talk this out," Max says in a soft voice. "You don't need to hurt us. Just put the gun down. I'll figure something out. I'll get your dad out of jail. I'll make sure you can keep your house." Liar. Does he think Willy is seven and believes him?

"Are you crazy?" She is at the point her voice is something short of a whisper-shriek. She lets out three long curses, and I don't have time to think because I see the shadow of a shotgun in her hands rise.

"Willie, no!" Beck's voice is hoarse. I know he must see the gun because now I feel his fingers wiggling around Max and on my right shoulder like he's trying to latch on to it, pull me back. "Don't do it!" *She's not much bigger than me. I can take her.* I don't know. I only know two seconds pass, then three and I do what any person would do that jumps feet first and then asks questions later. I take one bounding step and I tackle the shadow full force. I lunge on Willy Dunn. She takes two steps backward with my full weight because, for the first three seconds, my feet are two inches off the ground. My hands are clenched on her shoulders, and just as my toes smack the wood floor, we do this strange wiggle-dance before she just keels straight back.

BOOM! I should have expected the gun to go off. It explodes somewhere at our feet, and for just a moment, I've got the urge to grab my head with both hands. I hear gasps behind me. Willy makes this funny huff-screech as I hear the shell making a twanging bounce off the ceiling followed by a dusting of plaster that showers us in what feels like baby powder.

"Jesus Christ!" Max yells from somewhere at the top of the stairway. I'm thinking he's shot and I'm freaking out, tussling with Willy about three rolls toward the railing. Then Mikayla screams again from somewhere downstairs, and I swear I hear her feet padding toward the front door.

Willy is kneeing me in the gut, grabbing my neck with her fingers, and trying to roll me to the left to get off her belly that I'm straddling. The problem is that my left shoulder is already smashed into the railing and it hurts. I can only wobble my way to a half sit on top of Willy and just feign her blows with my flapping hands. When I finally see a break where she's rearing her elbow back to wale me again, I bring up my own arm and ready it to hit back.

"Stop!" Beck is the one who grabs my wrist in mid-air and ready to career down to Willy's face. "Don't, Harley!

She's a kid!" He's using his own arm to deflect her fists and telling her to: "Stop, stop, stop, please—stop."

I hesitate and shouldn't have. Yes, she's a kid. But she's Lester Dunn's kid and a little shit. So right when I turn to gaze up at Beck holding my wrist, Willy does this little buck upward using her heels and shoulders for support. Beck's fingers slide from my wrist, his fist tickling across my forearm. Willy thrusts me to the right into the railing and my shoulder and hip crash into the only barrier between me and the downstairs floor twenty feet below.

I see Max jump forward, slap his hands on Willy's shoulders. There's a sickening crack behind me and then the pop-pop-pop of eight feet of railing peeling away from the flooring holding it. The top handrail and six or seven wooden supports keel outward with my weight. I thrash around wildly, hands trying to latch on to anything stable and instead, my fingernails make a gritty scratch, trying to dig along the top floor to stop my skidding descent. Then, suddenly, I only snatch air while I feel my feet, legs, and everything below the belly start to slide along the wood over the broken banister and toward the first floor.

"Shit on a stick." Of all the things I could say for my last words, I suppose that wouldn't be the cleverest nor the most eloquent while I'm staring past Max holding Willy and to Beck who is staring in shock at me, taking one step forward. I'm not sure if that was the same thing Beck was thinking when I gave him one last, pleading blink. Then, I feel my body sliding downward. I tell him: "Don't let those be my last words, Beck, please—don't let that little dumbass be the death of—" Pop. Crackle—

Chapter 42

"Gotcha."

Yeah, Beck has me. But it is barely by the back of my flimsy shirt that is tearing its way up my back and toward my neck. "Help me," he says to Max who is hunkering down on one knee. But Max has a hand pushing Willy against the wall and holding her back. I can barely see Beck on hands and knees. He flopped down hard, extended one, long arm and slapped it on my back, catching part of my bra strap and my shirt. I'm dangling there, feeling my heart pound.

"Willy, if I let you go, will you stop for a minute?" Max is gently, softly coaxing the girl. "Please." She hasn't moved. She's just perched on her hands and knees about a foot away from Max like a little, stunned wren. I'm hoping to God he doesn't move forward. Because whenever he talks about his weight, I toss it aside. He is a little chubby. But right now he looks ten tons, and I know this perch I'm on won't hold anything over a hundred pounds. "Please. She's going to fall. Beck—Mister O'Sullivan needs my help. And—and you heard her. Don't let her last words be *shit on a stick*."

"They wouldn't be her last words. I think it would be, *please don't let that little dumbass be the death of me*. She was referring to me. So why should I help her?"

"I'm going to die here, Willy," I growl-choke. "Give me a break, would you?"

"She's not always this saucy, Willy," Max mutters.

"You're kidding, right? I don't have time for her to make a moral decision here, grow spiritually," I hiss. I'm going to die. I know it. "You're always offering cash up, Max. Give her fifty bucks, would you?" I wiggle my legs a little, hoping there's maybe something to latch on beneath me. There isn't. My eyes veer to the shadows where Willy is. "He'll give you fifty bucks if you grab my shoulder or something. I promise. Because I'll hold him down and wheedle it out of his wallet if I have to."

"*I'm* not the one always offering up my cash, Harley," Max contradicts me. "*You* are the one who nickels and dimes me for drinks and payoffs and bribes to unsavory characters like that homeless guy at the gas station." There's this long, long pause and a moment where I think the shirt easing up to the soft part of the neck below the chin is going to slowly strangle me. Then, it makes a leisurely stroll across my chin and I feel it touch my lip. "Okay, if I die, you've got to get Trevor's stuff out of my closet, you hear me? Max, can you hear me?" I try to wiggle enough to catch Max's eyes, and they are big and wide and scared. "You hear me?" I'm slipping. Beck is looking around wildly, trying to snatch something that is stable. I see his fingers latch on to the last piece of railing and lean. "You're not going to fall."

"Haha," It's funny that I hear myself give such a hearty laugh. I choke a little with my shirt around my neck and play our old game. "If there were four, six-hundred-pound women, an old goat, and that eleventh-grade teacher who said you stole one of his math tests and you didn't, Max, and then there is me. Who would you pick?"

"Holy shit, the goat," he answers. "No." He seems to contemplate his answer like it's important. "Any one of the six-hundred-pound women." He says, and Beck's finger is peeling away from my shirt. "Are there any brunettes?"

"Two."

"Can I take two?"

I don't get to answer him. I do see an almost sad smile playing on his lips when he comes and leans over the ledge. Hell, he even knows I'm going to die. I do get to give him one doleful gaze while he slides in beside Beck and reaches a long arm over the broken ledge. Then I hear one last pop. Smack! Max's fingers latch on beneath my armpit. He's lunged forward, wrapped his legs around the last railing pole, and I feel Beck release long enough to swoop one arm in and slip it under my other armpit. I won't draw this out, but it hurt like heck on the tender flesh of my belly while they dragged me up and over, then spider-crawled backward to keep me from falling over that edge.

BOOM! Half the railing goes crashing downward while I kick my feet in a vain attempt to help. Then, there is silence. I'm laying half sprawled on Beck and half getting my face booted by Willy who is scooting back on her butt. "No, you can't take two brunettes," I hiss. I roll, sit up, and tug my shirt down. I sneeze twice, and Willy laughs.

"Your boobs are sticking out." It sounds strange and bubbly in the dusty air, a ping-pong ball banging across a metal table. Both Max and Beck snap their necks toward her. She's cupping a hand to her lips. She's wearing a dark jacket with a hoodie. The hoodie has slipped from her head to expose short, dark hair and super wide eyes with dark circles underneath. "Mom and dad quit fighting," she says. And now Max and Beck just start laughing like the girl hadn't, only minutes earlier, aimed a gun at our heads.

"You three are certifiably nuts," I mutter and push myself to my feet, carefully peering behind me to the blank spot where the railing stood. Then I point a finger at Max. "You can giggle it up all you want. She just tried to kill you."

"I didn't know the gun was loaded." Willy shoots up to her feet. "I was going to hit him with the barrel."

"Are you trying to convince me it is a more moral, wholesome gesture, then, bashing his head in with the butt of the gun?" I grunt. "Murder by gunshot or bludgeoning, I would guess, is still a felony in most courts." Willy puffs out her cheeks, snatches up her hoodie and pulls it over her head. I can hear the gritty sound of footsteps near the door and get a good bird's eye view all the way to the foyer.

"Is everybody okay?" It is Mikayla. She's peering around the corner, her feet firmly planted outside the bigger room. All four of us at the top of the stairs look at each other. I just roll my eyes while Beck pushes himself to his feet. "She's my hero," Max whispers. And that is funny because he's slipping in one of his classic lop-sided grins where his eyes almost disappear except a twinkle.

"Great, I'm surrounded by crazy comedian clowns and—"

POP! It sounds like Pop Pop's handheld nail gun, but only twenty times louder. And the floor makes this bumpety-bump beneath our feet.

"Oh, crap, this is where we die, right?" Beck cracks that like a joke and all four of us brace ourselves with hands held waist high like little wings we think we can use to fly.

"What the heck, Beck!" I wheel around, give Willy a shove with my hands toward the steps and we're trip-marching down the stairs as fast as we can. At what point the upstairs balcony skinned itself from the wall, I can't quite pinpoint. I wasn't looking, just feeling the nudge of Max's knuckle to the small of my back goading me forward. However, most likely, his eyes were hard and steady because when I heard his foot hit the bottom step behind me, I feel his hands give me a hard shove forward. I hit the floor on my knees just as the balcony buckles over. Beck is nearly carrying Willy in his arms before she rolls behind me on her rear just as the plaster and paint and flooring collapse in a heap not three feet from Willy's foot, which she withdraws to her chest.

I'm watching over my shoulder, a curtain of dust billowing up from the floor just as Max dives down next to me. And there we sit, staring at what used to be the balcony but is now nothing more than a flat wall with two bedroom doors gaping open and tunnels for hallways on either side.

"What's that?" Willy calls out and I follow her finger. My eyes veer to the right and to the little room containing the turret hovering over the front porch. I rise and take two steps, peer into the dimness and under part of a banister and thick, ceiling boards. It's an old humpback trunk, from which I peel back the debris. It has a metal overlay, carefully tooled with a leaflet pattern and three slats of slightly rounded wood on the lid. The handles are leather, and I kneel and touch one. "It's a chest," I hiss through my teeth. "Holy cow, it's an antique trunk!"

Chapter 43

"So this is what it's like to be up on the stage and not in the audience?" Beck is asking me while he lugs the trunk behind me and rests it on the back of the ATV. He wiggles it to balance it on the seat. "Because I thought we were going to die there for a minute." It is almost ten at night and getting dark although the moon is almost full. Its cool glow in the warm night air gently lights up the world even a bit beneath the canopy of trees.

"Pretty much." I listen to Max and Makayla leaving in his ATV, the drone disappearing down the gravel road. Mikayla started crying the second the trunk came to a standstill. She wouldn't stop and started hyperventilating, saying she needed her asthma inhaler. That was fine with me. If I had to listen to her huffed excuses for running out the door, I was going to ball up my fist and hit her.

"What do you think is inside?"

"I don't know. But it's locked." I poke at the locking mechanism on the front. There is no key. "I'm thinking I'm going to check online for a way to open it. I probably should soon before Max tells somebody I've got it and they confiscate it for the museum."

"I'm surprised he didn't want to take it."

"Max really doesn't care about this kind of stuff."

Willy is lingering by the road, pushing a toe into the dirt. She finally comes over and stops just short of Beck.

"Mister O'Sullivan, are you going to tell the cops on me?"

Beck looks like he's going to say something. I shake my head. "No, he isn't. As long as you don't try to kill us again."

"I didn't know the gun was loaded. I found it. It was behind the door." That gun is sitting against my ATV now. We all turn our eyes toward it.

"It wasn't your daddy's?" Beck asks.

"No, Daddy's in jail. He locks up his guns in his closet."

"It's an old Springfield Rifle," I tell both. "It's probably from the Civil War. I'm surprised somebody hasn't stolen it." I poke it with my finger. "I have a picture of Hans Branntwein holding one in a tintype I found. I wouldn't be surprised if it was his."

"It's worth lots of money?" Willy is eyeing it like it's a piece of candy.

"It doesn't matter. You're not taking it. You need to go home." Beck looks up into the darkness of the mountain. His stature completely changes when he's around Willy. He goes into teacher mode, stoic and with lips pursed. Still, he always has a little smile. "Isn't somebody looking for you this late? Do you want us to walk you there?"

"No, I'm waiting for my dad's girlfriend to go to the bars. She goes out drinking until two in the morning. Then she comes home drunk around five. She doesn't like me." Willy follows Beck's gaze, looks like she's going to bolt. "You're not going to tell on me or anything? Because she doesn't like me much and—I don't like foster care."

"No, I'll text Max," I say, "and tell him to keep this between us as long as you don't try to kill us again."

"I'm going home."

"Hey," I call out to her back as she turns. "If you want to help me open this, stop by tomorrow after seven. Maybe it's a treasure, and we'll be rich."

"Yeah, okay." Did I see a flicker of a smile? I don't know. Just like that, she fades away up through the trees. It leaves Beck and I standing there in the darkness, only the sound of crickets and the breeze sweeping through the trees.

"You shouldn't get her hopes up so high," Beck mutters, pokes at the trunk. He's smiling. I can see a flash of white teeth.

"Why not, Beck?" I ask him. "Her daddy's in jail. His girlfriend obviously beats her. Nobody ever does anything about it. What's wrong with giving her something other than worrying where her next meal comes from to think about before she goes to bed?" I sigh. "I didn't want to go look in the backyard when everybody else was here. You got a few more minutes to check something out?"

"What do you mean?"

"You know the old story of Hans Branntwein burying money in his backyard. He didn't trust anybody, and there weren't any local banks. People did it all the time, filled up Ball Mason jars with their cash and buried it in their yards, so it didn't get stolen. Especially around the Civil War."

"Yeah, I know the story."

"Everybody looks up on the mountain for his treasure. If he lived here, then this is probably where it was buried."

"Makes sense."

"I think Trevor may have found that out somehow," I poke Beck in the arm, snatch a bit of his t-shirt and drag him toward the backyard. "I want to look for shovel marks in the ground out back."

"Why would you think Trevor would find this?"

"Because maybe that's why he's missing."

"You don't think that's farfetched?"

"I don't know what to think anymore, Beck." I shrug and turn on my cell phone flashlight, start weaving around the yard. "This is just better than listening to everybody say he committed suicide and knowing he didn't." I poke my foot in the ground. It is thick, calf-high grass pocked with scrubby balls of brush and shrubs. It is difficult to see through the tangled mess. Beck snatches his phone from his pocket and starts winding his way along the side of the house.

"Or with my sister's kids climbing all over me."

"What kind of teacher doesn't like kids?" I ask him with a chuckle.

"I like kids. I just don't like three kids under seven in my face all day without boundaries to block them off. They follow me into my bedroom, into the bathroom. They are *her* kids, and it's hard disciplining them, you know? She gets mad if I yell at them."

"I guess. But you're going to have to deal with kids someday if you get married. Little blonde-haired blue-eyed ones if that girl who was Mikayla's friend has any say." I pause, stand up straight to stretch my back a second.

"Yeah, I don't know so much about that."

"Ouch. Tara might be different," I tease him to lighten the mood.

"Tara," Beck says her name like he's grimacing when he says it. "Yeah, she kept sliding over in the seat next to me trying to hold my hand, leaning against me every time we made a turn and stuff. I don't even know her. I met her at the fields last week when Max's girlfriend dropped off the uniforms for the tournament. She kept following me around, flirting it up—hey, I think I've got something—"

I can make out his shadow in the dark, follow the light from his flashlight to where he's standing near a huge oak tree. "There." He's squatting with an elbow on his knee, pointing to a clump of sod that has been worked up and then delicately replaced near a root of the tree. "There are four of these, at least. I thought it was just a mole or something digging up dirt. But it looks like there are some holes in the ground shaped like somebody was poking the pointy end of a shovel into it like maybe trying to see if there was something underneath." He looks up at me. "I do it all the time to test for rocks before I dig fence holes. Maybe somebody was trying to see if there was something underneath."

I squat down beside him, tug up a tuft of grass. There's enough moonlight here to see the ground. It pulls easily. But beneath, there is no hole, just a fist-size cavity. "It doesn't look like they found anything. I just don't see anything." I scan the yard with a sweep of the phone. It's too difficult to see even in the moonlight with the scrubby cover and tall grass. I tell myself I'll come back in the light and kick the brush around.

I see Beck looking up at the tree above our heads. The canopy is huge. It must be over two-hundred years old. He's rolling his hand over the bark. "You know, when everybody else's looking at this kind of stuff, they're thinking how much money a tree like this would be worth if it was cut down for timber." He pushes an arm out, rolls his fingers down the rough bark. "Not me. I'm wondering who planted it, who sat underneath it. Damn, it must be old. I can't even imagine the things it has seen. If it could talk, it could tell us all the secrets of the people who lived here."

I laugh softly, nod. His words repeat over and over in my head. I know what he means. I mean, I really get what he said because I'm thinking the same thing. The moonshine is falling on his face and he's absorbed in that thought before he turns his head to me. I snap my eyes away. It is that moment I catch the faint edges of something etched in the tree bark. "Can you see that?" I ask Beck. It is almost over my head. It looks like the vague shape of a heart. "Is it a heart?"

"No, shit," he says softly. I watch him lean forward and flash the light from his phone to the etching. "It's a heart. It has the initials M.B. and S.O. That's so cool, right?" It is laced with delicate vines around it.

"You're kidding me?" I think he's lying, maybe reading it wrong. "You think it is one of the O'Malley's kids who did that?"

"Or the Branntweins. I don't know all their names. Grant always focused on the Branntweins because they were still living here. Maybe Mary or something?" I shrug. "I hadn't really looked into it. I mean, there's only so much information my head can hold, Beck."

He gives me a gentle knuckle-knock on my head, then leans his hand above the tree again. "I can look into it," he says and sighs. "You may be busy dawn to dusk, but me, I've just got me and a house full of kids and a sister. You'd think I wouldn't feel so—" he shakes his head, tosses his hands in the air. "You know—"

"Lonely?"

"Bingo. It's hard to say, right?"

"I can't believe a guy like you is lonely, Beck, come on," I say softly, turn so my back is against the tree. "You've got

T.J. and Pop Pop and Zach."

"You know what I mean. Tell me you don't feel like something's missing sometimes."

I do. He's leaning over me, and I guess for the first time since I've known him, I look at Beck. I look past the haughty attitude in high school, past the too-buff I don't really like, and I look up at his eyes right then. They are deep green, like the color my mood ring would turn when it was denoting I was happy. And he's pretty; I won't deny that. And I'm caught up in the romance of it all, finding the heart etched into the tree. But he's Zach's friend. I sigh. It is quiet except for crickets and a lone katydid.

"I like you, Harley." Beck smiles gently like it is a summer afternoon and we're just sitting around on my porch sipping glasses of tea. He reaches out a knuckle and nudges me in the soft place between ribs and belly button. I grunt softly, fan his hand away. But I smile back.

"So, okay, I like you too, Beck. But don't do that. When I started dating Trevor, it really put a wall between me and Zach. I can't do that again. Ever." I tell him. "It's a really bad idea whatever you are thinking."

"Oh, okay," he replies, but he's got this strange half-grin on his lips. "Well, I mean I *like-like* you, you know? I'm stressing the like-like, see? I was lying in bed the other night when you called me, and I thought about it. Then I couldn't sleep." Again, he nudges me, this time a little harder and I take a step back. "I'm making my move."

"Your move? I mean, I like-like you, too. And if you do that again, I'm going to ball up my fist and beat the snot out of your upper arm—" I reach out and knuckle-nudge him just above the elbow. "Right here." Wow, I realize as my finger jabs him and stops, the man's got some nice, hard muscle under that slightly freckled skin and curly, red-brown hair.

"No, I don't think you're getting it." Beck holds out that stupid knuckle again and comes in for the nudge. I ball up my fist and just punch him in the arm like I do to Zach when he's annoying me.

"Holy shit, why'd you do that?" Now Beck is narrowing his eyes with irritation, rubbing his palm along between shoulder and elbow. "That hurt. I'm trying to tell you I *like* you. I'm not asking you to marry me, for God's sakes. We don't have to tell your brother."

"Uncle." I correct him "But listen to yourself. You're asking for a *Trial Harley,* right? Because I don't think I'm hardwired to be like some sample, full-version of software you buy online that expires after thirty days. If you want to use me for a limited time, I don't know if I can just stop functioning like I used to before you started the trial, get it? I can't hide stuff from Zach."

"I wouldn't use you. God, how could you say that?"

"Yeah, the way I see it, you would. You want to try me out and hide whatever goes on, but you want to be able to walk out of the relationship, just be friends again. Then you want to see if I come back. I can't do that. I tried one-night stands. I don't like them." I shake my head.

"I wouldn't use you. I'm lonely. You're lonely—" He deep-sighs and shakes his head. "Harley, look at me." He reaches out a hand, lets it lay on my cheek. I feel chills run down my arms. And they are the good ones. It surprises me, this reaction. I would have never expected it. Yet, I would have never expected Beck to be touching my face and showing a bit of soft, sweet, and gentle beneath the laid-back exterior. "I'd never do that to you. No trials. I am just enjoying being with you. And you blew me away—in that dress the other day at your dad's—your grandpa's house. Damn, you're beautiful—I mean in jean shorts—" He waves a hand at me. "Or in the dress. You struck me dumb. I know it's stupid. You get guys saying stuff like this all the time." He pulls his hand away, throws his head back and groans. "You must think I'm an idiot. Drop it. Oh, God, and please do not tell Zach I'm like—"

"Kiss me. Let's try this thing out." *What the hell am I saying?* I can't believe those words slipped through my lips. But my back is to the tree and Beck is facing me, his hand resting just above my right shoulder on the bark of the tree. The breeze wafted through, and I caught a bit of Beck-scent. And it is good. The kind of natural man-perfume mingled with the type of aftershave men who know women know how to pick out.

I'd like to say he hesitates right then. But I'm not sure the time lapse is uncertainty or an attempt to read my expression. It's only for three seconds before he leans into me and I bring out one hand and gently light it on his belly. I'm thinking this is the point of no return. Three seconds. Two seconds—and his lips touch mine, cool and soft and tasting a little like the cherry slushy he was drinking. It's like two quick pecks and he pulls away. I didn't realize he'd slipped his fingers beneath my jaw until he dropped his hand and my skin suddenly felt cool there. Oh. Yeah, I can say for the first time since I kissed Kayden Fields on the playground in first grade, I felt the fireworks exploding in my chest like they talk about in books. I mean, really, I thought the sensation didn't exist. It was only how I wanted it to be at age six. It's like butterflies bursting from a hand grenade in my chest.

"You in or out?"

"I don't know. Tough to tell, Beck," I say hoarsely. "It was only a little kiss." It must show on my face, though, my lie. Because Beck leans in and his eyes are slightly open.

"You're beautiful. And smart." I don't know whether to say thank you. Is that a thing? It doesn't matter. He kisses me again, long and hard, and this time makes a smooth move toward me and pushes a hand over my shoulder and around to my neck. It is heavy, and I realize he's so big, so tall, so smart himself and so not the kind of guy I like to date. I'm on my tippy-toes, for heaven's sakes and he's keeling over halfway. And more so, me, I'm tiny like the tattoo baby blue butterflies flitting on my shoulder. Maybe he's going to crush me in his fist.

"Beck—" I start to say it. He's out of my realm. He called me smart, so he obviously thought that one out. Because I'm not the type of girl who thinks she's pretty, so he had a backup. He's deep, I suppose, and he cares about stuff, thinks it out. He's not like the guys I usually end up with who lack a whole lot of moral values. He's the kind who requires work, I suppose. "Hey, Beck, wait—please wait a minute." My eyes must be big and wide looking up at him when he stops. I know I must be like an awkward thirteen-year-old compared to the girls he's used to being with. He always likes the tall girls, the chunky athletic ones who played volleyball and basketball. I know. I heard Zach and him talk about women all the time. Me, I'm scrawny and short and not anything like any girl he's ever dated or coveted mentally over beers in Pop Pop's garage.

"I won't hurt you, Harley. Is that what you're worried about? I mean, because I'm big. You're small."

And if he hadn't leaned over and kissed me on my forehead, pushed my bangs from my face right then with the gentlest swipes of his fingers, I would have pushed out my hands, halted the whole thing. Because people telling me I'm small or tiny make me angry. It's like they've found a way to cull me from their herd, show a weakness that I can't change. But he did, then he just reaches around me and pulls me up, up, up. And I wrap my legs around his waist. I'm in. Oh, I'm so in. My chest is bursting with a thousand butterflies. Is it the danger of it? If Zach finds out I kissed his buddy, I think he'll kill us both. I don't know. No, I know what it is. It's that he is moving me around like I weigh nothing, kissing the soft skin of my shoulders, and oh-my-God, rolling his tongue along my neck.

"You want me to stop?" he asks me, wiggling his fingers under my shirt. Because I tugged it up and pushed his wrist.

"What do you think?" I ask him, and he chuckles. It blends with the crickets and the katydids and the little spring peeper frogs making a shrill trill in the creeks.

We kiss, and we kiss until Beck's got me pushed up against the tree and I've got a feeling I know what comes next. I wiggle my legs down, start to tug on the button of my shorts. But it's like I can't get them off quickly enough for him. He's got his hands rolling down my hips, grasping my bottom, wiggling the shorts and my panties down to my thighs and then to the ground. I feel his hand slide back up, fingers tickling my belly. They continue downward, roll with a coolness across the warm cleft between my legs. I'm going from butterflies in my chest, to butterflies just below my belly button. Again, something I've never been induced to feel. He pushes my legs apart with his right knee, parting my thighs so I spread my legs, take a step outward. And I'm not embarrassed to say, just that alone is forcing my fingers into a fist on his t-shirt, towing him inward. I'm ready. I mean, right this second, I'm like in a mad race to make him feel like I feel right this moment, so we can get on with it.

I'm intent on his kisses. I'm intent on his finger parting the softness between my legs. He's slow and easy, a proficient artist painting a picture with his touch on my skin. Holy shit. I'm wet. Not yet. Please, I'm begging any entity that might have pity on me. I want this to last. I'm like wondering what I need to do to get Beck to this point because I'm going to explode. What the hell? I've never been ready before the guy. I always have to think up something in my head, some fantasy to get me to that point while he finishes. But Beck's finger just barely grazes my thigh. A trickle of sweat runs along my forehead while I push up his shirt, press my forehead against his lower chest. I kiss him. His belly is flat and salty-tasting. I bumble around the crotch of his pants like a virgin bride trying to figure out if there's something underneath the five silver buttons and—

"Here." I think after thirty seconds, he takes his free hand and in an accomplished twist, unbuttons the secret to expose what I've been begging to get.

"Harley—" he says that then just lifts me upward. "Put your legs around me again. Please, please—" And I do, and I know that's all it takes while he gently slides me down on him, slowly, carefully before he curses low on his breath. I am the one who pushes myself on him, taking him in while he rubs me up and down, up and down. Twice. That's it. And we're both making sweet sighing sounds along with the crickets and the katydids.

I suppose it's like a storm rolling over a sunny, summer day. It is there in a rush of thunder and lightning hard rain and then suddenly, the outburst ends in a soft, subtle silence. Beck lifts me and sets me down. He goes to kiss the top of my head, but I don't realize that's what he's doing and duck to get my shorts. He misses. I hit the tree with my rear and almost fall over.

"I'm sorry. It's been a long time." That's what he says buttoning his pants. My cheeks are red while I rise and slip into my panties, then my shorts. Then it is like it rolls over him, what just happened. "Why'd you let me do that?" Beck says. I look up, and he's got his hand on his forehead, fingers pinching his temples. I've seen him do this before at three events, all stressful: funerals, difficult tests in high school, and when Pop Pop would yell at Zach for something he'd thought Zach did, but Beck was really the offender.

"What?"

"You should have stopped me. Oh, God, I can't believe—"

"You told me you were lonely. Like me." Why did that sound so naïve coming from my lips? Why is he blaming this on me?

"Don't guys tell you that all the time? Harley, for God's sakes, it's me. I've used that line so many times."

Flummoxed. Pop Pop used that word the other day, culled from Nana Nisee's crosswords. It means thrown, dumbfounded, floored, stunned. I can't remember his sentence use. I just know it was the moment Zach must have told him he wasn't going to be on his team for the ball tournament. He rounded the kitchen, and the expression on his face was like he'd just got punched in the belly. I just know that word matches the feeling I am getting right now along with hurt, feeling used, and like I felt when I found the much thought-out and excited-to-give Christmas present I got Trevor one year sitting on the table of the church rummage-sale two weeks later in January.

I don't know what to say. Still, I muster up something like: "Yeah, but it's *me*. I didn't think—I didn't think you'd use it on me. I just thought—" It was real. Shit. "Well, you got a trial version. Good for you."

I stomped off and wiggled the trunk off the ATV. It slides down and it's heavy. I feel Beck shove his hand over my shoulder and slow its descent. It lands a little hard on the ground.

"Get off." I turn and hiss. "Get away from me."

"What are you doing?"

"I'm coming back with my jeep to get it. I can't drive and hold it on."

"I thought we could put it on the back and I could hold it while you drive—"

"*We?*" I feel my cheeks burning, feel this angry ball of hate in my chest that I know encompasses all the jerks who used me like him and Trevor. I walk up to him, give him a shove with both my hands. "You're kidding me, right? *You* and *I* are not *we*. *You* are an asshole and you don't deserve women like me who care and empathize and feel sorry for dumbass, bullshitting guys like you. You just stood here and told me you used me and that's *not* okay. Go to hell. Fuck off. *You*, Beck O'Sullivan, can walk *your* ass home by *your*self. It's only four and a half miles give or take. I'm going to drive back myself." *You're beautiful. You're smart.* What am I, fourteen and sitting under the high school bleachers with some nameless boy who wants to put his hand up my shirt?

"Stop, dammit!" Beck gruffs loudly. I do stop. I'm not scared of him. I know he wouldn't hurt me outwardly. I don't know if I can say that about any one of the other guys I've dated. Maybe that's why I stop and turn.

"Say it, Beck. And you better say it fast."

"Okay. I don't want the trial version, dammit! I meant that I didn't just want to jump into it like that! I didn't want it to be meaningless. Please. There's just so much at stake here. You and me, we are the epitome of complicated. I don't even know if we should go down this road." He looks up at the sky, maybe the moon. Because I see it light on his face. "But—the day you came home to your grandpa's, I was in the living room watching TV with Zach. We were eating your grandpa's stew. I heard your voice from the door talking to him and it was like I felt this rush of *something*. Like since I left Lost Hollow, there was something missing, and even when I came back, it wasn't—there. You're that *something*, Harley. I don't know why. I just feel it all the time when you're there."

"Okay," I say. I'm suddenly tired. I don't want to fight with Beck. "We're back to *we*. But can we just not think it out too much right this second?" My head is swimming. I don't know if I feel the same way. Or maybe, I do, and I'm scared. I don't want to get hurt again. I don't. Not at all.

Chapter 44

"I just wanted you to know I sold the house."

I'm in my office. I quickly switch the search engine to a different page and look up to Taylor peering into the doorway. I'm hardly working on updating the company website with new houses like I'm supposed to be doing as part of my job. I'm the first day of period-grumpy. I don't feel like doing anything but lying in bed. I don't feel like avoiding Theo who has been eyeing me suspiciously as if he knows I'm pre-dumping him because I've alluded his advances ten times already today. Instead, I'm researching the names, Hayward Jackson and Sean O'Malley.

"Awesome," I answer, wondering why she's telling me this while she slips into the room and looks up at my wall curiously. I mean, the senior sales rarely go around flaunting they sold something. I'm focusing on nothing today. I feel like my head is stuffed up in the clouds and is slowly filling with the misty vapor around me. Beck and I drove my ATV back to the house. We returned with my jeep. We didn't talk much. I was tired. He was tired. I think we are both flummoxed by the whole thing. I couldn't get the trunk open when I got home. I thought I had an epiphany—using the skeleton key Trevor entrusted Orv to give to me the night he disappeared. I ran to my room, dug it from my bed stand drawer and tried to stick it into the lock. Fail. I've given myself a time-frame of three days to use every internet search on how to pick an old trunk lock. If I can't by then, I'm going to call a locksmith.

"Here." Taylor takes a step forward and drops something on my desk. It looks like a check. I lean forward, pluck it up between my fingers and my long bangs slide across my eyes. I got a hair trim. I'm not used to having to style it, and I stood at the bathroom sink this morning trying to figure out how to make my bangs stay in place. I'd always just left them as long as the rest of my hair and just pulled them back with a swipe of my hand and a hair tie. I'm not quite adept at giving it the ol' flip with my finger like Lissette and Taylor do, but I try. "What's this?"

"It's a check for three-thousand dollars." She's giving me a half-grin and reaches out and pushes my bangs back like she can read my mind. Her hand lingers there, and when our eyes meet, I quickly pull my gaze away.

"You have such beautiful eyes, Harley." Taylor flirts with everybody, men or women. She's just got a way of doing it and being sexy about it. Everybody else seems to lounge in it like they are enjoying a spa day. I think it makes them feel special. Me, it just makes me feel uncomfortable like when Pop Pop's old guy friends flirt with me. I feel like if I lean into her touch, she'll get the wrong idea in the same way if I laugh at their stupid jokes, they'll think I'm wanting to go on a date. I'm just not into Taylor or her type—fake. Even though, I'm noticing, the longer I work at Central Independent Realty, the more I'm becoming like them.

So, "Thank you," I say abruptly, pull back, and look at what she is handing me. "It's not a real check?" I ask. "Is this a joke?"

"No, goofy. I sold the house that used to be the inn. There was a bit of a bidding war over it once everyone found out about its history. I made twice as much on the house because of you. That's your commission."

"Three-thousand dollars?"

"Well, minus taxes."

I'm staring at the check. Taylor must think I'm such a poor dweeb because my heart is racing. Surely, she's playing a joke on me. "This is really mine?"

"Yes, silly."

"So, if I cash this, it's not going to bounce?"

"No. And there are more of those if you can research the background on a couple other houses I've got that are historical. If I make a sale, I'll give you a percentage."

"Okay."

She bites her bottom lip. "You're not going to ask how much of a percentage?"

"Should I?"

"Let's say ten percent."

"Twelve percent."

"You're just bartering because you think you need to, aren't you?"

"Yes." I shrug and Taylor giggles.

"How about we go out to dinner and celebrate?" she asks me. I'm sitting there looking at a check for three-thousand dollars, and I've got goose pimples. I can pay off my rent for the month and my car payment and my college loan payment and—

"Of course. Yes. Please."

An hour later, Taylor and I are sitting at the local spaghetti restaurant. I'm vaguely aware I am dressing like her now, a smaller and blonde body-double. I admit dropping a gaze at the window glass while we passed to go inside. Horrors. We're both sporting four-hundred-dollar Nancy Lynn of New York jackets, blouses, and skirts. As the name implies, the outfits are stylish, sophisticated, and tailored to fit. I have officially been cloned by Central Independent Realty, and I'm now one of their aliens.

"So how did the training go with Theo last week?" she asks me, digging her fork past the spaghetti sauce and into the depths of the noodles. She's rolling her eyes, giving me a sly smile.

"Fine, really," I return. "But if Lissette wanted you to slip in a reminder to keep it discreet, he already mentioned it ten times. You know how he is all business when Lissette's around." I sip my soda pop. "He says to me—" I drop my voice to imitate Theo— "*So we probably need to talk about how we're going to do this little affair.*" I shake my head. "Then he winks at me—"

"Oh, you mean because of Lyndsey? Yeah, she dropped

off his lunch the other day when you two were out goofing off at one of the houses—"

"Lyndsey?"

She pauses, draws out a blank stare at me. I return the same gaze. "His wife, silly."

I was stone cold silent right then, unblinking and staring at Taylor who is still cutting a smile like we're sharing some secret. "He—what? He's—married?"

"Surely you knew that, Harley. You met her at the seminar. She was the pregnant one with the two kids who kept terrorizing the hallways."

So that's how I found out Theo was married. I'm not hungry anymore. I don't know why I even care. I mean, I was done with it, with him. But I feel used just like I felt used with Trevor and probably every other guy I've dated who dumped me for some reason or the other. Lyndsey was sweet and beautiful and flustered because she felt six months pregnant and exhibiting a baby belly. She told me that in a soft whisper when we passed in the bathroom, said she felt like a frog among all the realty princesses. I had told her it would pass. She would be skinny again.

"You know, Lissette's husband is a teacher at one of the middle schools." Taylor stares at me, still expressionless. "Most people think he's this really good guy. Not so. Lissette tried to leave him a couple times. He waits until she goes to work, then he and his brother take the kids and won't let her see them until she comes back. She works so much, she doesn't think she could get custody if she did get a divorce. And if she leaves him for a woman, everyone will know. At least that's how he threatens her, keeps her in his cage. So, she stays. And I stay. It's not a big deal. Some people get stuck marrying people they don't really love. They just don't want to hurt them. Others, they don't have a choice. What we do, you and I, is become somewhat of a lighthouse for them, right?"

Chapter 45

"Baby, you got to hit the ball harder than that." Pop Pop's a patient man, but I can see him getting a little annoyed at my hitting two days later. After weeks of batting practice with Pop Pop's team and with Taylor's help, I can at least hit the dang thing. Now, I've got to figure out how to hit it hard enough to do more than skid-bounce twenty feet out and, with the same ambition as a sloth dozing on a tree limb, stop just short of the pitcher's mound. However, I don't think it's going to happen. Every coach who didn't pick me for a team must have seen it. I just don't have the right stuff.

"We can all move up toward home plate," Buddy Peterson offers, does his limp-walk to the ball, and snatches it up in his fist. He's on first base which is probably good. He doesn't have to run hard to the ball because Timmy Jones is on second and runs up as quick as all get out, wheezing and coughing against whatever lung disease he's gotten from smoking three packs of cigarettes a day.

"Naw, I'll pitch," Zach stopped off to borrow Pop Pop's car because his still isn't fixed. He's standing at the raggedy fence and is kicking at the grass growing up between the little rungs. I don't know if Beck is with him or not. I'm not looking. "Her arms are so skinny, they're like two little twigs. She'd be lucky if she could swat a cotton ball with a pencil." He's also more than cocky recently with his new job. He started out laying roofs and putting the vinyl siding on the new homes he's building. Within a week, Max's dad moved him up to a construction site foreman position. Now he's rubbing elbows with the middle management guys at the sports bars and sporting a button-up shirt and brown khakis.

"How about if I pitch?" I toss out. "I mean, I could try." I've gotten a bit better. I haven't told anybody else I'm taking pitching lessons from Taylor and her old teammates. Pop Pop doesn't know that, nor does he care. I suppose I'm thinking I'll hide my pitching secret until he's six games in and his team is losing so badly, they decide to forfeit. Then I'll stand up and tell all of them I'd been learning how to pitch, and I'll win the game. He'll realize I'm so good, he'll be begging me on bent knees and clasped hands to pitch for him because the crowd of onlookers—

"Are you deaf?" I feel a gentle swat of Pop Pop's ballcap on my head. "I asked you if you were deaf. You're like looking at me all dreamy-eyed and goofy. I said, no, we don't need a pitcher. What we need is more bottled water." He reaches into his pocket and pulls out a five-dollar bill. "Run up to Billy's gas station and get some water."

"Fine. I quit." I toss down the bat.

My feelings are hurt by Zach's words and Pop Pop's treating me like I'm second-class. It isn't *what* they said that bothers me. It's that Zach's moving up in life, swimming the fast current in a stream and never really cared if he did or not. I wanted to move up, and I'm paddling like crazy in stagnant water barely keeping my head up.

I know I say that I quit, but it isn't like I'm even a part of the team to begin with and that makes my cheeks turn red. I get it now and probably quicker than I did as a freshman in high school when I got turned down for track and volleyball and softball. I'm just the girl who they pity-pick to run to the store to get their bottled water and who has the old pair of shorts in the back of her car to provide third base because nobody can afford the real throw down bases like they've got everywhere else. That's where I'm always going to be. Nothing has changed since high school. I'm not good enough to play. It's not just being a girl. "I get it," I say to them. "Alright. You've made your point. I couldn't do it in high school. I can't do it now. I'm never going to get a home run or even get the chance to try."

"That's no surprise," Zach huffs and makes a run toward me like he's going to take my position.

"Zach, that's enough," Pop Pop says, and he waves at me. "Get and go, Zach. Flea, give him the money. He can get us water. You stay."

"And that's why she's never finished anything," Zach yells out. They all laugh like it's a joke. It infuriates me, then makes me mad because now if I walk off, they'll all talk behind my back that I never finish anything I started.

"At least I didn't sell myself out to the man who is abusing the use of eminent domain to get rid of The Bottoms. Blood money, that's what I call your paychecks. Every time you accept his money, you're stabbing everyone down here in the back." Silence. Zach's jaws are churning while he stares at me. "I'm right. You know it. Nick lost his job along with half of these guys here. You get what he's doing, right? Take away the jobs, they can't pay taxes or fix their houses—"

"You better watch what you say out loud, Harley," Zach finally hisses. "And it has nothing to do with him. You're mad because you can't hit the ball. You never could. You act like nobody ever picked you for a team because you weren't rich. Well, that ain't the real truth, is it?"

I shrug. I want to burst into tears. I swallow the ball in my throat. Maybe he's right. I suck at everything. "Well, maybe so," I say and look out at the men on the field trying to do anything but get involved in our battle. Nine men are staring at me like they are waiting for me to say more. Not a word comes from their lips. Zach laughs and holds out his hands for the bat. "Gimme. I can show you later how to hit. Let me get some balls out to these guys before it gets dark. They're going to need all the help they can get."

I start to hand it over to him and I hear Buddy clear his throat. "Don't do it," he says. And that's all he says. T.J. Atkinson is on third base, and he's rocking back and forth on his feet. He's hard-eyeing Zach, his arms folded across his chest. I know the only reason he isn't playing with the boys up on the mountain is that they think he's too old. But he's Zach's buddy. Still, "Don't do it," he repeats what Buddy says, regardless of his usual loyalties. I suppose he sees the cocky change in my uncle too. "You ain't gonna learn by passing off the bat." Zach grasps the tip of the bat. I've still got the handle. My eyes are on each of them, one by one. "It's like you're handing our team off to The Brandy. You want to do that?"

"Hell, no," I respond, feeling Zach tug the bat.

"I'm not from The Brandy." Zach looks mad. "You know what? It's all one mountain. We're all the same. Nothing's changed." He's eying all of them like he's trying to figure out which one to punch in the face first.

"It used to be like that. Not so much anymore." T.J. bangs his fist into his glove like he's impatient to play. I know what he's insinuating. Since John Matthews has come to the mountain, he's slowly and diligently built a rift that hasn't been there between the upper and lower for a long time. I hear Pop Pop talking at his Sunday dinners. It's not a secret. Still, we don't say it too loud. Maybe we're scared he knows those little secrets on how to get rid of the whole lot of us down in The Bottoms. Maybe we know he's got the lawyers and the clout to make a right-of-way through the center of town for some *much-needed* park or electric line or natural gas pipeline.

I see a sudden and strange expression on Zach's lips like he's realizing that he just might have sold his soul to the devil by joining the Brandy Mountain team. It's that moment of comprehension that I jerk the bat back. "Get and go, Zach," I say. "You made your choice. I'll figure this out on my own."

"Loser," he says to me. It's no surprise. "You're all losers, you know that, right?" He doesn't look at them now like he did a second ago. I'm a bit empowered by it all. So, I make a bold comeback: "We'll see about that."

Later, when I walk to the church parking lot with a baseball bat in one hand and a plastic sack of everybody's trash in the other, I see a truck parked next to mine. I'm the last to leave, so there are only two vehicles in the lot. It's not difficult to see it is Beck sliding out of the door and standing there.

"So, Zach's ticked off at everybody." He's got his arms crossed and he's staring down at his feet before he looks up. He's smiling a bit.

"He'll get over it."

"I suppose. He's just trying to figure out where to go with his life. You're kind of hard to compete with going to college and all."

I lean against my jeep. He leans against his truck. "Are you telling me I'm wrong for sticking up to him?"

"No. It's brother-sister stuff," he says. I start to protest. Beck holds up a hand. "Yeah, I know. You're not brother and sister. But you were raised together."

"It's fine." I wave it off. "You're Zach's friend. You always have his back. I never worried about him because of that. I'd expect no less right now."

"I feel like a kid caught between fighting parents. I don't know how to do this. I don't know where we are—" He waves a hand between us. "—you and me. I don't know."

"Makes sense."

"You're taking this a lot better than last night." He winces, maybe waiting for some impact. I shake my head.

"I've been kind of emotionless since Trevor ditched me. I put up walls. It hurts. Maybe you won't get it. You've got two parents that love you, probably jumped up and down when they found out they were pregnant with you. Me, I've got a mama who left me on my grandpa's doorstep. I don't love her any less for it, but I got a whole truckload of bricks I have stored up here to start building my walls—" I poke at my head. "If my mama doesn't want me and my daddy never claimed me, how can I expect anybody else to want me?" I can't look at Beck. So, I stare at the baseball bat in my hand, give it little kicks with the toe of my tennis shoe and watch it swing out, then come back in. "I don't want to get hurt again. I don't want meaningless sex either. I don't know. This is really hard for me, Beck." I absolutely hate opening up. I don't know why I am. But there's something in the pit of my belly screaming I could lose something important right now that I'd regret later if I don't toss out my feelings to him. I feel like I'm tossing off my clothes clean down to my bare, pale skin so he can see the real me. He could take me in and laugh at me. For that, I am terrified. He is standing there staring at me patiently when I peer up at him. "When we were at that tree all alone in Lost Hollow, I, um, felt something again. I don't know. Call it what you want and don't freak out like you owe me anything. Maybe that's just all it was, and because I've known you forever, I trusted. And it was just that, maybe it's time for me to stop putting up walls. I don't know if it is more terrifying knowing I'm putting up those walls, or that I've got my hand on a brick ready to tear it down."

"That's what I came to talk to you about."

"Are you breaking up with me?" I tease-mewl at him. "Already? We aren't even a thing yet, are we?"

"Do you want to be?"

"Do you?"

"Listen, I'm supporting my sister and three bratty kids. My house is always a mess, I'm three weeks behind on the electric and water bill, and I think I've got more emotional baggage leftover from my ex-wife than you do with Trevor. Because of my old leg injury, I'm nothing more than back-up for the ball team in case they lose somebody. I know Zach will lose it completely if he thinks I'm asking you out."

"I know all that, Beck. Zach gives me mean eyes if I come into the same room with his friends. Besides, you're talking to the batgirl for Pop Pop's team." I hold up my trash bag, wiggle it between us. "I pick up after everybody when they leave. I'd probably make more money as a realtor if I didn't point out all the stuff about the house like broken pipes. I'm not good at it. I have no clue what else to do."

"So how about we hang out for a while, see where we go. We don't tell Zach anything until we've tried it out."

"A trial Harley. I thought we hashed that out. You got it. The free trial has ended."

"What do I have to do to extend the plan? Pay? Because if you say that, you don't know how much I've got invested in this relationship already, Harley," he says. "Think what you want. But I've been crushing on you since third grade when you bit me on the swing sets, then punched yourself in the arm and told the teacher I hit you."

"Zach squealed on me so he could be your friend."

"You stuck around with Zach at the hospital after my wreck. I know you got dragged along with your Pop Pop and your uncle when I was doing my therapy—my mom and dad had to get second jobs to cover the hospital stuff, and so Pop Pop drove me. You probably don't remember."

"I just remember you whining in the back seat all the time and everybody being quiet around you."

"Yeah, well, you were the only one who told me off, told me to grow some balls because shit happens. Either move on and stick it out or die. You didn't want to be in the car for another two-hour, one-way drive, much less listen to some pansy-ass bellyache about himself the entire time. Your Pop Pop made you get out of the car and walk."

"Yeah, I remember that. I'm sorry for that. I mean, I'm sorry I said that stuff. I was mean." I watch him reach around, tug out his wallet from his back pocket.

"I walked because you made me mad. I didn't want you to think I was a pansy ass." He opens it and pulls out a twenty-dollar bill. "Here. Twenty bucks. It's the last one I got in there. No sex, just hanging out. Maybe sticking it out. I'm not sure what Harley program that gets me, but I'll give my last dime for it."

"Shit, Beck," I'm staring at his hand. He's got this serious look on his face. "I'll extend the free version a little longer." I reach out, gently push his hand away. I suppose most people would think Beck was eluding a relationship. Not me. I don't know a whole lot of what he went through with his ex-wife. However, I do know that it is the one thing I don't jump into feet first anymore and that's a relationship with someone. Still— "Okay, I'm in."

Chapter 46

I know a little about Max's father. It isn't because Max talks about him even when I am blowing off steam and ranting about something Pop Pop did or didn't do that bugged me. He doesn't say: *Well, you think that's bad? You should hear what my dad did* or *Well, it's not as bad as when my dad-blah-blah-blah*. I suppose if it was anybody else other than Max, I would find it strange. But it *is* Max who doesn't really tell anybody anything unless you work hard at wheedling it out of him.

"Listen, I think what my dad did was shitty," he says in the light of my front porch lamp and juggling a brown cardboard box. "I just want you to know." I admittedly think it odd when I find myself face to face with Max who is standing at my door at five-forty on a Wednesday morning and apologizing for his father when I open the door to charge out to my jeep to leave. I jump, startled. I had paused long enough, dangling in the door frame to wiggle on my right sandal slipping off.

"Holy crap! You just scared the shit out of me!" My heart is racing. I'm in a mad rush to get to work, so I've got a foamy toothbrush stuck between my teeth, a dribble of blue-white toothpaste on the front of my deep red dress that I'm trying to rub away with a musty-smelling washrag in one hand. I'm juggling my purse in the cleft of my arm because I was digging inside for my backup cherry red lipstick because I'm in a cherry red lipstick kind of mood today and mine rolled down into the open heater vent and I don't have time to dig it out.

"Sorry. I wanted to stop by and tell you Mikayla's fine. She just hyperventilated. She does that sometimes."

He acts like I care. "That's cool. I'm running late."

"So, did you open the trunk?"

"No, not yet. Max, I'm late for work. What did your dad do? Surely, he hasn't wiped out our entire hollow yet, right?

Can you sum it up in less than thirty seconds?" I'm perplexed. "And what's in the box?" He doesn't answer right away. With a hooked forefinger of the other hand, I'm leaning over and doing a funny balancing dance, so I can wiggle on the dainty strap of a red high-heel sandal on my right foot. The one on the left sets me up higher. I am having a hard time balancing without hopping toward the porch at the same time. Max, with hair askew, looks like he just walked straight out of bed with his clothes on. His button-up shirt is wrinkled, and the parts he usually tucks carefully beneath a belt are dribbling over the waist of his khaki pants. "Oh, you look like hell, dude." I wiggle on the sandal and stand up straight. I'm still a foot shorter than Max in six-inch stilettos. I take out the toothbrush and wince while I swallow the toothpaste for lack of a sink to spit it out. I scratch my head, lean against the doorframe. "You been out drinking? Don't leave me hanging. What did your dad do?" I prompt him again.

"No, I was in meetings until ten o'clock last night, and then I couldn't sleep. It was a rough night." I look down, make one last swipe with the washrag just over my right breast that doesn't completely take out the stain, and toss the smelly rag into the room behind me. "Lay it on me."

"You've got toothpaste on your chin."

"Thanks." I swipe at my chin with my wrist absently, wiggle a hand toward my jeep. "Walk toward my driveway. I'm twenty minutes behind schedule. And oh, my God, Max. What—did he do?" I also catch the shoulder strap to my purse on the doorknob momentarily and dump my lipstick, a set of keys from my office and an open pack of mint bubblegum on the floor between us. "Shit."

"Here, I'll get that," he says, swinging the box to one arm and kneeling while I follow the descent of two more items: a cute little box of hot pink condoms with brown lipstick lips on the cover and a comb.

"Oh, don't," I grunt, waving my hands between us. But he's already kneeling and plucking up my stuff between two fingers of his right hand. He rises and holds out his palm for me to take them, doesn't make a comment about the contents.

"You didn't hear?"

"I would assume not because you're making it sound bad and I haven't heard anything bad," I tell him, grabbing up the condoms and comb in his palm in one, big fist and hoping I got it all on the first swipe. "What?"

"I'm sorry. Your grandpa sent a check and the form to play in the league. Dad sent it back to him. I figured you hadn't texted me because you found out. I miss you."

Honestly, I did text him. Five times. On the fifth time, I get a terse message back: *Harley, this is Max's girlfriend, Mikayla. Stop texting him or else.* Or else, what? I didn't know. I stopped. I make a sloppy shove of the things in my fist into my purse. "Why would I blame you for that?"

"I think you call it: guilty by association."

"Oh, yeah, that old thing," I laugh softly. "Well, that's come back to kick me in the butt, hasn't it? Considering everybody thinks I stole the stuff." Then I stop and think it out. "Do you want me to text you? I mean, you've got a girlfriend. It's a gray area, you know. Girls texting guys who have girlfriends. It's probably not a good idea." I wave the conversation away. "Regardless, what's going on with Pop Pop's application? Why'd your dad send the form back?"

"The obvious."

"The obvious?" I hold out my arms questioning.

"You guys don't have a ballfield. I mean, a *real* ballfield. It's been sixty years since that baseball diamond in The Bottoms has been used by anyone other than Little League or church—and I think the church just used it as a picnic area." He wavers there like he's expecting me to stop his chatter. I don't. I see where this is going. "Harley, I don't know. I don't make the rules. But I guess to be in the league, you must have a board of six people who are not on the team, a legitimate sponsor, insurance, and a set of drafted bylaws.

They don't have the proper equipment. The league is for—"

"Alright!" I stuff the contents into my purse and toss my toothbrush toward the porch. Max follows its descent to the first step where it lands with a plop before falling to the gritty concrete below. "I'm late. Shit, shit, I can't be late again." I catch his eyes. He looks like he is going to say more. I stop him with my hands out. "I get it. They are old and poor—"

"Or a girl." He tries to make light and pokes me with his finger on the shoulder. It is a little too hard, and I grunt.

"Ow, dumbass, that hurt." I rub my shoulder. "I hope you're not telling me that girls can't play in your stupid league too. Because I think there are laws against that."

"I don't know. There just aren't any playing. I figured you were playing to stir up the pot or something."

"No, Max, because I'm not on the team. I just hit balls for them." I look up at the clock. "Listen, I don't want to be late. If that's all you wanted, to tell me my grandpa is poor and old and out of shape and—hell, I don't know, but I already know that. *He* already knows that. I think he just wants to feel young again."

"Is everything okay? You're acting strangely."

He's right. I can't seem to shake the Theo thing. It even trumped three-thousand dollars in my bank account that's laying there begging to be spent on frivolous things. I suppose the moment that Taylor told me he was married, I dove head first again into that old mucky pool of inadequacy. Because it's not the first time I wasn't enough of whatever it takes to be the prized possession, someone who is cherished enough to not dump on someone else's lap who probably didn't want me either. I mean, who gives a kid away? I can never seem to shake that I'm some kind of cheap, plastic dollar store doll whose arms don't flex and whose hair is accidentally sticking into the air in a big clump of an awful shade of bright orange and was somebody's last minute purchase on Christmas eve when there aren't any good dolls left on the shelves of the retail stores. They pull me from a stocking, eye me up and down, then set me on the floor.

Later, I'm piled up with all the other unwanted cheap toys. Maybe Beck's the one holding that doll right now.

"I'm late, Max." I stop at my jeep door and open it, start to slide inside. Then I feel bad because he's just standing there like a pup I just abandoned on a lonely, dark highway. I get ready to close the door, toss my purse to the passenger seat.

"Can you text me when you get home? I'll come over. We'll hang out."

"No. Your girlfriend told me to stop texting you."

"Mikayla? She called you?"

"No, I texted you. She texted me back and told me to stop. And so I did as not to ruin your budding relationship."

"You mind if I come over?"

"You think your dad was right for barring my Pop Pop? Tell me the truth."

"I don't know, there are health issues—" I start to close the door between us. I honestly have always believed Max has been brainwashed by his dad. John Matthews has all the airs of the fat, old tyrant, King Henry the Eighth. He just hasn't cut off the heads of his two ex-wives, nor completely kicked out all the staff working in the Brandy Mountain administrative offices who have come from The Bottoms, only to replace them with his own court.

"Speak from your heart, not your dad's ass."

"Okay, I like your Pop Pop, so I want to see him play. But here. I'm going to toss this in the back of your jeep. It's a bunch of old stuff my mom left in the attic from her side of the family that dad would never let us get into." He marches around the jeep, slams open my passenger side door and tosses the box in the back. "Text me."

Chapter 47

"Drum roll," I say to Beck. I nod to Willy. "If you'll do the honors, Miss Dunn, we'll pop the lid on this puppy."

Beck is sitting on my worn couch later that evening, looking comfortable stuffed into my old cushions and throw pillows even though he just plopped down two minutes ago. He's got this contented smile on his face like Pop Pop gets only moments before he takes an unanticipated, blissful, nap in front of his TV. I've been so busy at work and practicing ball with Pop Pop's team, we haven't even been able to do much more than subtle flirting through texts and once last night, catching each other's gaze in Pop Pop's garage for less than ten seconds.

Willy is kneeling with me on the floor in front of the old trunk. Beck holds up the forefingers of both hands and does a pretty even beat on my coffee table before ending it with a wag of one finger toward the trunk settled on the floor in front of me. Willy latches on to one side of the lid. I snatch up a corner of the other, and we both open it slowly.

Just like the locksmith at Pete's Lock and Key told me (who charged me $65.00 and spent less than ten minutes wiggling the lock and doing his magic while the chest was settled on his counter), the hasp popped open without a hitch. I would not allow him to flip the lid. What fun would it be opening it with a stranger? So now and for the first time in a long time, the trunk opens with a gasp like a long-closed coffin and the stale scent of exhausted mothballs spews into the air. "Oh, gross." Willy Dunn slaps a palm over her nose, scrunches up her face, so her lips make a kissy-purse. "It smells like something died in there."

She has been showing up on my front porch for the last three days, every late afternoon when I pull into my gravel drive from work. She settles in on an old wicker chair I've got propped near the door and probably spends an hour while she waits for me peeling the white paint shedding off my banister because there are three fist-size mounds of stripped paint lying on the porch floor. When I pull in, she jumps up to greet me like a loyal pup and asks if I figured out how to open the trunk. Then she looks dejected when I tell her that I have not opened it like I gave her a bone, and just before her teeth latched on, I tugged it away.

I wasn't so sure, at first, if she was really interested in what was inside the trunk as she was intent on getting a free meal every night before I left for practice at the ballfields. She has been following me inside and plops down in the living room when I get dressed and then follows me into the kitchen while I make supper. Then we both spend a half hour perusing the internet on my laptop, trying to find ways to open the trunk, and then taking breaks looking up information on people in Hans Branntwein's journal. Willy told me she wants to be an artist someday. She also said her dad is in jail for his third DUI and his girlfriend, Terry, doesn't like her, so she won't let her in the house. She's been sleeping at the abandoned home in Lost Hollow. When I leave to hit balls for Grandpa's team at the ballfield, she tags along and huddles on one of the old picnic tables at the church a stone's throw away. Willy pecks at my cell phone and keeps eyeing me to make sure I don't desert her there.

I take a breath and hold it there until I realize I'm dizzy with anticipation. Inside the trunk, there is a top drawer with pretty white paper liner patterned with blue flowers. Within, there are two sides to the drawer. One is holding a folded and faded blue jacket. I reach out, roll my finger along the coarse woolen sleeve.

"What is it?" Willy's voice is high-pitched but still soft.

"It looks like a Civil War uniform," I say, carefully latching on to the shoulders of the jacket and tugging it out. I hold it aloft, shake it gently to open it fully. It is tiny and Willy eyes it with a narrow gaze. "That's really little."

"It is," I say and peer out of the corner of my eyes at Beck who is leaning forward with as much anticipation, I think, as both Willy and me. I am surprised he scoots down the couch and to the edge so he is next to us. He carefully takes out the pants and holds them up. "These are for a little kid, right?" They flip open and don't look much bigger than the size Willy would wear. "I've seen pictures of kids wearing soldier's uniforms for pictures like dress-up to look like daddy."

"Well, yeah, but I'm not so sure that this isn't for a soldier," I mutter. "The average height of a man back then was a lot smaller than now. I think I read it was like five feet and eight or nine inches." But I'm thinking about Hans Branntwein, and he was in the Civil War when he was somewhere between the ages of twelve and fourteen. My finger runs to the right shoulder. There is a small tear in the material. "Beck, I think this might be Hans Branntwein's stuff. Look. There's a hole right here."

His eyes work to the material, and he scoots up slowly on the couch. "A hole?"

I look at Willy. Then I look at Beck. "Can you two keep a secret? At least for a couple more weeks? You can't tell anybody."

I stand and walk into my bedroom. I return with Hans Branntwein's journal and set it on the coffee table. "This right here is Hans Branntwein's diary from the war. He was smart and was forced by some southern guerilla soldiers to blow up bridges. Later, he did the same for the north."

"He changed sides?" Willy asks.

"I'm not sure," I answer. "I mean, he mentioned in the journal that he didn't know which side to choose. When he finally did, well, that's where the journal stops."

"Where did you find—?" Beck starts, and I hold up a hand.

"Don't ask. I didn't steal it." I watch Beck roll his fingers across the leather, slip a finger into the pages and open it wide. He seems to breathe it in the same way I did, taking in the scent of old books with a long, drawn-out sniff. "It is real. Max knows about it." I take great license with those words. "But Hans Branntwein got shot in the shoulder in November of 1864. He was probably fourteen years old at the time. That's when the entries stop in the diary, so that's where his story ends for me. There's nothing but a few newspaper entries about him."

"You didn't have anything at the museum?" Beck asks almost absently while he tickles the cover with his fingers, narrows his eyes almost seductively at the journal. I've never seen him react so fascinated to something, not even to one of Zach's models-in-bathing-suit posters my uncle used to tack to the wall of his bedroom. "I thought there were pictures and stuff with him in it."

"Not that I've ever seen. Lost Hollow and Brandy Mountain didn't have their own newspaper, so news was sparse. Back in the late 1800s, this was a poor area before the coal camps. Not many people had cameras."

"Mister Lebowski said Hans was rich. He started everything here and buried the money because he didn't trust banks," Willy says to me.

"Well, he only lived another seven years after the war. Beck and I found the old historic sign where the tunnel was that collapsed. He died inside, Willy," I tell her. "At least he lived that much longer." I poke at the tear in the jacket. "He thought he was going to die from his wound. He also said he had a secret." I smile at Beck. "But what? I don't know."

I place the jacket on the table and carefully pull the drawer out to expose what lays beneath in the belly of the trunk. Our heads lean in, and I tug out a green, woolen blanket and then, a pair of small leather shoes. Beck slides a little back on the couch, leans forward, and rests his elbows on his knees. I see him peering into the depths.

"Oh, okay, this is cool," he finally says. Suddenly, each of us is reaching within, then, because there are trinkets and knick-knacks—an old lead bullet, a tiny doll, a cotton chemise with lace along the bottom. There's a box Willy holds up that isn't bigger than her palm, and she carefully wiggles a tiny hasp to expose a tin cup and—

"Oh, shit," I exclaim. "I know this—I know what this is!

Don't tell me." I close my eyes. "I remember reading about it. Hans got this box from Irish." I turn to Beck. "That's the name of the Federal soldier who Hans saves, and then Irish took care of Hans—well, until he got shot. It had two soldiers made of lead and two marbles."

"Yeah, yeah it does!" Willy holds out her palm with a piece of woolen blanket and the objects lying within. "How'd you know that?"

"I read about them in Hans' journal. He got sick and Irish brought it to him. Hans said he kept them in his pouch along with a Rebel hat and a Yankee hat."

Then Beck just says: "Tell me about him." I look up and Beck is staring at me intensely, but with little other expression. I tell Beck and Willy the story of Hans Branntwein, about his Civil War. They stare at me rapt, and it makes me feel good to get their attention.

Later, the three of us watch a sitcom. About ten minutes into the show, I pause the TV. Willy goes to the restroom, and I walk into the kitchen to get some snacks. I'm juggling a bag of barbecue chips when I come back out toward the living room. Beck stops me with his hand on my arm, peers to the dark recesses of the back hallway where Willy disappeared.

He reaches out, rolls his finger along my cheek. I look up, he looks down. He doesn't say a word, just stares at me. I feel my tummy jump like it used to when Zach and I would set up a board on two bricks and use it as a ramp to jump off our bicycles. Right at the peak where both wheels were off the ground, that's when I felt that the wonderful jumpety-jump between belly button and ribs. That's where I'm feeling it now when Beck reaches up with his free hand and tenderly rolls his fingers along my jawline and leans in. "You have the lips of an angel, Harley," he whispers. "Like the ones on the pictures at church. I feel almost like I'm walking hallowed ground when you kiss me. Like I'm in heaven." Then he kisses me—his two gentle pecks and then a deep kiss sending my mind into blissful nothingness.

"That's a lot of sweet talk. I thought you said not to listen to your lines, Beck." He's close. I catch his scent. I still feel the taste of his lips on mine. I'm reeling from the kiss.

"I just want to kiss you. I'm trying to be romantic."

"I'll turn on some music," I say, "so we can dance."

"Have you ever seen me dance?"

"No."

"It is because I don't dance."

"Then you'll never take me dancing?"

"Probably not. I suppose I feel comfortable saying that to the woman who clearly maintains she will never dance for a man. Does the fact I don't dance matter that much to you?"

"I like to dance. But no, it isn't a big deal. I don't even know why I brought it up. If we start dancing in the kitchen, Willy will have a heart attack." I hear the door to the bathroom open, and we push away. Maybe it just reminds me of the empty junk Theo lustily and too hotly whispered in my ear. It was meaningless.

"So, I guess I know you like to go to the clubs. I don't really. Is that a game changer?" That's what Beck asks while he rights himself and backs up. Willy's walking down the hallway and I know he must have read my expression.

"No, that's fine."

"Oh, *just fine*," he forces a smile. "That's what every man wants to hear."

"I'm sorry, I'm just not that girl who—" I can't finish. We break away. I hear the gritty sound of big tires crunching on gravel in my driveway. I stuff the chips in his arms and tell Willy she can grab a soda from the refrigerator. I walk to the window, peer through the curtains to the front lawn.

"It's Max." I'm not sure of his reaction to the company I've got tonight. I don't know if he'll be mad I opened the trunk without him. I don't know if he'll mention to Zach at ball practice or work that I'm hanging out with Beck. I decide to deflect him and slip out the front door on to the porch.

"You didn't text me back," he says, getting out of his

truck and looking like he's going to settle in at my house.

"I got busy at work. I'm tired tonight—"

"Mikayla's working tonight. We can watch some TV."

I don't know why Beck decides to show himself right then. He comes up the foyer and stops behind me. "Hey, Max," he says just like that. I'm disconcerted. I see a spark of realization while Max's eyes hover over my shoulder at Beck. Then he goes expressionless.

"Hey, Beck," he says, then drops his eyes back down to me. "Looks like you've already got a TV date."

Beck says nothing. I even crane my neck around a bit stupefied waiting for him to come up with a lame excuse. He just smiles at me like an idiot. "No, not really," I mutter finally, turning my head back around. "Zach was supposed to come down. He's just not here yet." Strangely, I hear my back-door slam. It crosses my mind Willy is leaving. But I'm focused on Max. "You want to come in and hang out?"

"No, no." He shakes his head. "I'll catch you another time. Tomorrow, maybe."

"What the hell?" I half-hearted gripe at Beck after Max pulls out of the drive. "Could you not just stay in the kitchen? What if he tells Zach we were hanging out?"

"Do you really care?" he asks. I'm cutting through the living room looking for Willy.

"Yeah, I do." I do. I'm walking a fine line right now with my brother-uncle as it is. I don't want to walk into every family function and have him walking out of the room because I'm there. "Beck, just give me a few to figure out how I approach this if—"

"If *what?*" he asks. "If this doesn't go any farther than sex?"

"Well, kind of." I check the hallway and peer into the kitchen.

"I can't believe you just said that. Stop and talk." The back door is slightly ajar. I stop, turn and look at Beck.

"I-know-I-didn't-mean-it," I say fast and furiously and put my head in my hands. "Beck, the guy I was just dating was married." I blow out a puff of air between my lips and look up again. "How the hell do I *not* know that? Trevor was dating ten girls when he was dating me. Max was like—" I drop my voice in that sarcastic tone again. "*It was pretty obvious, Harley. He had girls' panties stuffed in his glove box, three shelves of porn in the basement, and I can't tell you how many times you picked up the phone and it was a girl on it, and you handed it to him.* In my defense, I thought he worked with them."

"Emma knew how I felt about having kids. She got a divorce, married some guy in two months. Now they've got three boys. We've got bruises from the past. We can't just assume we're the same as them. I know you. You know me."

"I really don't know you," I answer. "I don't know personal stuff like your favorite color or—"

"It's green."

"Haha, I would have expected you to say blue like my eyes." He laughs. I jab a thumb at the door. "She's gone. She left. You think it was Max or—"

"I don't know. It was strange. But she's a little strange. She walked out of my class a couple times like I wouldn't notice she was gone. I did."

"But she asked for a soda pop like she was going to stick around." I say, puzzled. Beck comes up behind me. He smells like aftershave. I take it in like I take a long whiff of the candy bar rack while I'm waiting in line to pay for my groceries at the store. "She stays up at that old house a lot."

"I suppose it is better than home." He cups a yawn in his palm. "Can I finish that kiss?"

"You sure you want to? Zach's right. I'm broke."

"You're not broke, Harley. Everybody else around you is broke. Not you."

"Really?" I ask him. "Because I'll remind you I got fired doing the job I love, and I'm stuck doing the job I hate. My car got stolen, and I'm under the scrutinizing gaze of the local cops for stealing something I didn't steal and, perhaps, murdering a man I didn't murder. My only source of solace is throwing myself into an old Civil War diary."

"And me, right? Unless you didn't recognize that I came to the door when Max pulled in. I'm sorry. I'm not the jealous type usually." He leans back, looks up at the ceiling and makes a groan with a funny grin on his lips.

"What? You mean coming up behind me at the door and almost peeing on my leg to show your territory? We are going to have to set up boundaries."

"I know, don't say it. It doesn't bother me you've got friends."

"Max is my friend. He's got a girlfriend. We've never been a thing, and neither of us wants to be a thing." I sigh. "But for you, big guy, I'm wearing peach panties with black bows. I wore them because I figured I'd see you tonight."

"Oh."

"You can peek at it if you want," I say, and I just reach around my arms and peel off my shirt. "But if peach doesn't appeal to you as much as—"

"Green," he finishes before me with a throaty whisper. "I—I must have been wrong. My favorite color is peach." He tells me looking down while I flip my shirt on to the floor.

"Or maybe you want something more substantial to build a relationship on," I say fondling the little bow in the center, then unclasping the clip holding it together. The bra flips open exposing my breasts. "I mean, I can talk smart, or I can talk relationships and put my shirt back on."

"Holy shit." Beck leans in, rolls his right hand over my breast, pushes a hand up to the wall and leans hard into me. "No, baby, don't do that." He sniffs a laugh. He called me baby. Oh, hell, I like that. Baby. I like being somebody's baby. I can feel his heart beating against me. "I could listen to you chatter all night about that history stuff and be as excited as my sister's three-year-old waiting for the ending of that cartoon about Red Riding Hood even though she knows the wolf doesn't eat the girl. But right this second, Harley, you can talk, but it will probably be like blah-blah-blah because I can't think about anything but your tits. And they are damn nice tits."

He must really like them because he kneels and nibbles gently on each, then gives them kisses leaving me groaning with the tickle-itch his lips leave. It ends with kisses to my belly before he tugs me down to our knees on the floor. We kneel there kissing, kissing, kissing.

"You know, sex is a lot like dancing," I tease him, give him a wink."

"Oh, no, I am not—"

"Take off your pants," I tell him. He wriggles them off straight down to the skin, eyeing me cautiously.

"Let me take a moment." I hold out my hand between us, take Beck in with my eyes. In one of my art history college classes, there was a picture of a vase with Roman soldiers parading after a triumphant battle. Half-clothed men draped in little more than cloth marched along the clay for eternity. Each one was incredibly detailed, each muscular limb carefully defined. It was beautiful. They were beautiful. Beck is buff and beautiful because he looks like one of those soldiers who had just paraded off the vase.

"You know you're beautiful, right?" I ask in something like a whisper looking up. "Like a piece of art I remember from college." I know I usually feel three inches tall, a runt. Inside, I dread taking off my clothes because I'm not big-boobed and well-rounded anywhere on my body. Right that moment, I realize it isn't all about me with Beck. It didn't faze me to whip off my bra. I do not know why he makes me feel like I'm perfect even if I'm not in my eyes. He doesn't tell me that, he doesn't fake-flatter me.

Such, right then, I realize at that moment while Beck looks back and forth between my eyes, he is the one questioning my genuineness. *Is she just saying that?* He is the self-conscious one. "Can I show you a dance right now?"

Because he's not so worried about how other girls perceive him. He's confident that he fits into their mold of what is sexy. He's worried about just me. Me. Because he knows he's not my usual type—skinny guys, smart guys, guys who are cocky, a bit feral, and rough.

I don't think he even knows how to answer me. He doesn't. He looks about as confident as a squirrel with a walnut in his little fists being treed by a beagle. If he bolts, he loses the nut. If he stays still, he gets eaten. I gently nudge him, so he knows to lay on the floor while I wiggle off my underpants. "I'll do all the moving. You just have to put your hands on my hips, work them up and down. It's like a tango, just naked and close."

The floor. I really don't notice it is wood and hard because Beck rolls to his back and plops me on top of his waist. I straddle him naked with my knees on the floor and slide down, so we are as one. His skin touches mine. Mine touches his. And I feel him inside me, and my hands tighten into fists. I start to move, rub back and forth. I just pretend I'm dancing and I really think that Beck is starting to like dancing too. He starts moving with me, rolling his hips until we're back to our mewling moans.

We lay on the floor for an hour, me cupped in his body chattering about stupid stuff and old things that are funny we remember. We try to find things to divulge about ourselves that maybe the other doesn't know. I tell him I don't have a favorite color, but if I must choose, it would be orange. I like sunrises. I like storms. He likes the video games where soldiers fight in apocalyptic battles. He likes pizza. I already knew that. One of his favorite things is sitting in Pop Pop's garage doing nothing and waiting for me to stop in.

"Beck, I'm scared someday you'll wake up and see me how I really am. You think I'm crazy?" I ask him. He doesn't say anything. He's fallen asleep.

Chapter 48

It's three in the morning. I wake up to tires grinding across the gravel in my driveway and the flash of headlights in my window. The throaty drawl of big muffler sounds like Max's truck. I sit up in bed, then slide my legs over the side. Beck awakened about an hour earlier, dressed, and made a sleepy walk two blocks over to his house. A car door slams and I stand up quickly, look down to make sure I'm dressed. I'm wearing an old tank top and stretchy shorts, an outfit suitable for answering the door. I peer out the window, see Max leaning over a bit and stepping up to my front porch. I open the door just as his knuckles knock the wood.

"Oh, hey." That's what he says nonchalantly while I blink sleepy eyes at him. The porch light is spilling out a warm, yellow haze filled with bugs.

"Oh, hey?" I toss back at him and open the door with my shoulder. I swat away a mosquito. "It is three in the morning. Did somebody die?" The sound of a truck roaring a few blocks over is followed by a dog's deep-throated bark.

"No, I'm just—Harley, I can't stop thinking about you. I guess I want to get to know you better."

"How much more can you know me, Max—?" I start to laugh, then it occurs to me what he's saying. "You know everything about me—well, except maybe what size bra I wear." I tease him, then let his words sink in. Is he asking me out on a date? "Oh, you want to—"

"Well, for one thing. I do know your bra size. You used to lay your bras all over Trevor's bathroom. I know you don't want me to remind you, but there was a certain incident where you walked buck naked into the living room and sat down on Trevor's lap—"

"I didn't know you were there," I interrupt him. I had just taken a shower, and Trevor had called me out with something like *Babe, can you get me a beer when you get out?* I walked right through the hallway, around the living room, and into the kitchen to get him a beer without a stitch of clothes on and not even noticing Max sitting in the recliner. *I'll get you more than that,* I'd said.

Max had said something like: *Can I get one of those too?*

"You want to go out on a date?" Max swipes away the memory with his words. "I could show you what it's like to go out with a nice guy, you know?"

I furrow my brow. "You've gone through more girlfriends since I've known you than all the guys combined that I've gone out with. And you already have a girl."

"Beck O'Sullivan is better? You know how many girls he hustles into bed. What was he doing over here earlier?"

"None of your business." I push my hands over my ears. I feel a bit irritated at his words. And neither of us are moving from where we're standing in the doorway even though gnats are homing in on fresh flesh to bite. He reads it, tries to readjust. "I told you he was waiting for Zach."

"Zach went out with Angel Ferguson. If Beck fed you that line, he was lying. He knew that. I don't do that to girls anymore, Harley."

"Yeah, you do."

"Why does everything have to be such an issue with you, Harley? I'm just asking you out. Say yes or no. It's just a date. One night."

"No." Now I'm holding out both hands. "I'm not like your girls, Max. You know that."

"That's why I'm asking you out. I'm thinking I've got this small window of time right now where you're not going out with anybody and I'm—"

"Let's just drop it for now. I'm going to bed." I don't let him reply, start to close the door. "You're my friend, Max. I want to keep it that way."

"You're like—you're like Joan of Arc." Max holds out his hand, stops the door with his fingers. "Or—or Grace O'Malley, right? Nakano Takeko. You're fierce, a warrior."

"What are you talking about?" I ask, but it is sinking in.

He looked up all those badass women to impress me. All were women warriors that I'm hardly equal to in class, and yet I'm impressed he is comparing me to them.

"You saved my life the other day in the hollow."

"From a fifteen-year-old girl."

"That fifteen-year-old had a shotgun, and you didn't know if she was going to kill me or not." Max holds out both hands stopping me. "Don't make it any less than it is. You didn't know it was a fifteen-year-old girl and you literally attacked her to stop me from being murdered in cold blood. You put your life on the line for me."

"You want to base this relationship on hero worship?"

"Call it what you want. I take it you are telling me you're not interested." He looks upwards like he's taking in the sky. "Okay, you're beautiful, that way you're looking at me now— um your head tilted and your hair in your eyes. I don't know, it's sexy as hell. It's not like I'm noticing it for the first time, this new you in dresses and makeup and the hair thing—" He waves a hand at his head. "You're always dating somebody. I'm always dating somebody—"

"You are *still* dating somebody. Am I correct?"

"Well, yes and no."

"No, Max." I shake my head, close the door. I don't know when he turned and walked away. I try to wrap my head around the whole thing, him and me. Best friends, kind of. I suppose it sounds stupid that I know I love the shit out of him. And I don't want to ruin all that because I know his past, know his record, know his list. And he knows me and all my weaknesses.

Chapter 49

The road along the old hollow is already rutted from the rain. Nobody bothers to patch up the street that eventually turns to path after Dave Sanford's house at the far end of town anymore. It's a rough climb up the road with Nana Nisee grinning in the back at every bump and hanging on the seats. I don't know if anyone has told her that our little piece of heaven down here is going to get swallowed up by new houses and condos. Maybe she knows. Maybe she just hopes she's dead and gone before John Matthews builds a castle for himself at the top of the mountain. My back tires are a bit worn out, and I need a new set. Such, they don't catch gravel sometimes and wheel us sideways right or left.

Beside me, Willy Dunn is playing dark princess in the passenger seat because she has, for some reason, attached herself to me. Three days ago, she was snuffling about Trevor being dead again, and so I dragged out Hans Branntwein's journal and let her start reading it. Now she's as obsessed with it as I am.

I have to drive four miles from town to get gas at Dusty Road/Lost Hollow Grocery and Gas because Nana Nisee wants another crossword puzzle book and I think they've got a shelf along one wall with coloring books and newspapers and crossword paperbacks. After I get the gas, I stroll inside. I'm a bit carsick. It is hot in my jeep and it bumps and bangs on old, big tires. I grab a pack of gum to settle it. I'm standing at the three-level magazine shelf with arms crossed, and there's one dusty crossword booklet that I snatch up with my hand. I pause as I pull back. On the bottom tier, there's a spiral-bound tan sketchbook packaged in plastic wrap. It's oddly settled there and stuffed between the teen magazines, word puzzles, and coloring books. I think of Max and how we used to sit at the park and he would draw on lined, spiral bound notebooks while I spun around and around on an old, rusted merry-go-round chattering about stuff I figure he probably never listened to because he was deep in his artwork. I think the summers spent sitting in the park with the hot metal of the playground merry-go-round searing my bottom and the sun on my shoulders while staring at Max deep in thought were the best summers of my life. Just seeing the sketchbook makes my tummy feel the soft glow of that memory. We've hardly done more than argue with each other at the door since Mikayla came into the picture. Maybe I should just let him go. But I want to bring back those summers in my mind, so I count out the bit of cash I've got in my purse while I'm standing there. I've got enough to maybe buy my old dream through that sketchbook, the six-dollar set of three art pencils settled in front of it, the crossword booklet and the pack of gum for me and a candy bar for Willy.

"I'm glad somebody bought that. The Lawsons asked me to order that last year for their kid's art class, and they never came and got it. I almost tossed it." Bill Armstrong owns the gas station. "You're not an artist, are you?" He's a chubby, hairy man with smiling eyes. "I need a new logo for the grocery. We're getting new signs." He's working the register today. He jabs a thumb behind him to a 1950s-looking poster. It is torn. I shake my head, slide the money over to him. "No. Max Matthews-Branntwein does that kind of stuff."

"I think he and his dad are too busy buying out everybody west of here." His eyes aren't smiling anymore. "Don't see how he has time to do piddly stuff like draw." Bill rings up the register. "They're really pushing my dad to sell his house over on Lost Hollow Road. He's been living in it since the forties. He bought it from the Branntweins when they were selling their estate. He bought it good as gold. Now if he doesn't pay his water bill or his taxes two days early, they are knocking at his door asking him to sell before he goes bankrupt. Who does that?"

I pat the sketchbook. "Maybe this will take up more of his time so he isn't thinking so hard about gobbling up our town, huh?" I smile. Bill smiles back.

"You're a good girl, you know that? Just because you got more earrings and tattoos than a sailor doesn't make you bad, right?" He pokes my shoulder softly with three chubby and black-hairy fingers where my little baby blue butterfly is sticking out. "You watch out for that Matthews-Branntwein family. They are up to no good. If we all stick together and don't sell, they'll stop bothering us. Maybe they'll go somewhere else."

"Maybe." I smile and pat the counter. "I got to go. My grandma's waiting for me in the car. It's getting hot." He hands me my bag, and I turn, head for the door.

"Hey," Bill calls out to my back. "I heard about your job at the historical society. You need another job; you got one here. I could use a few days off now and then."

"Thanks." I push the door with one hand and hear Bill call out a *hey* again. I pause mid-step. He's leaning on the counter, looking down the rows of shelves, then turns a straight-lipped gaze at me. "I saw him up in the hollow."

I'm tipping my head to the side and turn slowly. "*Him*?"

"Trevor. It was the same week he came up missing," he says firmly. "Maybe it was a day or two before he disappeared. I rent out that old cabin up the hill where the Dunns live. I hiked it up the side of the mountain along the road leading to the mines instead of driving to pick up the rent. He was carrying a plastic tote in his arms coming down the road. It was odd, it was. I mean, I wondered what the hell that boy was doing in the middle of nowhere lugging around a plastic tote."

"Was it dark blue?"

"Yeah. I didn't stop him or nothing. I don't even think he saw me. It was just plain odd. He was in a hurry—"

Chapter 50

John Matthews is called Big Johnny by his friends. It is for good reason—he's a big man at six feet and six inches and two-hundred and ten pounds. He's impending sitting in his office chair in the spotless white police station room set aside for the mayor's office. It is a starkly bare room barring one wooden desk and two cabinets on either wall, perfectly parallel to each other. His desk takes up nearly the back wall of what was once the kitchen of the revamped home. He sits behind it like a king at a throne with two stacks of paperwork on either side of his elbows so carefully collated and laid upon his desk, it is almost like they are reams of copy paper fresh from the box.

There's a tape dispenser and a jumbo size pump-bottle of hand sanitizer. I watch him reach his palm up and cup it beneath the hand sanitizer before pumping it twice with his free hand so the liquid spurts out a clear puddle. He rubs his hands together briskly. Then John Matthews proceeds to touch his finger to his right nostril and take two, hearty sniffs. Just to the right of a desktop calendar lying flat atop his desk, he's got a Newton's Cradle—five shiny, metal balls hanging from strong, thin, transparent cord. He drops his hand and lifts one ball of his contraption to the side and lets it fall just as my right foot steps to the door. It hits the rest, and the far ball on the opposite end is set to motion as my left foot crosses the threshold of the room. *Clack, clack, clack*— the balls hit each other in perfect synchronization to the tread of my feet. I catch the overbearing waft of the ammonia and lemon-scented multi-purpose cleaner my Aunt Ruth uses to clean her bathroom. It is so heavy; my eyes burn a little. *Clack, clack, clack.*

I've only been in the mayor's office once to drop off a manila envelope with bills from the historical society from Grant. John Matthews wasn't in at the time. I just plopped them on his desk and hightailed it out of there as fast as I could. I was stopped by Dispatch Carla who wagged a finger at me. "You didn't just toss that on his desk, did you?" she asked me while I nodded dumbly. "Because he'll call Grant on the phone and make you get your butt back up here and lay it on the tray straight as can be. Then he'll write you up and give you a poor performance review. I mean it. Even if you're a hundred miles away, he'll hunt you down and make you put it in straight. He's got something called W-A-H-G-O-C-D-B-H-D. You know what that is?" I shook my head back and forth. "It stands for *Won't Admit He's Got OCD. But He Does*. Get it. He doesn't like things out of place. And he's dirty-mean about it. He's got a *thing* about it."

"You're kidding me, right?" I'd said. Because although I had not been in that particular office, Pop Pop has been in there more than a few times for more than a few things from disputing a parking violation to demanding our streets in Lost Hollow get paved. That and there were at least six times I had to sit in the principal's office and listen to him blame me for his son getting in trouble for one thing or another at school. Honestly, he was probably right. However, Pop Pop was always my knight in shining armor and refused to believe his five foot and two-inch, ninety-five-pound granddaughter would talk a tenth-grade honor student into tossing firecrackers into the toilets or taking the screws out of everyone's seat so when they sat down in math class, the chairs fell apart. But I could hear John Matthews screaming and Pop Pop screaming back and the principal trying desperately to keep them from murdering each other. One time, John Matthews tossed a chair at Pop Pop in the office. He scares the shit out of me.

Accordingly, when I pass the threshold of the doorway on Friday afternoon and come face to face with him sitting at his throne, and the *clack, clack, clack* of the shiny metal balls stealing my focus, my mouth goes completely dry. The room is stone-cold white and smells of fresh paint. It is chilly. A window air-conditioner is blowing on high on one wall. I keep telling myself that he's the same size as his son and almost a body double. But he's not. While Max could be compared to a gentle Saint Bernard, his dad could be compared to an angry grizzly bear. Oh, and one with OCD.

"I was wondering why you sent back my grandpa's application to play in the Brandy Mountain Classic Big Ball Tournament." I hold up the envelope with his returned application and check and wiggle it between us. "He really wanted to play. He had a team and everything. They've been practicing." *Clack, clack, clack*

John Matthews looks up. I try not to squirm because he is tightlipped and has a bit of bored detachment in his gaze. "Miss Davidson, I think we all know why I sent it back. We have certain age requirements—" The balls on the little contraption finally come to a stop. He reaches out and taps his nose twice, then drops his hand and slowly pulls one on the far end back and lets it loose again. *Clack, clack, clack.*

"I didn't see any age requirements on the papers we received. It listed the guidelines and rules." I insert my forefinger into the perforated edge of the envelope and wiggle out the sheets of paper within. *Clack, clack, clack.* A tiny piece of the serrated envelope edge breaks free and flutters to the floor. I quickly kneel, pick it up, and feel humbled that I'm so scared of this man, I'm kowtowing to his tight-lipped stare at me. "My grandpa picked up the forms available at the post office." I rise and fumble with the piece of envelope. "There was no—" *Clack, clack, clack.*

"Because we never expected any of the elderly in the community to sign up, Miss Davidson. The age policy was added in the last couple weeks. The tournament will be for ages nineteen through forty years of age. It isn't that we are limiting anyone of other ages, it is just that we are offering the tournament for this age group. In fact, after the tournament, we will be opening it up to the little leaguers starting at age four and the baseball league for players up to age forty-two. The insurance company believes that pitting those over the age of forty against young men in their prime, say twenty to thirty, would only make for injuries. It isn't my decision, of course, it is made by the insurance company."

Clack, clack, clack. The balls stop, and he reaches out and touches his nose, then John Matthews pulls one back. I feel the hair on my arms rise while he lets it loose again. *Clack, clack, clack.*

"I think it is *your* decision," I retort. "I don't think it is right or fair. My grandpa—we have all been working hard to build a team." *Clack, clack, clack.*

"You cannot convince me otherwise," he sighs and picks up whatever paperwork he was reading when I came in and feigns going back to work. *Clack, clack, clack.* "I understand feelings will be hurt by our policies. But we can't afford to ruin the entire league so we can let old and out-of-shape people play. Our insurance would skyrocket. Let's be honest. You and I both know that the men on your grandfather's team are hardly going to be able to properly compete against men in their prime. I don't like to lose, Miss Davidson. I don't plan on doing so as not to hurt feelings or provide a sense of community among those who don't lift a finger to work in the first place."

"So just young people can play ball, is that what you're saying?" My fingers are plucking angrily at the envelope, picking off little teeny-tiny pieces that are slowly slipping to the floor. One. Two. Twelve. I watch John Matthews eyeing my hands closely, see him leaning slightly to see them fall.

"Again, I don't make the rules." *Clack, clack, clack.*

"Can't you make an exception?" I ask. "You're like sixty, don't you want to play?" Okay, I know Max's dad isn't sixty. He's like forty-five or fifty. And it quite possibly was the worst thing I could say to make my point. But I was pissed. *Clack, clack, clack.*

"Miss Davidson, I will ask you to leave. I am not changing any policies. And you don't have any grounds to stand here and mock me. If you decide to stay, I will simply walk over to the police department next door and have you escorted out of here. That might be a change for you, wouldn't it—getting escorted *out* of a jail rather than into it? Or in the case that you should decide to be unrulier, we can simply make you feel more at home by allowing you to spend a few hours in one of our two homey jail cells here while you cool off and rethink the situation."

He makes a point of picking up the telephone and wiggling it in front of him. "It's your choice. Oh, but here's an idea." He taps his chin and gives me a snarky smile. "If you don't like the way we run things in this community, go find another one to live in. It isn't like you or your kind do anything to be a positive influence on our Brandy Mountain. Maybe somewhere else, you can start your own league with what you call *old people*. I'm sure with your background in finishing projects you've started, you'll make a wonderful manager. Now, get and go."

I'm stewing. I'm up to about sixty pieces of paper littering his floor. I think he is on to me because he hasn't started up the little metal balls again. "Well, we'll start our own down in the hollow if you won't let them play." I mean, I can feel fireworks in my chest right then while I stare at the smug face staring back at me. A dribble of sweat creeps along my forehead even though the window air-conditioner has not stopped running since I walked in here.

"I'll never let it get past this office, young lady." He snickers, starts to poke his finger on the phone dial pad. I turn. I don't know if his threat is good or not. "But the odds I'll even see the paperwork on my desk are about as great as the odds Grant Lebowski said you'd stick around to finish your internship with him. I think he gave you a resounding four percent chance. He sat up here holding your application for the summer internship and asked me if we really had to hire someone as a summer intern if it *had to be* you." I stop and pivot on my feet, staring at him. "He warned me from the start he was concerned things would come up missing. He was right." John Matthews sighs, bumps his knuckle to his nose twice and reaches out to adjust the tape dispenser on the desk. "I told him it was a requirement for the Appalachian Rural and Historical Development Council. It's the only reason he took you. You realize that? Because you're local and he had to hire locally first, or we lose their funding." He waves a hand at me, looks me up and down and pauses just above my eye. "You don't know how far down on the list you were, do you? The last, just so you know." He sniffs twice again, adjusts the tape dispenser on his desk. "You don't even have the professionalism to take off that silly thing on your eye or your nose. You look like a bull. Who wants to look at that?"

He chuckles like he's funny. It catches my attention while I turn, take a step, and then momentarily pause at the door frame. "The day my son and the Woods boy stopped hanging around with you was the day they both became men I'd be proud to have in my community. It's people like you and yours that hold people like us back. Between you and me, it was the stupidest thing we did selling those homes in The Bottoms instead of keeping the property. I can't wait for the day your grandpa sells his house and we can get rid of the whole lot of you down at the bottom."

I swallow hard, rub my chin. He doesn't say The Bottoms. No, he tosses *the bottom* out like we're the bottom of the barrel or we're at the very bottom of a septic tank. He's raising up his fingers and taking two sniffs. He's three seconds from setting the metal balls into that damn clacking. I should just turn and leave. I don't. I'm that stupid *jumps feet first girl*. I take three hard steps forward and stop just short of his desk. I watch his fingers come out, and I reach out, snatch the balls in my right fist. "Let me tell you something about those people you call *the whole lot of you* and are the ones who are too old or too out of shape to play ball." I stare at the top of his head because he is staring at my fistful of his shiny, metal balls. "Because obviously, you don't know who pays your salary. There are twenty-seven families living in what you call the bottom that you are supposed to represent. They work and pay taxes—"

"I'm well aware who lives in our community." He nods to the door, then turns his gaze to my hand holding his Newton's Cradle.

"Oh, no, I don't think you are." I can see his eyes narrow angrily. "Roy Adkins, who you might know, used to run the sewage and water plant. He was replaced by one of your contractor's sons. Now, he has to drive forty miles away to get to his job at Morris Curbing. He used to work six days a week and sometimes seven if there's a problem at the water plant. We never went a day without water. When he isn't there, he helps collect toys for the Secret Santa thrift shop. Now, ten times a year, we have to boil water because the pipes aren't working, and nobody knows how to fix them. T.J. Atkinson owns a contract business—"

"Enough—"

"No. T.J. works some months. Some months, he can't find work. But when somebody's water pipes blow, and they don't have the money, he fixes their pipes for free. Last Easter when we had that big storm, he didn't sleep for three days cleaning trees off the road." I take a breath and ignore John Matthews picking up his phone. "Billy Stinger was on active duty in Iraq, and a fourteen-year-old boy tossed a handmade grenade at a vehicle with three soldiers in it. He was able to kick it before it exploded and saved all those men, but he blew two of his toes off in the process. That doesn't stop him from mowing the grass at the playground and washing the windows here a couple times a month for free." I'm facing John Matthews who is rising to his full height with the phone in his hand. "Let me ask you what you've done for your community that isn't paid, that you do out of the kindness of your heart to help others. Buddy Peterson helps build houses for people who can't afford it during two weeks of the summer."

"Carla!" he yells over my shoulder. I stand steady.

"Buddy mows old Missus Rinehart's grass. He shovels the road up on Brandy Mountain and doesn't get a dime for gas. My Pop Pop fixes cars. Most folks pay him in homecooked meals."

"Carla, get one of the officers in here!"

"They all do things to make a community. I can be damn sure that they notice you don't do anything but sit on your fat ass up here in this office and do nothing but tap that damn toy of yours. But just so you know, there are over forty houses full of hardworking people down here. There are only six houses up on the mountain that you've built. When it comes down to voting, what do you think the numbers will look like if *we all* vote and *they all* vote. Who do you think will win? You're a bully, and you take advantage of your position. The whole lot of us aren't going anywhere soon, no matter what you do to get us out."

"Dammit! Carla!" John Matthews is cradling the phone to his chest and starts poking at the little keypad. I hear footsteps in the hallway, two sets.

"So, before you decide to go bullying around those of us at The Bottoms and you leave us out of certain events like baseball, or you replace us with outsiders on jobs when we're perfectly capable of working them, remember this—it isn't just me holding your balls in my hand right now, is it?" I see him look down at my fist. John Matthews's face turns a deep, deep shade of red and he shivers. "We all do different stuff together to make Lost Hollow a community. And we've been doing it for over a hundred and fifty years, and our roots are deep here. But the one thing we've got in common is we all *vote*. You understand that, don't you? You should. Because there's more of us than you." I release my fingers to expose the five little balls in my palm. "You don't *own us*. We, in fact, *own you. We've* got *you* by the balls, Big Johnny."

"Get her out of here!" John Matthews's voice is like a winter storm full of thunder. I feel a hand on my shoulder just as I drop the balls. I reach down and gently tap his tape dispenser three inches and flick his Newton's Cradle so it tips.

"You need to leave." It is Officer Washington trying to herd me to the door.

"I'm going." I hold up my hands, pivot on my feet. Then I release the last of the little shreds of paper in my left fist and let them trickle to the floor.

Chapter 51

"Uh oh, look what the storm brought in." Arnie O'Malley is sitting on a stool at the counter of Big Dee's. "The restaurant's closed for the night." He's got his elbows propped on the counter. He's drinking a coffee from a white teacup with two hands on either side like a queen sipping daintily of tea. His cowboy hat is settled on a napkin holder.

There are two other men standing there. One is the New Grace Fellowship preacher, Harvey Oakley. He's a quiet man with a balding head and a big smile. He's got a couple boxes next to him on the table. Inside, I know there are today's leftovers of food from Big Dee's that the preacher takes around to those who need a little help this week. Big Dee is leaning over the register with both hands on either side. My mama is leaning against the counter with her rear and wiggling a white washcloth in her hands lazily.

"Do you ever move from that position?" I ask Arnie as the door shuts behind me. "I mean, every time I come in here, you're sitting there. Don't you have water pipes to fix and roads to clean?"

"You are grumpy tonight, Flea," Mama says to me.

"She's always like that," Big Dee knocks a knuckle to his nose. "The apple doesn't fall far from the tree."

"What does that mean?" I roll my eyes. Everybody's quiet a minute. Big Dee looks at Arnie. Mama's eyes get wide. "Now that's enough. What's the matter, baby girl?"

I plop down on a stool next to Arnie. "Okay, so John Matthews told Pop Pop he was too old to play ball in the Brandy Mountain Classic Big Ball Tournament. He sent back the form and changed the rules so the guys who have been practicing forever can't be a team."

"There are always rules with any sport," Preacher Oakley says softly.

"Yeah, if it has to do with the Branntweins," I grumble. "It's like just because Hans Branntwein founded the town, they think they've inherited it and all of us like we're junk left in an attic for them to sort through or send to Goodwill depending on how they feel about us that day."

"Let me tell you something," Big Dee mutters. "That mayor ain't got a bit of Branntwein blood in his veins."

"Yeah, well, his son and daughter are full-blooded Branntwein pups," I reply. "Max and Ashley's mom was a direct descendant. Folks see him as a Branntwein by marriage."

"That boy and girl don't have Branntwein blood. They were already two and three years old when John Matthews married Katie Lynn." Big Dee looks at Arnie and snickers. "They came from some other mama from Ohio. Katie Lynn adopted them, God love her. She raised them like her own until the marriage soured. They aren't blood. The only reason that jackass is mayor is that he put himself there, used her name like it was his own."

"We never had a mayor until he came here, and he decided we needed one. We couldn't afford one." Arnie adds.

"So why are all of us letting him buy out homes?" I'm still letting the realization sink in that Max and Ashley aren't Branntweins by blood. It's like I'm finding out the prince and princess of some great kingdom are only there because their father, the king, by some foul play, conquered the country.

"You think he's not running it right by heredity, why don't you be mayor," Big Dee grunts. "Take that throne. Nobody else wants it."

"You'd toss me under the train? Why don't you? Nobody should want that asshole in there," I spat. "Everybody's too afraid of him to do anything. They think you've got to be related to the Branntweins to take his throne. It's like a monarchy."

"Why? Because if that's the case, *you* got more claim than me and them—" Big Dee starts. I see mama want to pipe up. I swing around on the stool and look at Big Dee.

"Don't. It isn't the time or the place." Mama lets her rag slap the counter. "Come on. We need to close up."

"What?" I ask her. They shut up. Big Dee starts counting the money in the register. Arnie sets his teacup down and excuses himself. Mama and the preacher follow him to the front door and the two men step outside, leaving her alone at the door. She doesn't lock it behind them, just stands there with it partially open. "Baby, you going too? It's closing time. I'll watch you to your car."

"She has a right to know." Big Dee says while I slide from my seat. "He's a slick bastard."

"He's still married," Mama says. "I can't."

"What's this big secret!" My voice is a hoarse shout. Mama won't tell me. I just shake my head. "Yeah, I'm leaving." I walk to the door. Mama opens it. I walk outside to the parking lot. Arnie's starting his truck next to mine. He's wearing his cowboy hat and adjusts it on his head.

"It ain't going to change anything," he says. "I told her not to tell you because you'd go blasting your mouth around town. Don't. It wasn't supposed to happen. It was a mistake I regret. I won't claim you. I'll deny it. I told your mama that. She's been good to go with that from day one. It wasn't my fault, and I gave her money to end it, so we didn't have to be a part of any hurt. Then I gave her money to shut up. And look, here you stand. Don't know why suddenly she's decided to fly the coop."

So that's how I found out Arnie O'Malley was my daddy. I wouldn't think I'd be so thunderstruck watching that piece of puzzle sliding across and slipping in beside Mama's. I must have looked stunned standing there. I didn't move, felt the blood drain from my face. Mentally, I suppose, I was using my forefinger and thumb flicking his puzzle piece away while he starts his truck and drives off in a spray of dust on me and my jeep. I look back toward the restaurant. Mama's closed the doors. I think I stand there two more minutes, then get into my jeep and drive off.

Chapter 52

"You need another one?" Jake Ringgold is tending bar again at Damon's Bar and Grille. "I mean I can fill that up all night for you." He's referring to my soda. I'm not really into dancing on the table and closing the bar down anymore. I'm sitting on a barstool when he walks past. I'm alone.

"Naw, not yet," I reach out and latch on to my glass. The glass is sweaty and tepid. I've been sipping on it for forty-five minutes. The bars were always my go-to place when I wanted to wash away the trash rolling around my head. Now, not so much. It is probably why I'm here—just to feel something of the old me again even if it is just the surroundings and not the girl dancing until the bar closed.

I guess I kind of want to be anywhere but my dead silent house. There, I'll sit in a tub of lukewarm awareness of a new identity I never really cared to know in the first place. If I go to Pop Pop's, Nana Nisee and Pop Pop will know I'm being too quiet and question me until I divulge this new secret. I feel like I'm suddenly shoved from my third-class seat on a plane up to first class. But the first-class folks don't want me there, and I certainly don't fit in.

But the strangest thing happened when I came through the bar door. I ran right into Lauren Peterson who was coming out. Lauren, I will add, was one of the girls in the pictures I found Trevor was sleeping with when I caught him in the shower with Lila. She stops and gives me a big smile. "Hey, I have not seen you in—?"

I want to tell her since I saw her with an arm slung around Trevor in a picture. I don't. "It's been five years."

"It's been more than that. I haven't been back to West Virginia since I left after high school. I went to California, and it stuck with me for a while." She looks me up and down. "Wow, you look all grown up." She looks down at herself. "I guess I do too." There's a guy pushing his way through between us. She clings to the door to open it wider. "Hey, I just wanted to say I was sorry to hear about Trevor. I thought of you when I heard the news. You guys were such a cute couple." She gives me a sad smile.

"We broke up almost five years ago." I lean back. "How long did you say you were gone?"

"It's been eight or nine years this October."

"Let me ask you something. You didn't date Trevor while I was dating him?"

"No," she laughs a little. "No, of course not. Who told you that? We went out on a date our freshman year. That was it. Why?"

"I don't know. I just thought—forget it." I think about those seventeen photographs I found that day I came home to Trevor in the shower with Lila. I always assumed it was one of the other girls who had collected them up—maybe from Trevor's drawer at his house. But now, it seems a foolish assumption especially since there would be one person who had full access to them just about any time— Max. But he denied giving me those pictures. I think he lied to me. I think he lies a lot now. Maybe those girls were all made up.

Forty-five minutes into my soda, my mind shifts from those photographs to the ones at the railroad tracks. I've looked at the pictures that Robby took a hundred times. I'm scrolling through them again. I've made them larger, tried to make out anything that looked like Trevor. I get nothing. The dead guy looks like Orv Saylor. His clothes match the pants and shirt I remember him wearing. The dark, long hair and thin, older-man build looks the same. Anybody who knew blonde-haired Trevor Woods would never identify the dead man on the tracks as him. Jake takes my glass, exchanges it for a fresher one. "This one's on me. Where's your buddy, Max?" he asks me, swatting my hand with a fusty smelling washrag.

"He's probably with his girlfriend." I look up, smile, and cover the phone with my palm.

"He ever tell you what went on that night?"

"You mean the fight with Trevor in Baker?" I rub my face. He narrows his eyes at me.

"No, about Trevor and him coming here—to the bar."

"The night—he disappeared?"

"You're friends with him, right?" Jake asks me. "I'm going to tell you something. You need to watch your back with him. Because he's not telling you something."

"I'm getting that feeling."

"Yeah, none of them are. When you came in with him asking questions, I was like really caught off-guard. I didn't say anything because I just don't want to get the bar shut down by his dad and his buddies. I don't want to end up dead." He pokes me in the arm. "You going to go running to him if I tell you something?"

"No."

"It wasn't Paul Davis he was looking for like I said. Paul got busted by the cops a week earlier. He was in jail. Trevor came in, and he was looking for Max. That's who he asked for. He was drugged out, goofy acting. He turned around and said *they are here*." Jake looks up, scans the room. "I went to close the door after him. I looked out, and that red car of yours was right out front, parked sideways in the first parking spot, across the yellow lines. Next to it was Max's dad's truck. Max jumped out and he was looking around. There was a woman in the truck yelling at him. She had this whiny, high-pitched voice. Then John Matthews got out and grabbed Trevor by the shoulder. It was dark. I'm like closing the door, trying to do it slowly so they think it is just shutting on its own. But I thought there was going to be a fight or something. That Matthews dude pushed him toward the truck, made the woman get out and drive the car Trevor came in."

"No shit," I say softly. I turn my phone around, show him a picture of the dead man on the tracks. "Does this look like Trevor to you?"

"Oh, God, where'd you get that?"

"The same place I got the information just now from you. I don't know. It just showed up." I hint to him.

"That is not Trevor. I can even see it. With brownish hair like that? No. No way. This guy's skinny like—"

"A homeless person."

"Yeah.

"Well," I announce. "This guy is the one they buried in the Brandy Mountain Cemetery."

"You know who identified the body?" he asks me. I shake my head.

"But I know how I might be able to find out. You'll keep this between us?"

"Are you kidding me? I don't want to be dead."

"Yeah, me either."

"Then," Jake leans forward, elbows on the counter and head low. "Harley, I suggest you contact the new cop at Brandy Mountain. That's all I'm going to say. And I didn't tell you that."

I start to slip off my seat. I stop and look up at the corner. They have surveillance cameras set up at every corner. "Jake, can you get me your surveillance tapes from the end of May?" He hard-stares me. "Listen, if you know what you know, then John Matthews knows you know it. You get what I'm saying? You want to be dead next?"

Chapter 53

"Pop Pop, is it true?" Pop Pop is kneeling in his garage next to a motorcycle. He's rolling his hands across the exterior. When I walked in, he was googly-eying it and whistling low on his breath, murmuring over and over *this is a classic* like a lover whispering sweet nothings into the ear of his beloved. He looks almost like he's worshipping it. Strangely, I don't find that strange.

"Pop Pop!" I huff at him. He seems to break from a dream, blink at Beck who is settled in on a lawn chair and chuckling. It's been almost three weeks since we hooked up. I'd be lying if I said I'm not sure where we stand. He is as deadpan as he used to be when he's around Pop Pop or Zach. They are the only two in the room. Such, I don't mind baring my soul if I have to right then.

"This is a vintage Harley Davidson, little girl." Pop Pop rises slowly, using a hand on his knee. "You should respect it like you respect that professor you're always rattling on about that knows everything."

"Professor Williams."

"Uh huh," Pop Pop mutters. "These motorcycles took men to great places. And they let others dream of someday doing the same."

"I know it's the kind Evel Knievel used for his *death-defying stunts*, as you called them. You've told me that a thousand times. You made me watch them on old shows since I was born. I hope you're not thinking about getting out Zach's old bike ramps and doing something stupid."

"Um," he grunts. "No, it isn't mine. I'm doing some work on it." Pop Pop sighs then leans over so he can see me in the light. "You been crying, baby?"

I don't answer his question, just look him in the eyes. "So, Arnie O'Malley just said he's my dad. Is that true?"

I'm not sure I've ever seen Pop Pop speechless. He stands up straight, takes an even breath. I see Beck eyeing him prudently before his gaze slowly roams back to mine and settles there.

"He said he'd deny it," I go on. "Arnie said he gave Mama money for an abortion and she wouldn't go through with it. He didn't want me."

"I wanted you. Your grandma wanted you," Pop Pop says. "Your mama wanted you in her own way. So, nothing else matters."

"Nothing else matters," I repeat. I wish I felt that was true. Beck rises, and I suppose he was waiting for Pop Pop to come over and hug me or something. But that's just not Pop Pop's style. Beck comes over and pushes a hand on my shoulder, sweet and gentle and brotherly to anyone's eyes but our own. It makes me feel better. I smile at him and Pop Pop says: "How about we all go inside and make chocolate chip cookies?"

I laugh. Pop Pop's answer to fixing everything—chocolate chip cookies. "Yeah, Pop Pop. That sounds good."

Chapter 54

I step into Taylor's office the next morning and tell her she doesn't have to teach me to pitch anymore. I feel old and tired like Aunt Rita always says before she takes a nap. None of the surveillance tapes show Trevor coming into the bar. I spent four hours last night staring at people drinking and dancing, watching two bar fights, and four people stealing bar waitress tips. I tell Taylor Pop Pop's team isn't getting on the tournament roster. We're only three weeks away. They changed the rules and added an age restriction. She looks letdown in the same way Pop Pop did when he tried to coax the old guys out on the field after church yesterday. Nobody really felt like playing and they waved him off. I think they all just felt a little old and dejected. And I really think Taylor's enjoyed using me as an excuse to get together with her old friends.

"We can still sneak out for practice, though, right?"

"I don't know," I say. "What's the use? Once my grandpa told his team there was an age requirement and they don't take girls, none of them even feel like hanging out and hitting the ball at the field."

"That's illegal, discriminating against women and the elderly." Taylor's body is suddenly rigid and angry. "You know that, right? You need to march right down there and file a complaint or get a lawyer or—"

"Okay, for one, it is simply an age requirement—"

"—that was added after you turned in the forms."

"I don't have a million dollars in cash to pay an attorney, and I don't know many in our region who would fight back against John Matthews. Everybody's afraid of him. For good reason. Taylor, when someone goes against what our mayor says, there's always a backlash. I looked up the rules on discrimination in sports. There is some protection, but not for us. Title IX of the 1972 Education Amendments Act is a federal law prohibiting gender discrimination. But it is only at high schools and colleges getting federal funds. The Brandy Mountain league is a private club. They can restrict their members, either by gender or age. They just can't be tax exempt."

"Okay, so why don't you do your own league, your own ball tournament?" Lissette has snuck up on us again. She's eyeing me, then Taylor. I can't read her expression. It is vague in the least when she slides into the room and holds her hands at her waist. Taylor's face flushes. She doesn't turn around and obviously didn't know Lissette was standing outside the door. She gives me this funny twist of lips. "And Taylor, why don't you tell her why you were sneaking around playing ball with her, dragging her to the bars? Because you are in love with her."

"I'm not—in love with her." Now Taylor turns around. And I'm wishing I could just sink into the floor, dissipate like August raindrops on a hot sidewalk.

"Okay—" Lissette coughs up a cynical laugh.

I take the moment to jump up from my seat. I make a hasty retreat to my own office, glad to be out of the electrified, ready-to-storm air in Taylor's office. I quite possibly opened the door to my own office too quickly. Theo's leaning hard over Lexie and she giggles just as he jumps and jerks his hand away from her where it was clasped gently on her shoulder.

"Just updating her on the—*stuff*," Theo mumbles, and they both laugh like they've got a secret joke. "I'll follow up with your *stuff* this evening at what? Eight?" The two laugh. I retreat to my chair, plop down.

"I'm all done." He ambles past me, whistling the National Anthem and gives me a wink before he slips through the doorway, closing it behind him.

"You know he's married, right?" I say while I turn on my computer. I keep my eyes plastered on it.

"It didn't seem to bother you, Harley. You jealous?"

"I didn't know, Lexie." I meet her dull reply. But even as

we speak, I'm doing a search on starting a ball league.

"Oh, I think you did."

I call Lance Washington like Jake Ringgold suggested. I get a distinct feeling Jake must be the local informant so I'm keeping my mouth closed about how I got the suggestion to do so. Lance answers his cell phone. "How'd you get my number?"

"I got connections," I kid him. I guess I do. I called Aunt Rita to ask her who owns the ballfield in Lost Hollow. She tells me that actually, the land was donated by the Branntweins in 1954 to the school as part of a playground. After Grant Lebowski got the old church to use as the museum, the church was granted ownership of the old school and playground. She gives me Preacher Oakley's number and I tell him my idea of starting a league of our own. He says that just might be a good idea. He says, though, that to use it as an event, someone must be a member of the church or at least attend once or twice a month. If I wanted to attend church, we might be able to come up with a deal. Besides, the church could run a concession stand and make some money for the New Grace Fellowship Women's Society, so they could buy new hymnals for the congregation.

I told him I could probably come to church once a month and bring Pop Pop. But he'd also have to give me Lance Washington's phone number. He gives the number right to me. I'm sure he's down on his knees within seconds of hanging up the phone with me, praying for those hymnals and thinking he's gained some heavenly leverage from above for hooking a heathen like me.

"I'm trying to find out who identified Trevor's body," I tell Lance. There's this long silence. Then I hear a big sigh. "Why would you possibly want that information?"

"I just want to know."

"It was John Matthews. Trevor's dad was out of town, and his mother was too distraught."

"Thank you. You don't think it is odd?"

"No. He is a close friend of the Woods family."

"Was there an autopsy?"

"The coroner decided that it was not needed. John Matthews explained to him there were special circumstances due to the family's religion."

"Their religion? You're kidding me, right?" I laugh softly. "They go to the same church as everybody else up there, the Brandy Mountain Holy Community Church. They've got the same rules as everybody else. Folks up there get autopsies all the time when they die. Even Preacher Oakley's mother did when she had a heart attack years ago."

"I don't know what was discussed about the religion. I only know it was the reason there was no autopsy done."

"What if I told you I don't think that was Trevor's body buried in the cemetery," I toss out.

"Then I'd say what my mom would say—you're grasping at straws." He sighs. "Do you have any basis for this wild claim, Harley? Because you can imagine the laughs I'd get if I walked into John Matthews's office and told him your theory. And for what purpose would it serve? Why would they identify the body as Trevor's if it wasn't his body?"

Because maybe he's running from something or someone. Or maybe John Matthews killed him and he's trying to cover it up. "I don't know." I start to say, then sigh. "But if it was John Matthews who said it was Trevor, I would hardly recommend you tell him my theory or any theory you might come up with. I'd keep it to yourself."

Chapter 55

There's a message on my cell phone when I get into range heading home. It is Doctor Williams from Southern Tri-State Community College. I return the call. He says he's got some interesting news for me. Can I come into his office or meet him for coffee somewhere? I feel like a poor servant in a village who is asked by the king to visit his castle. I stutter out something that sounds like *yyyeth*. We hang up, and I turn my jeep around, head to a halfway point for us both. I'm intrigued to the point I'm running a good ten miles per hour over my usual ten miles over the speed limit.

I meet him at an off-highway diner. I'm a cup of coffee in before he gets there carrying a briefcase and looking rather pleased with himself. "Ah, Miss Davidson in the flesh," he says, extending his hand to shake. I rise to greet him and return his shake and almost spill the contents of my coffee. "No, sit, sit, sit," He tells me and flags the bland waitress over, orders a grilled cheese sandwich and an iced tea. "You need anything?" he asks.

I shake my head. "I'm too nervous to eat." I don't tell him my tummy is all jittery because I'm in his presence. He thinks it's because of the information he's found. Such, he points a finger at me, then pulls some papers from a leather case at his feet, shuffles them, then sets them in front of me.

"This doctor you talk about, Bobby Brown. He wasn't what everybody thought he was."

"What do you mean?"

"Well, I did some researching because you piqued my interest in your old coal mining town. It's Lost Hollow, right?" I nod. He reaches out a forefinger and pokes it on one page. I look down. The tip of his finger is settled on a hand-drawn image of a man's face—he is dark-haired and balding and wears glasses. Beneath the image is a name: *Dr. T.A. McLaughlin 120 Main Street, Toledo. Oh.* The advertisement states: WEAK MEN READ THIS. It is one of a page full of old advertisements for everything from curing baldness to cocaine drops for toothaches. There are some ads with the same man's face. There are others with a woman's image. Each has a different address and name.

"He was a man of many faces, your Doc Brown. He was what they used to call a snake oil salesman, a man whose fire and brimstone sermons sold fake medicines. None of these images with the fake cures showed the true identity of the man, his character, or his greed. He wasn't a real doctor. Bobby Brown got his degree from a diploma mill, a fake college. His name was Robert Brown, but during the late 1800s, he also went by Harold Dunkin, Missus Cora, Hannah Coffman—it seems endless." Doctor Williams flips through an inch-thick layer of papers offhandedly. "All of these alleged remedies and cures were nothing more than cocaine, heroin, and cannabis mixed with God-knows-what. He got his start with nothing more than a fourth-grade education working in a pharmacy somewhere around 1875 when he was twenty. For almost forty-five years, he worked in several cities and posed as a doctor, selling his pharmaceuticals in the newspapers."

"You're kidding me? My grandma and all the old people talk like he was the best thing since apple pie."

"Okay," Doctor Williams chuckles. "He must have been quite a charmer. He was married four times. He was arrested several times for deaths of people who took his medicine, including two children who were given cocaine drops for earaches. He had a nervous breakdown after several malpractice and wrongful death suits. Around 1914, the use of cocaine as a medicine became illegal. But he was an avid proponent of the drug. I'm sure you can understand the reason. His customers were hooked. They kept coming back for it. Even after he was stripped of his license to practice medicine in Ohio, he moved to Indiana, then showed up again in West Virginia three years later. And in the small mining camps that were set apart from most of society in the wilderness, he started all over again."

I'm mesmerized, almost speechless. "So, he was probably poisoning people in Lost Hollow while he was poisoning people in the U.S. with his newspaper remedies."

"I would more than assume that," he says. "I read a newspaper article where he actually was asking for test subjects to try new cures for coughs, influenza, smallpox, asthma, pneumonia, and malaria—"

"And tuberculosis," I add. "I wonder how many people in our little cemetery died of his cures and not the disease." I feel my face flush. "Oh, I wonder—" No, it couldn't be, right? "I wonder if he killed that baby they found in the trunk at the church and maybe, Reverend Mills and Annabelle Easton. They died about the same time." I chew on this a moment. "—and maybe Clyde Hatfield and Mimi Edwards too."

"The only way you could tell was if you exhume the bodies, possibly do some testing on them."

"The baby and the trunk were part of the stolen items. Now, it could be done with the preacher and Missus Easton. But Sheriff Hatfield and Mimi Edwards disappeared. There are no bodies to dig up for them."

"Well, that doesn't sound coincidental." No, it didn't. Not at all.

He orders a piece of blueberry pie before he leaves. I order a piece of homemade apple pie. We both dig in with gusto. I'm starving, having missed supper. "You know, if I had to guess which piece of pie you'd choose of the four or five they had on the menu, I'd have guessed you'd pick apple."

"Why is that?" I ask, taking another bite.

"I read an article once that said people who pick apple pies for their choice of dessert are usually independent thinkers and empathetic to others. They might take longer to do things they set their mind to because, well, they aren't as focused on just one thing."

"I do find that when everybody else runs away from something, I'm the idiot that stands there trying to see what they are running from. Pop Pop, that's my grandpa, tells me I jump feet first into everything. It's not always the best thing to do. As far as empathy, I was raised by my grandpa with seven older and much bigger uncles, barring one who is two months younger than me. I was always the last one in line for the bathroom, the last one to get the smallest chicken leg left—you get where I'm going?"

"I do."

"What about blueberry?" I poke my fork at his plate. "What does choosing blueberry pie say about you?"

"I think things out before I do things. I'm open-minded and easygoing. I was flexible when you missed my last three classes. I let it slide, right?"

"You knew that?" I watch him nod. "I was living in my car. Don't tell my Pop Pop." I keep my eyes focused on my apple pie. My cheeks burn red. Why am I divulging this to him? I didn't tell anybody else.

"I'd like to see you get your degree. I don't think a few minor setbacks will stop you, considering you like apple pie and all." He pushes his blueberry pie over toward me, waves his fork at it. "Now try a bit of blueberry." I hesitate. I don't know why. "Go on," he says. "You said you do everything feet first. Jump."

I look up and nod. "But this time, take a second and think it out. You might not like it. You might drop it halfway to your mouth and it lands on the table. You get that, right?"

"Do you not want me to take a bite?" I ask. I'm confused.

"It's your choice. Just know that it may take a couple tries. No big deal. If you drop it, there's another bite there. If you don't like it, you can add more sugar and try it again."

"Okay," I say. "But I feel there is a lesson coming after I do it." I push my fork in, work up a bit on the tines, then take a bite. It's good. It's sour.

"You might be an apple pie kind of person, but you can mix it up now and then." Doctor Williams says. "You're afraid of new things, of accomplishing your goals. That's why you jump feet first. You can't claim you thought it out well and then failed. But, young lady, you need to be like a blueberry pie kind of person occasionally. Try something and know it might not work. We learn more from our failures than our successes, you realize that? Don't worry so much about failure. If you fall, pick yourself up and try again. Life's like that. Screw everybody else who doesn't have a clue how hard it is because they've never done something."

"Like running a ball league?"

"What?"

"We've got these old ballfields where we live. They are left over from the old mine camp days. The mayor up on Brandy Mountain decided to start up a big ball tournament, try to bring back the glory years of mine camp baseball."

"That's cool, Miss Davidson."

"Well, the idea is cool," I tell him. "But the mayor follows that same pattern you see all over. He and his buddies are out there to make their own kids shine. We've got this coach, his name's Niles Gates. He has two boys who played all the sports. They weren't that good. He used the other boys to build up the team, then thrust his kids out when it came time for athletic scholarships. And now, with this new league the mayor's starting, it's the same thing all over again. My Pop Pop started a team with a bunch of players including him and his old guy friends. When the team up on Brandy Mountain didn't have enough good players, he shut my Pop Pop down and took the young guys to use for his own. He told the rest they couldn't play because they were too old." I shrug, reach out and give a teasing smile while I take another bite of blueberry pie. "I want to start a league of big ball, have a tournament for all those guys, even from other towns, who got ousted by the mayor's new rules."

"Blueberry pie it," Doctor Williams tells me. "Look at you. You're already finding it's not so bad—"

Chapter 56

"Pop Pop, I want to start a big ball league and begin with a tournament the same day as John Matthews has his tournament. I know it is late season, but we could run it short like five weeks and make it informal. It'd be for old guys and girls and anybody who wanted to be in it. I know I can. Doctor Williams said so, and he said if I can eat blueberry pie, I can pretty much do anything."

He's standing at his front door looking at me standing on the porch. It is vaguely familiar to my return last year. It is probably not helping support my position. Pop Pop gives me *that* look. It's the one I always get when I want to start something, and he knows I'll never finish it. Ballet lessons, homework, Taekwondo, college—it's a peer upwards with his eyes and his lips pursed tightly. It's the kind of expression people use when their sensible, practical side wants to scream out a resounding NO! but their kindhearted side mewls all those impractical reasons like maybe he'll hurt my feelings.

"Well, why don't we all eat blueberry pie then, Harley?" Pop Pop offers with a slight smile. "Do you want to tell me why you're so gung-ho on this idea suddenly?" he asks me. "Because just a month ago, I was dragging you kicking and screaming to the ballfields."

"Because your idea of me playing was sewing uniforms and cleaning up," I tell him. "I'm going to play. I've been learning how to pitch so I can pitch, and all you guys have to do is lose weight and get in shape. Besides, I want to get back at John Matthews. He's a pukehead."

"Oh, for the love of God," he moans. "Is that what this is all about?"

"Historically, there have been sillier reasons for wars."

Pop Pop stares hard at me. He's trying to think out his words carefully. "You'll never win a war against that man all by yourself, sweetie," he says softly. "Did you hit your head hard enough you came up with this preposterous idea?" He shakes his head. "Come in a second, let me show you something."

"Preposterous." I laugh. "You've been listening to Nana Nisee while she does those crossword puzzles." I stop laughing quickly when he shows me a letter that came in the mail today. "Mayor Matthews offered me a deal. If I sell out on the rental properties, he'll give me nine-thousand dollars for each. He had an appraiser look at one of the properties and gave me an estimate. It is only six-thousand." It's like the world stops for me right then. I try to think of myself living in the city, living somewhere else.

"Are you going to do it?" I ask in a wispy whisper.

"What do you think I'm going to do? Everybody else got these letters too. You're the one who left, went to see that big world of yours."

"I wouldn't have come back here if I liked it better out there. I don't."

"Then, hell, no," Pop Pop says with a twang to his voice. "This is my home. I'm not going out without a fight. And we're going to start a big ball league and get these folks charged up about getting our lives taken from us."

He gives me goosebumps. "You took that old Harley for a ride, didn't you Pop Pop," I ask him. Because he is charged up and that is what he always says a motorcycle does to him.

"Yep," he smiles. "I did."

Chapter 57

Nana Nisee told me she wanted to go through town. That meant the old part of Lost Hollow. Beck and Willy are tagging along on our little journey. Beck's in the front and I watch him watching her try to peer out of the back windows that are more like baking paper with grease on them. I think he's having more fun enjoying my grandma taking in her old surroundings. He keeps looking at her, then looking at me and getting this sweet smile on his lips.

"What?" I ask him.

"I don't know. You two look alike."

"I think Mister O'Sullivan likes Miss Davidson," I hear from the back. I mean-eye Willy through the rear-view mirror. She's making a heart-shape with her fingers and thumbs pushed together.

I look over at Beck. He's got a silly smile on his face looking at me. "Yuck," he says. "She probably has cooties."

"Cooties," Nana Nisee laughs. "Old Doc Brown used to come into class and check us for cooties," I hear her tell Willie with a giggle. I haven't the heart to tell her about Old Doc Brown. She gets this sweet stare when she says his name. Who am I to tell her that her beloved doctor was a quack, a murderer. "That's what he called them. But Danny Coon was this little fat boy in our class, and he always had head lice and passed them on to all the other children." She pokes at her head. "But Doc Brown had his little cures for it he tried out on us. Some worked, some didn't. Those lice didn't go away until little Danny did." She seems satisfied she has creeped us all out when we each scratch our head.

Nana Nisee smiles smugly, then leans hard and wags a finger between us. "Welcome to Lost Hollow," she announces to no one in particular. "Lower Brandy. That's what we used to call it. *A place called home. A place where dreams come together.* There used to be a sign right there. That's what the sign used to say."

It doesn't look like a place of dreams anymore. Maybe Nana Nisee knows that. If so, it doesn't show. Her eyes are sparkly while she takes in a deep breath of air. "Home. It smells like home." She points out where Old Doc Bobby Brown used to live and where he died an old man, a home that's on a steady decline with windows knocked out and glass laying on the porch. She points out where the Eastons lived and where the preacher's house was before he died. I notice Willy's eyes suddenly widen in realization. "Those are the people from your story when you worked at the museum," she says. "So, it *is* real?"

"Yes, do you think I was lying?"

"Uh huh."

Nana Nisee laughs in the back. I can't tell if she's laughing at us or just at some ghost in her head. "Stop here," she says. I come to a careening halt while she hard-pats the back of my seat. "Get out while it's not raining for a minute." I look at Willy. Willy looks at me and shrugs. Nana Nisee is pushing on the seat. I get the feeling she's going to dive over her if Willy doesn't move right now.

"Look here." We both follow Nana Nisee out into the front lawn of one house. "Everybody back in the day worried about the color of somebody's skin and how much money they made. They hated you for the side you took in the war or didn't take in the war. They looked at most poor miners and turned their heads away. Lots of them died, you know. My Uncle Matthew and my best friend, Billy, were killed in an explosion." She stops, closes her eyes, and smiles softly. "But all that silly stuff about people being different, it wasn't like that in Little Brandy—well, Lost Hollow. Mama told me that my papa said they all came out of the mines the same color, black from that coal dust. When slate fell, or men got blown up, they couldn't tell one part from the other, a Rebel from a Yank, a poor man from Germany or a rich man from Virginia. We were prideful of ourselves for knowing we were all the same, we all had the same dreams no matter who we were. That's why the Branntweins and the O'Malleys put up the sign way back after the Civil War. *A place where dreams come together*. The men, they all got paid the same no matter who they were or where they came from. When new folks came, and they were highfalutin and thought they knew more than us, we taught them they weren't."

It's the most I've heard Nana Nisee talk. She's suddenly like one of the little toys I got with a kid's meal when I was little that fell down the furnace vent and every time Pop Pop stomped through the room, it chattered and chattered and wouldn't stop until Pop Pop got a coat hanger and dug it out. I'm staring at her, probably unsmiling just because I'm almost stunned. Because she shakes her head like Willy, Beck, and I are senile. "Well, come on. I want to show you something. Don't look so stupid, all of you."

There are eight houses left in Lost Hollow still intact. I'm assuming because as soon as somebody drives through who isn't from here, somebody from town comes and chases them down. "Here." Nana Nisee stops at the bottom of one step. "I was ten going on eleven when Clyde James Hatfield disappeared. He was the local police. Me and Jenny were best friends with one of his little girls, Charley Rae. She was only two months younger than me with the prettiest curls and freckles on her nose. Look on the stone there."

Willy and I follow her finger to an old concrete step in front of the porch. There are three little handprints side by side. "If you look around, every house had a step with the handprints of their kids or their families. It was something we used to do back in the day." She turns her attention to the handprints in front of us. "That step belonged to the Hatfields. The first one is Charley Rae's little hand. And the next is mine. The third is Jenny's. Charley Rae's daddy made that step and let us put our hands in the concrete while it was still wet." I find myself kneeling and pressing my hand over Jenny's handprint. Willy leans down and pushes hers on Charley Rae's. Nana Nisee chuckles and leans over, shoves her hand next to Willy's before she stands up straight. "Charley Rae was a daddy's girl. After he went away, she'd sit on that step for hours waiting for him to come home. After a while, they had to move away."

"Did anybody know where Clyde Hatfield went?"

"I don't know. I just remember every wagon and every car that came through town, she'd get these wide eyes. But it was never him. Her mama cried. We could hear her when we sat on the porch." Nana Nisee watches us rise, and she steps past Willy. "Everybody was scared then. We shut ourselves off after Preacher Andy and Missus Easton died. There was an outbreak of TB. We just figured the doctor could fix it. He always fixed us when we were sick. He was kind of famous, you know. He made medicines and sold them through the newspaper—" BOOM!

A crack of thunder careens across the sky, and we all jump, then our laughter echoes in almost perfect synchronization to a gentle rumble. I can hear the patter of rain in the trees far off, then quickly moving toward us. We make a quick retreat to my jeep and sit inside, waiting for the storm to pass over.

Nana Nisee slips into the back even before Beck could protest. I'm not sure he even would. He likes sitting there next to me. I look into the rear-view mirror, see my great grandma lugging a leather-bound journal with rawhide bindings from the box. "What's that?" I ask. She pats it with her hands.

"It was in the cardboard box in the back." She unclasps the binding and opens it up. "I can read it while we wait for the rain to pass. It's a story, somebody's story."

"Somebody's story," I repeat. "Yeah, Max found that stuff in an attic or somewhere. He said his dad put it away when his mom left. I forgot about it." I did. I had peered inside the other night in a hasty retreat to the house after dark and a long day of work. I didn't see anything but a couple old record albums from the 1970s. "Sure, go ahead."

Nana Nisee presses her fingers to the paper, and I sit back in the seat. Willy is in mid-push of cell phone earbuds into her ears. She stops, leans back against the door. Beck is staring out the windshield and tapping his fingers to the beat of the storm on his knee. I'm soaking him in like the first taste of cotton candy at the fair.

"I came back to Germany Mine the twentieth of March in 1865 with nothing more than hand-me-down clothes on my back. I suppose, in all rights, it wasn't really ever my home. It was Papa's stopping point after he sold the store in Columbus. I didn't live there but two months and by then Uncle Otto had taken over Papa's things because he was sick. Mama had been dead since I was a baby. He found out that Asa and I had been meeting and that I had a baby in my belly. He sent me away, I suppose, to avoid the shame. And now, I bring it back to him while I walk right in on a labor dispute between the coal miners in the little community—"

"Hmm," I mumble. "Does it say whose journal it is, Grandma?" For the moment, I'm more interested in Beck pretending to rest his elbow between our seats while he fiddles with my radio that is off. He's leaning and blocking the backseat. I feel his fingers come over, brush on mine. They pause there barely touching before he clasps my fingers in his own. Damn, he makes my tummy tickle sneak-doing that.

"No." She pauses long enough to look up, then squints back at the book. "—Two Union guards dropped me like an abandoned pup in a crate on a front porch step. Except my crate was a set of iron shackles around my wrists and the front porch of the church was the only place the guards could find Uncle. The stunned look on his face is burned into my brain for life when a room full of screaming men were parted to let us through. I called out his name, and the room became silent. Faces stared at me, so many strangers. He'd forgotten to pick me up at the train station. At least that was what was said later. I think the guards were right. He didn't want me. Nobody did. But General Isaacs said they weren't allowed back until I'd been signed over to my kin. And Uncle, he was my only kin left after the war." Nana Nisee stops. "Where did you say you got this?"

"Max brought it in a box for me. It had a bunch of his mom's junk. It was a peace offering for—" I see Beck eyeing me. He lacks expression. But it says a lot about him. He doesn't move his hand though. "—his dad being mean."

"Hmmm," she says and goes on. "So here I am now in a land I don't know once again. I go through each day under Uncle's stern gaze. I sit, and sit, and sit. My hands go to waste. My mind goes to waste. And I can only think of the war while it bangs in my head over and over. Everything that was Papa's is Uncle's now. Asa is dead, and I don't think our baby girl ever made it home. I've got ideas in my head to make this mining community work. Uncle laughs at me and spends Papa's money on his wife who is spoiled and came from Virginia. He is sixty-two. She is fifteen years old and still plays with dolls and has temper tantrums. I hate her so. She pulls my hair and tattles on me like we are toddlers and Uncle locks me in my room. Her name is Priscilla, and I call her Prissy just to be mean. He said a man came looking for my brother. He was an Irishman with a limp and was probably after money. He was poorly dressed in nothing more than rags and carried with him a bundle of clothes—a uniform, shirt, fiddle, and a small box that he said belonged to the boy and he was honored to return them. He said Hans was a partisan ranger with him in the war—"

"Wait, wait, wait—" I hiss. My mind is churning while I wild-eye Beck. "Is it Hans' sister? I thought she was dead. But the Irish man with the limp must be the Irish who Hans knew, right? What the heck? I'm confused."

"Why would he bring back Hans' uniform?" Beck asks. "He lived, right? At least until 1870. That's what you found out." Nana Nisee waits patiently while we talk back and forth, then holds up a hand and continues: "When I heard the knocking, I ran to the window to look out," she reads. "I peered through the curtain and watched my uncle talk to the man who was sure this was the place Hans talked about coming from, the place he would go after the war. There was no need to be angry because Hans was a Federal soldier and not a Rebel one. He fought valiantly. And Uncle got angry and said Hans never made it to the war. He died in 1859 in Cincinnati. He turned the man away—"

"What?" I jump to attention. "Did you just say it said Hans was dead? Hans?"

"It says that *Uncle got angry and said Hans was dead.*" Nana Nisee says. I turn and see her staring back at me. "In 1859." Grandma continues reading: "—I think he saw me at the window. And for that, I am scared. For my Irish will not give up—"

"Do you think it was Hans Branntwein? I don't understand."

"If you let her read, maybe we can find out," Willy says in her gruff tone.

"I'm sorry, but that kind of changes the course of history, Willy," I grump back to her. Grandma bends over again, pushes a finger to the words in the journal. "Asa's father runs a tavern in his house—"

"Asa?" I ask. "Hans talked about an Asa in his diary."

"They live upstairs, the tavern is downstairs. I snuck out tonight to talk to Asa's sister, climbed out the window. Laura is her name, and she looks just like her brother—tall and with fiery red hair that sticks out all over. She took me to Asa's grave and we laid dandelions on the tiny stone. We never had anything in common but him. I asked her if she knew if a black lady ever came and brought a baby to my uncle. She said there are so many miners coming and going, she wouldn't know. So now, I've got nothing but Asa's grave to stare over. He never made it to the war. He died of dysentery three weeks after I left and never made it past Ohio. And to think I looked for him in every Rebel soldier uniform for four years straight, thousands of soldiers. I was looking for a ghost, and I didn't know it. She asked me where I had gone. I told her Papa got sick. He and Uncle Otto married me off to a man whose wife had died before I started to get the little bump on my belly. I didn't tell her that he was almost sixty and he never touched me. He found out about the baby in my belly because he didn't put it there, but he didn't send me away. He said he liked to talk with me over the table because he could have any woman, but they all seemed so dull. I suppose he had a lot of women, too, because he was gone almost every night. I had a baby girl with fiery red hair just like her papa. I called her Gingersnap. At first, I didn't want anything to do with her, but one of the slave boys had a mama who helped me with her. Then when Rebel troops looted the house and burned it down, I had to hide. I gave the baby to Hayward's mama and sent her out in the middle of the night. Laura said the baby's probably dead and that's sad. I think it's sad too. Then she said she knew two men in the mining camp whose name was Hayward. She'd ask if it was the Hayward I knew."

Nana Nisee turns the page. "You want me to go on?" I nod. "There was a picnic after church service. Uncle Otto said I must go and help serve the lemonade. He is desperately trying to get rid of me. He doesn't want to share Papa's money from the store and the mine. I hear him trying to barter me like an old coon dog to every man to whom he speaks. He even talked to an old strikebreaker, trying to get him to take me. Then today at the picnic, I'm ladling lemonade. I don't even know anybody's watching me. I feel his hand on my cuff just as I reach to take a dip of drink. I freeze because I know who it is standing there. Pony. That's what he calls me, and I tell him no and Uncle comes marching to the table and tells him to unhand me. But right before he does, the soldier tugs on my cuff and I know he sees it. He saw my tattoo, the vine, and the *J.G.*—"

I blink and then it is like I'm woozy with realization. "Holy Mother of God, did you just say *J.G.?*" I hiss like I've got no air in my lungs. Hans had a tattoo on his wrist that Irish put on it. "Nana Nisee, can you hand me the journal?" I'm wagging my hand in the back, feeling flushed.

"What?" Willy's looking at me like I just grew wings and I'm trying to fly next to her while I snatch the journal Nana Nisee is handing me. I can't get it quickly enough, slap it down in front of me. My fingers alight on the cursive and I gasp softly. "My God," I whisper. "This is the same handwriting as Hans Branntwein's." I think my chest is going to explode. I'm staring at it, and my heart is thumping in my chest. I flip a few pages, slide my finger down one page and then look within the front cover.

"I don't understand," Willy says.

"Mila." I poke a finger on a name ten or so pages in. "This can't be." Then I read the sentence where I have found the name. "—*Her name is Mila Branntwein. That is what my uncle told him. There is no Hans here. He has been dead for years. But the red-haired soldier knows better. Why? Irish asks me. And I tell him the truth that I've told no one else. Because I had to do it so Bad Bill and his men didn't do to me what he did to the two servant girls. They beat them, and all took turns, and I could hear their screams until they couldn't scream anymore. And one, she sounded like a piggy snorting and squealing and the men they laughed at her and made it worse. I heard her while Hayward's mama shaved my head and Hayward got me clothes from a boy who worked in the stable—*"

"What?" Beck holds out his hands. "What's the matter?"

"This is Hans Branntwein's journal too."

"It's a woman's journal," Willy adds.

"Yes, you two. Did you know this, Nana Nisee?" I don't let her answer. "Hans is a *girl*, Grandma. I think—I think— she was *Mila* Branntwein. She had to have been. The man who founded the town was actually a woman."

"The names on the tree." Beck sits erect. "You remember the heart carved into the tree?"

"Yes."

"It was M.B. and S.O. What if the letter M stood for Mila? Mila Branntwein and Sean O'Malley."

"There were vines around the heart." I look at Beck. "The only way to find out is to see if their graves are in the cemetery. Then we can see if there is anything about Hans dying before the war—"

Before we leave, I ask Nana Nisee to show me which house Doc Brown lived in again. I drive along the rutted ground, my old worn tires spinning wildly at a few spots. She wags a finger at the largest home right across the street from the home we found the trunk. "That's where the Browns always lived. Doc Brown's kin lived there through the forties." I stop the jeep and get out and make a mad dash through the rain while the others watch through the windows.

The porch has sunk in, the wood sagging and broken. But the door is still there, and I push on it, step inside. It is almost empty save the raggedy furniture. It still has the feel of a doctor's office—there is a large room and two rooms on either side to receive patients. I step into the kitchen. It is eerie. There are still dusty plates, cups, and silverware on the table like someone just got up one day and walked out. The gingham curtain on a back doorway is ripped and torn. I can see the rain coming down outside a tiny back porch.

I step around pieces of curtain and a broken pitcher on the floor and walk into the living room and up the stairway. At the top, there are three rooms. It is the third that holds the prize for which I am searching. I hear the door grunt downstairs. Beck calls out my name and tells me the road is getting deep with puddles. I tell him I'll be right there while I sift through an entire room of stacks of newspapers, old baskets filled with paperwork—and Bingo! At the back of the room, I see a vintage Globe file cabinet with dark wood and copper-colored handles. The top two tiers are glass and beneath, are twelve pull-drawers to hold files.

I debate running my hand along the exterior. It is beautiful, but I hear someone honking the jeep's hard-to-honk horn. It bleats like an old sheep two times. I do so anyway, rolling my fingers across the still-shiny wood. I peer into the glass and there are some old medicine bottles, an antique syringe, and a couple old newspapers. "Alright!" I say to no-one in particular, then open one drawer, take in the sweet scent of old books and dust.

"Come on, Harley," Beck has traversed the steps, leans in the open door. I didn't hear him until he muttered something about *didn't she learn her lesson about going upstairs in old houses the last time?* "If you're going to make love to that old file cabinet, make it quick. We need to get off these old roads before it gets too muddy."

"Haha, you just want to watch," I muse. "Just so you know, this must be Doc Brown's patient files."

"Here?"

"Yeah, why not? Places like nursing homes and hospitals close all the time and just leave boxes of people's personal stuff. If you give me two minutes, I'm looking for a couple people."

"Okay—?"

"It is Reverend Mills and Annabelle Easton." I look up and catch green eyes in my own. The dark clouds of the storm have covered the sun, making it dim inside the room and such, his green eyes more piercing against his light skin. I blush. Why am I so goofy around him? "They are the two who died when they found the baby on the church porch." I carefully pull open the drawer for the letter E in the cabinet. Inside are the files of Doc Brown's patients. I flip through the files, find the name of Easton, Annabelle. I tug it out and look at the three cards in her file that are carefully printed for each date she saw Doc Brown. Then I do the same for Reverend Mills. The cards are small and only allow a minimum of wording. Each has a date, a reason for the visit, a diagnosis and medicines given. Strangely, the last three entries for both are the same. "Look here, Beck." I wave him over to me.

"Okay, what is it?" He doesn't question me, doesn't roll his eyes. I think, right then, I'm really in LOVE.

"Why are you looking at me like that?" he asks with a furrow of his brow. "Did I misunderstand you?"

"So, you're not going to ask me why I'm foraging through somebody's old stuff?"

"No, why do you ask? Isn't that what historians do?"

"I'd hardly call me a historian."

He laughs. It's like this big guffaw that startles me enough to jolt.

"Oh, geez, I'm sorry," he says, reaches out a hand and lays it on my shoulder. "But it was funny what you say. Because anybody who can get thirty-two bored students, ready for the school year to end, to take the earbuds out of their ears, turn off their music, and have a deep well-thought-out debate is a historian and a good one for knowing how to get kids interested in learning history. Their conversation on where that dead baby came from played out like a whodunit complete with character plots on their bus ride back to the high school and continued into the classroom."

"Oh." I nod. I'm hiding my zeal at his words. Inside, I'm doing this dorky dance. However, I reply a humble thanks. "Thanks."

"No, thank you. I didn't have anything planned for them that afternoon. I was winging it. We had a big debate and came up with a solution to how the baby died."

"And that was—?"

"Becca Sayers won the debate. Her angle was that the dead baby was the illegitimate child of the preacher and Annabelle Easton. Upon finding out she had a child; the preacher killed the baby. Clyde Hatfield was the gun for hire by Preacher Mills's wife who found out about the affair and the baby. He murdered Annabelle and Preacher Mills, then ran off with Mimi Edwards."

"Why Mimi?" I ask with a chuckle. "There were plenty of other women in town."

"She was from money up on the mountain. That's why no one has ever found Branntwein's treasure. They took it." He leans in with an elbow resting on the file cabinet just as the jeep horn honks again. "Finish here. We'll hit the cemetery next—what you got there?"

I show him where it lists: *Sunday, April 01. 1934. Exposed to Tuberculosis patient. Drug regime: coca pun, hydrargyrum.* There are three dates thereafter over a two-week period which show: Patient deceased. "They match almost perfectly from the date they were exposed to the baby on Easter Sunday and were started on the medicine treatment. They both died on the same day." I nibble my lip. "I wonder what hydrargyrum is? I'm assuming coca pun is cocaine."

"Was there anybody else exposed that day?" Beck asks. "I mean, surely, you could look them up and see if they caught it too."

"How about this? Grandma said Clyde Hatfield and Mimi Edwards disappeared. Maybe they didn't disappear. Maybe they died too."

"Why would their deaths be hidden? That doesn't make sense."

"Doc Brown was a quack, Beck," I tell him. "He made his money selling medicine. Just like pharmaceutical companies do now. He wasn't about helping the patients. He was about making money. It almost sounds like he was testing stuff on the people in town, then selling it as a cure if it worked. If someone found out he was using them or even if he killed them with his own medications—" A pop of thunder rumbles across the sky. We both jump and laugh. Beck leans over, gives me a peck on the cheek. "Dig out the rest of them, and we'll get out of here, head down to the cemetery. Let's try to figure out the mystery behind Hans Branntwein first. Then we'll work our way seventy years later to the dead baby and Doc Brown."

Chapter 58

I'm standing with my arms akimbo in front of an old white headstone. It is as tall as me and weathered. It is also slightly lopsided, so we're all keeling our heads to the right. It is the oldest section of the Brandy Mountain Cemetery and up and over a small raggedy hill with knee-high grass and leftover autumn leaves. It is almost like the older mining camp graves flooded the earth there and the overflow was swept down the mountain to the new section.

The grass isn't mowed here. Many of the gravestones have been knocked over by trees and years of neglect. Nana Nisee pointed out two old headstones. One was her baby sister who died when she was six. Another is Danny Coon. He was eleven. The third is Jenny's grave. She lingers there the longest. "How'd she die, Nana?" I ask her softly. She is pale and stares at the grave.

"She died giving birth to your Pop Pop, sweetie."

I turn my head. "I thought you were his—"

"I raised him. I'm his mama. He's a good man. That's all that matters. Her blood runs in your veins now. You are the spitting image of Jenny, feisty. She'd like that."

I let that sink in. Then I reach out and hold her hand. "I am feisty." We stand there for a few more minutes silently. Then Nana Nisee sighs, and it's almost like all the sadness washes from her face. "Jenny never let cloudy days get her down. So where were we. We were looking for a couple graves—"

Now after a five-minute trudge through the weeds, we stop in front of one grave that is surrounded by perhaps six others. Willy reaches out, touches one name. "It says Mila Augustus O'Malley. 1846 to 1931. Age 85. Beloved wife of Sean O'Malley."

"That answers one question," Beck says. He lays his hand on the grave, then while his fingers gently roll around the obelisk, he swings around to the other side. "And here is the other. Sean O'Malley. 1836 to 1929. Beloved husband and father." He leans in and Willy steps around the headstone, sidles up beside him. "It's got an inscription. It's hard to read," he tells us. "It says—*But those who hope in the Lord will renew their strength.*" He lingers there, leans in and out. "I can't read much more. Maybe it says—*them—?*"

Willy kneels next to the stone. "No, it is *they*. It says *They will soar on wings like eagles; they will run and not grow weary—*"

"*—they will walk and not be faint.*" I finish for them. They both peer around the stone at me. "It is from the book of Isaiah in the Bible. When one of Irish's men, he was just a sixteen-year-old boy, was going to be shot by Savage Bill, Irish kept reciting it to him to comfort him. Then when Hans saved them, he recalled the verse. It obviously had great meaning." I sigh.

"How do you think she hid it, being a girl?" Willy asks softly. "She had to stand up and pee, right? That's not easy. And all the other girl stuff."

I sigh. "Pee through a tube?" I offer. "Or maybe she just peed away from everybody else. If you think about it, the Victorian era had rigid rules of covering the body fully. In the 1860s and during the war, they avoided exposing themselves in public latrines and most slept in clothing and bathed privately. I know Hans said a doctor noted he—I mean, she," I correct myself, "was malnourished enough her growth was stunted. Maybe she didn't even have a period because of it. I didn't my entire first year of college I was so stressed out. And Hans disappeared all the time. I read where Irish would get mad at Hans for just leaving."

I still want to check to make sure Hans really died. And so I tell them that. I'm almost tired from digesting all the news. "So, who is up for a road trip to someplace tomorrow?" I ask all of them. "I'll pay for the gas and the lunch. I just need the company."

Later, I walk Beck home. He's got ball practice. I've got eleven of twenty-two more teams to call that were scratched from John Matthews's Brandy Mountain Classic Big Ball Tournament in two weeks. Pop Pop sweet-talked Dispatch Carla into making him a copy of all the teams that were cut. I think, but I'm not sure, part of the bargain included a date. Pop Pop was whistling Dixie after the call and that only means one thing—he's in a happy place.

Now, I'm calling each to see if they would like to compete in a tournament on the same day as the one on the top of the mountain. So far, they are all coming including six teams that heard about it through word of mouth.

Whereas John Matthews is basically playing baseball (including using major league baseballs instead of softballs), ours is going to be played just like the coal camp baseball our grandpa's and great-grandpas used back in the 1930s and 1940s—we're using the mushy and oversized sixteen-inch softballs. We won't use gloves, and instead, bare hands. The bats will be softball bats. We've even got vendors coming in to sell vintage food and souvenirs. Taylor sent out advertisements about the tournament. We've got people from the church who are going to do the stats, and they even passed the offering plate around this week to help get the fields into shape.

Beck's sister is sitting on the porch and I know she sees us holding hands. She has this silly grin on her face, and two of her boys come out singing—*Beck and Harley sitting in a tree*– until Beck chases them away.

"Hey, Brittany," I holler. She's a big girl, six feet and God-knows-what. Then I go and sit with her and she tells me stories about stupid stuff Beck did when he was a little kid. He is getting dressed, but he hears her and tells her to stop from somewhere inside the house with a whiny voice.

"He must really like you, Harley, if he quit that job for you," she divulges. "Be nice to him."

"I am nice to him."

"You know what I mean. Because I know what people are saying—"

"About me?"

"No, goofy, about the donation my grandma gave. That wasn't the reason Beck got the job. He's smart. He got the job on his own merit."

"I have no clue what you're talking about." I shake my head, lean in. "I don't think he's stupid at all."

"He's stupid for you," she laughs. I laugh too, then I lean in. "What did your grandma donate?"

"She did this reverse mortgage thing where the city buys her house and land, and she gets to live at home until she dies. They also pay her a small stipend while she's alive. Then, when she passes, they get ownership. She doesn't even live there. It's one of the houses way back in the holler. It isn't worth much. I mean, it's junk land—but there were ten or twelve old people that have done it. I know a few of them. They are in the Willows nursing home up by the highway with grandma—Helen Murphy and Edna O'Malley."

"Do you know that John Matthews is planning on building a subdivision here for millions of dollars?"

"Well, no. How can he?"

"I think he's *not* using the money for the city. He's pocketing it. Did she donate anything of value?"

"Well, everything. She didn't want us to have to sort through it. She's in a nursing home—"

"What did she donate, Brittany?"

"She inherited silverware and crystal, the good stuff from back in the 1800s when her dad helped run the mine. They kept a bunch of company scrip from when the mine closed. I know that my grandpa collected baseball cards. They were supposed to use it in the museum."

When I get home, I pull out the inventory Beck had gotten from the museum. I roll my finger along the list. I see nothing donated by the O'Sullivans, nor the Murphys or O'Malleys. Nothing. So where did it go? I feel the irritation grabbing at my chest. I wonder how easy it was to coerce those old people into giving away their homes for free room and board in the nursing home—oh, shit. I snatch up my phone, poke in THE WILLOWS RETIREMENT HOME AND ASSISTED LIVING CENTER. I feel my stomach lurch. *Welcome to the Willows at Brandy Mountain. We offer full-service, resort-style independent senior living and convenience.* The pretty sketched picture of the nursing home on the front page doesn't look anything like the real, bland and dilapidated one-level, 1970s nursing home where Beck's grandparents live. I scroll to the little button that says ABOUT US. I take a breath. Staring back at me is a huge image of John Matthews, and below, it says*: John Matthews currently serves as the Chairman of the Willows Board of Trustees on which he has previously served as Vice Chairman. He is also the President and CEO. He is proud to announce that his son, Maximus Matthews-Branntwein, has been inducted as Finance Committee Chair-partner. Maximus was formerly with Tinsley Law Firm where he concentrated his practice in commercial and civil litigation.*

"Holy shit." I stare at Max's picture beneath. Why did he not tell me he was a frigging lawyer? Tinsley. That's Mikayla's last name. Hells Bells. How did I not know this? I feel a rush of anger. I want to pick up my phone and call Max, scream at him and ask him why he's been lying to me. Then, I realize that could quite possibly be the second worse thing I could do. That's the new me. So, I breathe in, breathe out. Instead, I do the worst possible thing, and that is be the old me. And I plan on finding out exactly what Max, his dad, and Grant Lebowski are hiding.

Chapter 59

It's a full carload drive to Cincinnati to search for Hans Branntwein's grave two days later. I called in sick to work, feigned a cough and a few gags. It's not far off. I can't sleep half the time. Lissette promised me she did not mind if I never puked on her office floor again. I found a death notice in a slightly translated old German Methodist newspaper from 1859. *Died: Hanns Branntwein was born on 2nd June 1841 in Frankfurt, Hesse 18 years old. Died on 17th June 1859. Preceded in death by his mother, Adelheid Branntwein. Burial will be held Tuesday, 21st June. 2 o'clock in the afternoon. [Funeral party leaving] Spring Grove Cemetery.*

On the way, I stop at Bakers Quickie Stop and Gas to see if Orv has been there recently. If he has, no one has seen him. I ask the girl inside, and she says she hasn't seen him in a while. She used to share her lunch with him and gave him a free candy bar. She says she thinks he must have just moved on, but she misses the old dude. She said Orv's been a steady fixture there for years. It is strange he isn't there anymore. I mull this over while we drive.

Spring Grove Cemetery in Cincinnati is enormous. There is grave after grave, a city of the dead within a city of the living. Carefully manicured, maintained, and mapped or not, it took me two and a half hours to weave my way to the older section and find the tiny grave settled in the grass.

"I knew." Nana Nisee is standing beside me at the headstone. It says: *Hans Adalbert Branntwein. June 17, 1859.* It is a tall stone and nearly over my head, a white obelisk straight and tall. To the right of it, is a second stone almost matching with his father's name on it—*Alfred Branntwein. Beloved father and husband.*

"You knew what?" I ask her. It is hot today, the sun baking on to my back.

"I knew, I suppose. I mean, when we were standing at

the cemetery it was like a light illuminated everything in my head, showing the truth. My grandma told me when her father first came to the mining camp at Brandy Mountain, it was run by a little man and a tall man with red hair. They lived together in a house. The little man was Hans Branntwein, and the mine prospered so well beneath him that the town got bigger and bigger. Hans was tiny. Everyone thought him odd because he was so small. He led mining strikers against his uncle, then forced him to sign papers over to him."

"Why is this not in history books?"

"Because someone might say that the land wasn't obtained legally." Beck is leaning against me with his elbow on my shoulder. He has been noticeably quiet. I keep catching him looking at me. I'm not sure if I said something or he's just burned out like Max and Trevor would get when I felt on fire with something, and they thought I was cool embers. "I would suppose—Hans had made sure that the property and the mining business would go to Sean O'Malley should he die—and his new wife and heirs."

"And so, he died in a mining accident," Nana Nisee says. "I would think Hans had to leave. She was pregnant."

"But if it was set up, why kill everyone?" I ask. Nobody answers.

"You know what?" Beck pats his chin, looks reflective. "If you're Arnie's kid and he's an O'Malley, that means you're a direct descendant of the Branntweins."

"That would make me a great-great-granddaughter of Mila, wouldn't it?"

"That's cool," Willy says and peers at me like I'm a movie star. Nana Nisee smiles like she's proud.

"They were really good people back then," she says. "Not like the Branntweins you know."

"Yeah, well, you know John Matthews, Max, and his sister aren't related by blood."

"You're kidding?" Beck leans in.

"Max's mom didn't meet Max's dad until those two were a few years old."

"Nobody knows that," Beck says softly. "Everybody idolizes them because they think they're rooted in the town. They aren't even in the town family tree."

"Well, it isn't like Arnie's claiming me, so—"

"So, what?" Willy says. "We know."

Why does it make me feel a little empowered that my roots are so deep in my town right now? It's like the little bit of embarrassment I felt for growing up grasped in the arms of what some call hillbilly and redneck seems rude instead of humbling. "So like I can be stuck up and arrogant now. Clear me a path," I tell them waving my arms in front of me. Nobody does. I get no more than an eye roll. I wave them toward the jeep instead. Willy lingers, pushes a hand over her eyes. I think she is overwhelmed by all the graves. "You could get lost in here. I've never seen so many graves."

"Tell me, have you ever been out of Lost Hollow?" Beck asks her. He is close to me. I can feel his arm graze mine occasionally.

"No, not really. Once in foster care." She drops her head, pulls the hoodie over her. Nana Nisee looks at her, and I can see she looks sad for her. She reaches out, takes Willy's hand. I almost wince. I see Beck's eyes widen a little. We both think she's going to jerk it away. But the two walk ahead, hand-in-hand even though Willy's shoulders look taut and uncomfortable. Beck puts his hand out, slows me down. "Let them talk. We need to talk."

"About what?" I slow.

Beck comes to a standstill, rubs the scruff on his chin. "I used to be that guy who hopped from girl to girl. Maybe I didn't make it clear to you. I'm not anymore. That was a long time ago."

"Why would you tell me that?" I ask him. I'm looking at his eyes. They are a lime-green today and a bit veiled. "Did I say something to imply you *were* still that guy?"

"No, Harley, not at all. Maybe you're just not there yet. Maybe you don't want to be—there."

"What do you mean, *there*?

"You and me. A relationship with *just* you and me."

"Am I doing something that makes you think otherwise?"

"Max made a remark in the dugout at practice. He implied you had a girlfriend where you worked, and he said he'd —you two, oh, God, don't make me say it."

"What?"

"That you and he were doing it like rabbits and he used his hand, you know the sign of grabbing the air at your groin and—"

"Okay—I get it." I stop him with both hands. "He said that in front of other people? Why would he do that? I haven't ever slept with him, you know that, right?"

"He said it to Will Grayson loud enough everybody heard it. Zach too. He was caught between wanting to kill Max and dive under the seat in the dugout."

"Well, he is lying," I say firmly. "Taylor is my friend, albeit she is using me to make her girlfriend jealous, so she latches on to me sometimes like a rabid kitten. Beck, I've never slept with Max. You can believe me or not. I *want* you to believe it." I turn on my feet, rub my hands on my face. "Listen, I assume you remember the pictures I found of Trevor with all those girls before we broke up."

"I heard."

"I think it was Max who secretly sent them to me. I was chatting it up with one of the girls in the pictures last week. The picture of her and Trevor was from *before* he dated me. I had no doubt she was not lying."

"You're going to have to let me know at what point I can hit him if he does it again," Beck forces a smile. "Because I wanted to kill him."

I'm just about to answer when I hear the door to my jeep shut. I look up and Nana Nisee is coming toward us. "I need to talk to Harley," she says and shoos Beck away.

"What's up?" I ask her when Beck nods and heads toward the little cemetery road.

"Walk, and I'll talk," she says. She latches on to my arm and tugs me with her. "You need to take care of Willy until her daddy gets out of jail. You've got an extra bedroom. She can stay there."

I'm listening to my great grandma and then look at the jeep window where Willy's face is staring at us. "I've told her she can stay with me. I know she's living—"

"She's living in the old houses, Harley. Her daddy's girlfriend has a brother who is forty-two. He chased her down and tried to hurt her."

"*Have sex with her* hurt her?"

"Yes. This lady blamed her and beats her."

We're at the jeep. I don't answer Nana Nisee. She doesn't understand it isn't 1930 and you can just move a kid to the extra bedroom. "I'll try," I tell her. "I will."

I have a little surprise for Nana Nisee on the way home. Her old friend Charley Rae Hatfield, now Charley Rae DuPont, is still alive and quite well at the North Vernon Assisted Living Center not far off the beaten path from Huntington. It's a halfway point on the four-hour return drive. When I tell her we can stop and see her, she gets this scared-excited look on her face. "She'll think I look old," she tells me. I imagine that Nana Nisee thinks her little bestie from the Lost Hollow mining days is still a little girl by the way she is acting.

We don't get to the assisted living center until three in the afternoon. But when we get there, almost the entire clan of Hatfields from The Bottoms who are still living are waiting to see my great grandma. It's like a huge family reunion and Nana Nisee introduces all of us to her old neighbors while we sit down in the small open area. They all make a big deal because I look like Jenny. They chuck my chin like I'm eleven until Beck laughs out loud.

Grandma spends an hour chatting, right in the middle of all them and getting all the attention. She's queen for the day. You'd never know that family had parted Lost Hollow so long ago. Beck, Willy and I sit on a couch and pretend we're reading crumpled, outdated magazines.

"So, Queenie, what you going to do to take back the Hollow," Beck teases me. He keeps bumping me with his knee, poking me with his fingers, and smooshing up close. It's like this new thing between us has opened a door for him to touch, touch, touch me. "Because I'm thinking you're just like that Branntwein chick, your great-great– I don't know how many greats—grandma, all badass fighting a war and everything."

"Why does everybody say I'm badass?" I mutter right before an elderly woman with steel blue hair settles in beside me. Nana Nisee introduced us earlier. Her name was Carla. She is Charley Rae's older sister by two years.

"Why you're the spitting image of Jenny," she tells me. "I bet everybody tells you that."

"Well, my grandma does," I tell her.

"She said the old town is still there, just a bit banged up and falling down."

"We found the old tunnel the other day, hiking up there," I tell her, pointing to Beck. "People don't talk about the mine collapse."

She sits back, eyes me thoughtfully. "Did you two find the door into the tunnel?"

"A door?" Willy asks. Her eyes light up.

"Yes, young lady, a door." Carla's eyes are pale blue when I look into them. She smiles at Willy. "They used to cover it up so kids wouldn't go in there. That was way back when there was a huge fear of tuberculosis, a lung disease. We called it White Death. I was ten or eleven that summer I started to cough. Mama knew because I was as pale as a ghost. She tried to hide it by rubbing rouge on my cheeks." She pats her cheeks. "Old Doc Brown knew, though. After church one Sunday, he pulled my daddy aside. He told him I needed to be away from everybody else in the camp. He said he had special medicines to make me better. It was right after they found the baby in the trunk. Everybody was scared. You couldn't sniffle without people running from you."

We all bob our heads up and down. "There were five others with the same symptoms in the camp," she says. "Old Doc Brown took us up away from the others to an old infirmary building just a short walk from the tunnel. He didn't want the disease to spread. At night, we walked over to sleep in a room just within the tunnel with hanging sheets to give us privacy. We were forbidden to get in contact with anyone else. Back then, they believed the cool, damp air from caves healed the lungs. And we couldn't afford a sanitorium."

"So, he had a cure?" I ask.

"He tried different medicines with us. Every week, it was something new. Some made me sick. Even my mama was taking the doctor's medicine because they were afraid she had caught it from me. I know my daddy didn't at first. He didn't really like Doc Brown." Her voice drops. "He was a strange old bird. Daddy told my mama at the supper table a week before I went to the infirmary, he would rather jump in front of a bullet than send me up the road with that man. He didn't trust him. They got into a fight. I know our neighbors heard them yelling. That's probably why everybody talked about Daddy leaving. But they got over the fight. Mama and Daddy agreed to visit the sanitoriums. They found they were too expensive."

"So, what happened?" Willy asks.

"So, my daddy would come and sit on my bed and talk to me. I was the only one allowed to have someone visit. Then Doc Brown decided the tunnel was making us worse and we stopped going inside." She laughs. "That shaft was full of damp, cold air and probably hazardous fumes and dust from the cave-in. Doc Brown closed it up and put a lock on it. It wasn't safe. Nobody was allowed inside with the germs."

I take her in. I take in her words. *He locked up the tunnel and wouldn't let anybody else go in*. Does she not hear what she is saying? She probably doesn't know anything about the old doctor and his seedy reputation. "That was just about the time your daddy disappeared, wasn't it?"

"It was. I was in the infirmary for a few months. I got really bad. Mama said that Missus Edwards, the lady from up on the mountain who was going to pay for the funeral for the baby in the trunk was just beside herself with worry about catching tuberculosis. She'd picked up the dead baby. She was trying everything but drinking Lysol to stop from catching it. But everybody was terrified—even more so when Harry Peterson and a couple miners that I can't remember their names died. Even my daddy would take the medicine when he came to visit me. Then he stopped visiting me. They didn't tell me my daddy had left, just kept saying it wasn't safe for him to see me."

"So, you said your daddy was overprotective."

"Yes."

"He didn't take the medicine until you were there?"

I know Beck is hard-staring me. I feel his eyes penetrating my skull like shafts from a ray gun. I know he doesn't want me to say it. But I think her daddy was testing out each stupid medicine, taking a bullet for his beloved baby girl in case it was poison.

Carla switches to small talk then pats my leg and Beck helps her rise. "Thank you, sweetie, for bringing your grandma to see us. It was such a nice surprise."

"Are you thinking the same thing I'm thinking?" Beck asks me when she is out of hearing range.

"Gosh, I hope not," I grunt. "I have no clue what goes on in that weird man-mind of yours." He glares at me. "Yeah, we need to find that tunnel door and see what's behind it."

"Like maybe—"

"Clyde Hatfield and Mimi Edwards." I nod. "Maybe they were trying anything to avoid getting the disease—even if it was at the high cost of taking Doc Brown's snake oil—that was more like snake venom. Maybe Clyde Hatfield was testing the medicine before his little girl took it to make sure it was safe for her."

On the way home, I call Doctor Williams. I ask him if he knows what hydrargyrum and coca pun is. I give him a nut-size summary of what I found on Hans and Mila Branntwein and updated him with the latest information about Doc Brown's scandal nearly sixty-four years later.

"So, a few people in your town are going to be a little upset?" he asks me. "I mean, considering the town founder was dead even before he founded the town. And *he* ends up being a *she*?"

"They do have a statue in the little rundown playground in town." I laugh. "It's a heroic Roman-like statue of a man the size of a pro football player. But I'm more concerned about telling them Doc Brown was a fake. All the old people get these little smiles on their faces when they talk about him." Like my great grandma in the back seat right now glaring at me through the rear-view mirror.

"I'll check with one of my colleagues who might know something about these two medicines, and I'll get back with you. Have you been dining on blueberry pie this week?"

"Yep, every day. We've got fourteen teams competing, and we're going to do it on one field. You can imagine how that's going to play out."

"You can do it."

I see Beck looking over at me. He's got a little smile on his face when I hang up a minute later. "What?"

"I just see why he's your go-to guy. He sounds encouraging."

"You're pretty even with him right now."

"Really?" Beck asks, and he gets this haughty look on his face when he crosses his arms. "Well, that's good to hear. That's really good to hear."

Chapter 60

The rain follows us back to Lost Hollow. It is a downpour leaving the backroads flooded and my windshield nothing but a sheet of water shoved hastily away by my old wipers, only to be covered again. Nana Nisee reads Mila Branntwein's journal to us, her voice soft and low against the patter of rain on the roof.

"August 3rd, 1865. The miners at the camp are going to explode harder than dynamite. Uncle Otto pulled in strikebreakers. I was hiding among the miners dressed in men's clothing, trying to help them turn the tide of this war. Uncle Otto keeps me imprisoned in his home like a frail doll as not to mar his reputation. None recognize me as the mysterious girl who came in chains and peers out the window and watches the world go by. He tells them I am crazy. I know I can make this camp a better one for the workers. It is the only way I can get others to take me seriously and gain their respect, trade my dress for pants, trade my name for Hans' name once more. They don't know my brother is dead and buried in Cincinnati. It is the only way I can free myself from Uncle's prison, sneaking out and being among them. I tell them how it can be. The miners, they want to listen. I saw Hayward shaking his fist at them. That's when he saw me. That's when he saw me like the old Pony boy he knew from the war. He dropped his fist. Then he stood there and stared at me. I stared at him. We were like blood one time. I could see it in his eyes. He wanted to hug me. I wanted to run up and hug him. Now we cannot even catch each other's eyes for more than a fleeting second because of the color of our skin, because I am a woman and he is a man—" Nana Nisee looks at me, then turns her attention back to the journal. "I want to see if he knows where his mama took my baby—when she left the night Bad Bill came, I never saw her again. I wonder if she found the camp and she is here or if she died and the baby with her."

"Oh, my, Hayward was the son of Mila's husband," I

almost sigh the words. "And it was Hayward's mother who took the baby. Nana Nisee," I peer into the rear-view mirror. "Look and see if they find them."

A half-hour later, Nana Nisee pushes a finger on the print of the journal. Willy must hold my cell phone up so she can read the words. "Here, listen," she says. "—Hayward and six men were sentenced to the penitentiary for murder. I promised him I would find a way to repay him. He just smiled and said he was the one who owed me for saving Minnie Bean on the train that day. Everyone knew it was well-deserved, Uncle Otto's death. You cannot send armed men into camp to drag out starving women and babies during a strike. Uncle Otto sat on that horse and fired randomly into that little house because the man and his family had no place to go. I drew my little line like I always did, and he raised his gun. I thought Irish was going to kill himself cutting through the crowd. Two shot Uncle Otto dead. My Irish, my love. And Hayward, the closest thing to a brother I will ever have and the only one who does not see me as some silly white woman. Hayward's papa would be proud of him."

About a half hour before we get home, Willy taps my shoulder. "Okay, I found two things at the very end," she says. "It says: I just want to walk the streets of Germany Hollow with my Irish. I want to hold his hand. I cannot do it wearing men's clothing." She stops and turns a couple pages. "It is time for Hans to finally rest in peace. His ghost has lived inside me for so long, I am weary of trying to be him and not being me. When I walked home today, and on the tree at the house, I see something carved into the bark. My Irish left his initials there within a heart and such, along with his are mine. He is standing there with a ring. *It took me a long time to come around, Pony, but here I am. I don't want to be with no other. We've been through hell together and for so long. Now let's hold hands until we go to heaven.* So I have hired out men from the prison. One of them is Hayward. It is time for him to finally be free. He fought well in battle. He deserves no less. I tell him the day Hans finally understood what he was fighting for in the war, was the same day he realized he would die for that cause. Freedom. And so, Hans would die. So would Hayward and his love, Minnie Bean, in that tunnel so they could be born again and wed. We would all be born again as someone else—but only in name." It is quiet. I think we are all waiting for some epic ending. Willy looks up. "That's it. That's the last entry. The rest of the pages are blank." She holds up the journal and wags a thick wad of pages between finger and thumb to display the empty pages.

"Well, that sucks," Beck chuckles. "It's like realizing you only taped the first three-quarters of a movie and missed the grand finale."

Chapter 61

I'm dying to get up to the tunnel to check for the door. But the creek's so high, I can't cross it. I sit in my quiet house, and I know there's more than a few people who think I hooked up with Max. I mean, in a small town, word travels fast. It has gone from one end to the other and back again. I'm not sure why he is doing this to me, but I am going to use it to my advantage. (*Bitch*, don't leave hand-me-down clothes in plastic garbage bags on my front porch with *homeless shelter* written on the front).

Because Mikayla is one of those who have heard the rumor and it is her knuckles that are knocking on my door the following morning. She's hotter than one of Pop Pop's marshmallows he always burns to a crispy black ball of charcoal over the bonfire. Mikayla *Tinsley,* that is, whose father owns the Tinsley Law Firm of personal injury lawyers. It appears within the last six months, Marcus Tinsley has been in a bit of trouble for applying false expenses to his clients' bills and claiming to work for three schools and four medical practices full time. One junior executive on his team included Max who suddenly stopped working for him only days before the shit hit the fan.

Pop Pop would call her *spitting mad* while she stands on my front porch and screams at me Saturday morning. I'm still in my fluffy white pajama pants with little pink hearts and an old t-shirt. She tells me I am the whore who stole her man and she's going to punch me down one side of the street and up the other. I just stand there and take it all in. Then, I pull on my old wide-eyed puffy-lipped face and burst into a ball of tears. It's not difficult.

"He played us both," I tell her. "I thought he loved me. He told me he did." Let me see, what is the line my beloved now *ex*-best friend always laughed at using on women. Oh yeah—"*Baby, this is me trying to pick you up. Is it working?* That sound familiar?" I ask her. I don't let her finish. She's stopped screaming and instead, Mikayla is shaking angrily with her hands in fists. "I should have known. He's always been like that."

"He loves me. He doesn't even *like* you," she hisses.

"Okay, you go with that," I tell her. I dab at my crocodile tears.

"You're doing this because Beck told you, aren't you?"

I'm ready to close the door. My curiosity gets the best of me. "What did Beck do?" I ask her with bored eyes. "Lay it on me." I know whatever she tells me will be a lie.

"He's been working with me and Grant. I know he told you he wasn't. Did you catch him lying?"

"Right." I roll my eyes and close the door. Twenty minutes later, I carefully use my photo editor and place a date on the bottom of some old pictures I had of Max and girls he met at bars, random shots I took when we were hanging out. I post them on her social network long enough I think she's seen them. I hide the post and delete it. Then, I wait.

Chapter 62

For an hour at lunch, every day and a half hour after work, Taylor, Paula Fitzgerald, and Tatum Morris have helped me set up rosters for the different teams playing. We use the kitchen at the office. Paula is an old pro at this. She's not only running a basketball league, she's also running a baseball league. We've set up maps for the vendors and have tied up everything with a pretty little bow. That is, except one thing—Lissette Baker.

Lissette is well-known for being a workaholic. She begins her day at 5 a.m. sharp and ends her day at 8 p.m. A couple times a week, she takes a breather at the local Sam's Steakhouse Bar for an hour. Then, and only when her kids are safely tucked into bed and are out of the way, she makes her way home. I imagine she tiptoes into the house with her heels in her hand to avoid any interaction with her family.

"She's using you, you know that, right?" Lissette leans over me while I'm rinsing a cup in the kitchen sink. "Eventually, she'll toss you away kind of like—" she jabs a thumb toward the doorway where Theo and Lexie disappeared. "—Theo did." Her voice is low because Taylor is sitting at the table with Paula Fitzgerald. Theo just stuck his head in the doorway to tell Lissette he was leaving. Lexie was in tow. I'm substantially grumpy. I can't sleep, and then I can't get enough sleep. I'm irritable and ornery and—

"So why do you think she's using me, Lissette?" I ask her a bit hotly. I say it loud enough everyone can hear me. "Because I'm not good enough for her and you are—*better* than me?"

"Shut your mouth, Harley."

"No, Lissette. I'm tired of it. You point a finger at me, and you really don't know me. You assume since I'm from a small town and an old house, I'm poor white trash. It isn't okay to treat me like that—like I'm walking around with head lice all the time." Lissette's face goes pale. She looks around the room. Paula is focusing hard on the paper in front of her, trying hard to pretend she isn't listening. Taylor, she's got that same smug look on her lips she always gets when Lissette gets jealous of me. But she's not looking at me. She's sucking in the hackles rising on Lissette's neck.

I knew Taylor has been using me to make Lissette jealous. I just didn't know the extent. She's not even really my friend. It's all an act. Every time Lissette would walk into the room with us, Taylor would lean in and give me the kind of look snobby, popular middle school girls give each other when the pimply dweeb walks past them. I never realized Lissette was using me too, this alpha female who runs the office wolf pack. I'm someone she can call a badass and strong. However, as dominant female, she knows she always holds the power over me—the power to make or break me in the business she runs. She can constantly show off her prowess as the leader of the pack of wolves she's raised in her office simply by snapping her fingers and making me do the humblest of jobs—*Harley, there's no toilet paper in the bathroom or Can you run a thousand copies?* I'm not just a pawn in Taylor's game. I am also one in Lissette's. I am a ping-pong ball being paddled from one side of the table to another.

"Baby, don't talk to her like that," Taylor tells me. "She's our boss." *Baby*? I turn to Taylor who has risen and is coming up beside me, reaching out her hand, laying it on my shoulder almost seductively. I pull away.

"Please don't do that," I say. She gives me a sad smile like I hurt her feelings. This, I know Paula notices. Now, I look like the bitch who is getting mad at the poor girlfriend who is stuck in the middle.

"What am I doing?" Taylor gets this weepy look in her wide eyes. "Gosh, Harley, I'm just trying to be nice." I see her hand, and I see Lissette swallowing hard. She hardcore loves Taylor. And I'm sick of being the pawn in whatever gambling game they are playing day in and day out.

"Stop."

"Stop what?"

"Stop touching me and fondling me when Lissette is around. Stop acting like you like me. You don't. You're just trying to make her jealous—"

"Shut up, Harley!" Lissette yells at me. Suddenly, she struts across the room and shoves me with both hands.

"Is that what you want?" she screams at Taylor while I stumble backward and land on my bottom between my chair and the table. Then in the two seconds that I grapple with the chair to rise, she kicks it out from beneath my elbow and pushes me with her knees from behind.

"You want me jealous?" she starts screaming. I see her pick up the chair. I don't know if she planned on hitting me in the head with it. It never happened. Theo comes rushing through the doorway, the top two buttons of his shirt unbuttoned like he was letting loose a little after work and then got to the top of the stairs and heard the shouts.

"Get out." Lissette is holding the chair over her head. Theo has wide eyes and grabs it in his hands just as she starts to let it fall on my head. "You're fired. Don't come back. I SAID, GET OUT!"

I turn to Taylor whose lips are all puckered and whose cheeks are pale. "You happy?" I ask her hoarsely while I mop up my papers from the table. "Is this the way your game was supposed to turn out? She's all yours, *baby*."

Chapter 63

At two in the morning, Beck sends a text. I just blink at it while I lay there holding it up over my head. It is self-explanatory. *Hey, I think we need to break this off before it gets too serious. I just don't feel the same way about you. I wanted it to work. I did. I don't want to lie. I've been texting with Emma. I think we're going to give it another try—I can't waste my life on somebody who is hooking up with anything that doesn't sit still for more than five seconds—*

What? I try to call him. There's no answer. I don't want to believe it. Still, it's like having my heart ripped from my chest. No, I'll keep trying him on the phone. It's not true. He wouldn't do that. Tomorrow, I'll talk to him. It overshadows getting fired. I told him I wasn't sleeping with anybody else. He looked like he believed me. Or maybe he was just saying that to keep the ride home less awkward. It's me who makes the guys I like turn out to be idiots.

At seven in the morning, I got a call from the company that does Central Independent Realty's payroll. The lady told me she was sending me a final check out. Nobody from my office called. Nobody seemed to give a rat's ass I'd even been there for almost a year. I call Beck's house. His sister answers. She tells me she'll leave Beck a message, but she sounds terse and cool about it. He never calls back.

I sit by the phone all day. The only person who calls me is Robby Pierson who had the dead-Trevor pictures from the train tracks. He tells me a truck has pulled up Joe Walsh's driveway three times in a row this week. It stops at the little gate at the bottom that clearly states: NO TRESPASSING and is closed most of the time. All three times, Joe's dogs have gone running out, barking and carrying on so whoever is in the truck can't get out without fending them off. He has gone out there with his flashlight as soon as the truck pulls in, turns on his front porch light. When he comes within a certain distance, the truck makes a speedy backing out and shoots on down the road. He's been trying to get the license plate number, but he can't even make out the type of truck or even the color.

That wouldn't be so strange, Robby tells me, but if you park right at Joe's drive, it's only about fifty steps from where they found the dead body. He thinks they have come back to look for something. What it is, he doesn't know. Robby says he and Joe had gone out there for three hours this afternoon looking for anything that they might have missed when they took the body. They found nothing.

So tonight, I'm going to Robby's. They are going to turn out the lights at Joe's house and park his car in the garage. He's going to put the dogs inside so they don't bark and carry on. Then, he's going to leave the gate open wide so whoever keeps stopping thinks that Joe is out somewhere and left it open until he returns. Robby and Joe are going to hide up in the grass and see who has been coming to the tracks. Haley is going to come and she thought I might want to come too. Maybe I could identify the person in the truck. They've put up three deer trail video cameras and have nighttime game binoculars.

Hurricane Hollow is only twenty-two miles from Guysville. I make plans to pick up Nana Nisee and tell Pop Pop we're going to the movies together. I ask if he's seen Beck. He says this to me: *I think he said he was meeting his ex-wife today. Why are you asking?* I told him nothing. But he's great with me taking my grandma to the movies. He thinks we've got some new bond going. I'm not going to the movies with her. I'm picking up Ned on the corner of Kempton and Reed in Guysville, then dropping them off at a theatre just outside town. While they are there, I'm going to do some surveillance with Robby, Joe, and Haley. If we aren't done in time, there's an all-night Waffle House restaurant next to the movie. Nana Nisee and Ned are going to grab a bite to eat and sip coffee until I get there.

It sounds easy-peasy. What could go wrong? At ten-fifteen, I am settled into the hillside with one of Pop Pop's baseball bats I loaded in after practice. It's my weapon of choice after Robby and Joe grab shovels from the garage. We're an hour and twenty minutes and one short train passing into the wait. It's warm out, but after the train bustles through in a roar of wind, I'm starting to get chilly in the damp air in my shorts and t-shirt. There's a misty haze coming up from the creek across the road. Joe is funny, has a buttload of jokes to tell us while we sit on our rears in the tall grass by the tracks, elbows on knees and frogs deafening the air from a pond by his house. I've decided this has got to be better than sitting around my house wondering over and over what I did so wrong that a nice guy like Beck dumped me via a text so he could possibly go back to the cruddy relationship he had with his ex-wife. And if Arnie O'Malley really gave Mama that money for an abortion. Mama called me later that evening. I didn't pick up. I just wanted to get away from Lost Hollow and all the junk going on there now.

At ten-twenty-three, three cars and a truck roar down the route. The third in line, a silver or white truck slows, then speeds up. Four minutes later, it comes back the opposite direction and pulls into the drive. We are far enough away from the vehicle that the headlights don't shine on us when it pulls into the gravelly drive. My fingers latch on to Haley's wrist. Her eyes are so wide, I can see the whites in the mere shine of a quarter moon above us.

Two doors slam. "Let's go." It's Robby and I who slide down the little embankment and peer through the weeds to the track. A train's horn blares at an intersection far away. I see two flashlights weaving and bobbing and stop just short of the place where Robby pointed out Trevor's body was found.

"Here. Here." The voice is deep. The beams from the flashlights work up and down. I take a breath, feel Robby's hand on my arm. I can't see anything in the bland light. The beam stops only inches from the toes of my tennis shoes. I can only make out two forms moving in the mist. One is big, one is bigger. The train is gaining speed. I see an arm come out and see something flash in the air.

"Hey, you boys are trespassing, you know that?" Joe Walsh's voice breaks the air. *What is he doing?* I see him sidling along the tracks, walking up to the two figures. Just as quickly, the sound of gunfire breaks the air in an explosion. I don't think Joe expected it. I mean, he's just a nice old guy who used to own a tax service. As soon as the gun goes off, I hear Joe's dogs barking at the house, hear him holler out a strange and surprised gasp.

Robby surges forward. I see him lunge upward toward the tracks. He starts yelling and hollering. I see the flashlights waggling wildly and I follow him like the dumb wolf pup in the pack who pads along naively straight down toward danger and not knowing the rest of the wolves are just posturing and are going to dive back into the woods. Because the next gunshot isn't aimed at Joe. It is aimed in our direction. I think it was probably a warning shot or fired simply willy-nilly toward the grass. Because that's where I am. I'm standing along the tracks, feel my shoulder just kind of jerk to the right before I feel something like a papercut along the flesh. I yelp, and it sounds nothing less than the yowl of a coyote.

"Shit, I hit one. *Gackk.*"

I suppose I dropped more out of panic than pain. I feel warmth on my arm. It was the shock that I thought I got shot and they were going to shoot again. But it wasn't before the voice just stops in a gag. I can hear the thud-whap of what I know is the sound of shovel to flesh. "Son of a bitch!" That voice, I know. I swear, it was John Matthews. I swear it. I push myself up to the sound of their feet running the track before it is swallowed up by the train. I feel moisture on my fingertips, warm and wet and dribbling. Haley comes running. I see her swoop down to me, snatch up her phone and hold the light toward my bloody arm to illuminate the wound.

"God, she's been hit!"

Chapter 64

"This is going to hurt."

I guess it is an advantage that Nana Nisee's boyfriend was a medic in the army. He knows how to stitch flesh wounds together. He does so on my upper arm, just inches from my collarbone in the two-story home that abuts his daughter's house next door.

It is less than an inch, the cut, but it won't stop bleeding until he gets the third stitch in. He's got a little medical kit. It isn't that I don't want to answer questions about getting shot at Joe's. I can't afford the visit to the emergency room. I don't even have the meager insurance Central Independent Realty offered. I'm also scared shitless it was really John Matthews with the gun. As Joe said, if he is stupid enough to shoot into the dark at strangers, he's probably stupid enough to chase me down and murder me if he knows it was me at the tracks.

It does hurt. Ned doesn't have anything to numb the pain. I just grit my teeth and cuss. Then he patches me up and gives me four ibuprofen. *Lovely.* Haley keeps texting me. I send her and Robby a text that I'm alright and a picture of me smiling a little too hard. Nana Nisee and I speed off into the night and between a call to Pop Pop telling him we'll be late because I stopped in for some coffee and I am a little tired, Robby Pierson texts me: *We found two .38 caliber gun shells. And we found this.* I have to pull off the road to look at it before I run back down into a hollow and lose cell phone service. I narrow my eyes at the picture. It's a gold wristwatch.

Look on the back. Does it say: To Trevor From Dad?

I wait in the darkness, listening to Nana Nisee snore gently in the passenger seat beside me. Robby calls me back this time. "Yeah, it belonged to him, right?" He asks me nearly out of breath. "Joe thinks whoever was there was trying to plant it for evidence. Why would they do that?"

"Because I don't think that was Trevor Woods dead on the tracks," I tell him. I've still got the pictures Robby sent me on the phone. I scroll through them again. Striped shirt. Dark blue jeans. Brown hair. "I think I know who it is, who was on the tracks. It was this homeless guy who used to sit at the gas station outside Bakers Quickie Stop and Gas and panhandle. His name is—" I pause. "—was Orv Saylor. He hasn't been there for a while."

"Joe's going to call the cops and tell them what's going on."

"Can you tell him to leave my name out?"

"Yeah, he suggested the same thing. He's just going to tell the cops somebody keeps stopping and he found the watch afterward."

It is two-thirty before I drop off Nana Nisee. I stop off at my house and grab a clean t-shirt first, one that doesn't have blood on it. Pop Pop's mad. I'm just in pain. I probably wouldn't have fallen asleep tonight easily anyway because of the ache in my arm and the sadness in my heart. But worse yet, I hear the rumble of a truck drive past my house three times. It sounds like the one at the railroad tracks. And I know it belongs to Max.

Willy Dunn came knocking on my door about four in the morning. She said Trevor's mom was fighting with Terry Gillis, her dad's girlfriend, about something in the driveway and threatening to burn the house down. One of them started shooting a gun. Four hours later, Bill Armstrong (who heard about the fight) came up and gave them an eviction notice because he'd had it with all the crap there. Willy climbed out her window and headed to my place.

"I have an extra room," I tell her. "I've got food in the refrigerator—"

"I can't go home anymore," she says so softly I can hardly hear her.

"So," I tell her, "stay here."

Chapter 65

I've snuck into the stands of the new Brandy Mountain Baseball Complex. My shoulder is sore. But I'm not letting it slow me down. There's an urgency in the air, and I don't know if John Matthews knows it is me he shot. There are four fields. Each is huge and as well-manicured as Lissette's perfectly trimmed and polished nails. Where I'm seated, it smells new like a still-packaged Christmas doll and has the feel of a miniature version of the professional baseball diamond in Huntington. It even has a pro-style electronic scoreboard the size of the billboards along the highway with MATTHEWS STADIUM, BRANDY MOUNTAIN FALCONS.

It certainly stands out more than our old-fashioned hand-made sign down in The Bottoms. Big Dee donated the wood from a barn he was taking down, and we dug out a couple old chalkboards from the old school in a shed behind the church. Buddy Peterson cut out little squares on the boards to place numbers for the score. Aunt Rita and Aunt Joy are going to be the scoreboard keepers. They will hand up the numbers to a handful of boys dressed in 1930s knickers, shirts, and newsboy caps who will put the scores in the slots like they used to in the olden days. Ours says: Brandy Mountain Spartans painted in white on the top because Pop Pop found the team name in some of his grandpa's stuff that had the name on their shirt.

"What are you doing here? Aren't you supposed to be at work?" Zach is not smiling when he comes up to the farthest corner of the bleachers. They are a shiny steel and provide enough seating for two-hundred. They only hurt my butt because I'm wearing shorts and it is hot. I must tug my eyes away. I was taking in the buff players in the same way a middle school athletic coach takes in the players from a rival team who have full beards and appear more like grown boys who have been held back simply to pad a team to win. All of John Matthews's Brandy Mountain Falcons are between the ages of (and I'm guessing because of their muscular size and their polished ability of play) nineteen and twenty-nine.

I don't answer him. There's no way I'm telling him I got fired. "I take it these boys must have played college ball? They look like a professional team."

"We're playing to win."

"Because John Matthews doesn't like to lose." I remember him telling me that in my meeting with him. "I've been told that." I look at Zach. He's as refined as the rest of his team with his freshly cut hair, styled like a magazine model.

"You really shouldn't be here. Everybody knows you started another league and you set up the opening day the same date as our tournament."

"What are you worried about?" I ask him. "Your team is cutting edge. You've even got players from out of state. I suppose John Matthews offered them payments to be on his team just like he gave you that job."

"So what? Again, we don't plan on losing. We do what we have to do."

"So everybody else you are playing against thinks they are playing recreation league softball. You're as close to a paid professional team I've ever seen. You think that's a respectable, an admirable way to win, running up the score just because John Matthews doesn't want to lose?"

"I want to win. I want to be a winner. I don't want to be like the rest of the losers in The Bottoms. Will you please leave, Flea?" He looks right to left. Nobody is bothering to look our direction. I nod and rise. "You know you're the best player on that team barring Beck, right? Max can't hit worth shit. It's like rec league baseball and basketball all over again. Coach Gates puts in you guys to run up the score. Then he pulls you out and sticks Max and his boys in to finish. They get the scholarships, you know, because nobody else wants them." I stare at him hard. "You know I'm being sarcastic, right? You get them on base, they score. It's high school all over again. Me and the kids who aren't related to someone or the coaches don't even get on the teams." He starts to leave. I grab his arm. "We're not going to be the best team out there. I know that. Don't think for one minute I don't want to win. I got Timmy Jones on Nicorette gum and I'm texting Billy Stinger every three hours to get him to stand up and walk to the kitchen and back. He's lost two pounds. Little steps—"

"Little steps for big losers. What do you want, Flea?"

"Nothing. I'm just saying."

"I think you've said enough. I'll tell you what you told me a couple weeks ago. You're not wanted here."

"If you change your mind, I'd like you on our team."

"You're not going to offer me something in exchange?" he sniffs caustically. "That's your usual M.O."

"You'd actually get to play." I deep-sigh and take a step away. "Whatever."

"I heard *you're* playing on another team."

"What do you mean, *another team*?" I twist my head.

"You know what I mean. I saw you hanging out with those women at the bar. The dark-haired one was all over you at your table. Beck and Max and I followed you to the park, then to the bar. Don't look at me like that."

"You followed me?" *Did Beck follow me?* I feel like I just got shoved into ice-cold water and my arms and legs won't move. "Like you *stalked* me or something?"

"Max was just worried about you. I hopped in his truck and we went for a ride." Zach stiffens in the seat. I follow his gaze and let my eyes lull on Beck's back. He's leaning in, saying something to Max. They both laugh.

"New best friends?" I try not to grunt while realization washes over me. Max and Beck. "You need to be careful around them. Beck isn't who you think he is."

"Yeah, right, Harley. It's always somebody else to blame. Never you. Max cares about you. He cares about Beck. He's letting him borrow his truck to go see Emma so they can patch things up. He'd never make it to Ohio, much less Michigan to meet her in his truck."

"This is sudden. I thought she was married with kids."

"She wants to be *unmarried* to the guy she's with. People regret the things they do, Harley. They need second chances. Beck, of all people, knows this and understands."

"Right." I force back a wince. Why the hell does my heart drop? "And suddenly, Max is your bestie?" I feel my belly jump, then almost growl. "That's why he said he was doing me all over the place—like rabbits?"

"You do have a reputation," Zach turns his head slightly away and spits a long line of saliva. His bored expression gives the impression of indifference. But I can read my uncle almost better than myself. The spitting is more out of disdain as if he is expelling the idea his sister-niece is actually a woman who might sleep with a man. "How can I expect any less, Harley? He might be the only one that has stuck around other than Dad and me. I wouldn't be playing him like a jerk right now."

"Or because he's filling your pockets with money."

Zach shakes his head. "Listen, you've been acting weird since the night you hooked up with Trevor. You're never home. You're out on the town. You got new friends. Why don't you just move uptown with that girlfriend?"

"You sound like Max."

"At least until you get over this new thing, whatever it is. Because if I thought for one second you were really attached to this girl, it'd be one thing. But it's not worth Dad going through whatever he would go through if he saw you two holding hands or kissing or whatever. I don't want to see him go through the crap he's had to go through for a kid that isn't even his and who doesn't give a rat's ass if he has to pick up after whatever destruction is following in your path after you storm through—"

"Shut up."

"No. I think you're just using that girl like you use Max and me and Dad and everybody else in this game you play. You want everybody to feel hurt when you feel hurt. You want everybody to feel unwanted when you feel unwanted. You only started your own league to hurt John Matthews, and he's a good man. But why am I worried? You'll never finish what you started anyway." He's going to say more. Then he clams up. I see the reason. Max has seen me. I see his eyes working across the field. I see him lean over, snatch up his phone and start to call someone. "Get out of here, Harley. I assume he's calling security."

"Security." I shake my head. They've even got security here. "Well, when you come back down from whatever cloud you're on, there's a place for you on our team."

"Yeah, that's not happening."

My feet make a bang, bang, bang down the steps and back into the coolness of the shade of the bleachers. The only thing I can think about is this image that pops up in my mind in eighth grade. It's Zach with his skinny arm slung around my shoulders while we rode the bus home from school. I got into a fight walking out of my last class. I had to tell Pop Pop and didn't want to do it. *I got your back, Flea, even when I know you're wrong. But could you just not be wrong so much?* Why do I feel like bawling like a big baby? It's like I can't get to my jeep quickly enough. I wiggle my keys, weave my way through the twenty cars parked in the lot. I'm not even focused when I pause for the full-size, white pickup. I'm just shoving back the baseball size ball of tears stuck in my throat and begging to be released. The sun is beating down into my eyes. I realize I'm sick to my tummy. I hate it when Zach is mad at me.

"Where are you going so fast there?" I hear two doors slam. I look up. Then I feel the blood run from my face. It is John Matthews. I see one big hulk of a man in a blue uniform like the kind the security wears at the mall. He's not a cop. But he's carrying a baton at his waist. "Keep an eye out for me," Matthew says. "Wouldn't you, Abe?" I look at his face. There are three nasty bruises between ear and chin. There's a scabby red on his forehead. I'm sure it is from getting hit by a shovel at the railroad tracks. It's not really a question. The security guard gives me a wide-toothed grin that looks akin to a shark readying to attack. Now, he doesn't seem interested in me. John Matthews nods at him, and the guard turns, seems to be scanning the parking lot filled with ten or twelve cars. I realize everyone is on the field. I'm alone out here with John Matthews and what Pop Pop would call his goon squad. Does he know I was at the railroad tracks?

"Excuse me, I'm going to my jeep." I back up a step.

"Well, no you're not. Not right this second." John Matthews walks up to me. He latches on to me between my collarbone and my neck and shoves me back against a gray truck. I'm so stunned, I just take the two steps back afforded to me until my bottom smacks against the door.

"Get off," I grunt at him. His fingers are warm against my skin, almost tepid like a plastic cup of milk left out on a picnic table and beneath a June sun. "I've been getting a few calls from folks saying you've got a ball tournament going on down in the hollow. It isn't going to happen, you hear me? You've got no right. That piece of property belongs to the city of Brandy Mountain. It isn't yours. You are having an event illegally. I intend to prosecute you to the—"

"I said, get the hell off me!" I try to push his hands off my chest, but I only end up peeling two of his fingers and one thumb upward an inch. It only seems to make him angrier. His lip twitches into a smile.

"I'm trying to be nice here, little girl. But you know how many of your—what's the word you bunch of dirty rednecks in the ditch call it? Oh, kin. That's right. I have half of *yer* kin on my payroll up there. I'll start firing them one at a time, one each day for every day you don't close that tournament down." He leans in. His breath is hot and smells like moldy bread. "Now, you know in less time it takes for me to drive from here down to your house, I can call the FBI on you and tell them I think it was you who killed Trevor Woods. It was you who stole all the stuff from the museum."

"Bullshit." I slide to my left, shove his arms to the left with both my hands. "I'm not backing off. It isn't your property. It belongs to the church." Then I kick out with my foot to his shins. "Touch me again, and you'll be sorry." John Matthews takes a step to the side, a little dance. I barely cuff him with my fingers, but it is enough to give me space before he pushes in again. *"Touch me again, and you'll be sorry,"* he repeats in a mousy, high-pitched voice. "See, here's how it goes from now on out. You're gonna—"

"I'm not doing anything for you, Matthews—" I'm standing erect. I reach up my middle finger and hold it up six inches from his face.

"You're not a good girl." That's what he says. Then John Matthews just pulls up his right hand. He brings it across his chest, then backhands me right across the face. I've honestly never been hit by a man other than Trevor the night he ditched me on the side of the road and stole my car. I've been pushed. I've been shoved. But the blow sends me reeling to my left in stunned surprise. I do this little march-dance with my feet, spin, and fall to one knee like a football player praying before the big game. I didn't expect it, and I don't expect John Matthews to snatch the back of my head and just cram my face into the hot metal of the truck. My cheek makes a *ker-chuch* against the door. I see stars while he holds my head there and I feel the burn in my flesh.

"Just so you know, there's more where that came from. You will shut down the tournament. And you will get your ass out of my town."

"It's not your town—" I feel the pressure getting harder. I know I am little and he is big. My only weapon to battle him is his weakness. That's his fear of germs. I roll some saliva around my mouth, chew it a little. I reach up and lay my palm on his face, then drag my fingernails from the top of his eyebrow and down along his cheek. Deep, my nails gouge him. It's nearly in slow motion while he pulls his face back. Then, I turn enough to spit right into his face. A long line of spittle drips down his nose to his lips.

He gags and bats it away with his palms. He's mad with cheeks a rosy hue. I was supposed to start my period two days ago, and I think it's holding up, building up in a big ball of anger ready to spew out on anybody in my path. I'm jerking to a rising position, almost standing when I hear the click-click of the truck door behind me. I turn my neck and my eyes take in Max just as he shoves the door open. He must have used both hands and pushed it as hard as he could because it smacks my hip and leaves a deep pang while I stumble forward almost into his father. I can do no more than stare at him with the same dumb gaze a mouse exhibits right before a hawk snatches it up in its talons. Then I'm snapping my attention to any spot I can make an escape.

"Sir, there are people leaving the fields."

John Matthews nods. "You just dug your own grave, girl."

"We'll see about that," I tell his back. And he does this bizarre thing. He pivots on his feet and comes at me fast with his arms in the air like he's going to belt me one more time with his fist. But he stops just short and leans his head in while I lean back, stare at him. "Nanny nanny *boo boo*, I'd watch my back if I was you-you."

I guess I take my anger out on Beck. I get on the phone, and I call him and just scream for five minutes on my way home. I call him a liar and a user and any other words that I can think of. Then I hang up.

Chapter 66

The front window of my house is broken when I get home. It is shattered glass strewn around the yard. There's a softball inside on the floor of my living room and none of my neighbors saw anything happen. I find that strange considering Missus Fields, three doors down, is peering through her curtains with her pug when I pull in the drive. Willy is nowhere to be found.

I'm stapling plastic over the window thirty minutes later when the Brandy Mountain Police Department cruiser pulls into my drive. I don't recognize the officer when he swings out of the car door, shuts it with a bang behind him. He's short and put together like a wrestler, but with painfully odd-shaped muscles that look like cantaloupes on his fore and upper arms. His clean-shaven head is tiny in proportion. He's not here to take a report of my broken window. He barely notes it.

"Are you in possession of a historical document belonging to the Branntwein family and a trunk and clothing belonging to Hans Branntwein?" He asks me, then holds up a warning hand. "And let me give you a hint on how you should answer. It is a journal from the 1800s. The trunk has a Civil War uniform. It was among the items listed as being stolen from the museum." He looks over my shoulder and into my living room. He doesn't know I've got a list of the items stolen and they are not listed anywhere on the document. "We can do this one of two ways. You can relinquish the stolen items from your possession immediately, or I can get a search warrant and confiscate the items with handcuffs on your wrists." He leans hard, pushes his hand over my head and rests it against the partially open door. I have to take a step back.

"Who told you I had these items?" I am looking over his shoulder. I can see Tim Webster across the street coming out on to his porch, leaning into the rails with his elbows bent.

411

To my left, Missus Fields has opened her curtains wide and she's watching over me. Ben Reynolds, Eddy O'Malley, and Ronnie Mills have also worked their way out their doors and are standing in their driveways near their trucks.

"That is confidential." The cop answers but doesn't seem to notice he's being watched.

"Well, I don't know what you're talking about," I lie. But Mikayla, Max, Beck and Willy are the only ones who know I've got both of these items. "You'll have to get a warrant. Get off my property."

He stands there, jaws churning. "I had a dog like you once," he says low and beneath his breath. "He must have thought I was a bone. It came after me. I had to shoot it."

"Too bad he didn't carry a gun like most folks down here in The Bottoms." I clear my throat, make a point of rolling my gaze from one neighbor to the other. "Because bad bones, no matter how big, can be buried in these woods and never be found."

"Are you threatening me?" He snaps his head left and right and growls deep in his throat.

"Are *you* threatening *me*?" I return. He takes a step back. Then he radios the police department making it clear out loud that he plans on returning within twenty-four hours. I'm shaken. I follow him with my eyes and see there is a car two blocks up that isn't typical in my neighborhood. It sits there while I force myself to finish stapling the window and my neighbors slowly scatter.

I get a text from Beck. He must have seen the police lights. *What's going on over there? You okay?* I don't answer, just delete him from my contacts. I wouldn't have believed the story about Beck going back with Emma if it didn't come from Zach's lips. I guess I was stupid to think there was more to every relationship of every guy I date. It's all about the sex. Then when it's boring, they are gone.

Chapter 67

Grant Lebowski paid the water bill for the Lost Hollow Historical Society Visitor Center on June 3rd. He paid the electric bill and has three invoices for sixty corrugated storage boxes purchased on June 12th. There are twelve weekly checks to Beck Allen O'Sullivan for two-hundred dollars each. I pause on these. Then Mikayla wasn't lying. It makes me sick to my tummy. There are fourteen donation intake forms in the last three months carefully filed under: DONATION INTAKES. Two of these are from the Matthews-Branntwein estate and include several pre-Civil War guns, miscellaneous books, and assorted Victorian clothing. He also rents a storage unit outside Ansted, a small town about twenty-two miles from Lost Hollow. There is also a box that says ACCOUNTING—BRANDY MOUNTAIN. I remember part of Grant's job is part-time doing the taxes for the town of Brandy Mountain.

I know all of this because I walked down the street at seven o'clock the same evening the cop banged on my door. Leland Wilson has unlocked the historical society building for me and let me into Grant's office while he cleans the rooms. I figure if there's nothing on the list worth selling, then maybe Grant Lebowski is *not* turning in items that are worth selling. And maybe, he's selling them under the table.

Leland is the cemetery grounds caretaker and the community building custodian. He also worked under Pop Pop, when he was foreman, as an equipment operator at the Brandy Mountain Colliery in the 1970s. He's tall and lanky and walks slightly bent. His hair is a fuzzy gray-black cap around the sides and back of his head and the top of his skull is shiny deep brown. This, he constantly rubs with his fingers when he answers a question.

He's got perfect teeth, except they are kind of yellowed. I can't help but think the entire time I talk to him how lucky he was to have straight teeth. Because everybody else his age I know down here has crooked teeth because parents couldn't afford braces on a miner's salary.

I'm shaken by what happened in the parking lot and on my porch. I don't want to go back to my house. I can't go to Pop Pop's. If he sees the bruises on my cheeks and chin John Matthews left on me, he'll go through the roof. Such, I went for a drive. When I passed the older section of the Brandy Mountain Cemetery on my way out of town, I stopped and pulled to the back. I sat for a while. Then I went for a walk halfway up the hill to find the old headstones for Reverend Mills and Annabelle Easton.

While I was swatting away the gnats, Leland came ambling across the freshly-mowed grass with a big smile on his face and a bottled water in an extended hand. I took it and opened the lid. "Well, look at you all grown up." He shook his head and held out a hand which he waved down by his knees, and then up to my head as if to show how much I've increased. "I remember when you used to sit in the pews at church with your aunties and turn around and stick out your tongue at everybody behind you."

"That was pretty much everybody because we sat in the front row." I smiled. "Aunt Joy always said, closer to the preacher, closer to God. I'm not so sure that helped me. If that's so, he saw all that goofy stuff."

"You was a good little girl in your heart, Harley," he said and patted his chest with his fist. "You made everybody in the back laugh. It kept most of us awake during those long sermons. God's got a job for everybody. Yours was keeping them awake so they heard the gospel of the Lord. What are you doing here today? Just strolling? Some folks like to do that in the cemeteries, just walk around because it's got a certain aura, a quiet feel to it."

"I'm just looking for a couple graves—two people who died in the 1930s when they had the tuberculosis epidemic, Reverend Mills and Annabelle Easton."

"Why, they'd be over there. Come with me. I'll show you," he told me. "My mama used to tell me Preacher Mills could start preaching in the morning on Sunday and go way into the night without taking a breath. He wasn't no fire and brimstone preacher. He was soft-spoken and kind."

As we walked, Leland stopped at almost every grave and touched it with his fingers. "I pray over each grave when I run my mower past it." He patted me on the arm. "I know most the names because I say it in my prayers. I make sure somebody remembers them."

He'd taken me over to the parts of the cemeteries that held the graves during the 1930s. Then he rubbed the top of his balding head and looked toward the roadway where a wrought iron sign with BRANDY MOUNTAIN CEMETERY hovered over the entrance. The dust was settling from a car easing off down the gravel lane. "You see that car?"

"Uh huh."

"That was Grant Lebowski sitting there while you was walking around. Don't know what he was doing. Maybe he thinks you're going to topple some of these old stones?" He leaned in. "He's an odd one, isn't he? I heard what happened with him booting you out of your volunteer work. That ain't right, ain't right at all. My grandson says you're the only one that ain't boring." I had kicked at the dirt a moment, not sure if our conversation was over. Then Leland said to me: "I'm going to tell you something. Something fishy is going on in the historical building."

"Like what?"

Weird stuff. Leland went on to tell me Grant and his new office assistant have been moving boxes in and out in the evening. Grant also told Leland he had to cut his hours because they were revamping the security system and refurbishing the building to keep it safer. Such, there would be higher costs involved in maintaining the security of the building and Grant and his assistant would offset the care. And yet, not a coat of paint had been used on the walls, nor were there any surveillance cameras or other equipment added. Leland also said Grant and the young lady helping him now weren't cleaning the place at all to cover the extra expenses. He still had to come in and the place was a mess. Now he just did it for half the time, half the pay. I asked him if he minded if I came in one evening and did a look-see.

And here I am now in the museum a few hours later, scanning the documents with my phone just in case they might hint at *something fishy going on*. I've got to be honest, after how Grant Lebowski treated me, I'd love to see him get caught doing something wrong. I've got pictures of receipts and scans of everything listed on the intake forms.

"Look, this is the stuff they are selling at auction to make more money. But if they're bringing in more money, I ain't seeing it. And it's stuff people donated."

"I know Grant had a clause in the intake form that stated once an item was contributed to the historical society, it belonged to the historical society. They could do with it what they wanted. It allowed the president of the historical society full control of its service. He could even throw away the items. Grant told me it was because they would get a lot of old junk like sweaters and broken plates. It was too much to sort through and contact the donor to come pick up. Besides, they didn't want to hurt anyone's feelings."

"Like this?" Leland wags his hand at me. I follow him down the hallway. He unlocks a double-bolted door and opens it wide. He shows me stack upon stack of brown cardboard boxes in one of the old Sunday school rooms, each carefully marked with a black indelible marker in bold print. I see one that states: JAMES—DOLL COLLECTION. They are taped closed. I kneel next to one: YOUNG—RBS SILVER. Then I peel the tape back and carefully lift the lids to expose the contents within.

"Holy shit," I mumble. I reach inside, pull out a fork and turn it around in my fingers. The handle is intricately designed like a building pillar with roses and vines twined and twirling at the base. "This is Raymond Baring Silversmith flatware." I poke my finger at the RBS embossed into the back, then reach in and grab a handful. "See? This is probably at least two sets."

"How much is something like that worth?" Leland mumbles, narrows his eyes, and focuses on the fork.

"For a full set, it can run fifteen to twenty thousand."

"For a bunch of silverware?"

"Not just any silverware, Leland. This is Raymond Baring, and the company stopped making silverware in the 1970s during the recession—"

"How you know all that?" he says softly, reaching out a slow finger to poke at the fork.

I glare half-heartedly at him. "I went to school for this. Why do you think I volunteered here? I spent a lot of time online looking up everything I could possibly find that was— old." I watch him roll a finger along the smooth surface and stop just short of the design. "I've seen a single steak knife go for four-hundred dollars on online auctions."

"Well, I'll be," he says. He pulls his hand away, looks around the room. "Wonder what's in the other boxes and what Grant Lebowski is doing with all this stuff."

"I don't know. But it probably isn't legal." I start to stand right then. My eyes are on a second box with: FIELDS- TEDDY BEAR, ORIGINAL IN BOX. HOLT-MONKEY HAND. KIRKPATRICK-ACTION COMICS.

"You think he's selling all this?" I ask Leland. "I wonder if he didn't blame me for stuff getting stolen and he sold it."

"We'd have seen it, right?" Leland walks over and leans down near a box that says: SPORTS MEMORABILIA- RUTH-SIGNED BASEBALL. And below, one that says: PARTS—HAND, FOOT, SKULL.

"No, not at all. There are private auctions going on all the time. There are private collectors who search out specific items and it is all kept confidential—like artifacts illegally dug up from Native Indian burial grounds. Look there," I point to a box that clearly states: CHEYENNE CRADLE BOARD. POT. SKULL. "That may be totally legal to keep and sell unless, of course, it was obtained illegally from what used to be called pot hunters, people who go in and steal from federal lands. I mean, people will do anything to get something of worth. Are you sure he's selling this stuff?"

"That's what I heard him say. I mean, I wasn't supposed to. I was in here cleaning—" Leland tips his head to the side suddenly. He holds up a hand. He looks like one of the little chickadees who alights cautiously on my Aunt Rita's back porch bird feeder she fills with seeds. As soon as one of those little birds settles in, it snaps its neck left and right to check for her old yellow tabby cat that pounces at the glass of the closed window. I hear the key rattle in the front door. I know that sound. Grant Lebowski has a specific way of jamming the key into the doorknob lock, so it makes a grinding sound. Then, he impatiently pulls and jams and wiggles it three or four times until the lock unbolts.

Leland snaps to attention, wags a hand at me. But the front door is only down the hallway. I wiggle my way between boxes just as Leland slips out the door, closes it softly behind. "What are you doing in here tonight, Mister Lebowski?"

"I've got some paperwork to take care of. If you're all done for the night, you can go ahead and leave."

"No, sir, I've got some more sweeping to do. Then I've got to put out the trash. I'm dusting the office—"

"Get to it, then."

I thought I was the only one Grant berated and treated like a child. His voice right now speaking to Leland, who is nearly the same age, is demeaning and makes the hairs on my arms stand up on end. I can't linger on their words. I hear Grant's footsteps easing by the doorway, and I push myself deeper into the boxes until I can't fit farther. That's when the doorknob wiggles. I hear it open, see the light go on and splash across the ceiling above me. *Shit. Shit. Shit.* I curse beneath my breath, listen as the footsteps get closer and closer—BOOM!

"What the heck—?" I hear Grant grumble and his footsteps patter away from my hiding place. "What is going on out—oh, for the love of God! Leland, do you know how much that display cost?"

I don't wait for Leland's answer, I clamber out of the boxes and set my sights for the open door. I stop just short, peering right to left. I can hear Leland apologizing, and I know by the racket he's making, he's trying to help my escape. "I'm so sorry. I'll get this mess cleaned up—"

"What are you doing, man?" Grant snaps. "Why are you yelling?" He's yelling to cover the sound of my steps toward the entrance. "No, I'll grab the broom. You just pick up the display—" He can't keep Grant in the room. I see his shadow, slip into the office because it is the closest escape. I know Grant is heading to the maintenance closet just inside the front door to dig out a broom. His heavy steps pass me as I slip past his garbage can and crawl on hands and knees beneath his desk. I see my phone laying on the corner of his desk. "Where is that broom, Leland?" Uh oh. It's still in here where Leland was talking to me.

I feel my face flush, stretch out my hand above me and snatch my phone just as Grant stomps around the corner, cursing. I can see the broom he is looking for. It is directly across from me. I squish into a ball, grab my legs between my arms and say a prayer in my mind. Just as Grant takes a third step toward the desk, the lights go out in the entire building. It just goes completely black. BOOM. He trips on the garbage can and nearly falls. "WHAT THE HELL IS GOING ON?" Grant screams. I hear a swish of clothing, then the sound of his foot booting the garbage can in anger. He doesn't just do it once. He does it twice. "Leland, are you completely incompetent? Did you turn off the switch in the circuit box? What are you doing? Are we having a blackout?" His last words are fading while he marches around the corner, his hands patting hard on the walls to guide his way.

I, on the other hand, rock forward and crawl from beneath the desk. I know I can't make it to the front door without exposing my whereabouts. If I open the door, the lights from the street are going to splash across the hallway and all the way toward the old sanctuary where Grant is now yowling at Leland to turn the damn lights on or call the cops or the electric company or—

Such, he doesn't hear me scramble toward the old kitchen and the back doorway—palms slapping and knees banging. I wheel around just as I hear his voice getting louder again and see the small doorway leading to the cellar. *Aw, hell no,* I moan to myself, *I don't want to go down there.*

I hear Grant coming this direction. Then, I feel my heart race because he gives a round of six, loud sneezes. Surely, he must know right now, it is me. He turns into the back room muttering something about incompetent bastards that are too stupid to know how to fix the circuit breaker box. But I know better as I hear the click, click, click while Grant flicks the switches on each circuit breaker, trying to figure out which one went off. I have thanked Leland with every bone-jarring thump of my knees on the hardwood floor. Still, as luck would have it, the door is padlocked to the basement. And just as the lights go on, I see my only escape. It's the old donation chute, a simple square window in the wall about three feet from the floor where clothing could be thrust-through. It would fall about twelve feet to the floor of the cellar below where there was a collection box. Now, I must assume there's nothing but solid concrete floor.

It has a little hanging door. I remember the chute. When I was little, I used to beg my Aunt Joy to look over her outdated clothes each week to find something she didn't want any longer so I could thrust it into the donation chute. I always imagined there was a big old church mouse down there that I was feeding and it devoured Aunt Joy's clothes. Now, it is devouring me headfirst. It's either that or Leland loses his job and I suffer through a breaking and entering, and time in jail. And so, I fall. But my descent is short as I ricochet off one set of high boxes, then another. I tumble to the floor in the darkness, then cautiously turn on my cell phone light. I blink. There must be hundreds of plastic containers and boxes carefully layered around the room.

When I hear only footsteps upstairs, I carefully peel back

one lid and then another. *Bingo*. The antiques upstairs were not the only valuables Grant Lebowski was hiding from the public eye. The cellar is filled with them. I meticulously take pictures until my cell phone storage is full.

Midnight. It is when I slide through the cellar window and out into the summer grass. Twelve-twenty is when I step on to my front porch. Willy is back. She's waiting for me on my front porch.

"Hey," she says, holding up a blank envelope. "Some guy named Jake dropped this off. He said to give it to you. I don't know what he means, but he says this one was harder to reach. They just got it from the building roof this morning." It is from Jake Ringgold, the bartender, I guessed. I take it in my fingertips and open it. Inside is a tiny memory card.

I tuck Willy into her room. At one-ten, I pop the memory card into my computer. I recognize the view as the front of Damon's Bar. I'm blurry-eyed staring at the surveillance tapes. I swear I've been staring at it forever. It shows the lights on the pavement for forty minutes. Then another ten. I'm falling asleep, my head dropping when I see shadow cross through the light. A car. A tiny car. I lean forward, stare at the bumper. Yes, there's the tiny dent I got running into Pop Pop's garbage can. It's my car. It is Trevor moving in a jerky walk toward the bar doorway. He disappears. One minute passes, then three. Then a truck slides into the parking spot next to my car. The door opens, smacks my car door. Out pops a man. I can see him walking like a bull toward the door. It is John Matthews. And yes, Max is following. They are yelling at each other. A shadow comes from the bar. It is Trevor. John Matthews grabs him up and shoves him against the truck. And Trevor, he falls.

Chapter 68

Max pulls into my driveway two hours later. I am shaking but trying to play it cool. I watched the tape over and over. Trevor did not rise. He had to be lifted and disappears into the shadows. I meet Max on the porch. He's got a wide grin on his face like nothing happened at all at the parking lot at the new ballfields. It's the grin he always gives when he's glad to see me, like a pup waiting for its returning owner at the door. I loved that grin. I loved Max. I hate him now. "I'm calling the cops in two seconds. Get the hell off my porch. How dare you tell everybody you are screwing me. How dare you even think you can come here after what you and your dad did in the parking lot to me."

"You deserved it. What the hell did you tell Mikayla?"

"The same thing you told me about Trevor and that he had a bunch of screws on the side." I laugh with a sassy pucker to my lips. "Because let's be honest, nobody could have gotten ahold of those pictures but you. It's payback."

"Bullshit. Trevor was screwing Lila from one end of the apartment to the other. I was doing you a favor." He pokes his finger at me. Then shakes his head, stops. "And something just happened at the museum. You know anything about that? You better not be trying to steal stuff."

"I never stole anything in the first place. You're the one trying to steal something that isn't yours. Like our town." Maybe Max will kill me too.

"I'm telling you right now you might as well let me on this property. It's going to be ours—I mean, the city's." He waves a hand in the air. "We've got all the papers filed, and we've been told we're good to go. No judge is going to deny our right. The use of eminent domain is such a wonderful way to confiscate private property for public use and for pennies on the dollar. It is so easy when it is for economic development for blighted property—"

"Beauty is in the eyes of the beholder. You know what

that means? It means beauty is subjective," I spit at him. "I find beauty here. Just because your idea is different gives you no right to steal our land."

"You and your poor neighbors aren't going to win. We're filing a lawsuit against you for trespassing on our property at the ballfields. You don't want the cops showing up while everybody is pulling in for your half-ass tournament and arresting you."

"The property belongs to the church. It is private."

"The church belongs to the city, as does that little museum that is going to get demolished as soon as we clear the land for housing down here."

I have anger boiling in my chest. I think it is going to spill over. "What happened to you, Max?" I say hoarsely. "What went so wrong you turned into this monster?"

"Monster?" he laughs loudly. "I'm your God damn savior, don't you see?" he tells me. "This place is trash. We're paying you to move and find a place somewhere else."

"Get off my property." I take my phone from my pocket. Ting. I see a message, but I don't have time for it. I flip past it, dial Lance Washington's number.

"What are you doing?"

"I'm calling the cops—calling Officer Washington to come and get you off my property."

"Well, good luck with that. He got fired." Max laughs. I stare at Max, hear Lance pick up the phone. "*Hello*?" he's saying. I back into the house, slide around the door and close it with my butt. "Hey, this is Harley. Is it true you got fired?"

"Yeah."

"Okay, we need to talk—" I say. "I'm going to call you back in five minutes. Please pick up." I hang up. Just then, there's a ting, ting, ting of more messages on my phone. I flick the icon for texts, watch a few images come on to my screen. I can't see them, narrow my eyes to focus in. Then, I see it. "Holy crap," I whisper. I can hear Max banging on the door. But I don't answer it. Just lock it tightly.

Chapter 69

Pop Pop knows something is wrong when I walk through the door the next afternoon. I've got Willy sitting in my jeep and Lance Washington in tow. He's not wearing a uniform. I see Pop Pop look from me to him questioningly with eyes slightly narrowed.

"Pop Pop, we need to talk," I tell him, setting down the plastic storage container I got in Trevor's garage. I hear laughter in the living room. It sounds canned like the kind for old sitcoms. It's not. It is Zach and his buddies. "And I need someplace safe for Willy to stay for a few days."

"What happened?" Pop Pop asks me, eyes now wavering at me, then to my jeep. He pushes his hand on the container. "What's this?" He veers back toward my face. Already, I've got a deep blue-red bruise below my cheekbone and one above my eyebrow. "Are you alright? Were you in an accident? Did somebody hurt you?" He's going to lose it. I see the look in his wide eyes.

"Pop, hush. I'm fine right now." I push a finger to my lips. "I'm fine now. Just listen." I saw three or four trucks outside. I recognize Beck's and T.J.'s truck. The other two vehicles are new to me. "Who else is here?"

"It's just the boys. Beck, T.J., Zach. Max is here, and so are a few I don't know well."

"Crap." My eyes snap to Lance, then back to Pop Pop. "Come outside with us a minute. This has to do with Max and his dad. This is an emergency. Pop Pop, you know Lance, right? He was the cop for Brandy Mountain. John Matthews just fired him. John sent him to pick up some evidence in Trevor's death. When Lance returned with it, he questioned John why they had not found this evidence earlier. The area was thoroughly examined."

"It was a watch given to Trevor by his father," Lance Washington divulges. "It would have been found."

"The watch was planted a couple days ago by John

Matthews on the railroad tracks where Trevor's body was allegedly found to make it appear it was Trevor who was actually killed on the tracks," I hold up my chin and say softly. "I was there when he dumped it." I hear footsteps. "We need to go outside."

Pop Pop nods to the door, looks behind him to the dark foyer. "Let's go to the garage."

"The night Trevor stole my car, he told me to get this container out of his garage. He said it had girly magazines in it," I tell Pop Pop. We have moved to Pop Pop's garage. The three of us are standing, leaning in and peering at the container. "So, I did." I open it, push aside the magazines to expose the six jars. "In it was Hans Branntwein's journal and these jars full of old coins and scrip from the colliery. I was kind of waiting for him to come back and tell me why he had me take them from his garage—why he had them in his possession. I just thought it was part of the treasure from the legend buried in The Bottoms."

"In a way, it was," Lance reaches in and grabs one Ball Mason Jar. "It might not be much by today's standards, but it was probably somebody's life savings passed on to their family. And it wasn't dug from the ground recently. It was probably buried years ago in the floor of a cellar for lack of anywhere else to hide money before banks. It was unburied and donated to the museum by family members."

"We think Trevor stole this while he was helping to steal stuff for Grant Lebowski and John Matthews. That's why he was murdered—"

"Murder? Grant and John were stealing?" Pop Pop seems to chew on the words. "All of this is hard to digest. Most look at those two men as pillars of our community. Trevor Woods came from a good family."

"Well, they aren't good men. I have a surveillance tape from Damon's Bar that shows John Matthews shoving Trevor against my car. Then he and Max drag him off. Trevor was probably stealing a lot, maybe for a drug problem—"

"He's been arrested a couple times for driving under the influence and having drugs in his vehicle," Lance offers. "He was probably skimming some of the profits of their thefts."

I thrust my hand out with my phone. "Here, this is a list of people who Grant Lebowski and John Matthews have been dealing with to sell donated items they get at the museum."

"These dealers take a percentage, then Grant and John place a small increment into city funds to make it appear they received some revenue for it," Lance adds. "The rest of the profit, they pocket for themselves with no tax deductions."

"Well, except what Trevor probably stole."

"Why aren't these men in jail?" Pop Pop asks me. "How did you come up with this?"

"They aren't in jail because they're connected to so many people, Pop Pop. I didn't know who to turn to for help. Big people—"

"Like Mikayla Tinsley, Max's girlfriend," Lance adds. "Her father owns Tinsley Law Firm. From what chatter I heard in the office, there was a falling out between Marcus Tinsley and Max Matthews-Branntwein over money issues. Max left and Mikayla, who he had been dating, left with him. Tinsley told Mikayla if she left with Max, not to come home. But Grant saw an easy way to switch Harley's job to Mikayla when Trevor Woods disappeared because she knew what was going on. I believe the whole plot behind the museum goods being stolen was to cover up for his disappearance and the goods being sold off illegally."

"The Tinsley law firm got into trouble for stuff like applying phony expenses to their bills," I cut in. "Tinsley is claiming, from newspapers I read, that one of his junior executives was a part of the scheme. I'm assuming that is Max. That's why he's here. He's in a huge legal battle and needs funds. Such, I think he and his dad were skimming money from the city."

"Okay—" Pop Pop leans in to goad me farther. "Keep

going."

"Mikayla's been doing inventory. I know that because she gave Beck a list of the stuff that was allegedly stolen the night I was at a big meeting with my realty company. But she told me in a text that after she gave the correct inventory to Grant, it was typed into the computer and ninety percent of the donations were gone. Then she sent me these copies of the deals late last night right when Max came knocking at my door. She texted me and said that she found these in John Matthews's file cabinet." I look at Lance.

"Why is she giving you this information?"

"Max told a bunch of people he was um, you know, sleeping with me. He wasn't." I can't look at Pop Pop, so I stare at my hands before I turn to Lance. "She heard it, too. I used it to my advantage. I sent pictures to her of Max with girls. I told her he was using us both. It ticked her off enough I think she just blew a gasket. She saw him leave to come to my house last night."

"But we've got no proof of the items they received versus what is not on inventory," Lance says. He scratches his head. "This is kind of our word against theirs—"

"Not necessarily." I nibble on my lip. "I, um, got these pictures of items from the cellar of the museum. I stood down there for good two hours and got a picture of almost all the boxes and a picture of at least part of the contents."

"How'd you do that?"

Breaking and entering. "Um, I was able to get access to the museum."

"I'm not going to ask. And I'm not going to ask how you got involved with the watch at the tracks."

"I got people," I say in a hoarse, deep throat, trying to sound like some mob boss.

"Then who do we take this information to?" Pop Pop ignores my imitation and turns his attention to Lance. "Where do we go from here? Because she's not safe. You're not safe."

"None of us are safe from the Matthews," I voice my opinion. "Pop Pop, you can't trust anybody."

"I'm going to call a few folks tonight who I worked with during my training. It's a hard row to hoe," Lance tells us. "Matthews has a lot of friends in high places. If I go to the wrong person, they'll tell him. It will be covered up. But I have a few people I can trust. Until then, I'd just watch your step. Don't go anywhere alone."

"And I need to ask a favor." I look to Willy peering from the jeep window. "Willy's not safe at home with her daddy gone. She wants to stay with me. I don't think it's safe right now. Can she stay with you and Nana Nisee a couple days or until—?"

"Will she stay?" Pop Pop asks. "That's my question. And why don't you come home too."

"She trusts grandma. I don't want to bring trouble here."

"You're never—trouble."

"I'm always trouble, *Poppy*," I try to tease him, clear the air of urgency. There's the sound of shoe soles skidding on gravel. I clamp my mouth shut. Pop Pop makes a quick turn, steps over to his mini-fridge and pulls out a couple soda pops and hands them to Lance and me. Just as I pop the lid, Beck's form fills the doorway.

"We're heading out," I mumble fast. "Thanks, Pop Pop. I'll call later." Pop Pop asks Beck if he wants a soda pop too. Beck shifts uncomfortably and tells him no. I know why he came out to spy on me when I see Max is standing on the front porch of Pop Pop's house as we step into the sunshine. I see him eye me, swing his keys. Then he makes a quick exit to his truck. Pop Pop starts to follow. Lance lays a hand on his shoulder. "Not a good idea, sir. Let him go."

I think we're all waiting for Beck to follow Max. He doesn't. It makes me uncomfortable. Maybe he's more uncomfortable because he slows and doesn't keep pace. Pop Pop rubs his forehead, slows, then turns to me.

"You're staying with me tonight," he says low on his

breath.

"No, I'm not." I watch Max's truck pull out of the driveway. He knows what is going on. We pause at the porch. "Pop Pop, I've got all my stuff at home to work on the tournament—"

"It can wait."

"I'll stay with her." Lance rubs the top of his head. "I've got nothing better to do than start calling some folks — obviously."

"Do you have cooties?" I try to make light of the situation.

"Yeah, probably," he tells me, scratches his arms. We stop at my jeep. I wave Willy out and snatch the overnight bag I put together for her from my clothes. "Pop Pop and Nana Nisee will take care of you for a couple days," I tell her softly. We discussed it and she'd rather stay with me. But she agreed only if I promised to come get her. "Then we'll work on something more permanent, okay?" She asks me if I'm going to be alright and I fake a smile, tell her—yes, of course. That's when Beck steps up, blocks me from following Willy toward Pop Pop.

"Harley, I need to talk to you." Beck eyes the bag and Willy, then Lance. Lance looks from Beck to me. He's suddenly got cop-eyes on for all it is worth without a gun and without a uniform. "Alone."

"No, Beck," I tell him. "There is really nothing you can say. I mean, I know you were getting paid by Grant."

"You're joking, right? Are you going with him somewhere?"

"Lance?" I ask him. "No, but it isn't any of your business. I found copies of your paychecks. There are twelve of them from the Lost Hollow Historical Society." I tell him and hold up a finger because he is opening his mouth as if to protest. "Don't, just—" I start to protest. I mean, I just want to lose it on him, scream until my lungs hurt. He knows it. I literally see him wincing outwardly, preparing for it. He's seen me lose it before. He's putting up a shield waiting for my blows. Then suddenly, I feel like a balloon with the air slowly wafting from a tiny hole in its exterior. "It's fine," I say softly to a face that isn't expecting it. "I wasn't invested. I wish you the best." I'm lying. I wish I could push Emma off a cliff. And yet, for the first time in my life, I actually want the best for someone I boyfriend-love. Shit and that's when I realize I really do *love* him. It isn't just an *I love you* tossed back casually after he says it to me. It is that I really, *truly* love him. Ouch. And it hurts.

"What are you talking about?"

"Emma. I heard that you and your ex-wife are getting back together."

Beck sniffs a caustic laugh. I see him reach into his back pocket, pull out his phone. "Did you write these texts? Answer me. That's all I ask." I pat my hand on the jeep door. Then I nod, work my way over to Beck. He holds up his phone. "Just so you know, these were allegedly sent from your old cell phone. They were forwarded to me by Max's girlfriend."

Harley: *Hey, bestie screw. Coming over tonight?*

Max: *Only if you tell me, baby, what u gonna do.*

"Oh." My eyes widen at the graphic detail following. I push the phone away. I mean, honestly, I've been known to talk naughty to a guy if that's his thing. I don't write it out. I whisper it in his ear. I'm not necessarily embarrassed by seeing this. It just isn't me.

"I didn't text him this."

"I didn't think so," Beck says. "I mean, at first, it caught me off-guard. Then I realized you were still using your grandpa's old phone. They were stupid enough to use *your* cell phone. The one that's still in the police evidence locker, I suppose." He steps back and away. "I'm not getting back with Emma. Max called her on the phone and told her I talked about her all the time. She called me and said that yeah, she'd like to give it another try. She's separated from her husband. I told her I had somebody in my life already. That didn't go over well—"

"How—how did they know about—us?"

"They've been parked in front of your house for two weeks. I just thought one of your neighbors bought a new car. I'm going to deny those paychecks. I was never paid by them. I'm assuming they were cashing the checks in my name. I tried to get ahold of you. You blocked my calls."

"I'm stupid." Realization slips over me. Beck's paychecks—Grant was making the checks out to Beck. Mikayla was cashing them in Beck's name so she could work and they still got the funding from the Appalachian Rural and Historical Development Council. "It was Grant illegally making out the checks to you and giving them to Mikayla—"

"No, you're not dumb. You don't trust. And it's not your trust issues I'm having a hard time dealing with; I can work with that. Everybody's got baggage." He gives me a smile. Oh. I know this one. It's the *that-was-a-good-screw-but-that's-as-far-as-it-goes* smile. I should have recognized it on Theo and Trevor, and well, I'm not making a list. "Harley, I'm sorry, but I can't deal with somebody who isn't afraid to walk across a swinging bridge, but won't open up, who wants to hide a relationship simply because she doesn't want to deal with the consequences. I assume that sums it all up. You don't believe it's worth it." He turns and walks away. He's not three steps away, and I'm getting ready to step forward when Zach slams open the screen door to Pop Pop's house, "Dude, what are you doing? We've got the game on hold." Zach doesn't even look at me. I just stare at Beck's back walking away.

Chapter 70

I didn't think he'd come. I told Lance I needed some time alone. He left. I called Beck, asked him to come over and talk. He just sounded far away. Then eighteen minutes and twenty-one seconds later (I was staring at the clock), there's a knock at the door.

"I was thinking I had one chance to kind of show you that I think what we've been working on is worth it. Will you hear me out?" I'm wearing one of my work business suits—a black button-up striped jacket and matching black skirt. I've got on my heels.

"I don't really feel like going anywhere," Beck answers like he thinks I'm dressed to go out for dinner. "Just say what you want to say." But he's here. So at least I know it's one step.

"I can't say it—" I watch Beck's eyes. "You'll have to come inside." They have a faraway gaze. He's got his hands in his pockets.

"I don't really want to come inside. Just say what you want to say right here. I can hear you from the porch just as well as inside your living room."

"Alright. I'm not asking. I'm telling you. I am going to say this once. Either get your ass in here Beck O'Sullivan," I say softly and firmly, "or I am going to pull out all my tools including biting, kicking, and screaming. You know what I can do."

"Harley, this isn't a joke—you can't say anything right here that will fix the situation."

"AND I'M NOT JOKING. GET YOUR ASS IN HERE!"

Beck is scary when he's mad. He gets a certain darkness in his eyes like they go from a deep, sparkling green ocean to a black, dark abyss. He has a tip to his chin slightly upward and sideways as if he is preparing for a punch. I've only seen him like this once when Gil Montgomery slapped his girlfriend in the hallway in high school. He beat the crap out of that boy, dragged him out the back doors and into the parking lot. Now, he is clamping down hard on his teeth.

I stare at him. He stares at me. "Okay," I say. Obviously, threatening isn't going to work. Perhaps bartering will. "I can't say what I want to say out here. If you come inside and hear me out—give me five minutes. That's all I ask. Five minutes. You can either stay or walk away."

He's not happy but gives one last look behind him before he comes in the door. "Sit, please," I say when he follows me into the kitchen. Beck hesitates but sits down on the kitchen chair I have turned around facing him. I lock the front door and he asks why I am locking the door, turning down the lights. "Just sit," I say and plop my phone down on the little table next to him. "So, this is how it goes—"

I swore I'd never dance for a guy. I thought it was subservient because I've known enough girls who have been forced to do it to pay for college or pay their kid's medical bills. I watched them die a little inside after they did. I'm not going to sit here and hash it out, justify what I'm doing. I'm just proving a point. And I'm not dancing for some psychopath pervert. It's Beck. And I'm willing to put my ego on the shelf and let him know how I feel.

"You don't have to—" He says, and that darkness in his eyes starts to fade away when I turn on a song on my phone.

"Shut up. I know."

I'm pretty good at dancing, gyrating around, wiggling my ass at all the right times and to the beat. I slip up two inches from his face, slide around him and rub my breasts against his shoulders, do every sexy move I can think of for four minutes. He's kind of stone cold, I guess until I wriggle out of the suit coat and skirt. Button by button, I pop until I reveal that old teeny weeny, two-piece bathing suit I still had stuffed in my top undie drawer for lack of funds to buy a new suit. By then, he's got a whiff of coconut sunscreen and Sweet Baby perfume. I still buy it. It's only $10.00 at the drugstore.

When the song ends, I snatch up the phone in my hand, walk over to the counter. "When you told me about what I

433

did to you back then, wearing this suit, leaning against the sink, it made my heart race hearing it." I lean my belly against it just like he should remember, rest my elbows on the counter. I roll my finger through my hair. "So, Beck, how did it play out in your head? How's this story end for you?"

He rises, makes his way over while I look over my shoulder at him. The anger has dripped away, replaced by a soft smile and twinkling green eyes. "You know, I can't—I could hardly breathe that day looking at you," he divulges. "I can't right now." He says in a deep, throaty whisper while he comes up behind me. He presses his chest against my back. I feel his heart racing while he gently places both hands on my hips. His right, he slowly eases it up and slips his palm under my bathing suit, rolls his fingers along my nipple. He slips a forefinger of his left hand into the strings of the bikini and peels it downward. Now I can feel his pants against my bare bottom until he brings his fingers up and unclasps the top button of his jeans, then rolls down the zipper. I feel him moving between the cleft of my legs, feel him against my thighs. "So in my dreams, Harley, this goes slow and easy and on and on." He chuckles lightly and heaves a wispy sigh. "But now it's real and you are so much damn sexier and so much more beautiful than I even imagined, I think it's going to be a little quicker than I thought." I never thought I'd think a guy moving too fast was sexy. But at this moment, it is quite logically the sexiest thing a man has ever said to me, and I'm getting ready to burst myself.

"So, big guy, let's make that dream come true." He gently spreads my legs farther with his hands, gives me a nudge, so I'm leaning slightly over. Our bodies come together. He thrusts himself against me until our soft groans mingle at the same time. The climax is grand, blissful-ripples beating beneath my belly. Then, simply that wonderful sense of joy and sleepy overcome me. I've got my elbows cutting into the counter and Beck's arms are on either side of me, I look up and he flashes me a smile.

"What?" I ask.

"Okay, you asked me how it played out in my head. So here goes—I love you." I know I blush. Beck looks scared, his eyes going back and forth between my own.

"Well, I love you too." Oh, my God. I said it. I feel it. I just busted it out without hesitation. I turn so I'm facing him, and he pulls his arms around me in an embrace.

"So that's the *perfect* ending," he says and kisses my forehead. "The one that went through my head. I've been trying to figure out a way to tell you. I'm just scared shit-less you were going to look at me and say: *What the hell, Beck? You're an idiot. I thought we were just hooking up.*"

"The perfect ending," I repeat softly. Strangely and wonderfully, it doesn't feel like the endings in my old sappy movies I once told Max ended sadly with the couple riding into the sunset and then, normal lives. "You want to spend the night?" I ask him, then sigh and hold out my hand. "Before you answer, Beck, I need more time to talk to Zach. He's slipping from my fingers and just out of reach. I know you know him probably as well as I do. But I am scared that rift between us, that span Max has left will push it too far if he thinks I took you from him. I'm not hiding *us*, just trying to figure out how to keep you and not lose him."

"Baby, I hear you," he starts to say. I think he is going to shake his head and tell me to choose. "I'll trust your judgment. I want to stay, hold you all night if I can. But just know that by hiding it from him, you're making his best friend a liar in his eyes. Just saying."

Chapter 71

At two-thirty-two in the morning, there's a bang-bang-bang on my door. Three huge cops dressed in full SWAT protective body armor including helmets and visors are shoving assault rifles in my face. A fourth, waving a paper in his hand, screams he has a search warrant, body slams me to the floor, and handcuffs me. I'm barefoot and in my fluffy pajama shorts and a t-shirt. I catch a faint image of Beck through the madness of full-grown men ruffling through every drawer, digging up my carpets, and tearing my little house to pieces. They've got him up against a wall, making him do the scissors to check for weapons. Papers are flying out of my cabinets, furniture is tossed around. They are less about searching for evidence and more ripping my things apart.

"This is how it works when you're dealing with the big leagues, Miss Davidson." I'm reclining flat on my belly on the cool linoleum floor of my entranceway. I crane my neck to peer upward. "Oh, no, better not move. They might think you're trying to escape and shoot you." I didn't know John Matthews had entered. He's hovering over top of me scanning the room with his hands behind his back and a smile on his face. He looks around, pushes his foot forward, then makes a hard swipe of the toe of one brown, leather shoe on my cheek.

"We got something." One of the cops comes out lugging the trunk with Hans Branntwein's Civil War uniform and effects along with a cigar box full of old postcards I had collected. "We've got shotgun shells. Found them in the drawer by the bed." Crap. The ones that were tossed in my jeep at Trevor's funeral.

"Well, look here. I guess we have our culprit." He takes the shells in his hand. "These are an exact match of what was dug out of Trevor's head. Thought it was a suicide. Guess we have a homicide."

"Don't say anything. Tell them you want a lawyer," Beck calls out. I hear him grunt. Twice. Then there's a bang like knees upon floor.

"Don't say a word or he might make a wrong move and boom! He's dead." I can't turn because John Matthews's foot is on my cheek. He leans over, squats with one elbow on his knee. "You understand—you're done, right?"

"Go to hell. I'm more a Branntwein than you are. Your kids aren't even blood—"

"Get her out of here."

I get paraded in my pajamas by armed guard to a bulletproof, armored SWAT van while my neighbors watch from their porches with their lights on. I'm shaking. I feel like I'm going to throw up. I think I'm going to end up on the railroad tracks like Orv Saylor.

They wouldn't let me use the phone for the six hours they keep me at the police station on Brandy Mountain. I think if Dispatch Carla hadn't clocked in at three in the morning, I would have ended up a broken body on the railroad tracks. "It's policy to have a female officer present in a closed room," she tells the three men who aren't even bothering to interrogate me. She points to the video cameras in every corner of the room. "I'd leave her out here in my office unless you want to deal with a lawsuit. You've got her cuffed. She's not going anywhere."

At four-thirty in the morning, there's something of a scuffle in the outside waiting area. It sounds like a chair hitting the wall "—because I'm going to rip the damn wall down if you don't release her, that's why!" It's Pop Pop's bark followed by Beck yelling along like a pup following the alpha male's howl. Ten minutes pass with voices yelling back and forth. Carla steps from the room, seems to stifle the yells. I don't hear anything for twenty minutes.

Then there is silence. Carla steps back into the office. She stands over me. "I have contacted Lance Washington. The security patrol are not commissioned officers. They have no right to detain you. Sit tight." She walks out into the hallway and I hear her talking to someone. Five minutes later, one of the armed guards comes into the office, uncuffs me, and tells me I'm free to go now. They will contact me. I don't ask for a ride. I just walk out into the gray edges of dawn. I've got bruises on my wrists and dried blood beneath my nose.

About a half mile down the road, Pop Pop's truck comes up behind me. Beck is in the passenger seat and gets out to let me sit between the two.

"Christ almighty," Beck is shaking, and he's beat to heck too.

"Carla called me. She said I'd see you walking down the road with pink pajamas with little puppy-dogs on them," Pop Pop tells me. He looks tired. "You okay, baby?"

"I'm not hurt. But, no." I push into him and Beck comes in on the other side, closes the door. Pop Pop drives off while I let the tears flow, little huffing sobs while Pop Pop takes me home. I feel Beck's hand come out, soft and gentle and lay on my own. "I've never been arrested before," I mumble.

"You weren't. They weren't even real cops," Pop Pop says. "Sweetie, I'm worried about you. I think we need—"

"I wouldn't worry so much about me. I'd worry about John Matthews," I say hoarsely. "Because he just screwed with the wrong girl."

Chapter 72

It's like the calm before the storm. Nothing happens for three days. Nothing. It's almost like Max and his dad are playing a game of cat and mouse. They drive their trucks through our little subdivision, slow at my house. Two days ago, they were taking a rented vanload of people up and down the streets. Pop Pop said they are probably investors. Yesterday, they had a crew of surveyors running through the entire neighborhood until Jimmy Young and Red McCoy ran them out.

Lance calls and tells me he has given the information to some federal agency. Maybe he's lying. Maybe he really is on John Matthews's side. I wait. I work on the tournament. I practice ball with Pop Pop's team. We're transitioning from the Easter bucket full of a hodgepodge of well-worn softballs and raggedy baseballs to real 16-inch big balls. The gloves are gone; bare hands are used. I lug around one of Pop Pop's hunting shotguns in my truck, a pistol in my glovebox, and a can of bear deterrent in my purse that might have expired last April.

Then Doctor Williams calls and tells me that his colleague returned his call. The Hydrargyrum that Doc Brown prescribed to his patients for tuberculosis is a form of mercury, and mercury is poisonous. Large doses can cause kidney failure. Coca pun was a name for cocaine. It was illegal after 1914 for the common person to buy and use it as a medicine. Alone, either could kill. Together and used for a treatment or to avoid getting sick, at the dosage given, it was lethal.

"You have got to relax." Beck is watching me tap-tap-tap my finger on the table in front of the computer when I hang up the phone. He's sitting across from me at the table reading something. It is only a week until the tournament. I haven't stopped. I have three unopened letters from Max, the attorney. I know they are demanding I stop Pop Pop's ball games.

"I know. I can't." I never realized how deep the friendship between Max and I was when we were younger. I can't shake it. I want to cling to the good memories and not the man who jammed his truck door on me and watched his daddy beat me up. "I'm trying." I know Beck must think I'm sappy. I change the subject— "Me and Doctor Williams have come to the assumption Doc Bobby Brown was using some of the people in town as Guinea pigs." He swipes at a smile on his face.

"What?"

"You sound smart."

"I *am* smart. I just can't let it come out in large increments, or I might scare dumb jocks like you away with my smartness." He knows I'm teasing. Still, I rub my face. "What's going to happen, Beck? You think John Matthews will send down his guards to arrest me when the vendors start coming in next Friday?"

"I don't know."

Willy laughs at something on the TV in the other room. She escaped Pop Pop's house for a while. I found her settled in her usual spot on the porch. Both Beck and I look toward the couch where she's cozied up with a blanket. Willy has a bag of potato chips in her hand and a soda in the other. She's wearing some of my hand-me-down jeans and t-shirts. But she doesn't have any new bruises on her face.

Two days ago, on impulse, I drove to a local attorney's office and told him about Willy. Yesterday, Pop Pop and I drove Willy to the minimum security correctional facility to see if Lester Dunn would sign papers for me to watch over her until he gets out in six months. Pop Pop talked to him a long, long time. When he came out, he said Lester would sign the papers. The lawyer was able to get me Standby Guardianship until her daddy is out of jail. Consequently, she's got the extra bedrooms at both Pop Pop's and my house and she goes back and forth depending on her mood.

"Have you ever heard her laugh?" Beck leans in.

"No, I don't think so."

"She must feel safe."

"I can't imagine why with all this crap going on. I feel like I'm just towing her into my problems."

"She's safer here than with her dad's girlfriend and Trevor's mom wanting to burn the house down."

"Maybe. Maybe not. Beck, I lost my job."

"Is that why you've been so antsy?"

"I suppose. Don't ask why. I just did."

"Okay."

"Will this ever end?"

Beck puffs out air from his lips, then pats his hands on the table. "Alright. You need a break." Beck stands up, towers over me. I feel like a little squirrel who ran under a grizzly bear. "How about we go for a ride up the mountain, look for that door that's supposed to lead to the room of the old TB infirmary."

"I've got Nana Nisee today, Beck. It's Saturday."

"She likes doing that, right?"

Nana Nisee wants to see Ned. Thus, Beck, Willy and I drive to Guysville to pick him up. Nana Nisee is beaming. She looks twenty years younger when he's around. I see them holding hands in the back seat, and I can see Willy peering at them curiously when they giggle like schoolkids at each other's old jokes the rest of us don't understand.

I have to take an old railroad bed from the opposite side of the mountain because the creeks are still high. The route takes an extra forty-five minutes. Then, I bounce along the edge of a cliff on an old logging road and I have to stop once so Beck can throw up the grilled cheese and tomato soup we had for lunch, and I can pat his back, gag, and tell him *everything's gonna be alright, big guy.*

It places us at an awkward angle on the mountain, but fifty feet from the tunnel. There's a jumble of huge stones that form a stream from somewhere above the very top of the mountain. It leaves a waterfall running hard and steady that we must traverse. Not so bad for Willy, Beck, and me. Ned and Nana Nisee opt to stay in the jeep.

We hike along the path in front of the crevice that was once the beginning of the tunnel. Even though we know we're looking for something, none of us can find a door. That is until Beck wrenches away three hefty boulders. When the mossy mud and dirt fall away with the stones, it exposes rusted metal roofing beneath an inch or two of dirt and old leafy debris and a crooked sign which reads: WARNING. QUARANTINED/CONTAGION AREA. CLOSED FOR ENTRY.

We peel away trees limbs and the rusted roofing. Beneath, there is a large wooden door made of thick barn wood. With a hand on a rickety wrought iron handle, Beck wiggles and heaves until it opens. It's like a giant sucks in a great breath of air when the door succumbs to his strength. It is dark and nothing more than a black hole with a rock wall while we don our cell phone flashlights and let them dance along the walls.

"There are still beds in here," Willy exclaims. There are eight cots, each with a bedside table. All of them are broken, decayed, and lying haphazardly on the stone floor. Rotted blankets rest on the floor. At the far wall is a wooden desk settled slightly to the left because two of its legs are broken. The drawers are open and falling out. A shattered chair rests sideways in front of it.

It smells of darkness and old things. It is nothing more than a chiseled-out cave not bigger than my kitchen. At least, that is what I thought until Beck grunts several coarse curse words that fall in the air like thick chunks of mud plopped to the floor. It is unsettling at best. He does not curse in front of Willy Dunn or any kids that I'm aware. Such, the goose pimples rise on my arms and I automatically take three stomping steps to come up beside him and latch on to his bare arm. He has surpassed the little room. I only saw his back until I follow his light toward a small room just beyond.

My stomach drops, and I make a quick flap of my hand to Willy who has come up behind me. "Stop," I grunt at her, my voice firm. She does as I say. I'm glad for it. Because before Beck, there are two sets of clothing and two mummified bodies, decayed heads with brown-red hair. They are settled against one wall, side by side. One is wearing a rotted suit. The other is barely clad in tattered rags that must have, at one time, been a rayon crepe dress, a navy-blue afternoon dress worn to town by someone of better means. A wide-brimmed straw hat lay at the waist, and the hands are still donned in gloves. What they both have in common is a small bottle resting on the right leg.

"Clyde Hatfield and Mimi Edwards." I know exactly to whom the bodies belong. I don't need to guess. I sweep forward, lean down in front of them. I take them in with my eyes like I eat up an animated creature in a horror movie for the first time. The faces are dried parched brown paper. It clings to bone in the same way a hornet's nest flakes its outer layer. The eyeballs are gone leaving only a dark, roundish crater where the socket once rested. I can see several missing teeth in Clyde's mouth. Mimi's mouth is pulled back in an eternal grin of perfect teeth. There is a pistol cupped beneath Clyde's dead hands and his lap.

"What's that?" Beck whispers suddenly over my shoulder. So, mesmerized by the bodies, I had not really focused on the sound of his shoes scooting across the gritty gravel of the floor. I jump, startled and glare at him. Then I lean closer. Balanced on each lap is a tiny, deep green bottle. I pick one up, hold it to my phone to make out the words imprinted on the glass. "Ant poison," I read.

"I—" Whatever Beck was going to say is cut off by a healthy and deep-throated BOOM! A blast of air gusts its way through the stones in the back wall, puffs and gasps creeping through every crack and crevice in the boulders smelling of damp stone and old, dead things. "Oh, my God!" That's what he huffs next, and I feel his hand latch around my waist, and he swings me around. "Explosives. Someone's blasting—" I faintly catch Willy standing there with a shocked look on her face and her arms out to her sides, a bird ready to take flight.

"Go!" I scream at her, trying to catch my footing, but only feeling my tippy toes catching the ground because Beck is falling forward with a second blast.

I can hear the cave grumbling behind us, the grunt of old stones rubbing together while we rush pell-mell toward the light of door. Then, it is as if the light goes out. The door slams shut just as Willy's wildly waving hands are about to break the surface to light. I yelp. I suppose it is the same reaction I would expect if I thought she was getting ready to have her finger smashed in a door. She wails out a banshee cry, a high-pitched scream that echoes off the black walls around us just as her elbows crash into the door and her fists bang, bang, bang. Beck shoves past me, leaving me taking two steps to the left and pawing in the last shreds of light to hook my arm around Willy. "Stop, it's okay!" I'm whisper-grunting. "Stop, stop—" Beck wheels around her just as the pitch black consumes us, and in that blackness, he hits the door with his shoulder and bursts through. It opens large enough that I can hear a grunt on the opposite side.

"Back up!" Shit, it is Max's voice demanding Beck's steps to retreat. Beck is keeling forward, hardly able to get his balance already when the sound of the gunshot goes off. It is thunderous, a piercing boom that leaves my ears numb and ringing. My hands automatically slap to my ears. My body bows forward. That's when I see Beck slip to one side, his hand reaching out pawing at the air. *Oh-my-God.* I can't move. I just stand there with my mouth dropped open while Willy starts backing away from my grasp. She makes this throaty grunt and I know why she's balking. Max has placed himself in the doorway a hands-width away from Beck who is sitting on his rear and grasping, groping, fumbling to get a grip on Max's legs. "I didn't shoot him! He did it! I didn't—!" Max is screaming. There is blood just pouring down through Beck's hair, a torrent of red making rivulets around his eye and along the bridge of his nose before dribbling from his chin. I'm shocked. I see the gun rise, and it is pointed at him.

"Why'd you do that!" Max is doing this funky step up and down and now he's yelling at Beck. He doesn't look like him. He's pale and grabbing his hair with one hand, dancing from one foot to the other. "Why'd you do that, man? What the hell!" I know what he did. I know Beck must have seen Max with that gun, jumped right in front of him to stop him from firing blindly at me and Willy.

"Don't, dude. Hey, Max, easy does it. Just—just—if you're going to hurt somebody, let it be me. Let them go—It's fine. Nobody's mad—" Beck's voice is soft and deep. He's blinking hard around the blood on his face. I don't even know if he can see me through the blood.

"Max, no—no—no—" my own voice sounds like a whistle. I am walking little, teeny steps to Max with my arms waggling in front of me like one of those windup toys marching-marching-marching until they fall off the table. "Put it down. Don't—" But he's not putting it down. I'm trying to make it to Beck. All I can think of is to stop the blood. Stop the blood. He's going to die. Because Beck is pale, and he's got this funny roll of his eyes. I hold one hand up in a vain attempt to fend off Max and push one hand on Beck. "Look at me, Beck. You're alright, okay?" Then the rumble of the earth behind me makes me flinch, open my eyes wide. "Max, I've got to move him! The rocks are going to fall! Please, Max, put it down. I won't do the ball tournament. I'll do whatever you want. Anything."

"Well, it's too late for that, isn't it?" He's balancing the gun in his hands. It's flopping right and left.

"Baby, just get ready to—" I look at Beck. It's like time is standing still.

"No, I won't leave you." I shake my head. Max hears, brings up the gun like a sword and ready to strike. Beck shoves himself upward. "Babe, Run!"

Chapter 73

I can see Willy running, bouncing each step ahead of me. Her hoodie has fallen, and her dark hair is bobbing up and down. She doesn't turn around. It's funny. I remember hitting the baseball the other day. When I ran to first base, I turned to see where the ball was heading. Pop Pop yelled at me and told me not to look back. Don't ever look back. It slows you down. Just set your sights toward the base you're running. I set my sights on Willy's back. Willy's got hers on the bridge. I don't think we'll make it. Whatever struggle Beck had with Max was temporary. Max is alone, he's twice our size, and he's almost caught up with me.

I'm out of breath when I get to the bridge. It is the only time Willy stops. "Go. Go." I hand her my cell phone, slip it in her hand. "Call 9-1-1. You're going to have to go across, then go up a bit higher to get service. But whatever you do, don't look back. Just keep running."

Then, I give her a little shove with my hand. "What about—"

"Go!" I scream it. "If he's chasing us, he isn't hurting Beck." Then I stand there, listening to Max's footsteps slapping on the mud. He's slipping and sliding a bit sideways. He's close enough to shoot me. Max has fired the gun blindly in our direction twice already and missed. Each time, I flinched and waited for either Willy or me to fall. We didn't. Surely, he can't have many more bullets. I take five steps out on the swinging bridge, slowly and carefully. I can't go farther for fear I'll tip the bridge and knock Willy into the chasm below. My hands are on the little ropes. Willy is walking. She must almost tip-toe, so she doesn't waggle the bridge right or left. Too much weight either direction and there's nothing but big boulders and a raging creek below us. One wrong move and the whole bridge tips and pours whoever is on it into the water.

I suppose I'm breathing hard. I just assume little me is

going to stop Max Matthews-Branntwein. He's not even concerned with me. He needs to stop Willy. I realize it just as she crosses the threshold on the other side and I back up and back up and back up until I am in the middle. Max takes two steps on to the bridge. He looks down, then he scans the bridge. "Come back and I won't shoot her."

I don't say anything, just take three more steps and feel the bounce from Willy's bouncing treads stop. She is on the other side. Max's feet step on the bridge. He uses one hand to hold the rusted metal fiber rope and takes a stride down until he's five rungs of wood in. He balances, raises his gun, and takes aim. "I'm telling her one last time, Harley—"

Steps. I remember Mila's story. She drew the line with Bad Bill that horrible day during the Civil War. And so, over a hundred and fifty years later, I am going to do the same. "Okay, Max. I'm gonna draw a line. If you're going to shoot Willy, you're going to have to shoot through me," I interrupt softly, drawing from the essence of Mila's journal to give Willy time to run. "If you stay on the other side of the line, I'm alright with it. If you cross it, we're gonna have words." He just laughs and I can't help but remember Bad Bill did the same to Mila when she was Hans and Bad Bill was going to kill Irish and his men. "If that's what you want—trouble," I go on, "then you got trouble."

Max snorts a laugh, lifts his foot. "What's that mean? Are you threatening me? I've got the gun. Hell, I'll shoot right through you." And so he crosses the line just like Bad Bill did to Mila that day she killed those Rebel soldiers. And so, trouble, he will get.

"If you ever listened to any of the stuff I tried to tell you about Hans Branntwein, you'd know." I grit my teeth. "But you didn't, so—" He's got no hold on the bridge. I do. I turn and face the ongoing water, grasp the rope in both hands in two tight fists. Then, I take every ounce of my weight, and I do a somersault over the edge. It's all it takes to flip the bridge. And it is so fast, Max can't do anything more than let the gun flip out of his hands before the bridge does a somersault too, flipping over as his weight careens to the end where I jumped.

The rope burns my hands as I bounce there, my armpits feel as if they are ripping in half before Max's weight catches on the rope and he topples right over and down to the boulders below. Smack! I hear the crash of his body against the boulders. It is a sickening thud while I dangle there helplessly trying to figure out what the hell I'm going to do now. I think he fell thirty-feet. He's screaming, and his voice blends with the splash of water. I drop my chin, look down. "Aw, crud." He's rolling there, screaming while his fingers reach for the damn gun that landed only inches from his own landing point.

And there I dangle, unable to move right or left. I'm just an easy target when he lifts the gun and crawls to a sitting position. I close my eyes, try to decide if I want to chance dropping into the creek. He's not that far below me. He's close enough if he has enough shots in that gun, Max is going to hit me. I don't think the water's that deep. But I couldn't get much easier as a target than this. How does this guy go from my best friend to worst enemy?

He's got blood on his teeth when I open my eyes. I know because he's smiling at me hard. It's not a nice smile, though. It's an I'm-gonna-kill-you-leer. I think there's no way in hell I'm going to mewl out, begging for him to drop the gun.

"I hate you, bitch—" he grunts.

"No, *bitch*," the voice calls out from above. "If you don't drop that gun, *you're* going to die." I snap my head to the front of the bridge.

"Grandma?" I say. I sound three years old. I suppose I'm allowed a certain amount of whining considering I really am about to die—either by falling or by gunshot. But yes, that's Nana Nisee pumping up my shotgun that was in my jeep and she's aiming it at Max.

"Yeah, Jenny, you just hold on tight there. Ned's coming. He's got to finish hog-tying the mayor."

I nod to her. "Beck's hurt, Grandma." I'm afraid not to

look at her because my shoulders are getting numb.

"Ned will get him fixed up, baby." She doesn't take her eyes from Max. "You want to put that gun down or do you just want me to pump you up a little first," Nana Nisee asks him. "One inch, boy, and you're gonna find out how mad her grammy can get when little boys don't play nice with my little girl, now. And I don't give spankings. I *whoop ass*. Because I used to run moonshine when I was eleven for my uncle. Might be more than a few like you buried up here, *if you know what I mean.*"

I'm dizzy. I think of Hans—well, Mila when she saw the train coming toward her that day. She didn't shirk. She just did what she had to do to save Hayward. But I don't have anyone to save. And my little fists are way past that tingling-asleep feeling I've been holding on so tightly. *Ting.* What was that? *Ting. Wish-swish.* Oh. It's the bridge railing ripping away from the rock wall holding it. Grunt-bang. And that's me and the bridge falling—falling—falling—

Chapter 74

I think I'm going to die. It isn't because I hit the ground hard. Instead, I dangled at the end of the bridge like a tiny catfish suspended above the water on a hook until the Baker EMS could rappel down to untangle me from the ropes on the walkway of the bridge. I watch the life flight helicopter take Beck to his destination at the hospital. I am helpless sitting on the mossy rock with water gushing around me. "I'll never fish again," I yell that up to Pop Pop where he is perched precariously close to the edge (two times, the police almost arrested him) and describing with great detail exactly how I should be rescued to the very capable rescue team.

However, I get a great view of Max Matthews-Branntwein getting arrested while they lay him on the stretcher. Willy sits on the edge next to Pop Pop and won't leave me until she had Zach drive around and pick her up. "I want to get an earring on my lip like you," she yells down.

"Your dad would kill me. Why are you asking me that now?"

"I don't know." She shrugs.

Now it is eight o'clock at night and I'm slinking down the hospital hallway to sneak into Beck's room. I guess it isn't sneaking. Nobody seems to care I'm here. T.J. and a bunch of the guys from the Brandy Mountain team have been going in and out of the room like it's a hotel lobby in New Orleans during Mardi Gras. Then again, I suppose maybe Zach might care. It's his laughter I can hear sweeping up the room and out into the hallway. He didn't bother to come see me.

I just checked out of the emergency room myself. I don't have to stay the night. However, they needed to monitor me for a few hours. Beck's got an IV in his arm, and Pop Pop said Max hit him so hard with the butt of his gun, he got eleven stitches in the top of his head. The hospital is keeping him for the night, his sister said, to make sure he didn't get a concussion. He got shot just once. The bullet grazed his right hip. More stitches. No surgery.

"Hey." I hang in the doorway. His TV is on quietly and he's lying in bed in a white hospital gown with blue trefoils on it. Zach is sitting in a gaudy orange, faux-leather chair. He looks up at me in the same way my Aunt Joy's bored cat little more than notices me with a yawn and a stretch from the top of her brown rug cat tree when I walk into her house.

"Hey, how'd you like the dance?" I ask Beck.

"You're kidding me, right?"

"I thought you'd say that." I feel my heart drop.

"What do you expect, Flea?" Zach shakes his head and reaches over to the TV remote device hooked to the bed to turn up the sound of the TV. "He had no clue what he was getting into when dad asked him to babysit you. I don't know what dad was thinking."

"You never complained hanging with me."

"Yeah, I did all the time. You were always daring me to jump ramps that were too big. You talked me into driving alone on my learner's permit. You gave me a cigarette when I was fourteen. I broke my arm hanging with you three times. I got grounded for a week with the permit thing. And those were the simple things." Zach reaches out, gives me a push with his knuckle. "Go home. He's trying to sleep or something."

I pretend I don't hear him, stare at Beck who is eyeing me noncommittedly "Well, I just wanted to let you know that Ned was the one who stopped John Matthews from putting another round of dynamite down a sinkhole at the top of the Lost Tunnel. That's why the tunnel was collapsing. He figured sooner or later, we were going in there."

"I heard."

"Did you hear they arrested him and Max?"

"Yes." Zach answers for him. "Yes, he heard everything. And we all want to thank you after our hard work for ruining the tournament."

I don't even know what to say to that. I ignore my uncle. "I called Doctor Williams. He agrees with me that the ant poison was probably put in Clyde and Mimi's hands as a decoy. They were probably trying out the TB antidote hoping it would save people in town and it ended up killing them because of the mercury and cocaine mix. Doc Brown knew if anybody found out, he would be in jail for impersonating a doctor without a license or degree and probably, murder. Just in case somebody decided to go into the tunnel, he was trying to make it look like a suicide pact between two lovers who couldn't be together. The coroner asked me questions. He's going to test for mercury in their bodies." Beck's just staring at the TV, doesn't turn around. "Well, thanks for jumping in front of the gun for me."

"Somebody had to do it," Zach answers for me. "Harley, go home. He's drugged up. Let him enjoy it."

I linger there, wait for Beck to say something more like: *Babe, that was the most exciting day of my life! I got shot at, solved an old crime, and we might have saved our town from being stolen out from beneath us*—but he doesn't. Such, I don't say: *Oh, by the way, before they gave me pain pills for my shoulder that I fell on, but didn't break, they did a urine test to make sure I wasn't pregnant and could take the pills. And guess what? Not only can't I take the damn pills, I'm turning out to be just like my mama. All I need is a different, bad boyfriend to beat the crap out of me every other week, a drawer full of weed, and you to hand me a few hundred bucks, so I get an abortion. And yeah, I know it's yours. I did the math.* But I don't say anything. Instead, I just say: "Goodnight, Beck. See you around."

Chapter 75

They pulled my car from Summersville Lake two days after John Matthews's arrest. Lance Washington came right to my door and told me. It is five in the morning, and I'm dressed, ready to make sure everything's in order for the tournament.

"And Trevor—?" I ask him.

Lance gives me a long look. "You want to sit down for this, Harley?"

"No."

"Trevor Woods was feeding an addiction to cocaine."

"Cocaine," I repeat softly. "I didn't know. Since when?"

"I don't know. I know from other police sources that he was on the radar for purchasing drugs in Baker for the past two years. He had been bailed out with the help of the Matthews family a couple times and went to rehab twice. They helped pay for an attorney. Such, John and Max knew about his addiction and used it to their advantage. They paid him to run the donations coming into the museum to different dealers for just enough cash he could buy the coke. The only problem they didn't think ahead of time was that Trevor Woods was skimming money off the top and only paying them a certain amount he would receive from the people selling the items for them. They found out and confronted him the night he was at Damon's Bar."

"That's what I saw on the tapes," I add. Lance nods.

"Yes. John Matthews slammed him hard enough against the truck to knock Trevor out. Trevor must have suffocated on his own vomit after they tossed him in the back of his truck. He was dead by the time they got to the house. They returned and got your car, placed him in the trunk, and dumped it in the lake."

"What does this have to do with Orv being killed?"

"He just came into Max's radar, I suppose. About two

weeks after Trevor was murdered, Pam Woods started pressuring Max for an explanation as to why he let her son leave the party that night, why he didn't drive him home. Max lied to her and told her Trevor was still alive and well and was going to be pinned for the thefts at the museum because he was the one who broke into the building. In effect, he made it appear that he was covering for him. Max convinces Pam somehow to make it look like Trevor committed suicide so he wouldn't go to jail, and he would just disappear for a while until they could make it look like someone else had robbed the museum."

"Ah," I say. "I was going to be the one they blamed."

"It appears so. John Matthews was going to pretend like he was giving Trevor money to hide out somewhere. They would blame the thefts on you. Then he told Pam that Trevor would reappear and just say he decided to take a break from life for a while."

"But they needed a body," I sigh. "They murdered Orv and set him on the tracks to look like Trevor. Then, I suppose, they told Pam when Trevor appeared again, Orv would have been properly identified. Since he was homeless, they could easily explain his death as a suicide or just walking the tracks drunk or something."

"Yes. We've arrested Pamela and Amos Woods and Terry Gillis for complicity to his murder." My heart aches. Orv. My friend. I shared a drink with him in the parking lot of the Bakers Quickie Stop and Gas. "Max Matthews-Branntwein enticed him into his truck. The four used his body as a cover for Trevor Woods, so it looked like a suicide. They just didn't bother to change his clothing which you identified. Then John Matthews found out you questioned the fact there was no autopsy."

"That's why they took Trevor's watch down to the tracks—so everybody would think they found evidence." I shake my head. "And Pam never questioned the reason her son didn't call or contact her?"

"Nope. I think she wanted her son to be alive so badly,

she convinced herself it was true. And the Matthews, I think, were probably going to find another body to use as Trevor when Pam started questioning the reason he didn't return. They made a full confession." Lance answers.

"Now what happens to everybody?"

"John Matthews is in jail. He's not getting out for a long time. Same with his son. Trevor Woods's mother and father and Lester Dunn's girlfriend will all get time in jail."

"And Grant?"

"He's been stealing from the folks of Lost Hollow and Brandy Mountain for a long, long time. I'm assuming his job position is open. It has been brought up by several people our task force has interviewed. I'm just going to tell you that folks are talking that maybe you ought to be taking the mayor's position and not necessarily working at the historical society."

I suppose I should feel like crying. And so, my emotional level being in pregnant mode, I do. I guess I have been preparing myself for this since the day Grant Lebowski confronted me on the steps. I never expected it to end like this.

"What about Orv? Will they leave him there where they buried him?"

"They are exhuming the body. After that—"

"I'll take up a collection and have him buried with us here," I say. "Will you let the undertaker or the coroner or whoever does the exhumation know?"

"I will. I'll throw in some money too."

"If you vote for me, I will hire you as law enforcement," I tease him and pretend to knight him with my arm. He laughs.

"I would. From what I heard, you solved two crimes and you got rid of Matthews. If I had a clue what he was up to, I would have run the other direction the day he hired me."

"Still—" I chuckle. "I never found the stupid treasure that everybody's been searching for."

Chapter 76

Pop Pop was seventeen when he started working at the mines. He was lean and mean, and probably could have played baseball for the Brandy Mountain company team. However, during the 1970s, the heyday of mining on our mountain was almost gone. Men were replaced by machines. With few bodies to play, the Brandy Mountain Spartans had faded away, and instead of men playing ball in the fields, the bodies were replaced by a meager number of little league teams. Even the big ball team had faded away with the good times when coal money was good. It was enough just to survive in a recession that nearly wiped out those of us who were already barely keeping their heads above water. It was just what the old men talked about while they sat on their porches and reminisced about the good ol' days of mine camps and baseball and being young again.

Pop Pop just worked the mines. He came home to his wife and kids, ate supper, watched the ball games on TV, then went to bed a few beers in. Then he got up again. I suppose something was missing. My grandma didn't see it. Nor did any of his kids—or the grandkid he raised. But while he rises to the occasion today his arm reaching high as a shortstop, I see whatever it was that got lost to his generation even when the sixteen-inch, leather cover, Kapok core big ball skims off the tip of his bare fingers and continues toward the outfield. It is what sitting in front of a TV, *watching* a Sunday game, and dreaming he was a part of it all could simply not replace. It was being a part of that dance, the show that was missing, misplaced or as Nana Nisee's crossword puzzles might state was *mislaid* for a time. It's spirit. Pop Pop's spirit. And the only way to get it back was to play the game. Even if he missed. Even if he failed. Because, at the end of the day, he still held the ball in his hand and became a part of a team. Win. Lose. It didn't matter. He danced. He lived the dream.

It didn't start out like that, our day. It took twelve hours for him to get there—

"Are you going to pitch our games or not?" Pop Pop asked me this morning while I was motioning Dave's Friendly Outhouses into the back section of the church parking lot. "Because I'm not going to do it. Them boys won't let me."

Willy is my shadow now, six inches from me at all times. Well, until Pop Pop comes around, then she's like a pup who knows who has all the bones to chew on. Because she interrupts us: "Can I go with Pop Pop for a while? This is boring." Pop Pop gets this big grin on his face because I know he misses having me and Zach under his feet all the time. He bobs his head. "You can be in charge of passing out the bottled water while we play," he tells her. The lot is full already and people are pouring into the registration desk. It's busy, and I can hardly hear Pop Pop over the crowd. "Are you going to pitch?"

"What about Jay?" I ask him. "I mean, I've been practicing mostly with a smaller softball." I don't know if he really wants me to play. He's going straight 16-inch big ball for the tournament after he found boxes of them at an online auction.

"You know it ain't no different," he grunts. "Jay hits the batter more than he gets the ball over the plate. And you can't catch a ball in the outfield worth crap with those teeny hands of yours." He tips his head a little and gets a teeny smile on his face. I don't know this smile. It is new to me. "Sweetie, you got to make your grandpa look good today. Can you do that on the field?"

"I ain't no sissy, Pop Pop. I just—?"

"Carla's coming to watch the game. I called her to thank her for keeping you safe and sometime during our talk, she throws out a little bet. If we win, she'll go out on a date with me. I really want that date."

"She's ten years younger than you. Can you handle that, *old man*?"

"Can you handle pitching, *little lady*? Can you handle a game of *real* ball without a glove?"

I'm like jumping up and down inside, my tummy's all aflutter. But I act really cool because I might start salivating like T.J.'s stupid basset hound he takes hunting for raccoons. "I suppose if I have to do it."

"If I have to," Pop Pop repeats in a sarcastic mutter. He knows better. "Well, that and your uncle told me I needed to ask you."

"What?" I stop wagging my hand for Dave to back up his outhouse truck and he jams on his breaks, nearly hits a truck. "Uncle— Zach?"

"He said to tell me he'd talk me into letting you pitch if you get your butt up there and run their show too. They got nobody to run it. It's a fiasco, Flea. He's not kidding. I know you probably want it to fail, but there's a lot of folks in this town who are stuck with the bills if it goes under. Matthews invested every last cent into that field, and he's in jail and can't run it. I think if you play your cards right and show them how good you are at taking something that's in shambles and figuring out how to make it work, they just might have a job up at The Brandy for you fixing up the mess Matthews and Lebowski made. I'd jump on that considering you ain't got a job right now."

"Aw, who told you I got fired?"

"A little bird."

"A little bird? What's that mean?"

"It's from the Bible. Ecclesiastes. It just means I'm not giving away the informant that gave me the information."

I don't get what he's saying. I wave it away. "If I'm running both, I won't be able to play ball, Pop Pop," I say. Does he know this, and he set me up so I wouldn't pitch? "I'm cutting it close anyway."

"Well, you do have a backup." He waves a hand behind me. He's not smiling or unsmiling, just trying to read my face. I lean a little, follow his pointing finger to the small crowd surrounding a couple cars. One of them waves a little timidly. "My little bird—birds."

"Taylor?" I whisper more to myself. It is Central Independent Realty's entire office—Lissette, Theo, Lexie, Taylor and a few others like Tatum and Paula.

"She said they are here to volunteer. Put them to work while you're playing—" he leans in. "The big girl says she plays catcher. That was Beck's position. He said he would, but he can't wear the headgear with his stitches."

"Alright," I turn back to Pop Pop. "You tell Zach that if I run the event today along with mine, I get to pitch your team and he's playing on it too—Beck can coach while you're playing. If he wants to play, we'll pad him up with t-shirts under his hat to protect his head. I also need Grant Myers, Bobby Kendall, and Allen McCoy to come down and play our last game with us."

"You can't do that. They aren't on our team list."

"Yes, they are. I added them just in case they changed their mind. I just didn't tell you because you're still kind of spicy over Zach not playing for you. But he did need a job, Pop Pop." I walk up to tell Dave to put the outhouses where he parked, and Pop Pop follows. "Why do I have to be the adult about this?"

Pop Pop gives me a teasing scowl. "Are you out of your comfort zone?"

"Okay, well, you think it out. Our last game is against the New River Falcons. If you look closely to the team list as I did this morning when they signed in, you will see that they have culled out some of the alumni players from three different teams including the Brandy Mountain Falcons— Niles Gates and the old coach that never let me on his team, Jim Simmons, are playing instead of coaching. They think it is a shoe-in winning because they've added a few choice players like they used to do in high school. I don't. Grudge or not, if we don't have them, the score will probably play out like a herd of elephants chasing a pack of hyenas. They are going to squash us. If you decide you wish to negotiate a deal for us, take my list of terms. If not, we'll just let it ride—oh, wait." I let my eyes veer to his. "And I get Beck for twenty minutes." Pop Pop almost pops a grin. "I want to talk to him. He's ignoring me, Pop Pop. The last three guys I've dated have been crappy like that. I thought he was different." I say that and drop my little workbook to my waist. Pop Pop's grin and smiling eyes turn to a reflective furrow of his brow. "I know you saw him holding my hand."

"He was in the hospital. He just got out. You've been working three days straight without stop. Maybe give him a little time to figure things out."

"I really like—" I let my head roll back. "I love him."

My grandpa makes this funny grunt like he doesn't want to discuss this sappy stuff. Still, he says: "Did you tell him—that?"

"Well, not in a couple days."

Pop Pop throws up his arms. "What time do they need to be here?"

"Four. Thank you."

"And what if they don't agree?" Pop Pop stops, puts his hands behind his back, and asks me. "Baby girl, what are you going to do if those young men can't or won't do it. I think it about killed him to ask you to help."

"You know I'll do it. Just be a good arbitrator. Don't tell him that at first."

"So, um, I don't think it would be conducive to the office environment if you came back," Lissette stands a little awkwardly in front of me twenty minutes later while I set her up handling registrations on Brandy Mountain. Pop Pop left with Willy on his heels like a happy pup getting ready for a long walk. "But I can give you a good recommendation for a job in the southern region—"

"Listen, I'm just not cut out for selling houses." Or being dumb-caught in the middle of a love triangle that could last a lifetime. I can't believe I'm saying that considering I'm jobless and broke.

"Let me finish," Lissette holds her hand out. "Or you can research some of the homes as a contractor for us with our historical homes section. You are good at that."

"You have a section for historical homes?"

"They are hot sellers, as you probably know. Since you've been giving Taylor information, our sales have gone up. Aw, I'll be honest, they've gone up tremendously. So, I am adding that section. It isn't going to be large at first. And you would work directly with me, if you know what I mean? Then—then maybe Taylor won't use her prowess to pit us against each other." She gives me a knowing smile. "I really don't have anything against you, Harley. Theo is right. I'm a hardass. I do what it takes to get things done, and I say how I feel. But you're kind of a hardass, too. We butt heads. I don't want my business to fail. If that would work for you, you could work from a home office."

"Okay," I say. I almost sigh in relief. "Okay."

So back to Pop Pop and his hand in the air—We played two games, then had a break. It's not like I got a break. I'm running back and forth from the top of the mountain to the bottom trying to run both the tournaments. We're even with the other teams. Our games are close. One loss, two wins. Pop Pop keeps making a whistle, mimicking my pitches after I strike someone out. It is the grandest compliment I can get from him. Such, each time, I beam.

But it is the last game we're playing that is going to make a difference. I mean, it isn't whether we win or lose. Pop Pop about shit a brick when I pitched the first game. That was worth the work. He got up and did this little dance on third base. It almost started a fight with the other team. It all comes down to Zach and Beck and whether they will really show up with the others from their team and play the *authentic big ball* with us. No gloves. Bare hands. Lots of heart, comradery, and teamwork. And a big ball with a soft core. It isn't even me. I think it is for The Brandy and The

461

Bottoms. We don't necessarily need a win. We need a team that's right down the middle, one big handshake that'll make us one again.

They don't show at three-forty-five. By four-thirty-five, the score is 11-0. It's a dismal way to end our day because Jim Simmons keeps taunting Pop Pop and sticking out his chest. *That's my boy!* He keeps yelling that about his son who isn't that much to flaunt over because, once again, he's sandwiched between the good players who make him look— well, good. Niles Gates keeps muttering we just ought to call the game. We're never going to catch up. There are more games I must watch over until seven. My shoulder is sore where I fell with the bridge. I'm bushed. Pop Pop keeps staring at me and his taunts to the other team are getting a little angrier. Roy Adkins tries to punch out the first baseman the third time he got out. Billy Stinger got nervous and couldn't eat and almost passed out before we got him some of his diabetic candy to suck on. We had to bring in Preacher Oakley to cover for Jay Short who is still saucy over Pop Pop letting *that girl* pitch instead of him.

"Hey, you gonna let us play or do we have to ride the bench the entire game?"

I look up and I see a whole gaggle of hard-worn players leaning on the fence. It's Zach's voice who calls out. "Our game went over." He yells out. "You know, because somebody's down here taking a break and pitching and not running the show up there." Beck gives me a little wave of his hand. Crap, I wonder what Pop Pop told him.

Pop Pop calls for a timeout, and I see him talking to the umpire. The coach for the other team comes stomping out, waving his hands in the air like he's trying to land a helicopter. I see there's a question to the reason we've got more troops coming in to play.

We all walk over to the bench to get a drink of water. Just as I'm taking a swig, Beck comes up and leans against one of the two little lean-tos we borrowed from the cemetery that they usually keep to store the mowers and equipment.

He waves his hand, displaying he wants me to follow him. I do, and he stops just outside in a bit of shade from the hot sun. "Zach said I need to talk to you for twenty minutes," he says, tapping his watch with his fingers. "Do I have to time it?"

"No. Why are you avoiding me?"

"I thought that's what you wanted me to do." Crap, I hear the umpire blowing a whistle. "And I haven't. I've been down here watching you play when we get a break. I don't know how much longer I can do this, Harley. It's just not me, hiding how I feel—hiding stuff from Zach. I want to cheer for you, hold your hand. I want to spend the night—"

"Hey, get your butts out here!" It's Zach rounding the corner and looking back and forth between the two of us. I see something in his eyes suddenly, like he realizes something is up. He doesn't look happy. I see a scowl starting on his lips.

"What do you want me to do?" Beck hisses at me. I just stand there trying not to think how bad this is going to go right now. It's the wrong timing. The wrong place. But isn't it always?

"Okay, I'm making the call. Hate me." Beck says that, and he wheels around to face the wall where Zach is standing. And he just walks away.

"Wait—" I tell his back. I see his shoulder get taut. He doesn't turn around. I'm trying to talk low so no one else hears. "Beck, before you make any call, you need to know something." Still, he doesn't turn. "I know you don't want kids. I know that's why you broke it off with Emma. And this is your chance to walk away. Just keep going. I'll say it belongs to someone else—"

"*It*?" Beck turns, tips his head to look down at me.

"I'm pregnant. I—I found out at the hospital," I stutter. "I guess—I guess—I didn't know you could get pregnant right after a period." OH GOD, WHY AM I SAYING THIS TO HIM? "The doctor asked me how I'd gone this long believing that old wives' tale without, you know, getting pregnant—I'm sorry. It's mine and yours. I'm sure. I think he overestimated the number of guys I've—oh, never mind—"

He's just staring at me. One day last winter, I was driving along the highway home from work on the interstate. I'd looked down to change the station on my phone. When I looked up, a big buck deer was staring into my headlights with this wild-stunned look to his eyes. SURPRISE! Beck's got the same expression.

"Where'd you hear that?"

Huh? I don't know what he's talking about. It doesn't matter, he pivots on his feet slowly and continues his way to the dugout. He stops just short of Zach. He leans in and he's like six inches from Zach's face. Zach just stands there while Beck says something low on his breath. I see my uncle's eyes work slowly, carefully past Beck's and take me in. Aw, shit, he's telling him what a screw-up I am and what I did! I want to protest. Instead, I'm just worn out. I watch Beck keep going and I push myself forward, past Zach and—

He stops me with his hand on my elbow. I look up and Zach is just staring down at me. "What did he say to you?" My voice is hoarse.

"He said he loves you." Zach pushes a finger to his neck, wags it back and forth to crack it. I'm waiting for it. I'm waiting for him to explode into a million pieces and stomp off. But he just sighs. "He's nice. And you're—well, you're—you tend to grow on people like thorny wild roses that grow on the fences in the woods behind Dad's house."

"Are you going to tear me off? Pop Pop gets mad at the roses and makes you get the cutters out all the time and shear them to—"

"Huh?"

"I mean, you're implying the fence are the people in my life like Beck. And I'm the rose bush clinging to him like a parasite you cut away."

"Oh, no, where'd you get that?" He looks at me like I'm crazy, holds up his hands questioningly. "I just meant you guys are good together. I was thinking symbiotic. You remember that from high school? It's a mutual relationship. You're different, but you like doing the history stuff." Zach looks behind me. Beck is gone. "Where'd he go? Did he leave?"

"I don't know what that means?" I tell Zach's back, follow him out. "I don't understand you and your friends— you're all weird and stuff—"

We're such a mixture, this new team. I mean you could say we're old guys mixed with young guys. But it isn't that way at all. It's like everybody's got their thing they add to the team. Zach tends to not think things out when he plays outfield. T.J. thinks things out, but he isn't as fast on the ball. Pop Pop's playing second, and he's five inches shorter than Bobby Kendall who tends to focus more on the girls in the lawn chairs than on the ball.

Such, we're pretty good. Especially with Tatum telling me which balls to throw because she knows my strengths and weaknesses and has a good feel of the batters and how they are going to react. It isn't difficult for us to work our way back into the game. By the end of the ninth, we're 17-18, one run up from them. The only thing we need to do is hold them off. I don't honestly think it is going to happen. There's a man on first, a man on second, and the batter is none other than a hot-under-the-collar Jim Simmons.

Beck's the coach while Pop Pop's in the field. He calls a timeout. I hear the groans of the other team. They have it all tied up in a bow. So what? He waves me and Zach and Tatum in. He stops me with his hand.

"I love you." That's what he says just like that. "I'm good with everything. You got it wrong. It was Emma who didn't want the kids. I do. I'm like freaking out—in a good way. We're pregnant, you and me. *Us.* Like when you found a way around the bridge and said it wasn't you or me, but *we.* I knew something good was going to come out of that. We found a way around and it was scary, but I did the jump. I reckon I like the dance. Did I say I love you?"

"You called a timeout to tell her that?" Tatum laughs. She looks over at the impatient umpire tapping his watch.

"Freaking out about what?" Zach rubs the sweat off his face. He only caught the tail end.

"Nothing." I shake my head, lie. I am not announcing this out on the field. "We just need to figure out a schedule so your playtime with my uncle isn't messed up. It'll be alright."

"Oh, that's easy. I get him for Sundays from one in the afternoon to five." Zach pokes me in the arm.

"That's fair. Then I get him Friday nights through Saturday—" I hold up my hand. "And Sunday mornings because that was part of the deal. We all got to go to church."

"No, way. I'm out. I'm not getting up out of bed on the only day I've got to sleep in." Zach shakes his head.

"Can we do this after the game?" Pop Pop runs up and pats Beck with his hand.

"In a minute. We're working something out. You don't have a job, Zach. Don't play that bullshit to me. Matthews's business is wiped out." Pop Pop tugs on my arm, so I walk backward, then turn to follow Zach's back with my eyes while he jogs back out to left field.

"Not so—some of the contractors asked me and a few other men from The Bottoms to finish the contracts for them. So, I'm starting my own business."

"*Men,* that's funny," I laugh. "Okay, I'll do your bookkeeping for you. I get to sit by Beck at church—"

Tatum is still just standing there, looking at Beck with questioning eyes. "You can go back to catching. This is how they roll," Beck informs her. "If you sit back long enough, they'll haggle it out and move on."

"Over you?"

"This time. Harley always gets the better of the barter each time. She goes whining to her grandpa if she doesn't."

"Hey, screw off, Beck," I tell him. "Or I'll just take Sunday mornings and you'll be snuggling up with Zach—" Oops, too loud. Everybody's staring at us. My face turns red.

Beck's face turns red. I lean into Tatum who thinks it is funny. "I'm going to throw a screwball," I tell her.

"No offense, but you're horrible at that one. This guy's going to hit it and send it out to left field."

"We are one up. They have two on base. Now correct me if I'm wrong, but the odds they are going to score is good unless—"

"Someone catches the ball and gets the guy out on first." She looks over my shoulder. I know she sees Pop Pop standing out there on second base. "Harley, he's got to catch it *and* get the guy out on second base."

"He'll catch it." I look at third base. "If not, he's got back up." Simmons is whining. He's yelling at the ump, yelling at us. Oh, how I hate that guy.

"They weren't kidding when they said you were a wild one."

"Don't harass me. I need your chatter to the batter."

"Chatter to the batter. I like that. And hell, yes, that's my job." She shrugs, backs up to the plate and settles herself into a squat. I can see her muttering stuff. I'm not sure what she is saying. Jim Simmons is up to bat and I can see his face getting redder and redder. He's a hothead. I turn, then pitch the ball. One ball. Two balls. The third, it is high, but I know Simmons just wants to get his son home who is on first base. He rears back, then gives the ball a good, hard hit.

It sails over my head, right for second base. But it is just two inches over Pop Pop's reach and he jumps, and it pops over his hand. I see it fly past. I see Zach blink like he's surprised it came his way. Then, my uncle, he tears down the field, reaches up and catches the ball right in his fingers. Smack. It isn't two seconds later as Simmons sits-behind-a-desk-too-much-pudgy son goes running, Zach sends the ball right into Pop Pop's palm. Boom. Boom. We just need two to have three outs. We've won.

"Hey, nice job."

I don't have long to linger. I weave my way to set up for

the final games up on the mountain. A hand on my shoulder stops me. It's Doctor Williams. I freeze, smile at him.

"You came to my game?"

"I guess I came to congratulate you," he answers. "I saw in the newspapers you decided to eat that blueberry pie like we talked about at the restaurant. They painted a wonderful picture of you doing it, too. Solving crimes isn't always a historian's aspiration. And two crimes, at that. We tend to hide behind computers or books or the likes."

"I couldn't have done it without your input."

"That's my job. I just don't always get to see my students succeed. I kind of toss them to the wind when they are finished with my classes. This was truly a very enjoyable experience. I'm hoping you'll do more."

"I need to find an internship, so I can graduate."

"Oh, yes, that—" He reaches into his pocket and tugs out a folded piece of paper. "No worries. You're good to go. I signed off on your internship. I think you more than exceeded what we're looking for in our students using the tools we give them by taking on an internship."

"Huh?" Well, I dragged that out a mile or so and probably diminished any idea he thought I might be smart.

"You are officially a graduate."

It was only made worse by me snatching up the paper, pivoting on my feet, and screaming out at Pop Pop.

"I did it! I did it!"

Chapter 77

Lance knocks on my door Tuesday morning. He's back to his police uniform. I'm still in my pajamas. Beck comes up behind me, swiping his hand through his hair. Willy is watching cartoons on the TV and laughing with a snort.

"Hey, Lance. Got your job back, huh?" Beck gives him a dorky thumbs-up. Lance is holding a miniature trunk.

"You're not here to arrest me for something, are you?" I ask. Beck gives me a poke on my arm like I shouldn't have said that. He knows better. There's always the chance. "Well, usually when a cop comes to my door, he's holding the twelve speeding tickets I haven't paid."

"You've got outstanding speeding tickets?" Lance asks.

"I'll get them paid," Beck shakes his head. "Is that what you're here for?"

"Seriously?" I ask him. "I don't have twelve—" I sigh, wave the conversation away. "What can we do for you?"

"I know it hasn't been but a few days, but I got called in by some of the town commissioners Monday." Lance swipes the gnats away from his face. "We went through everything with some attorneys. It's a mess, but we've still got the town intact. John Matthews bought up over twenty different properties in the name of the city in the name of eminent domain. There's some sort of clause that states properties can be bought up in blighted communities. But then, he purchased them for himself at a fraction of the cost. He was in the process of building cabins on each piece of land and reselling them." Lance looks from me to Beck. "Then, he built the practice and pro-size ballfield up there using his boys from his contracting business but paying them with the money from the town property taxes. From what I got from the FBI and the attorneys, John Matthews and his son are going to be in jail for a long time for embezzlement, murder, and countless other violations. Grant Lebowski's under arrest and blabbering like a little baby on everybody. But that's not the point. Your name keeps coming up. Folks think you'd make a good mayor. They want to petition to put you in the office until the end of the year—"

"Me?" I laugh. "Is this a joke?"

"No, it is not a joke. And I'm just the bearer of the news. There are only a few hundred people who live here. You know your way around." Lance sighs. "Think about it. You'll get free reign of the museum."

"Uh oh, you're bartering. Nobody else wants to do it."

"It's a big mess up there."

"Have you seen her bathroom?" Beck chuckles loudly. "Her laundry basket is sky high and her sink—well, let's just say it is scary."

I elbow him. "They also said we could offer up a free spot for Orv Saylor at the community cemetery along with a stone. And—" Lance offers up something else. "You said you didn't find the treasure the other day. I think you did. You just had the tip of the iceberg in that plastic container. Here, we confiscated everything in Trevor Woods's garage and at the storage unit in Ansted."

"Did the baby in the trunk show up?"

"It did." He nods. I sigh out loud. "It was actually discovered in a locked room in the basement of Grant Lebowski's home along with the company scrip and a few boxes that were in the initial report. You would think he would have more sense—but he was in deep. It would be hard to move those items considering we knew about them. And there was this." He hands me the small chest, not much larger than a shoebox. "Come inside," I tell Lance. "I think I have the key for this." I wave him in, then go to my bureau drawer before heading to the kitchen. I set the trunk down on the table and I push in the little key, turn it in the lock. The lid opens to expose the contents within.

Pictures. I reach inside. Within is a lifetime of family pictures. One is a small baby with big ears and a wide grin in a long, white christening dress. It flows down the baby's legs and drops to the woman's legs who is holding her. Above are two young boys and a man with dark curly hair and a hat. The baby. It is Mila. I scan down the image and see this carefully printed at the bottom: BRANNTWEINS. HANS. ULRICH. ALFRED. ADELHEID. MILA. 1847.

There are more pictures and little trinkets—it is like I can see the family's life before my eyes. Lance pulls out the picture of a little girl settled alone in a chair posing. A picture is drawn in pen of a cat. Then, I pause on one. I sigh. "Beck, Beck, Beck!" I say. "Look!" It is the image of a beautiful young woman dressed in a white and puffy wedding gown. Beside her with a hand on her shoulder is a tall, gangly man. And to her right is a black woman dressed in a fancy light-colored dress. "This is them." I know them even before I take in the names printed beneath each one.

"It's a marriage photo. The groom, it is Irish—Sean O'Malley." I turn to Lance. "Our town founder, I have found, was a woman and not a man. She pretended to be a boy during the war and afterward continued her disguise, so she could start the mining industry on the mountain. Then, she ended up marrying a man who was in charge of her troop in the war. I can tell this is him." I poke at Sean O'Malley's face. "He has a scar beneath his eye. Mila mentioned it in her diary. He would be my great, great grandpa. And Mila is the bride." I gently roll my finger over her face.

"She looks like you." Beck laughs.

"Yeah." I agree. She does. "But look here—these men, they are all dressed in Union colors. They are all John Grey soldiers—the ones who fought with Hans—I mean Mila and Irish. See here, this is Sean Kelly. He had a father who was from Ireland, and his mother was a slave. I know it is him even without the name below because he's wearing a preacher's collar. Mila mentions they called him *Preacher* and after the war, he wanted to become a minister. This one must be Teddy. Look at his eye. It is white. Bobo is the tall and skinny one and—okay, Beck, meet your great, great grampa—Callen O'Sullivan."

"No, shit." Beck follows my finger to a man with wild red hair. It is curly, and he's as big as Beck. I reach up, wiggle my fingers in his hair. "Is your hair that wild without all the junk in it?"

"Let's not go there," he mutters, but he can't take his eyes off the man.

"I know it is, goofbutt."

"This is Hayward," Beck points at the image. "And that must be the girl he met, and he saved on the train—Minnie Bean. The one who went into the tunnel before the collapse."

"It was all a fake, them dying in the tunnel, only to be reborn again," I say softly. "Even the mine. Oh, that was when the name was changed from Germany Mine to Brandy Mountain Colliery."

"But who is the kid?" Beck holds the picture up a little. Leaning into Mila is a little girl in a flamboyant dress with little black shoes peeking out of the bottom. She is perhaps six or seven years. Underneath, there is a name. "Gingersnap." It is the baby Mila had left behind and searched for—she found her.

It is quiet. We stare at the picture. I sigh. "I have some things I'd like to return to Max, Lance," I say softly. "Stuff from high school. You think you could get it to his family or—him." Lance nods. I look to Beck. "I want to get rid of the whole lot of him." He smiles. I go into my bedroom, drop to my knees and reach beneath my bed to draw the little shoebox of Max's things I had placed there after cleaning up the mess from John Matthews's security guards. Inside are Max's blue-tinted sunglasses, red bandana, bobble-head Hawaiian girl and a few other items I collected belonging to him. I reach into my bedside drawer and pull out the picture Max had given me of the chubby wren clasped in hands I had kept on the refrigerator. I place it on top of the box. I linger just a moment, stare at it. Then I sigh and lay it atop the shoebox and take it to Lance.

Beck's hand on my wrist stops me. I turn my eyes to him. "Where did you get—that drawing?" he asks me.

"Max drew it for me. We used to sit at the park while he drew. I found it in his writing tablet. He gave it to me."

Beck pokes a finger on the little wren and says: "She was but a wild, little thing. I wanted to keep her in the clasp of my hands and pretend her wings were broken. But they weren't. So I let her fly."

I am staring at him somewhat confused, dumbfounded. "How—how did you know that?"

"I drew the picture," he answers gazing at me. "That verse was underneath. It was erased." He picks up the picture, holds it up. Sure enough, I can see where someone had written something beneath the hands. "We had to take that art class in twelfth grade. The art teacher told us to draw something that reminded us of home. I don't know. I thought of your Aunt Joy's wrens. I was always the tallest. When we went to her house for Sunday lunch, she always made me fill the feeders. Then when I drew the bird, I thought of you." Beck shrugs. "I threw it away because I thought for sure everybody would laugh at me for something so sappy. He must have found it in the trash."

"It's my favorite picture," I tell him. I give the shoebox a little push with my hands toward Lance, clasp the picture to my chest. I'm still amazed.

"You two are one lucky couple to have each other," Lance shakes his head. Crap, I know that look he has. I had it until Beck and I got together.

"Hey, we're planning on heading up the mountain later," I say to Lance. "You want to come along after work?"

I think he's unsure, but Beck nods. "We'll grab some sandwiches, make it a picnic."

Later, Beck, Lance, and I take a ride up the mountain with Willy and Nana Nisee in tow. We came to watch the county coroner take out the bodies of Clyde Hatfield and Mimi Edwards. Then, they are sealing up the tunnel and moving any rocks that had fallen. What can I say? There's not much else to do in Lost Hollow in the summer.

When we ride back down, we stop at the Branntwein home and Beck gets out of the jeep. He tells me to follow, and I hear Willy and Nana Nisee giggling in the back. Lance is giving them questioning gazes while Beck snatches up my hand, weaves me around some thickets and we stop at the old tree. His hand is cool and he's shaking. I don't point it out. The feeling is mutual. I see the initials and heart with M.B. and S.O. laced with delicate vines around it. Then below, I see a new heart and a new set of initials: H.D. + B.O.

"It's beautiful," I say. "When did you do this?"

"A week ago. I was going to bring you down here the day we went inside the tunnel." He pats his head where his stitches are. "We just never made it. So—there was something else I was going to do. I never was one for catching fireflies. I liked to watch them light up. My mom told me once they were little angels flying around. After that, I was afraid if I caught one, I might kill its spirit. You're like a firefly flitting all around me, all wild. I want to catch you. I don't want to kill your spirit. I want to marry you, but I don't want to stop you from being all that wild and stuff that keeps me from being too careful—that keeps me coming back because honestly, I love all that about you."

"Okay."

"Okay, what?"

"Okay, I'll marry you. I love you. I like it when you don't want to do something, and then you do it because I ask you. I like laying with you in bed. I feel safe with you. I like it when you give in and make a big deal of it like when you gave me the keys to your truck. I like that you like me and Pop Pop and you know where I'm coming from when I tell people I live in The Bottoms." I sigh. "I'm telling you all that because I know you know I don't want to be like my mom, going from boyfriend to boyfriend. But that isn't the reason."

"Does that mean I still have to do those things?"

"Yeah, Beck." I look into those green eyes, and my lips want to stutter. "Will you marry me, too?"

"Hell, yeah," Beck says softly. "I will."

www.ingramcontent.com/pod-product-compliance
Lightning Source LLC
Chambersburg PA
CBHW030848030726
47495CB00005B/1422